DEFENDERS
OF THE
BLACK CROWN

CATE PEARCE

Cover design by Elizabeth Jeannel

ISBN 978-1-956037-07-4 (hardcover)

ISBN 978-1-956037-01-2 (paperback)

ISBN 978-1-956037-96-8 (eBook)

First Edition

First Edition: November 2022

This eBook edition first published in 2022

Published by Hansen House

www.hansenhousebooks.com

HH
Hansen House

Calamyta

Scablands

Lox

Candor

Schinen

Candeo

Hawks
Keep

West Twin

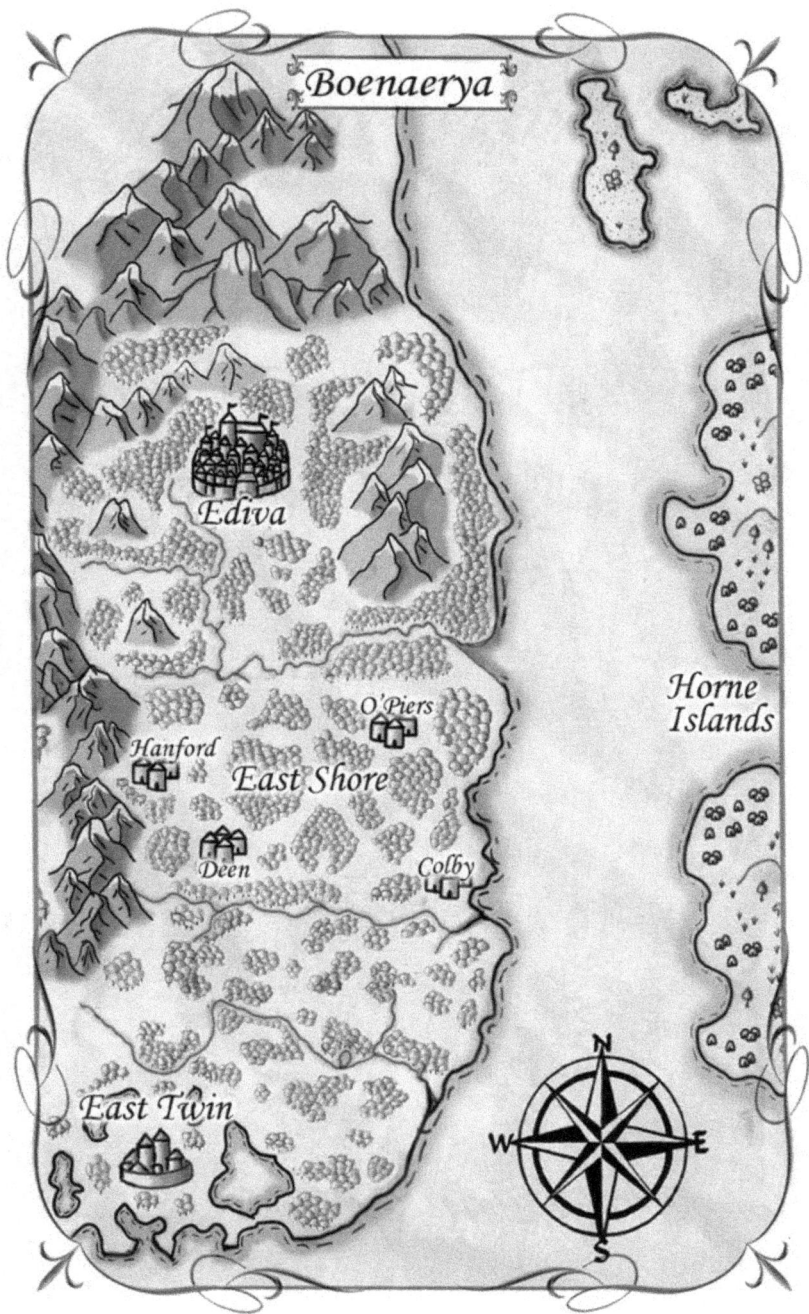

Boenaerya

Ediva

O'Piers

Hanford

East Shore

Deen

Colby

Horne
Islands

East Twin

Everything I do, I dedicate to my mentor, role-model, leader, and inspiration
John Nicholas Pearce IV
September 22, 1952 - August 4, 2014

CHAPTER 1
RAENA

The Womb

They called it "The Womb".

At the center of every castle or keep in Ediva was a courtyard with seven hallways, like purposeful spokes that extended out in all directions. The Womb was a gathering place for major events: weddings, childbirth blessings, funerals, and executions. The latter was the reason the people would assemble today.

Raena had avoided The Womb all morning.

She knew seeing 'King' Zander's head removed from his neck would be resolute, in a twisted way. But she also knew that Queen Zarana's death somehow didn't give her the satisfaction it once had.

Raena had been provided a room on the upper floors of Salish Castle after they arrived in Ediva. It was gaudily decorated by her account, as most Edivan buildings were. Every piece of furniture had tasseled pillows, fabrics dyed in rainbows, and hanging flags of every pattern. It hurt her eyes, so she kept all candles and oil lamps extinguished and she avoided the room during daytime hours when the sunlight crept in.

Except today.

Raena lingered in her quarters. She asked the servants to bring her tea and books from the library, and she sat atop her bed with both. She wore a heavy woven shirt, though the weather was warming. The Edivans had a lack of leather animals to skin into fur and tunics, like they'd worn in East Shore. Here the tailors spun threads from the wool of spurlings and gruts and wound them together on looms into fine clothing. The thick top served to keep Raena warm, but most importantly it covered the feminine parts of her body she still kept concealed.

There was a knock near the door frame and a familiar face caught Raena's eye.

"Almighty's breath," Bell cursed, "Rowan, why is it black as night in your quarters? Are you fully evolving into a Boen? Maybe we ought to ask King Micha to build you a cave room below the keep?"

Bell went to the windows and pulled back a curtain to allow in the sun.

"Thank you, sister-cousin, for insisting on changing my room to suit your liking." Raena set her book on the bed and stood up to receive her guest.

"Seems I ought to," Bell retorted, "since leaving you unsupervised results in disaster. Do you have some explanation for why you are here and not gathering with the rest of us?"

Raena shrugged.

Bell rolled her eyes. "That's still our king and queen receiving their sentence. We might be free to live here without most royal obligation, but we can't change who we are and our loyalty to Candor. Especially today."

"What difference would it make? They will be put to death whether I'm there to see it or not."

Bell paused, leaning back and studying Raena with skepticism. "I thought you didn't want to be there because you feel guilty. Now I think it's something else. You've been wishing for the demise of the Paytons most your life. What is it?"

"It seems flat, now. This feels empty."

Bell nodded, "I see. You wanted to be the one to put your knife to their throats in a blaze of vengeful glory, is that it? Well, even if it's a formal affair, we still owe them our respect. And Aven will want you by her side."

"Will she?"

"You know she will," Bell said.

With a sigh, she stepped forward and began inspecting Raena's shoulders. Tiny feathers from the bed pillows were clinging to the woolly knit of her shirt, and Bell picked them out with tedious attention.

"I don't know," Raena muttered.

Bell's mahogany eyes glanced into Raena's, then back to the task of removing feathers. "Maybe you should make more efforts to go speak with her about it, then. She's an easy woman to read if you just try."

"She doesn't want to talk to me about the Queen."

"When was the last time you tried?"

Raena bit her lip and turned her face.

"There," Bell said, stepping back, "I think that's all of them. Now you won't look as if you just fell out of bed when you go sit with the Edivan nobles. Though you may want to wash your face."

"What's wrong with my face?"

"Everything," Bell quipped, "but mostly how tired your eyes are. Give it a wash, I'll wait."

Raena scoffed, "So you leaving me to continue my day isn't an option?"

"No. We all put this queen up for execution, now we pay respects and will watch the axe swing."

Without another protest, Raena stepped into the bath chamber and filled a basin from the resting water in the tub. She sprayed it with a bottle of rose oil, then dipped her hands in the liquid and rubbed it on her cheeks.

Bell lingered in the doorway, playing with the feathers she was still holding.

"Do you think we'll stay after this?" Bell asked.

3

Raena didn't straighten up from where she was bent over the basin to catch the excess water. "Stay in Ediva?"

"Aye, it's not the right place for Aven."

Raena stiffened, "What is the right place for Aven?"

"What do you mean?"

Raena splashed her face twice more, then coated her hand with the water and ran it through her long blonde hair to train it back. Satisfied, she set the basin on a table and shook her head to shed the remaining water. Water still dripped down the sides of her head where her hair was shaved to her temples.

With a heavy sigh, Raena answered the delicate question. "Candor will soon become a lawless wasteland. News of our role in testifying against the King and Queen will travel like wildfire. There is nowhere in our home kingdom we could ever be safe, not even in Hawk's Keep—"

"But my father—"

"Let me finish, please."

Bell crossed her arms and gave Raena a challenging glare.

Raena continued, "Even if we are under the protection of the people and the nobles excuse us, there will be thousands who disagree and may try to kill us in the night. We have no guarantees of protection against assassins or hired cutthroats. Then there is East Shore—"

"Boenarya."

"Right," Raena consented, "there's Boenarya. We can't take refuge there for obvious reasons. So, what does that leave us? It leaves Ediva. And I don't know about you, but I'm tired of running for my life and looking over my shoulder. The last few months here have been blissfully free of danger and threats to my wellbeing, which I've enjoyed immensely. I think you might feel the same, even if there are a few snags."

"Snags?" Bell scoffed.

"Nowhere is perfect."

Bell lifted her hands to the ceiling and shook her head in an exaggerated display of disgust.

4

Raena patted her chest and looked down to inspect herself. She pulled tighter the cord holding up her leather trousers and then let the bottom of her shirt fall over it again. "How do I look? Manly?"

Bell shrugged, "Like a selfish ass."

Raena tilted her head with disdain. "Come on, cousin. Why don't we talk more tonight, after the feast? We can bring in the others and we'll all talk together. All right?"

Bell grumbled a response.

"Thank you. Now, truly, how do I look?"

With her eyes narrowed, Bell gave Raena an honest inspection. "It's odd that you're wearing pants from East Shore and a shirt from Ediva. It's as though you don't know where you belong."

"I don't have any Edivan trousers."

"Good, they're rubbish. They itch and pick up all of the leaves and brambles from the ground. Some things shouldn't be made with wool."

Raena nodded, "So, I look manly, then?"

"Aye. As much as ever."

"Thank you."

Raena stepped forward and extended her elbow. With a heavy, resigned breath, Bell placed her hand in the offered nook. Together, as knight and lady, they proceeded out of the chamber en route to the courtyards.

The nobles of Candor and Ediva were gathered in a half-circle around the courtyard: The Womb of Salish Castle. At the entrances stood the Kingsguard, keeping back the hordes of commoners who wished to see the executions for themselves. The crowds of citizens packed the many hallways that stretched outward from the courtyard like seven spokes of a wagon wheel, the same way every city in Ediva was designed.

Every Womb had a unique flair to represent the noble house or castle it served, or so Raena had been told. In Salish Castle, the domed interior seemed to stretch to the heavens, with stone walls covered in murals of every color and variety. Wrapped within to cover nearly every surface were beautiful trees and plants in homage to the seven gods. It was a gorgeous menagerie that smelled of spring in a rainforest. It reminded Raena of when she had first arrived in East Shore, though that seemed like a lifetime ago.

Raena stood near the front of the spectators, representing the nobles of Candor along with Bell, Allyn Lox, and Finn, who was propped up in a chair. Otherwise, Raena saw the unfamiliar cheeky faces of Edivans in all directions. There were a few hundred of the native lords and ladies, foreign-looking with their woven blouses, thick hats, and heavy boots.

At the center of the giant terrarium stood King Micha, a few paces behind Queen Zarana and her son 'King' Zander. Both of the Candorian rulers were bound to stools with blindfolds over their eyes. Raena was surprised to see Zander wasn't struggling. She wondered if they had been given substances to sedate them.

"Thank you all for joining me today," Micha addressed the nobles, "this is a somber, but necessary occasion."

Raena shuddered at the mention of necessity.

Micha folded his hands in front of his stomach. "Out of respect for the Princ—my apologies, the King and Queen, I will share in their native tongue, then repeat what I have said in Edivan for the benefit of all others."

Raena glanced from side to side, hoping to see Aven. It had been almost fifteen days since they had last spoken face-to-face. Everything else between them had passed through Bell as their messenger.

"Yesterday, you gave me perspective," Micha continued. "Most of you advocated for mercy. But I have a difficult choice as ruler of this kingdom to prevent a war and also to appease my lords. I'm also in the delicate situation of satisfying the Boens now, it seems. All those choices weigh heavily on me, and have brought us to this day of change." Micha allowed a short pause, then began repeating his speech in Edivan.

Raena turned to see several nodding heads from the nobles behind her. She followed the line of people, slower, scanning every face for one in particular. The droning sound of Micha's indistinguishable words wore on.

Then, at the corner of the sea of wide Edivan faces, Raena saw a pair of gentle hazel eyes surrounded by pale Candorian northerner skin. Aven was staring back at her with warmth and openness that melted her steeled heart immediately. The familiarity between them caused Raena to ache but yearn all in the same breath. It was like the first time she had seen Aven all over again, except with so much hurt and understanding layered over the simplest of gazes.

Raena checked to see that King Micha wasn't paying attention, but he was engaged in his speech and had locked eyes with a group of Edivan knights. As casually as she could muster, Raena slipped back into the crowd of nobles behind her, putting herself behind layers of lords two or three people deep. Without a word, she bowed her head and weaved through, staying close to the middle where she hoped she would stay unnoticed. Every few steps she cast a glance back toward Micha.

When Raena was a meter from her destination, she spotted the familiar broad shoulders and unruly auburn hair of a Colby boy.

"Barton," Raena whispered, "it's Rowan. Don't turn around. Walk with me?"

Barton nodded once to acknowledge he heard her. Raena placed her hand on his elbow and pulled him sideways, creeping closer toward her target, keeping his bulky body between her and Micha's line of sight.

Micha had switched back to speaking in Candorian. "Our tradition to choose your own fate is as ancient as Ediva, and it is right for a king to have this honor. I have asked King Zander for his last wishes, and I have asked him what death he considered the most noble. He was given the right to choose for himself, and also for the Queen."

Barton had stopped moving, frozen in place. Raena was still a few paces from Aven. She looked to see what had captivated Barton, peering around his neck.

7

Micha stood in the same spot but was joined by two men, each holding shining scythes. They had slipped behind the Candorian rulers, undetected.

King Zander and Queen Zarana were still. They were peaceful. They didn't even tremble at the slightest.

"King Zander chose to have the quickest, most-painless death," Micha said, "and he chose a torturous fate for his mother, the Queen. It seemed cruel to me that he would ask her death be dragged into suffering, but that was his wish."

Micha paused and stepped forward. It was silent in The Womb.

Raena felt herself holding her breath. She stepped out from behind Barton as if she was stepping into a nightmare she couldn't wake from.

There was no movement, no sound. Despite over a hundred gathered, no one whispered or broke the suffocating silence.

Then, there was a choke.

A garbling, heaving sound.

Raena couldn't tell where it was coming from, but Micha looked down at Zander, and all attentions followed his blue eyes.

Zander was trying to pull his arms free from the stool as he folded forward, coughing and sputtering.

"I heard his wishes," Micha said, raising his voice, "he wanted his death to be the quickest. So, we poisoned him, hours ago. We gave him a fine meal to enjoy, with plenty of wine."

Zander gagged violently. He convulsed, and a spatter of blood flew from his lips.

Micha shook his head, "I gave him the most-fitting thing, and he ought to appreciate it. I have it on good authority that poisoning is Zander's preferred way to deal with his enemies."

Raena glanced at Aven to see the former duchess was holding strong. Her eyes were steady, though her lips were rigid and her fists were clenched. Despite all the pain Zander had caused, it was certain that Aven hated to watch anyone suffer.

Micha began to speak in Edivan once more, perhaps repeating what he had said, or perhaps saying something else entirely. Zander jerked forward and spasmed, toppling face first onto the tile. For the first time, the crowd gasped. The young King was shaking as though he were in a seizure, spitting more blood.

"Curse you!" Zander shouted into the floor. "Almighties curse you!"

Micha did not falter, only raised his voice. The Edivan language was poetic and monosyllabic, with many dragging tones. It sounded as if he were chanting a low prayer.

Zander could no longer shout, as his words were drowned by wet, choking, gags.

All eyes were on Zander as his gagging turned to gurgles, and then slowly transformed into short gasps. Perhaps a full minute passed, and his skin began to tint as blue as the night sky.

Raena moved without hesitation until she was alongside Aven, where she'd wanted to be. She let her hand fall to her side and she waited. There was a space between them but Raena could feel the familiar pull of Aven near her, as though a light gust of wind would be enough to throw them into one another's arms. Raena was steady, and then she felt it— Aven's gentle fingers brushing against hers, tentatively asking permission for more. Raena obliged, and gripped Aven's hand with security. She prayed no one might see, but all eyes in the great room seemed to stay transfixed on Zander's final breaths.

Micha turned to address the Queen. "Your son has only seconds left. Is there anyone you wish to name your successor? I am giving you this final chance."

Queen Zarana wet her lips, "Trevin Schinen."

Raena's heart raced.

"You have named a dead man," Micha said. "You are ill, dear woman. All of House Schinen was slaughtered under your command. Do you wish to name any other successor?"

Raena felt her throat dry and her skin flush at the mention of her family. Even after sixteen years, she was haunted by the Queen's massacre of every member of her father's noble House.

"Trevin Schinen," Zarana repeated.

Micha sighed, "I will now read your last blessings." He stepped back and pulled a roll of paper from his pocket no larger than his forearm. He began to read from it in Candorian, but his voice knit the words together, like a song.

Aven's grip on Raena's hand was painfully tight.

From behind Zarana, the knight stepped forward and raised his scythe.

Zarana was a vision.

Her silver hair framed her face. Though the blindfold covered her brown eyes, her demeanor was tender and open. Her shoulders and arms were relaxed. Her mouth was turned up with the pleasant expression of someone who has let go of everything that once burdened them in life. Her lips remained that way, even as the scythe sliced into the sagging, wrinkled folds of her neck. Even as that slight smile became separated from her body. Even as her dead weight slumped forward, and her head rolled to the ground.

Zarana was at peace.

The crowd was alive with screams. Perhaps some were of joy. Perhaps some were of dismay. The sound was overwhelming as it echoed through the domed space.

Raena stared, unable to reconcile all of the emotions gushing inside her like a flood breaking a dam. She had her revenge. She should have felt whole. She looked at the bloodied stump spurting its last pulses of fluid life where Zarana's face had been only seconds before. She dared herself to feel any vindication for the death of her father, her cousins, her friends. This was the resolution she'd waited most of her life for. It was empty.

"Stop, he'll see you," Barton said.

Raena had been so focused that she hadn't realized Aven was in her arms, sobbing against her chest, until she heard the warning. She jumped away.

"Sorry, I'm sorry," Aven muttered, holding her hands to her chin. Tears streamed down her face through trails of dirt.

Raena felt a pang of anguish. She wanted to reach out again. But she caught a familiar face at the opposite side of the crowd and felt the burning glare of his chestnut eyes upon her. He had seen them together. He had seen Raena holding Aven, even though it was for a mere second of time.

"I have to go," Raena whispered, "I'll send Bell to you."

Aven gasped as a sob escaped her. This time Barton came to the former Duchess Aven's aid, patting her arms with his clumsy, boyish hands. She seemed to reach for Raena, but Barton was between them.

Raena turned and walked through the chaos of the crowd, now disintegrating into an amorphous shape. The Womb was raucous with chittering Edivan voices, shouting and calling out in the language Raena didn't understand. Zander's body had been removed, and Micha was nowhere to be seen. She spotted Finn in his chair being carried out by two strong guards, and she curved her path to follow after them. It felt as if she were swimming upstream as the Edivan nobles pushed inward, trying to get closer to the execution site.

She was nearly out of the courtyard when she saw him. Out of the corner of her eye Raena spotted his telltale armor, black with thick chainmail. He was impossible to miss—his hair and skin several shades darker than any Edivan. He was her perfect opposite in this way.

"I saw you," Sir Jonn said, falling into step alongside her.

"I'm aware," Raena snapped.

"We will speak tonight."

Raena scoffed and turned to mutter a reply, but he was already gone.

CHAPTER 2
RAENA

A Feast

"It's morbid to have a feast after that," Sir Allyn of Lox groaned, lifting his goblet.

"Yet here we are," Raena replied.

They stood together at the side of the Great Room, drowning their worries into the endless servings of lukewarm kelpi. The drink was a blend of sap and rye, fermented until it resembled a bubbling tea full of floating particles. Raena and Allyn were on a binge of it, despite having avoided it in the weeks prior. Around them was a party and a feast. The boisterous men of Ediva wore thin linens made from pulp that barely hid the fur and hair covering their skin. They fanned themselves to keep from overheating due to alcohol and being packed in the Great Room like fish fry bursting from a nest. For men of religion, valor, and purity, the Edivans were certainly eager to lose their stuffy morality and imbibe for the sake of celebration.

"Have you seen Sir Jonn?" Allyn asked.

Raena grunted into her glass, "More times than I'd wish."

"Don't piss with him. You'll fuck it for all of us."

"Such language for a nobleman," Raena taunted. "Don't let Bell hear you be as profane as a night watchman. She'll tell Micha you talk like a commoner and he'll send you to sleep in the bullocks."

Allyn rubbed at his upper lip where his elaborate, curled mustache originated and spanned out to his cheeks. He seemed to debate with himself for a moment, then sighed and returned to guzzling from his goblet.

The lull in conversation gave Raena a chance to observe as more Edivan nobles took part in the feast, which was a strange affair. All of the food was piled onto a singular table at the center of the Great Room, without a chair or bench to rest on. Nobles grazed at the table, coming and going, walking up to partake before they would wander off again. There were wooden scoops and picks to use as utensils, and the nobles would toss them to the floor when they were done. Most of the foods were cut into pieces small enough to finish in one bite, which Raena found frustrating because of the number of times she had to return to the table before she felt her hunger subsiding.

"Bell's here," Allyn remarked. He rubbed his fingers over his mustache to curl the tips.

"Huzzah, someone else who wants to tell me everything I'm wrong about." Raena punctuated her disdain by swallowing the dregs of her kelpi, including the pulp.

Allyn dug an elbow into Raena's side. "Well, maybe don't be such a dolt, then. Do you mind getting me another goblet of kelpi?"

Raena shook her head and walked away. "Refill your own glass," she tossed over her shoulder.

After another pour from the kelpi bowl and helping herself to a few dips of bean paste, Raena approached Bell and Finn. Finn was upright in his chair thanks to supports at the side to keep him from slumping. His disposition was brighter than it had been since his injury, and the light in his brown eyes had been returning to nearly what it was before the Boens. In the same vein, he could hold his head up and his shoulders appeared taller. At first glance, someone who knew him may not know he was a man without the use of his legs, and merely think he was accustomed to sitting longer than most.

Their conversation trailed off and they both nodded in Raena's direction, then Bell seemed to catch herself in her surroundings and dipped into a curtsy.

"Right, this shite," Raena muttered, bowing in return.

"Well, it's the shite we agreed to," Bell said through clenched teeth.

Finn's dark brown eyes scanned the room before he spoke. "Bell and I were just estimating how long it will be before one of us is poisoned the way Zander was today. I guessed about 47 days. Do you want to wager on it?"

Raena chuckled, "How will you collect on the wager if we're dead?"

"Oh, that's part of the wager," Finn quipped, "you hide the money in your undergarments and if they kill you, we know where to look for it."

"Fair enough," Raena said, "I'll wager ten quorrils."

"You cheap ass."

Raena's eyes twinkled. "Nah, I just haven't room for more than that in my tight trousers."

Finn guffawed at that, throwing his head back with glee. Raena shot a crooked grin of apology to Bell, who was rolling her eyes at their familiar banter.

"I forgot how stupid you both are when you're together," Bell complained.

"You see us every day," Finn said through chuckles, "albeit we're not usually this drunk. Why don't you catch up to us, oh Lady Islabell?"

Bell sighed, "After watching that gruesome execution today, I'd prefer to stay sober. The last thing I want is to blur the edges of my mind that are keeping me from envisioning it in full detail again and again, for the rest of the night. Enjoy that image while you boys are hunched over your chamber pots in a few hours."

"Don't underestimate me," Finn countered, "I can hold my kelpi with pride. It's the little floating bits that come back up."

Raena burped on cue.

14

"The both of you belong in a barn," Bell muttered.

Raena grinned, "You love us so fully. If we weren't in front of all these puffy, fuzz-face Edivan nobles, you'd be slathering our cheeks with kisses."

Bell cooed and reached out as though she wanted to bat Raena on the arm, then pulled away at the last second. "Aye, a bit. I miss that. Some days I think we'd be better off fending for ourselves in Boenarya."

"Rowan would," Finn said, "blending in with his golden head. The Boens love pale-skinned neighbors like him and Micha. Maybe you could ask the Boens to give you a nice little cave corner for us to live, Ro? How about you see if they'll leave us a cluster of trees in the woods? Surely, they'll toss up a morsel of horse now and then."

"At least then we'd all be together." Bell raised her eyebrow and hit Raena with a daring stare.

Raena looked back and forth at both her friends, who wore matching expressions of challenge and curiosity. She took a drink of her kelpi, stalling. It was enough to wear down their patience.

"Have you seen Aven, lately?" Bell asked.

Raena swallowed and shook her head.

Bell lowered her voice, "Perhaps you should tonight, while everyone is drunk and occupied."

Raena turned to scan the room. King Micha was engaged in a rousing conversation with a handful of nobles, but Sir Jonn was nowhere to be seen. "I might," she muttered, "if I can."

"You need help," Finn said, "let your friends help you."

Bell was quick to echo the sentiment.

Raena shifted, scratching at the thick collar of her woolen shirt.

"Ro, today was painful," Bell said quietly, "it was ugly for all of us, simply to be in the room when their last breaths were taken. We have each other to lean on. She has no one with her tonight to comfort her in her pain, and Queen Zarana was akin to her. Whether it makes sense to us or not, Aven was raised in that castle and has fond memories of the Queen."

"I know that," Raena muttered.

15

Finn raised his eyebrows. "Then why are you here? Why aren't you with her?"

"Sir Jonn already saw me with her once today," Raena frowned, "I've no doubt he is patrolling the hallways to catch me leaving the Great Room."

"We could stage a distraction?" Finn said. His eyes brightened and he cast a playful look toward Bell.

"Please don't," Raena responded, but both Bell and Finn were already locked into a wordless, grinning exchange.

Finn chuckled, prompting Raena to make her request a second time. She was about to reach out and slap his arm, but before her hand connected, he toppled forward. Finn's chair went tumbling behind him, the opposite direction of his body, as if a powerful spring had propelled both of them with great force. Finn caught his fall with his forearms, slapping the floor with a loud bang. He began crying out, wailing like a child. Bell made a show of gasping.

"Sir Finley!" Bell screamed with more gusto than necessary. She fell to her knees and patted his body fervently as if checking him for broken bones.

It was absurd.

The Edivan nobles turned their heads, various states of curiosity and surprise written in their expressions. All attention in the room was drawn to Finn and Bell. Raena sighed, unable to be cross with them when they were so determined and capable in their manipulative goals.

Bell escalated her disdain into full-blown anguish, crying as though Finn had died right there in the middle of the party. "Help him! What are you doing?" she screeched to no one in particular.

In the commotion, Raena slipped to the outer wall of the Great Room. She kept her face toward the crowd, and someone caught her eyes, giving her a momentary freeze of panic: Allyn. His familiar face melted into a knowing smile, which Raena returned with a slight wave. Allyn engaged in the charade, shouting something about Finn being "too young to die" as he shoved through the crowd.

Raena neared an archway that led to the hall and she gave a final glance through the room. She saw no one looking back at her as she stepped out of the Great Room.

The hallways weren't deserted, but they were less populated than an average night. Raena wound out of the royal wing and down the towers into the 'elevated floor': the nobles' quarters. Her lodging was there, within a few steps of three of the King's knights, Finn, and Allyn's rooms. Bell and Barton's quarters were one floor above them.

Raena took an Edivan outer cloak from her boudoir and draped it over her shoulders, then she donned a thick gray cap to cover her white-blonde hair. It wasn't that cold of a spring evening, but Raena had no other way to disguise herself. Surely the wrong guard might remember her for her Boeny skin and hair far longer than they would remember seeing someone mildly overdressed in the halls.

It was a long walk through the castle to the 'bullocks'. Raena kept to the shadows as much as possible, winding past the royal kitchens, the places of worship, the armories, and then to the courtyard. She had no choice but to pass through the room where Zarana and Zander had been executed. It felt eerie in the space, as if death was reaching out a hand to remind her of its toll. She avoided looking toward the center, though she wondered if perhaps their blood still stained the stone tiles.

When Raena entered the hallway opposite where she came, the castle structure changed rapidly. The murals were faded, and paint chipped on the walls. The ceilings were lower, cramping the corridors, and candle sconces were spaced further apart. Raena saw multiple guards milling around, and she gave them a nod of her head.

"*Hu krau fillas?*" a guard said.

Raena recognized the word *filla*, as 'healer'. She coughed on cue, answering through the sputtering. "*Filla Gourl Dunchak.*"

They nodded and turned away. Her coughing fit had been satisfactory to explain her reason for being in the lower corridors where *Gourl Dunchak*—the dark healer—could be found. Raena's smidge of

Edivan was improving every day, but she still only knew a few phrases, and her accent wasn't convincing.

Past the guards' stations were the peasants' quarters. They were near the stables and Raena noticed the pungent smell. It may have been a few weeks since she visited Aven, but the stench was a reminder.

A woman stood near Aven's door, holding a screaming infant. Her breast was exposed though the woman made no effort to bring the baby to it, instead she stared off into the distance as if waiting for the infant to correct itself. Raena ducked her head to avoid the woman's gaze. Normally she would have knocked at Aven's door, but the impropriety of being seen as a man entering a woman's room would certainly alert the unwanted loiterer. Raena continued past, down the walkway. A few paces ahead was an alcove, displaying a tapestry to one of the Almighties—the one over the air and birds, maybe. It was likely a violation of some custom, but Raena tucked into the alcove, hidden from view, and waited.

At least a dozen minutes passed. The infant's wailing echoed through the stone corridors. Several times Raena wanted to shout at the woman to comfort her child. Servants walked by, engaged in conversation, carrying barrels. Raena tried to occupy herself by thinking about what she might say to Aven, but the thought made her heart race more.

A guard came into view, leisurely swinging his spear. Raena flattened her back tighter against the stone wall, holding her breath as he neared. When he approached the alcove, she could see his brow furrow with disdain, but he remained fixated on something ahead in his path.

The guard walked faster and called out several things in Edivan in a gruff voice. Raena recognized simple words in his sentences: *bajïn* was 'stop', *ru* was 'no'.

The woman was arguing, and their voices escalated. The baby screamed louder, which Raena hadn't thought possible.

The shouts continued but also drifted farther away. After a few seconds, Raena could tell their voices were coming from a further corridor.

She wouldn't risk someone else coming along and ruining her chance. Raena jumped out of the alcove and bounded down the corridor. She didn't bother to knock; she opened the door and entered Aven's room, swinging the door shut with equal speed.

Aven was on her bed, and she jolted upright. Raena held out her hands.

"It's me, I'm sorry," Raena blurted out, "I didn't want to risk being seen."

Aven's bed was low to the ground and Raena crouched to meet her eyes, but she looked past, searching in the darkness.

"Sir Jonn and his guards," Aven said, "you can't be here."

"No one saw me," Raena whispered. She leaned forward and let her knees fall on the mattress, then reached out to place both her hands on Aven's forearms. "You've been crying. I'm sorry."

"It's nothing," Aven said, "and it's everything. You shouldn't be here. What if they find you?"

Raena shook her head, then realized Aven couldn't likely see. She inched forward until they were flush together, wrapping her arms around Aven. Raena pressed her cheek to Aven's, feeling the warm wetness of the tears on her face.

"I miss you every minute," Raena whispered, "I would gladly resign my nobility if it meant they would leave us in peace, down here together."

Aven rested her head on Raena's shoulder. "You would hate it here. It's often loud and the smell of the stables is rancid on slaughter days. You would rather be in the forests to reckon with the Boens than in the bullocks."

"You sound like Bell. She said something similar this very morning."

Aven sighed, then pulled away. "Why are you dressed like you're going for a midnight ride?"

"Pretend I am," Raena replied. "Pretend we're leaving here tonight and we'll disappear in the mountains. Where would we go? Tell me anywhere you want to go, and I'll take you."

"But you're happy here." Aven placed her hand on Raena's chest, over her heart. "I see you sometimes with Micha, when you're out in the courtyard. I've helped the servant girls weave blankets for the lords and carried them to the elevated floor. I've seen you, and Finn, laughing in the swordplay rooms while I filled the fireplace with coals."

"I'm sor—"

"Don't apologize," Aven pressed her fingers to Raena's lips, "I'm not angry with you. I'm not even hurt. I was glad to see you, even if you didn't notice me there. It brought me peace to see you smiling and relaxed. I was so afraid that you wouldn't be able to hide who you are here. I kept worrying when I didn't see you that maybe their customs forced you to bathe with the other men or you'd been discovered. I tried to find any reason to go to the elevated floor, otherwise, I'd have to wait for Bell to find me."

"But I've come here to visit you."

"You did, the first few days after we arrived."

Raena leaned back, resting on her heels. She pulled the gray cap off her head and scratched at her skull through shaggy blonde hair. "It hasn't been that long, has it?"

"It has," Aven said in a soft voice, "it's been twenty-five days. But I've seen you nearly a dozen times, enough to feel like I know how you are, and how you've been, and to get a sense that you are happy."

"Should I feel guilty for that? I know that Bell does."

"Why would you feel guilty?"

It was quiet for a long moment. Raena remained settled on her haunches, a space leaving cold air to drift between them. The lack of touch when they were in such close proximity was odd and noticeable.

Raena let out a long breath through her teeth. "I don't mean to feel any certain way. I only mean to live free from worries. I've watched over my shoulder for so long, and something changed me when I was in that prison in Candeo. It's as though I know I may not have to fear the Queen, but now there is something greater I fear, and I will always fear."

"You don't have to fear it in Ediva?"

"I do," Raena whispered, "Sir Jonn says they have beaten and raped women for pretending to be men. It's against what they believe the Almighties created."

"Then nothing has really changed, you are still afraid to be who you are."

Raena shook her head, "I am not. I know my enemy, and I know the risk. I know that I can hide myself from them, the same as I hid myself from everyone. It's easy to continue what I've always done. It's easy to settle into this place with Bell and Finn, like we're back home. I have everyone around me that I love, and no one is in danger. Except me. And it's a danger I can live with. I can control it and keep it from collapsing in on me."

Aven nodded, swallowing hard.

Raena could see the broken expression on her face. She reached out and cupped Aven's face in her hands, wiping away the remnants of tears with her thumbs. It was hard to discern if the tears were from the pain of the day's tragedy, Raena's words, or another hurt entirely.

"I'm the one keeping you in danger," Aven said, so quiet her words were almost inaudible.

Raena moved in and kissed the wet spots on Aven's cheeks. "You're not. I'll always be in danger until I can find a place to stop being Rowan. Now that Zander and Zarana are gone, that day will soon come. It just won't be here, I think, but I'm not certain."

Aven nodded, melting into the touch. They came back together, embracing once again with less reservation. Raena wrapped her muscular arms fully around Aven's back, squeezing her with all the vigor of a long-overdue reunion.

"You feel warm," Aven mumbled against Raena's neck.

"I'm boiling. It's all these layers I wore for a disguise."

Aven stroked her fingers through Raena's hair. "Take the layers off, then."

Raena remained still, holding Aven but going no further. For a short moment, neither of them moved, lingering in the embrace. Slowly, Aven slid her hands to the collar of Raena's cloak and pushed it back. Raena dropped her arms and let the cloak fall to the ground. In the pitch-black darkness, Aven reached for Raena's face, fumbling to feel her way. Raena relented, knowing she could see far better in the dark, and allowed herself to accept the intended kiss. Their lips came together in familiar warmth. The second that Raena surrendered, Aven's tender kiss evolved into a demanding hunger. With both of her small hands, Aven gripped Raena's shirt and fell backward onto the bed, pulling Raena down on top of her.

"Oi," Raena whispered between the sudden barrage of kisses they shared, "we don't have to—we can talk. Do you want to talk? About today?"

Aven shook her head and slid her hands down Raena's chest and stomach. She grabbed for the bottom of Raena's shirt, pulling it up. Her fingertips trailed along Raena's hard abdominal muscles then to the layered chest bindings Raena wore daily. Aven pulled at the clasp and Raena drew in a sharp breath.

"Are you sure?" Raena asked again.

Aven answered with another hungry kiss.

Raena was out of Aven's chamber before midnight. She hoped the party was still going so she wouldn't encounter anyone on the elevated floor. She moved like a shadow through the corridors, easily sneaking past guards when she went from the servant's wings to the courtyard.

When Raena reached the top of the stairs in the noble wing, she saw a familiar figure leaning against the wall between her and the entrance of her chamber.

Sir Jonn was taller and brawnier than most men, especially the pudgy Edivans. He had paled from sixteen years living in the frosty northern near-tundra, but was otherwise the same as Raena remembered from when he was a knight in her father's service and had saved her from the Queen's executioners.

Raena bristled herself to get the conversation over with. "To what do I owe the pleasure of your visit, Sir Jonn?" she asked as she approached.

Jonn grimaced, "Don't play idiot with me, Rowan. I know where ye've been."

"Oh? How's that? I didn't see you at the feast."

Jonn gestured to her cloak and hat, "You dressed for winter at the feast? I think nah. Let's go talk, shall we?"

Raena slumped her shoulders and reached for the chamber door. They entered together and Raena remembered to light an oil lamp for Jonn's benefit. She shut the door and motioned to an ornate lounge for him to take up in the boudoir, while she sat across from him on a stool. The difference in height allowed her to tower over him, which was an unusual dynamic but she appreciated it.

Jonn crossed his arms over his padded knight's tunic. "When are you going to understand what's at risk here? You've been given every chance. I've risked my life to save you, and I'm not convinced you're a day older than the eight-year-old girl I dragged out of House Schinen."

"Fuck you—"

"No, fuck you, Raena," Jonn snapped, "quit acting like a child. Sylas raised you to be a man, so act like one. I don't have to worry about Finn or Allyn running around this castle in the middle of the night to bury their pintles in a woman. And they're men with urges you wouldn't even struggle with."

"Well, you just said I should act like a man, so which is it?"

Jonn rose from his chair, slamming his fist into his palm. "You already exiled yourself from one kingdom, do you plan to make it a habit? I protected you all your life, and you're determined to find any way you can to challenge it. It's my duty to treat you as your father would have wanted, as long as I still live and serve his memory. And I know for certain that Henry Schinen would have wanted me to beat you for how you've acted. You will get far worse from the King if he finds out even one thing about who you are, or what you've been up to with that pig farmer's girl."

Raena shook her head. "She's a duchess, even if your fussocked kingdom laws don't recognize the truth. She has more right to be treated like a noble than you and I."

"I know you care for her, but we can't change her bloodline, just like you can't change your own birthrights. Lord Brande was kind enough to claim you as a bastard son when Sylas asked him. That was the best we could do. It's enough to keep you safe, and I can't give you everything you want. Every day that you live as Rowan is a threat to your safety. I would've turned you and your friends away if it weren't for my loyalty to protect your House. It's clear that loyalty means nothing to you."

"The opposite," Raena asserted, "loyalty means everything. It means more to me than frivolous laws which benefit no one and harm those I love. If Ediva cared for loyalty then it would reward those who have served and ruled, not focus on blood and nobility, which mean nothing. Any froll's ass can be born of noble blood, look at Zander! What Aven did for House Colby is more honorary than half these nobles would be for their own duchies. She risked her life time and again to preserve Colby and save her people. You can't undermine all that."

Jonn scoffed, "You act as if this is my choice, Rowan. You act as though I am a puppet master who controls Ediva and the whims of King Micha. He may be a fair man, but he's inclined to live within the bounds of his rule. He will not upturn a law which benefits him. And while you may disagree with the rules of nobility in Ediva, you also must be intelligent enough to admit they are far improved over Candor."

Raena narrowed her eyes at him. Though he neared her space and she was tempted to stand, she remained seated on the stool, her arms crossed in defiance. "I fail to see your point, so indulge me with your opinion."

Jonn let out a huff of air, then relaxed back into the lounge, some of his indignance fading. "You may have been farther from the crown when you lived under Sylas. Hawk's Keep has done well to stay isolated from much of the…there's nothing else to call it but what it is, horseshite and politics."

Raena nodded for him to continue.

"You never knew, but I visited Hawk's Keep many times. After the Black Spring, the crown suspected you were still alive, but no one outside Candeo remembered my face."

"You have one of those faces," Raena said.

"Maybe," Jonn agreed, "but I was careful regardless. I met Lord Sylas at the edges of the Western Founts, every three years. That was how he came to have letters for you."

"Aye, you've told me this."

Jonn scratched at his greying beard. "I suppose so, but you're not privy to how he saw the kingdom change under Zarana's rule. It may have felt slow to him and the other lords, but that's the thing about visiting a place once every three years, innit? You recognize right away the differences no one else would see. It feels drastic when everyone else thinks it small. King Lyam had wanted to make the kingdom stronger by weeding out the weak. He knew that building up the best of a kingdom allows only the best to grow. It's the same as breeding rounceys or warhorses. You don't give your mare to your lowest stallion or you'll never have the steeds to take into battle."

Raena cringed, "People aren't horses. We don't breed for war."

"Why shouldn't we?"

She felt she had an answer, but couldn't think of the words. Raena bit her lip and rubbed at her neck with fervent energy she tried to subdue.

Jonn shrugged, "It's not up to us, thank the Almighties. I couldn't be the king and decide who should live or die. That was Lyam's duty, and he was the best suited for it. Under his rule, the infirm and crippled and deviants were killed among noble families. You don't remember, because that trickled off like a dried-up stream when he grew ill, and Zarana didn't have the stomach to rule with that same authority. She turned a blind eye to it."

"By your accounts, the King himself ought to have been put to death."

"Perhaps he was."

25

Raena raised an eyebrow. "What do you mean?"

"I don't mean anything," Jonn waved his hands, "forget I said it. I don't mean anything more, except that Lyam hated the idea of being a sickly man. He would have asked for a death on the battlefield if given the choice. I suppose none of us do get to choose our birth, or our death. It doesn't make for a fair world; it only makes for a better one. Power sits in the hands of those who are capable, and believe me, if we pollute every bloodline with the weakest peasants and serfs until no true nobles are left, our power will be corrupted. You will see every kingdom fall, just like East Shore fell to the Boens."

Raena stood from her stool, knocking it to the floor with a clatter. "I'm done hearing this. Your coldness is sickening."

Jonn chuckled, not moving an inch from his place on the lounge. "It's good we made you a knight and not a lord. You haven't the stomach to rule. Leaders must make hard choices or watch their people starve or be conquered. You have been afforded too much luxury in your young life, I reckon."

"If you don't leave now, I'll drag you out, old man." Raena pointed her finger in his face, and he eyed it with a glare.

Jonn shook his head and rose with a sigh, taking a few lazy steps toward the door. When he was nearly to the threshold, he turned back toward Raena. "You can choose whether your duchess lives or dies. I stayed by your room tonight and when Micha came looking for you, I said you were in this chamber with too much kelpi in your gut. I won't do that for you again. I won't lie to my King on your behalf. The next time you wander down to the bullocks, go ahead and be discovered. They'll kill her without a second thought, simply for being a commoner with a nobleman. You'll be lucky if you survive the beating."

Raena grabbed for her oil lamp and raised it to throw, but Jonn moved with newfound urgency, rushing out into the hallway.

CHAPTER 3
RAENA

The Jin

It had been two weeks since Zarana's execution and the feast.

To Raena, it might've been hours. She couldn't stop the flood of imagery rushing back to her. Zarana's head separating from her body was constantly threatening to burst into Raena's mind, along with a guilty feeling that rushed up much like vomit builds after a night of drinking too much. Coincidentally, drinking too much was also the remedy to force the disturbing memory at bay from her consciousness. Raena had occupied herself with daily swordplay and kelpi from her first waking moment until she passed out near dawn. Edivans talked so much about moderation in their religion, but they encouraged her newfound habit with enthusiasm. Raena seldom imbibed alone.

Her rowdy drinking partners and fellow knights were enjoyable, but Raena was growing to loathe every other detail of Ediva. As a kingdom, as a climate, as a culture: Raena was sick to death of the pompous charade. It had taken her the few weeks to analyze the layers of their society, but once her eyes were opened to their ruses, she couldn't see Ediva for the false pretense it strived to project. Edivans wanted the world to believe they cared most for democratic decisions, but their religious leaders had all the say. They wanted the world to believe they were compassionate, but they treated their peasants worse than King Lyam had in his prime. Edivans offered peace to the other kingdoms, but their version of peace was simply withholding war and invasion brought by their own armies.

Sir Jonn loved the twisted hypocrisy, that was clear. Raena avoided him so obviously, walking away whenever he approached, it had become a joke amongst her friends. The only person whose company she avoided more—albeit for different reasons—was Aven's.

On another brisk and bleak afternoon that blended into all the others, Raena had awakened after the mid-day meal and drank a few goblets of kelpi in her chambers. She was preparing her swords for the training grounds when a guard entered to summon her. King Micha requested her presence in his royal sitting room. A ball formed in her throat at the notion that she would go before the King for such a formal meeting.

After all, the last time Micha had requested her audience for official matters, the end result had been her Queen's execution. The blood. The sound of ripping flesh. The gasp of the crowd. Aven's hand, clammy, tight, clenching Raena's.

It was flooding back to her again. Raena stumbled for her cabinet and poured another goblet of kelpi, the drink sloshing from the jug and splattering. She rushed to finish it and answer the King's summons.

When Raena was numb inside and out, she made her way to the royal sitting room. She raised her eyebrows to find Allyn, Bell, and Finn waiting in shining copper chairs. There were four seats vacant, leading Raena to speculate perhaps Barton and Aven would join them. Raena took care not to slump or stumble as she sat beside Allyn, loosely aware that she'd lost control of her finer motor skills in her effort to calm her nerves.

"How long have you been waiting?" Raena slurred, earning a glare from Bell.

"Not long," Allyn said. He sniffed the air and tilted his head toward her, raising one eyebrow.

Raena glanced away and breathed through her nose, conscious of the kelpi on her breath. The drink wasn't the only problem; the others were dressed in their finer garments, suitable to meet a king. She hadn't thought to change. Raena was in worn woven fighting gear, ready for a wrestling romp or swordplay on the training grounds. Her cheeks were warm at the recognition of her error.

Bell leaned forward, chasing Raena's gaze with a targeted stare. "Do you know why he's asked us here?"

Raena shook her head, her lips tightly pursed.

As though on cue, King Micha's entrance interrupted them. He was dressed in his heavy blue council robes. His shoulders were tense and he mumbled greetings under his breath, waving his hand to indicate they should not stand or bow on his account. He took the centermost chair in the circle, opposite the Candorians.

Raena tried to read Micha's mood from his demeanor, wondering if he was angry, sour, or stressed. Before she could make a determination, they were joined by Sir Jonn and one of Micha's spiritual advisors, Weft. Behind Weft was an additional small entourage of three.

At first sight of the three men, Raena had to bite her lip to keep from shouting with surprise. Beside her, Bell gasped aloud.

Their straw hair. Their skin; so pale it was nearly translucent. Their eyes grey like the stone they burrowed and lived beneath.

Micha spoke before anyone else could. "This is The Jin. He leads the Boens. These are his two advisors, he calls them Jotu."

Bell had one hand over her mouth in shock. Finn squirmed from one side of his supportive chair frame to the other. Raena didn't dare look at Allyn, certain that his reaction would be extreme.

Micha said nothing to quell the discomfort of the Candorians at the sight of their enemy. Instead, he gestured to the three empty chairs, staring expectantly toward the Boens.

Raena had never seen them move anywhere but in nature, flitting and scuttling out of the earth. In this space, as standard men, their arms and legs glided smoothly. They almost appeared to float into their seats alongside the Edivan King.

Everyone in the room was sizing each other up and casting studious, skeptical glances.

Micha began, addressing the Candorians. "I know you didn't expect this, so I apologize for surprising you. As you might imagine, I cannot reveal everything. I've promised these Boen leaders safe passage within my walls, and I've brought them here in secrecy today."

Raena saw Allyn tense, his fists balled in his lap, but no one dared to interrupt the King.

Micha continued, "My kingdom is at risk. Your kingdom is at risk. We have much to discuss and none of it can be taken lightly. After this meeting, I will speak with each of you individually. It's critical that in the next few months everything is handled delicately and executed perfectly. If we waver in our goals or our mission, we will fail, and the kingdom will fail. What's worse is that your kingdom may crumble and fall."

Raena raised an eyebrow and glanced at Finn, who was doing the same.

Micha rubbed his temple, "As you know, I've given a peace treaty to the Boens. In exchange for Zarana and Zander, I allowed the Boens safe passage of their families through Ediva. Not all of them have traversed through yet, but I'm told the final wave will take the easternmost road through Guamish within a fortnight."

"My people," The Jin spoke, "we owe a debt to you all. We are thankful. Our elders, our children, our babies, they have been returned to the home of our ancestors."

Raena bit her tongue at the notion that anyone had been given a choice to surrender Boenaerya to the Jin's people. She pictured Guon, the noble and gentle warrior of House Colby. Her side ached at the physical memory of him pressed against her while they fought a horde of Boens together, slashing desperately, their very survival at stake. Her scar ached with the sting of the blade that entered between her ribs. When the image of Guon's body on the ground entered her thoughts, it rolled to reveal Zarana's head severed in the dirt of a foreign land. Raena cringed, blinking her eyes, forcing the unwanted vision away. With a sly glance, she checked to see if the others had noticed her visceral reaction, but their attention was fixated on the Boens with blatant scowls.

"Balance is restored," Micha said, "an ancient debt has been paid. There will be no more fighting from the Boens, and we will be free to pass through Boenaerya as long as we keep moving and do not harvest crops. This treaty has been signed this very morning."

"Your Majesty," Finn interjected with a bow of his head, "pardon me for speaking out of turn in front of your...guests. But may I inquire about this treaty? What mutual assurances does it make?"

"Simple ones," Micha stated, "we don't want a war, and neither do the Boens."

"That's a joke," Allyn muttered.

Micha leaned forward with one eyebrow raised. "Is that how you address a king, Sir Allyn?"

"No, Your Majesty. It's a joke, Your Majesty."

Raena raised her hand and spoke quickly before the men could erupt into harsher words. "Your Majesty, I believe we might be skeptical, but please forgive us. We've lost many of our dearest friends to the Boens. We lost our best warriors. I lost my duchy. Our kingdom lost legions upon legions. We want to see peace, but a great price has been paid."

"Then join me in welcoming the end to that price," Micha said. "I've no other choice but to trust they'll honor their agreements. I've no other choice than to trust that you're not Candorian spies. And I've no other choice than to ask you to trust me not to banish you to the Scablands or send you back to Boenarya to fend for yourself."

The tension in the room shifted as the Candorians fell noticeably silent, none of them inclined to draw additional implications of disloyalty from the King.

Micha held up a hand, "Jin, if you'd please, could you relay to my companions here the urgent matter you and I discussed?"

"Of course," The Jin mumbled. He stared with his hollow grey eyes and spoke in a slow, droning tone. "Boenaerya is ours. We will build it again. We will make it new. All the kingdoms and kings will come to find that Boens are peaceful. We are good neighbors, and live quietly under the surface. We do not want more death."

Micha rested his elbows on his knees. "In addition to this treaty, Jin has asked for my help. They want to rebuild the kingdom they lost three hundred years ago. They want to have a fighting chance at a peaceful home. But they can't secure their foothold without us. I have considered how I can meet their request, and it will require a message of unity. If we allow attitudes and fears to fester, our kingdoms might be fighting the Boens for generations. That is why Ediva will declare peace with the Boens, and I will call upon Candor to do the same, before the war."

Allyn scoffed, "Pardon me, Your Majesty, but—"

"War?" Bell interrupted, "What war?"

"The war that will come," Micha answered.

There was a heavy pause.

Allyn leaned in and pointed at Micha. "You made a treaty. You just said you are calling for peace. You appeased the Boens, and they have their land. Why would there be a war?"

Micha shook his head, but Allyn wasn't satisfied.

"What was the point of your treaty and executing our King and Queen if it didn't prevent a war?" Allyn blurted with disdain.

Micha's pale skin reddened. "You misheard me. This will not be a war with Ediva, at least, I'm trying to ensure it won't be. The war will be the Hornes, coming to take what they believe is theirs."

Allyn slapped his thighs, "The Hornes! Now I've heard everything. They are primitive men, at best. Little gnats who flit around and bother the farmers. They cannot bring on a war."

"You're wrong," The Jin spoke. "You do not know the Hornes. They are mighty warriors. They brought us onto their islands, big rocks, wet with ocean. They took us on their boats, under the water, hidden from your rangers. Thousands of my men were ferried from the wastelands onto the Horne's island. We waited there until the Hornes were ready. When they unloaded their ships onto Boenaerya, we sought to go underground and take the land no one wanted; they were first to take the land belonging to Boens."

"But you didn't go underground," Allyn said. "You burned down keeps and killed innocent families."

The Jin snarled, exposing teeth sharp as fangs. "The Hornes killed them. We wanted to make a treaty, but we were ready to fight if attacked. We had no choice but to fight once the Hornes started. We do not kill children. We do not kill women and old men."

"Liar, I saw you—"

Finn held up a hand, "Allyn, please. I want to hear the rest of this."

"Yes, the rest," The Jin said. "We had a deal. The Hornes are not honorable. The Hornes will not keep a pact. The Hornes will not honor an agreement. The Hornes will not keep peace. They take prisoners and slaughter them. They feed beasts of the ocean with bodies. They feed children to monsters. When they take the surface, no one will be safe. Not even Boens."

"Why would the Hornes want the surface of Boenaerya?" Raena asked. "They can't live there. They are sea-people. I've seen them from Colby, and they can hardly breach above the ocean for more than a minute. Like a fish."

"They have a way," The Jin muttered.

The room waited to listen for the Boen leader to elaborate, but after a moment he'd said no more.

33

Finn looked to the Edivan King. "Your Majesty, what do you ask of us?"

"Simply?" Micha asked. "I won't lolly around it, I need you to convince your new king and his advisors to enter a treaty with the Boens, the same as I've done."

Allyn laughed.

"Majesty," Raena said, "we don't yet know our new king. And we have no influence in Candor."

"You don't," Micha replied, "but you will. You will know your new king, and you will have influence. You must, actually. Because if you do not do this, then no one else will. And the Hornes will come back for the land of Boenaerya. When they do, they will push the Boens forward and out. You will no longer have safe passage above the ground, none of us will. Boenaerya will become a lawless place that bridges the kingdoms. I need not remind you that every kingdom relies heavily on the resources contained there, even the lower East and West Twins."

Bell addressed The Jin, "And where will the Boens go?"

The Jin shook his head. "There are not many lands we can inhabit. Our home is below Boenaerya. It is called Boenaerya because that's what it is; land of Boens. Without that place, we will not return to the wastelands. We toiled there for three hundred years. It is time for us to rise and stop starving beneath the ice and rock."

The room fell quiet. It was clear The Jin had not answered the question, and the answer seemed like something to dread. Raena felt her throat going dry and she wished she had more ale to take the edge off, though she knew she'd drank quite enough for so early in the day already.

The Jin rubbed his lithe fingers together. "There is one other place the Boens may live. We once had caves beneath Calamyta, though we could not farm the land above. We stayed below; the sun was too hot. We could be there again. If there is no other choice."

"So, you want to live beneath Candor?" Bell asked.

Allyn chuckled but had the good sense to say nothing.

"As you've heard, I have no intention of letting that happen," Micha defended, "I believe that we can explore many possibilities before it gets to that point. There are strategic options."

Raena recognized his passion but wondered if she could see it because his demeanor was similar to hers. Sometimes watching him was like looking into a mirror.

"What exactly would you have us do?" Bell asked.

Micha sighed, rubbing his chin, "To be honest, I have considered two things. On the one hand, I wish for you to do this willingly, and enthusiastically. You came here to my kingdom because you wanted refuge, and I have believed—or perhaps hoped—that you would repay me for the favors I've extended to you. I've treated you as well as any Edivan noble. Sometimes, I've treated you as friends. I haven't done it in jest. On the other hand, I could foresee you going home to Candor and forgetting about all we've done in this short time and the trust we've built. Don't take me for a fool, I know that people are prone to forget their loyalties when their environment changes. So, if I trust you completely, I'll ask you to return to your home and be ambassadors for peace with the Boens until your leaders agree it's for the best."

"What if it isn't?" Allyn said.

Raena wanted to reach out and slap him for being so disrespectful. She tried to give him a signal with her eyes but he didn't see it—or didn't care.

"We have appreciated your kindness," Bell said. "I haven't taken it lightly, for one."

"Right," Micha mumbled, before turning his attention back to Allyn with a harsh tone. "Let me ask you something, Lox. If a war on Candor is the only option, do you think the four remaining kingdoms will remain neutral? Do you think anyone will escape unscathed?"

Weft spoke for the first time, "The Hornes were smart to attack East Shore. They must have known what to expect. It won't be long before they return to take all of Boenaerya."

"What of it?" Allyn snapped. "We're not afraid of squashing a bunch of barbaric seamen and you shouldn't be, either."

Micha's eyes narrowed. "As I said, this is bigger than fighting the Hornes. Try to expand your mind to see beyond the worries that fit inside your ridiculous mustache, for once."

Weft held out his hands as if predicting a fight and hoping to hold it back. The tension between the two men was thick, but they did little more than glare at one another.

Raena looked at The Jin and his eyes locked with hers. "Do you believe the Hornes will come?"

"Yes."

"And when they do, what will happen?"

The Jin sighed, "The Hornes will force us out. They are vengeful. They think that we took the land for Boens and Hornes to share. We wanted Boenaerya only for Boens. No Hornes. Now they say we must give them the land, or they kill."

Raena nodded and glanced at her companions on either side, who all appeared to understand the implication.

"Couldn't you share?" Allyn said.

Bell held up a finger. "If I may interject. There aren't enough resources. The Boens need the dense vegetation of Boenarya to farm and thrive, though they live underground. There isn't enough to support more."

"Yes," The Jin said, his grey eyes alight. "And we wish to honor agreements to share with Ediva, to share with Candor. We can share the minerals. We can share the wood from trees. We can give."

Micha elaborated, "We can make such pacts, I think that's clear by how amicably we can agree within this room. We will get no such assurances of economic mutuality or trade from the Hornes. We know the Hornes can't honor their agreement, because they made one with the Boens to move the Boen people from the wasteland to the Boenarya coast. The Hornes were asked to clear the way by attacking the fortified keeps the Boens couldn't reach from underground, such as Colby. But they took everything too far. We may not all see eye-to-eye, but everyone in this room can agree that the Hornes are our enemy. I trust the Boens. You trust me."

Allyn shook his head, "It's a lot of trust. You're asking a lot."

Micha didn't say anything, but pursed his lips and shrugged.

Raena sensed the opportunity to ask a question that had been nagging her. "If we do decide to enter a war with you against the Hornes, or if we simply convince Candor into a peaceful treaty, then how would we fight? Under what flag would we ride?"

"Boen flag," The Jin said, "this war is Boen against Horne. My armies will ride first, and die first. You will follow."

"That's an easier pill to swallow, at least," Raena muttered. "I might be able to convince a king to follow, but not to start a fight against a land he's never cared about."

"But how?" Finn asked. "How will the Boens fight above ground? If Candor sends an army into Boenaerya, then our legions must fight the Hornes. The Boens can't hold a front line when that line is under the surface."

The Jin smiled. "We have been preparing." He nudged the Boen man beside him.

The second Boen reached into a canvas sack and pulled forth a piece of armor. Raena could sense immediately that it was a helmet of some kind. Her memory flashed back to when and where she had seen it before; it was almost the exact replica of something she had seen buried in her family's artifacts, saved under Hawk's Keep. She avoided Sir Jonn's gaze, afraid that he may also recognize the item's significance as a reminder of House Schinen.

"We have adapted," The Jin said, gesturing to the helmet. "We can fight in the sun."

The second Boen pointed wordlessly to the tiny slit of an eyepiece. The metal was thick and would cover a man's entire skull, except for that one narrow opening. Indeed, it could block out almost all light for the wearer.

Raena stared at the helmet and for a moment found her thoughts wandering. She tried to picture Boens running through an underground tunnel and emerging with the helmet and a weapon. But every time she tried to picture a warrior, she saw a clear image of herself in her mind's eye. As it had felt when she held the similar helmet under Hawk's Keep, Raena longed to reach out and slide it on. Micha caught her attention and when she glanced at him, his eyes darted away. She wondered if he must be wishing the same thing for himself, or perhaps he was envisioning Raena among the Boens and making a comparison.

Weft stood, holding out his hands. "It's time that each of you sat with King Micha alone. Please leave the room and I will come to get each of you. Sir Finley, you'll stay first."

Raena, Allyn, and Bell bowed as they stood and waited until the three Boen visitors had been cleared from the room. With a nod from Micha, they went into the walkway to wait together. Allyn had a sour expression but Raena had no interest in hearing more of his opinions. She turned to Bell to start talking before Allyn could launch into a release of his negativity.

"Have you eaten yet?" Raena asked.

It was their code for if Bell had seen Aven.

"Recently? No." Bell replied, not elaborating.

"We should, together. After this."

Bell made a curious expression. Raena noticed that she seemed very tired, perhaps even down. There were dark circles under her brown eyes that Raena hadn't noticed before.

"You were quiet, in there," Raena pushed.

Bell glanced away, "Not much for me to say when you lot have all the answers."

Raena bristled, "That's never once bothered you."

"I suppose I've never had to defend my every thought to men before."

Raena scowled, the dramatism of Bell's comment seeming excessive.

"D'ya think he's trying to turn us against each other?" Allyn grumbled.

"How do you reckon?" Raena asked.

"Bringing us in alone," Allyn replied. "Who knows what Finn is saying in there. Maybe he's asking each of us to pledge to him and report on each other."

"I doubt that," Raena said.

Allyn shrugged.

Weft came out of the room and called for Finn's two barons, who were never far, and who carried him and tended to him day and night. They were kind and gentle with him, though they couldn't speak or understand him. They slid a strapped device under his chair to move him, mumbling to one another in Edivan and patting his shoulders to warn before they hoisted the chair with him secured to it. When the barons and Finn were out of the room, Weft called for Sir Rowan.

Raena returned to the chair she'd occupied a moment before, across from Micha in the room. Weft closed the door, then sat to the side, perhaps to give them privacy even though he would listen to everything.

"I regret we haven't spent more time together," Micha said, "of all my Candorian guests, you are the hardest for me to get to know."

Raena stiffened, not sure how to take the comment.

"Despite that, I'm sure you speak your mind." Micha leaned forward, "I want your opinion on who I should send back to Candor, and who should stay here."

Raena paused, thrown by the sudden change in topic. "You want...first of all, Majesty, you're not sending all of us?"

"I hadn't planned to, but if you suggest that I do, I'll consider that as well."

Raena paused, her brow furrowed, taking another moment. "Why would any of us stay here?"

"To entice you to return, for one," Micha said, "and so I might utilize you as my allies. I see a number of ways that you could all benefit me, greatly. That's why I approved Sir Jonn's request to shelter you here. It's not by accident."

"Of course not, Majesty."

Micha smiled, "Just because I don't understand you doesn't mean I haven't noticed that the others think highly of you. In fact, they look up to you. Bell and Finn in particular are loyal to you beyond anything I've ever seen. If that's the kind of credibility you have in Candor, I think you'd do fine to convince your king into a pact with Ediva."

"Thank you for the kind words," Raena said without emotion. The words might have meant something to her if she believed them. Micha must have been sensing their affinity for her from the past, not the present, and it gave Raena a pang of grief that tightened in her chest.

"You must understand my position," Micha continued, "I'm the youngest king to sit on this throne since Ediva was established three hundred years ago. The people chose me. We've allowed the people to choose since before the Equinox Wars. But the pressure..."

Raena was still reeling from a dull pain inside her. Thoughts of how she couldn't protect Aven. Her inner voice taunted her that her loyalty meant nothing if she couldn't be loyal to the one woman she swore herself to. She didn't deserve his praise. His words continued but they droned into the background. It was only when Micha stopped speaking that Raena realized he had asked a question. She caught his periwinkle eyes, open wide with expectation. "I...I beg your pardon, Majesty?"

Micha rubbed his face, "It's hard to explain and I couldn't do it justice. I think someday we could sit down and talk about everything I've had to forfeit and all the things I've gained. Out of everyone, I know you'd understand what I mean. There is a reason the Almighties have brought you and I together, but perhaps we are meant to be apart for the next piece of this great journey."

Raena blinked hard, trying to sober herself. She searched her mind for clues. Foolishly, she nodded, forcing her face into a tight expression to feign reflection.

"Do you need more time to consider it?" Micha asked.

"Consider?"

"Who I should send."

Raena bit her lip, "Send back to Candor, yes. No, I can judge that. I don't need more time. More time to consider, of course, I mean, I can have that answer without thinking much at all." Raena realized she was babbling and took a deep breath, willing herself to speak with some semblance of eloquence.

Micha pressed his fingertips together but was otherwise still as a statue.

"Majesty," Raena stated, "my answer is, I believe you should send Bell and Allyn."

"Really? Explain your reasoning."

Raena leaned back in her seat and took care to choose each word. "Both Bell and Allyn are close to succession. They have a lot of influence due to their bloodlines. If Bell's father, Lord Sylas, returns to Candor, he may likely be the next king. She will be able to speak to him as an equal, or at least to tell him all her opinions and he'll consider them."

"Is that something women can do, in Candor?"

"Not particularly, but that's the relationship Sylas has with his wife and daughter. Perhaps because he never had any sons of his own."

"Interesting. But that is contingent on Lord Sylas returning. I may ask Jonn if he's heard any different, but I don't believe Sylas is in Candor. Wasn't that a reason you said you could not return?"

Raena nodded, "It is. If you remember, Zarana claimed he was in East Twin, but I don't know if that's true."

"She would have no reason to lie, so close to death. What about Allyn, why should I send him?"

"He knows the library; he's trusted with history. He will be able to make his case for the next king. His family may have already determined who is entitled next for the throne…but Allyn can complete the records with any gaps. He knows the lineage better than any nobleman; it's been his sole purpose outside of knighthood."

Micha rubbed his fingertips together and paused for a long moment. He shifted in his chair, as though uncomfortable, but he provided no comment.

Raena waited, hearing the murmur of her friend's voices from beyond the door, suddenly aware of how she could distinguish the brushing sound of clothing each time she or Micha moved in the slightest. The silence was filled with casual interruptions, but she dared not press the King to hurry with his next words.

Finally, he spoke again. "Why shouldn't I send you?"

"Me?" Raena scratched at her chin and her mind flashed to Aven. Aven, alone in the bullocks. Aven, left behind in Ediva. Would Raena even be able to say goodbye? She stuttered over her words. "I—I am banished, first of all."

"You were banished by Zander. He's dead."

"Of course," Raena paused. She squirmed and rubbed at the back of her neck, struggling to find the words. "It's hard to say if his ideas would be vanquished, though. The people who followed him…"

"You should have a fresh start. Rowan, I can see by the way you are with the other Candorians. They all feel partial to you. You're a leader, with a strong voice. People gravitate toward you, even if you don't recognize that. I know if you go, then you can lead them."

"So, you do plan to send me, then?"

"I haven't fully decided, but the more I think about it, the more I lean that way."

Raena sighed. She wanted to insist that if she go, Aven must come also. But Jonn had made it clear that Micha detested the idea of a commoner and a noble together. As much as Raena wanted to believe that wasn't true, she had no way of knowing Micha's true thoughts or demeanor beyond the rigid persona he projected. "I would do my best to follow your orders, Majesty."

"Good," Micha said, "we are agreed, then. I will consider your recommendation."

Raena gave a half-smile and bowed her head, but didn't stand. She sensed their conversation nearing an end and felt torn. With a heavy sensation in her chest, she resolved that she couldn't leave the room without at least trying. If she received punishment perhaps it would stop with a stern warning.

Micha rubbed his hands together and gestured toward the door.

"Majesty," Raena blurted before she lost her courage, "forgive me, but, what of Duchess Avenna?"

He raised his eyebrows, seemingly taken aback. "What of her?"

"Would she stay? Surely, it makes as much sense for her to return to Candor? She hasn't a life here, perhaps anywhere, now that House Colby is gone. But her family is there in Candor."

Micha rubbed his pale neck, making a pained expression. "I wouldn't presume to ask her to stay or go. I'm providing the caravan and if she chooses to take it..."

Raena felt a lump in her throat as she swallowed. "Thank you, Majesty."

"Is that all?" Micha asked, then quickly asserted, "I'm not rushing you; I value what more you have to say, but I'd like to hear equally from the others."

Raena was afraid to say more and break the little bit of assurance she'd gained. "That's all, Majesty." She offered a bow as she scrambled up and returned to the hallway. Before she even noticed the others her attention drew immediately to the added presence of Sir Jonn.

He was further down the corridor, leaning against a wall. He made such a point to separate himself from the others, and Raena couldn't tell if it was his annoyance with them or a need to be seen as superior. Had he not been there, Raena would have slipped away, down to the bullocks. She could tell Aven the good news that they could return to Candor and stay together. Aven would need to know when the caravan left so she might join it. Perhaps then they could put this all behind them and be together, the way they might have been if Colby had never fallen to the Boens.

When Allyn took his turn to talk with Micha, Bell seemed eager to discuss something. Raena eyed Sir Jonn and shook her head, asking if it could wait. Bell understood and chose to ramble about how hard it was to choose a dress from Edivan tailors that didn't itch, while Raena nodded and thought of other matters. Throughout the dull conversation, Raena could feel the gravity of Jonn's dark eyes on her, following her every breath.

If Micha's offer gave Raena a chance to escape from under the weight of this scrutiny, then Raena supposed she may prefer it; but that meant finding a way to ensure Jonn stayed behind.

CHAPTER 4
SYLAS

From ships come scales and gills

"Do you think the rumors are true? Is it possible?" Lady Isla bit her lip as she stared off into the horizon at the setting sun. Dusk cast an orange glow to her skin, interrupted by the reflection of rippling ocean waves.

They were at the bow of their simple vessel: a cog. She was sturdy, yet beginning to wear from the multiple voyages they'd taken along this route already. Aboard the ship behind Sylas and Isla was the ever-present and steady creak of wood and the rhythmic grunts of their shipmates hard at work.

Sylas gazed at his wife. He recognized the toll of the last year, written in fresh crow's feet around her eyes. Yet he could see her face every day and never find a flaw, even as she aged and carried the stress of their constant evasion of the crown's murder squads.

"Sylas," Isla said, staring him in the eyes, "did you hear me?"

"Of course, love. I was only thinking. You asked if it were possible. Erm, is what possible, again?"

She sighed and placed her hand over his, resting on the ship's tall bow. "Is it possible the Queen has been executed? This last group of refugees sounded certain of the fact."

"Oh, that," Sylas grumbled, "you know how the peasants are. How many of them have we taken to Haven by now. A hundred? Two hundred? I've surely lost count. Every last one of them brings some rumors from Candor that sound promising or dismal, and then you know what happens; we get the next batch of them and they all swear to something that contradicts the last."

Isla sighed, "Then you ought to speak with Sesca yourself. She is wiser than all of them."

"Which one is Sesca?"

"The matriarch. The old woman."

Sylas squinted and glanced over his shoulder at the handful of peasants working above deck. He didn't see any old women as he scanned, only Sir Cames instructing a few teenage boys and scattered crispy elders at the stern, messing with rope.

"She's the healer," Isla continued, "remember, husband? She saved the boy with the broken leg and told us the story of how the soldiers were…assaulting the young women and she—"

"Right, right. That one. The one with the bad eye."

Isla let out a short breath through her nose. "Yes, the bad eye, but more importantly she's the one with all the beautiful stories of how she's watched over her people as Candor has fallen to ruin."

"That's remarkable."

"Yes, I agree."

"Watching over people with only one good eye."

Isla groaned and slapped Sylas on the shoulder. She opened her mouth to say something and Sylas braced himself for it, but Cames joined them in an opportune moment.

"Lord, Lady," Cames began, "the old man, Bein, has told me more news from Candeo."

Isla shook her head, "I suppose he told you that Zarana has been executed by the new young King in Ediva?"

Cames raised a thick black eyebrow, "How did you know?"

"So, like your type," Isla groaned, "you men will hear the same news, over and over, from the mouths of women. Yet the instant you hear it from one of your own, it's credible? Now you believe it? How astounding."

Cames giggled, raising his shoulders with a sheepish expression.

Sylas clapped a hand on the young knight's arm. "Don't let her get to you, lad. Before you know it, Isla will have you apologizing on account of every man whose ever been born, and possibly some who haven't yet."

"And I'll do it," Cames said, "because I know I'm a dumb boy compared to her brilliance."

Sylas both groaned and chuckled. "Oh, come off, now I know she's been bribing you with sea rations. What's she slipping you, lad? Is it the good fish? It's the marler, isn't it?"

Isla bristled, "I would never. I dole out all our rations fairly, based on work and weight. If Cames received more, it's because he earned it and is still a growing lad."

Both men laughed, sharing in the joke at her expense. Isla waited, red-faced, for them to finish.

"I'm sorry, love," Sylas said through laughter, "I've been particularly hard on ya today."

"Well," she muttered, "it's nice to see you in good spirits. I suppose this means you're feeling confident about our voyage."

"Aye," Sylas caught himself and took a long breath. "We have strong winds to thank. I might be a poor sailor but I know good fortune when I see it. We've been particularly blessed on this run."

Cames nodded. "It's true, Lord and Lady, I remember those rocks. We passed them at dawn on day three of our last few voyages. Now we are nearly to them on our second day's dusk. I'd say that's a twelve-hour lead."

47

"A six-hour lead," Sylas corrected, "we left East Twin at midnight the last few runs. Remember this time we left before nightfall. It's not about when we get there, it's about how long the journey takes. It's still the same distance to measure. It's still a twenty-day journey from the lowest tip of East Twin to Haven at the edge of Boenaerya."

"Well, twenty days minus six hours, at least," Cames said.

Isla shook her head and waved at the two stocky men. "You men could have this discussion all night—I'm off to sleep. It'll be another long day of cooking, for me. Goodnight to both of you."

Sylas gave his wife the expected kiss on the cheek and wished her goodnight. When she was out of earshot he chuckled, letting out a long breath.

"Well, Cames, how about it? Are you apt to sleep anytime tonight?"

Cames shrugged, "I haven't had night's watch since we set sail."

"Why don't you rest one more night. Tomorrow will be your chance. I can stay up and navigate with the stars."

Cames bit his lip. "Are you sure, my Lord? I've got plenty of energy. I can manage."

Sylas grimaced playfully. "You trying to say I'm old, eh? That stings a mite. Why don't you hold back your insults, baby-face."

"That—that's not what I meant! My Lord…"

Sylas erupted into a fit of laughter, clapping Cames on the shoulder. "Come off, lad. I'm only teasing. You're a worried goon. Now go on to bed, I'll take the crow's nest and watch until relief comes."

"Yes," Cames muttered, "of course. Easy enough."

With a few heavy sighs and great care, Sylas climbed the slippery pegs to the crow's nest, knocking his knees along the way. He was sore, and of course he was tired, but he refused to do less than his part.

At the top they had hitched a cloth that hung across, making a seat that could also serve as a hammock. Sylas lowered himself into it and leaned back, rubbing at his sore kneecaps. He stared up at the stars, familiar by now with their constellations as if it were the freckles on his own body. Quietly to himself, he began to sing a shanty. It was the only shanty he knew, as he was not a real sailor, but it felt right to sing it whenever he had the chance.

Pick up yer maiden, and gimme her time
Dunnot come here sober, nor give up yer wine
Carry your burdens, lay them down low
And th' moon will embrace ye all th' way home

Come to me maidens, we cherish th' dead
Remember the souls we once lost instead
Carry your burdens, lay them down low,
And th' light will embrace ye all th' way home

Hold me now maidens, lay in the light,
Forget not our days we carried th' fight,
We lost our mothers, but gained our sons,
Now the burdens we owe to the Almighty ones

Sylas felt the rock of his hammock, swaying. He smelled the sea. The gulls above were cawing with some enthusiasm, likely after a mollusk or another scrap of garbage they hoped to snatch off the deck.

But the gulls.

Sylas's eyes jolted open. It was daybreak. The sun had been up for several minutes, by the tint of the sky. He scrambled to rise from the hammock, tangling up in the fabric for a moment and tripping forward. He caught himself on the edge of the crow's nest, kicking his feet free.

When he looked out, spinning around, all he saw was the ocean, in every direction.

"Who's on the helm?!" he bellowed, searching the deck.

A few of the peasants were about, mucking around. They startled at the shout and gazed up to Lord Sylas.

"Who is manning the helm?" Sylas repeated, louder.

Davyn replied from a spot near the rigging. "I was, but we're sailing true. I have been checking it from time-to-time."

Sylas groaned words that Isla would have slapped him for. He swung his leg to the post and climbed down as fast as he could muster, banging both knees at every step. Near the bottom he jumped to the deck. "Do you've any idea how far we are from shore? We are out too far! You numb dunce!"

Davyn bowed his head. "I thought we kept a straight heading. I tied the wheel so it stayed in one direction."

Sylas ran to the helm and found that indeed, a rope had been tied through the wheel and rigged around two boards on either side. "The shore isn't a straight line, and we weren't right alongside it! Did you not notice we were getting farther and farther out?"

Davyn fell to his knees to begin undoing the ropes, but Sylas shouted at him to move away.

Sylas was still fiddling with the ropes feverishly when a familiar woman's voice chided him from overhead.

"Husband, what on earth has happened to our course?"

"I'll correct it, Isla," he grumbled.

"I don't know if you can. I'll fetch Cames."

Sylas looked up to shout a protest, but she was already rushing to the cabin. He returned to his task, ripping at the rope so hard he felt his fingernail tear. He ignored the pain, grimacing, but pushing through.

"Sesca, get up to the crow's nest," Cames was calling out orders from the deck. "Davyn, help me with this rigging. We are going to turn the ship faster if we let out this sail. Lady Isla, please help Sylas with the helm, we need all hands!"

Sylas noticed droplets of blood falling from his finger onto the wood and rope below. He didn't let up, breaking the first side free. He reached for the next section of rope, but Isla's thin hands beat him to it.

"Stop that," she snapped, "tend to your wound. There's blood all over the place."

"I think I ripped a nail off."

"Take care of it, you sap. I can manage this."

Sylas huffed and stood, wrapping his hand around his finger. He realized how much it hurt now that he could focus on the pain. His legs felt wobbly but he held it together as he stumbled across the deck.

Cames and Davyn were near the mast, their eyes fixated upward. Sylas followed their gazes all the way up to the crow's nest, where Sesca's frail frame was a dark outline against the stark white of the overcast sky. Without a word, Sylas stepped closer. His finger throbbed, but something about the look on the men's faces made his insides clench, and a swelling pit of dread bubbled up within him.

Sesca was pointing out toward something in the sea, off the bow. Cames and Davyn were shouting to her, but there was fear and urgency coating their bodies. Both men appeared poised to leap into action.

"Grab the oars!" Cames shouted.

Davyn ran across the deck, slipping on a wet plank and skidding forward before he regained his balance.

"We can throw something!" Sesca yelled down from the crow's nest before returning her attention to the sea.

"What's happening?" Sylas called out to them.

No one responded to the query. The men were running about the deck and Sesca was scrambling to descend the ladder of the crow's nest.

Sylas spun back to the helm where he had been a moment before, to see Isla staring ahead at the chaos. Her eyes were alert and her hands were raised.

"Sylas," she called, "do you see it?"

He shook his head, spinning around to look over the hull.

"Here, my Lord." Cames said. Without explanation, he shoved an oar into Sylas's hand, forcing him to let go of his wound.

The blood rushing back into his finger distracted him, and by the time he tried to ask Cames what the oar was for, the young knight was bounding away toward the bow.

"Find something else to fight with!" Cames directed Davyn, who nodded and ran for the rigging.

51

At the use of the word 'fight', Sylas jolted backward. He whipped his head around to the space ahead of their ship. He was no longer searching above the water for land, but he scanned the waves for signs of anything in or below.

That was when he saw it. That was when he knew. His chest clenched in knots immediately.

Skimming through the water were three dark shadows, nearly breaching the waves. The crafts were long and thin as far as Sylas could tell. They were aligned to the bow of the cog and gaining fast. By his estimation, they would intercept within seconds.

Cames shouted below the deck for Autrum, who emerged frazzled. All of the ship's passengers were a flurry, rushing about to grab anything that could be thrown or wielded for battle. Sylas could merely stand and stare.

With a sloshing rush of water peeling away, the tubular crafts broke through the surface. The outer two came up alongside the cog, while the third had slowed beyond the bow.

Sylas couldn't track everything that happened next. Davyn and Sesca were at one side, heaving a barrel to the deck railing. Cames was hunched over, dragging spare rigging across the deck toward the mast. The chains and shackles clanged.

Sylas heard a whooshing sound at the bow, then a creak. His body set into motion as his legs carried him with unwanted force to a destination his heart screamed at him to avoid. He thought to run back and protect Isla, but his only chance would be to run right into the fight. If they boarded the cog, the fight would be over.

He peered off the bow at a sickening sight.

The tubular ship had fully risen and floated atop the water. The head was split open like a pierced belly, revealing the contents inside. Dozens of barbaric Hornes were swarming within the dark mass of the wooden ship, scrambling for a single point. Sylas's eyes followed their movement to find their destination—a roped netting that had been secured to his cog with metal burs. Frantically, Sylas bent over the edge of the bow and grabbed at the rope, trying to yank free a bur's grip on the hull.

A firm tug on the netting from below ripped the rope from Sylas's hands.

The Hornes were upon the rope, climbing.

They were a sight of terror.

Every man wore sleek black hides, tight to their skin, wet from the spray. It was as though they were coated in an oily sea monster's flesh that gripped and caged the muscle beneath. They had long black hair and eyes of fury, dark as night. Their thick necks were gilled—their exposed fingers and toes splayed and webbed. As they clamored up the rope, the sunlight reflected on their cheeks, revealing glints of a mosaic, their skin displaying a patterned hint of scales.

Sylas's heart pounded in his chest and he grasped the oar in his hands, rolling it in his grip to prepare. As if there were anything he could do to save or protect himself.

And Isla.

And Cames.

They were all doomed. Oars and barrels would do nothing for any of them. His only hope was to kill enough of them on their way up.

He stepped backwards and readied the oar. He would strike them one-by-one as they breached the top of the hull.

"We have to surrender! Sylas!" Isla screamed from behind him.

The thud of more burs sticking to the deck slammed and echoed on both sides. Sylas heard the men's shouts and battle cries closing in around them.

Sylas readied the oar. He envisioned the sharp end stabbing into their gilled necks. He glanced back to see Cames with rigging and braces, poised to throw them over the starboard side.

Isla screamed again. "Sylas! Surrender!"

This time he found her; Isla's eyes filled with dismay. Her mouth was open and steam clouds of breath swirled out of her into the frosty morning air. No doubt she was filled with adrenaline. He would have applauded her for the power and beauty she exhibited if it weren't for the fact they were likely about to die in a gory, abrupt execution.

"It's the only way," she pleaded, "they won't spare us if we fight!"

He shook his head and let out a stifled wail. "What are you saying?"

"We're surrounded. They'll slaughter us."

Isla's chest heaved with a deep breath. Determination filled her eyes, fixated on her husband as though willing and begging him to join her resolve. She was beckoning him with tranquility in every breath, their souls tied together by countless strands that wove into strength no one could break. Their connection, their love, could speak without words.

The same realization washed over him and his muscles relaxed with resignation. All that was left in his frame was anguish.

"Fall back," Sylas choked, then raised his voice, "fall back! Drop everything, we must surrender. Come round to me, now!"

Cames, Davyn, Sesca, and Autrum looked to him, respectively confused, from opposite sides of the ship. Cames was first. He opened his hands and the bracing fell against the deck at his feet. As though entranced by a spell of obedience, he lugged across the boards toward his leader, his Lord.

Sylas tossed his oar and wrapped his hand around his bleeding finger, once more. He headed toward the center of the cog's deck and was joined by the peasants he knew well, and many he did not.

"Here, around the crow's nest," he instructed.

They were assembling still when a war cry pierced the air. Sylas jerked around to see them, over the bow and standing tall on the deck. He'd never seen a Horne, but they were magnificent in a terrible way. Now that they were on his ship, Sylas realized how long and sleek their bodies were, as though they would stand a head taller than any Candorian, if not for the way they all hunched forward. They certainly appeared shifty and uncomfortable out of the water.

"We surrender," Sylas called out.

He held up his hands, in case they didn't understand.

There was a gurgling sound from the Hornes. On all sides, they were raiding the ship. Within a second there were half-fish men at every angle, surrounding them. Sylas felt the others tightening up and huddling behind him.

"We surrender! Do not harm us! Take what you want from our stores!" Sylas shouted. He gestured toward the door to the galley.

One Horne emerged from behind the others, dragging a spear behind him. He whipped his arm forward and lodged the blade into the wood at his feet. He was a monstrous man, his bulky muscles twice the size that Sylas's ever were in his own prime. The Horne had curling hair like the waves of the ocean and midnight eyes. He stared at Sylas, blinking, his gills fluttering.

"Please," Sylas said, this time quieter. "You may have anything you want from the galley."

The Horne laughed, revealing teeth that were surprisingly normal to Sylas. He hadn't expected that.

"Oh, land-dweller," the Horne growled, "we'll take what we want."

CHAPTER 5
AVEN

The bullocks, or absolute humility

It would soon be summer in Ediva, and Aven was told the sparse trees would bloom, though she saw no buds or leaves. She longed for the deciduous trees in her childhood kingdom of Candor. She longed for the thick kelly clover of East Shore. It had been so long since she'd seen a blossom of any color. She speculated that a flash of natural pink or yellow petals might fill her with such warmth she would be overcome for days. No such flora appeared in the landscape. Her horizon remained grey for rocks and white for ice.

Except of course for the few brown sticks that passed for "trees". The broom-like plants clung to cracks, desperate to survive. What a hopeless fate, Aven thought. Their existence was a flash— the span of time between winters. Ediva was one long winter that bled into the next.

Aven woke each morning forcing herself to count her blessings and name the things she was grateful for. She was still alive, when so many people she loved were gone. She wasn't being beaten, like the serfs and peasants clamoring and toiling below her window. Ediva's king, Micha, had been generous to give her one of the best rooms in the servant's chambers, all things considered. But the view of "the bullocks" was horrific. The brutalization against Ediva's backbone of commoners and servants was a heinous reminder that she might be tossed out of the King's favor and treated like filth at a moment's notice. What separated her from them? She was also common-born, as she was reminded more harshly than ever before.

Aven was grateful each morning that she was spared and left alone.

She was thankful for her ornate wooden bench covered in bright, colorful fabrics, and she spent many afternoons sitting there beside her window. After thanking the Almighties, she prayed.

She prayed for the peasants and serfs as they were whipped by guards for working too slow. She prayed for her brothers and father, thinking of them farming pigs back in Candor. She prayed for the leaders of Ediva to have empathy and compassion, and for their hearts to change.

Raena.

Aven prayed for Raena.

She felt the coldness of Ediva wrapping around her heart like icy fingers and burying the love they'd once shared. The last time she'd seen Raena, they had touched like two hollow bodies that lacked souls, and Raena had not since returned to share her bed. It stung like a dagger driven through Aven's center. But she couldn't let go of her prayer that the fire of compassion in Raena's heart would not be snuffed out by the freezing oppression of Ediva's nobles.

The irony of her prayers to the Almighties was not lost on Aven; that she might call for a blessing from the same gods that Ediva's commoners were oppressed in the name of.

After a morning of gratitude and prayer, Aven watched the serfs below her window bring out the scraps from the midday nobles' feasts and throw them into a pen. Frolls would come to eat the waste. Aven didn't know the word in Candorian for the boar-like beasts, but they were common livestock here. Feeding the frolls meant that soon someone would bring her a cold meal—if they remembered.

Aven set to her daily needlework, the sounds from the window as a background. Each day, she stitched a new panel to the tapestry she was creating. It told the story of House Colby: of Andres and Gracia, of their sons, of the council, of the nobles, so that they may be remembered forever.

There were thirty-one panels.

It had been thirty-one days since she'd spoken to Raena. Since they had touched.

As Aven moved the needle, she contemplated how in thirty-one days, she'd been visited by Bell and Barton more than once. Neither of them spoke of Raena, as if her lover and knight didn't exist. As if they knew that the mention of "Sir Rowan" would tear Aven's delicate heart into pieces that none of them would want to help clean up. Aven didn't want to clean up the pieces either, so she didn't ask.

The knock at Aven's door startled her. She dropped her tapestry and the needles clanged against the stone. Her heart filled with hope as she rushed to open the door. But she let out a sigh of disappointment at the sight of the mustached and flourished Allyn of Lox. Aven caught herself, quickly dropping into a low bow, in case anyone was behind him in the corridors.

Allyn offered no formality or greeting, "May I enter? We'll leave the door ajar."

"If you wish," Aven said, raising from her curtsy and stepping aside.

Allyn burst in with a purpose. He wandered the chamber for a brief moment, scanning the meager surroundings with a terse expression. When he focused on the discarded embroidery, he raised an eyebrow.

"I dropped it," Aven muttered, suddenly wishing she'd taken a moment to shut it away in her wardrobe. She gathered a fistful of her outer skirt and squeezed it in her hands.

Allyn smiled, his mustache going lopsided. "You work fast. I recognize the colors. It's Colby, there?"

Aven nodded, grateful that he wasn't picking it up to observe it closer. She wasn't sure why, but her cheeks flushed.

"Rowan told me about your colors and sigil," Allyn said, turning his back on the tapestry to focus his eyes on Aven's. "You have a lot of lore in that House. Silly, really. The sorts of things the weak-minded would believe in. I don't think much of legends like that. But Rowan was fond of the legend of the sea-wolf, as he described it. Sounds like the things you tell your children to make them obey. 'Don't disrespect your father, or the garons will eat your legs.'"

Allyn chuckled, looking at Aven expectantly. She bit her lip.

With a sigh, Allyn sauntered over toward the wardrobe and then leaned against it, crossing his arms. "What do you do to keep yourself busy here?"

Aven felt her brow tighten, "What do you mean? You've seen me…we've seen each other, out in the yard. I've passed you at least a dozen times." She neglected to mention that she'd seen Raena, as well. At a distance, but close enough that she knew both knights had noticed her presence in the expanse of the castle.

"I know, but you're never busy. You're always watching the rest of us, or looking interested in someone else. So, explain it to me. How do you pass the time and still feel…valuable?"

Aven swallowed the thick ball forming in her throat, struggling to think of a response.

"Well, I've been…returning to the roots of my beliefs. Remembering what my mother and father taught me about the Almighties. The gods of Calamyta."

Allyn chortled, "How quaint. I can't seem to escape toxic religion no matter where I turn. The Edivans have their Statera, and you have your Libre, is that it?"

Aven felt the familiar heat of shame brewing in her chest. "It isn't 'mine', and I'm not sure I even follow it closely…I was raised to follow the principles of Libre. I left that behind when I married Eathon. I adopted the belief in terra and the power of land from Colby. They worship nature around them."

"What's the difference? You might as well pray to a plant or pray to a being. None of it will change your fate the way that determination or hard work will."

"Hard work?" Aven raised her eyebrows.

"Well, hard work and your bloodline. Or your husband's bloodline? Sorry. I forget who I'm talking to."

Aven could think of no way to redeem herself from that comment. She stifled her anger, visualizing burying it into a pit. With care, she replied, her voice stable. "My father was a strict Libren, so much that he was appointed as a diacon to care for the farmers around us and teach them the ways of the Almighties. We honored them in Candor. It's not only about prayers and offerings. You learn how to treat the land, to grow crops, to bring new life from death in a practical way. Libre teaches you how to balance your life and your relationships. It can be a powerful way to heal. Candor would fall without the scaffolding that Libre provides."

"Perhaps that's why I find no use for it. I have no need to grow crops, and I have nothing to heal from." Allyn paused, scratching his chin. "But I suppose it's something for you to pass the time. It gives you purpose? That's great. It would be something though if you had a way to contribute your leadership skills to someone other than yourself, holed up in this little room, praying and being sad."

"I suppose you mean that as a compliment. I think I am making the best use of my days as I'm able."

"The best use?" Allyn scoffed.

"It's not running a duchy," she muttered, "if that's what you mean—"

"It's precisely what I mean! How many people were under your charge? You ruled a duchy, giving purpose and prosperity to thousands of men before breakfast. Why haven't you fought for your place to be treated as equal with me, Bell, and Rowan? We've never led anyone, it seems unfair, doesn't it?"

Aven felt herself struggling to keep up with the rapid and changing pace of his rhetoric.

"Listen," Allyn said, extending his hands, "I'm surprised no one has advocated this for you. All I heard for months was how we had to save you, because you were a critical ruler who could have been spared from the Boens. We all risked our lives to bound everywhere through East Shore, or Boenarya, whatever we call it now. Good men died because we needed to rescue you and Lady Islabell. But for what?" He threw up his hands and slapped them hard against his thighs.

The sudden sound made Aven jolt.

"I have no answer," she replied coolly.

"Why would you?" Allyn gestured toward her chest, "Really, why would you? Why is it up to you to advocate for yourself, when you're seen as common born? How can you go make demands for treatment when you won't even be heard because of your parentage?"

"I understand, but bringing me this does nothing to solve it."

Allyn pushed a breath through loose lips and shook his head. He began to pace in the chamber, though it was a small space to do so.

Aven was about to ask him to leave, but he spoke before she could.

"If I had any say, I'd demand it. I'd demand that you be given all the same rights and voice that we are. Do you know that we are asked to consult on what is done with Boenarya? Me, and Finn, and Rowan? The audacity! How are we able to consult on the very lands that you ruled over? I've hardly been, and Rowan knows little except some specific vulnerable fishing places he brings up. How are we meant to make decisions on a land with so little knowledge, when here you sit."

Aven felt a sting behind her eyes. She shook it away. "I appreciate your visit. I'm afraid I haven't...I'm not informed about any of these 'consults' you speak of. Neither would I be invited to join them. So, I'm afraid I have nothing to offer to this conversation. Now, if you don't mind, I'm afraid I'm not feeling up to company."

Allyn idly twirled at a corner of his mustache, making no move toward the door. "I wanted to tell you about the caravan to Candor. Unless you already know?"

"I don't."

"Oh, well I'm glad I thought to tell you. Here I thought maybe Rowan would, but then I knew he hadn't been to see you."

Aven's insides clenched as if a fist had pummeled into her gut. "What is the caravan, then?"

Allyn sighed, "We're going back. Micha has charged us to return to Candor. He has arranged safe passage for our caravan, not to be harmed by the Boens. They will escort us to the Calam Mountains and we will ride to Candeo."

"And Rowan, he is going to Candeo?" Aven's voice broke against her will.

"Yes. Rowan, Sir Jonn, and I. Micha chose us to go and advocate for a peace treaty with the Boens. Finn is to stay behind, under Bell's care. Barton hasn't decided, though I think he's content here. The choice was left for only him to make, and the rest of us have no say in it."

Aven wanted to reply about Barton, but didn't speak for fear she might let loose the well of emotion swirling up inside her.

"You may join us, or you may stay. But when I thought of you here in the bullocks and the way things have been for you, I thought you must be unhappy. There's no chance you are satisfied with how things are in Ediva."

"You're right," she whispered. To keep him from seeing the tears threatening to flow, she went to the window and stared out at the froll slaughterhouse below. It was not unlike the pig farms of her childhood home. Allyn was so quiet behind her, Aven hoped perhaps he had left. She watched two men wrestle a froll to its side and brand it with a flaming hot iron. Her stomach roiled at the familiar sweet smell of burning flesh.

Allyn shuffled behind her, breaking the silence. "Has no one been visiting you?"

She rolled a shoulder without turning around.

He sighed, "I'm so sorry. I've been busy lately, learning about the Boens. We're trying to understand them so we know what to expect, I suppose. If we can get into their minds, we can guess the next moves they will make, and perhaps keep them from attacking..."

He continued to explain to Aven's back as she felt a tear fall. Soon another followed. She didn't wipe her eyes, she stared at the farmers below. She easily remembered the last time she'd spoken to her mother. It was before she'd met Raena, one of the times she visited Candeo and held council with Queen Zarana. Aven had gone to the pig farm where her parents and five older brothers worked. It was the first spring after Eathon's death, and Aven had still felt tender and broken. When she went to her family, she implored them to leave Candeo and come to House Colby. Aven's mother, Gailia, had been angry and cold, spitting on the floor and insisting she'd rather serve a true queen than be humiliated by bowing to her own "snooty daughter". Aven thought that was the most pain she would ever feel; how naive she'd been of what true grief was yet to come.

"...and we're meeting beside Painter's Lake tomorrow. You may join us."

Aven snapped out of her faraway thoughts, "Tomorrow? The caravan?" She glanced over her shoulder and saw him nod.

"If you're there, I'm sure you may go with us. That way you could stay with Rowan, if you still want to." His tone lifted as though asking a question.

Rowan.

Aven spun to face Allyn straight on, and she felt the dam break inside her. Her fingers began to shake and Aven clenched her fists to keep him from seeing. She raised her chin, not caring if a remnant of tears remained under her eyes. Inside her, everything twisted and turned like a hurricane, growing in volume.

"I don't want to," Aven snapped.

Allyn flinched.

"I don't care about staying with Rowan," Aven clarified, stepping forward with arms flexed. "I don't need him. I don't need any of you to help me. I didn't need you to come in here and tell me any of this, I was doing just fine."

Allyn raised his hands, "Aye, all right—"

"You're misguided and wasting my time, at best. Rowan is even worse. I'd prefer you stop coming around to tell me about him. I'll be on that caravan because I have family and business to tend to back in Candeo. No other reason. Let yourself worry about your own politics next time, and leave me out of it."

He sneered under his mustache with thinly veiled disgust. "I'm trying to do you a favor."

"Save it. I don't need favors."

Allyn balked, his jaw dropping.

Aven knew that the switch in her demeanor was unwanted. Allyn appeared afraid, or intimidated. Either way, it didn't matter to her. Aven would not be a little helpless girl anymore. Not for Raena, especially.

Allyn muttered to himself, then repeated it, louder. "Suit yourself, Duchess. Come back with us, or don't."

Before Aven could lurch forward to bark another word of spite, he was bolting from the room, huffing aloud as he did.

Aven paced the tiny chamber, keeping one eye on the door as if daring anyone to come through it and face her wrath. Part of her wished Raena might appear, begging her to join the caravan, so Aven could roast her alive with words. She shook her hands to ward off their shaking at the thought.

With a set of her jaw, Aven's mind was made up. She would take the caravan, but not to unite with her old noble allies. She would do it on her own, the same as she always had, relying only on herself.

Unburdened for a moment, Aven returned to the labor of her tapestry. She stitched the story of her councilors: Angeline Mondraken, Thadeon Cross, Eljoy. She recreated their likenesses with as much justice as she could manage. But the panels with the garons taunted her, reminding her of making Raena's tunic. Raena, proudly wearing the tunic. Aven paused several times, wringing out her fingers, willing them to steady. When she couldn't ignore her tremors any longer, she stood, leaving the needlework for another day.

"That's enough," Aven whispered to herself in a chastising tone. "What do you owe them? What do you owe her? Nothing. She'll continue to give you nothing. You've already made the right choice."

She poured herself a cup of water and brought it to her lips, sipping, willing herself to focus on the sensation of drinking.

At the mindlessness of the act, it loosened her emotions. The reality of what Aven felt burst from within her like an epiphany.

Fear. Fear that if she entered that caravan, it would be the final act that would drive her and Raena apart, forever. Fear that Raena would continue to be ice cold. Fear that only a tiny sliver of intimacy would remain between them and Aven would weaken herself to grasp for it.

Fear. Of losing Raena.

A pained groan escaped from deep within her chest. Aven ripped it back, turning it into an angered growl. She took another drink of water and washed her emotion away with a gulp.

Slamming down the goblet, Aven shook her head.

She would go to the caravan.

She would return to Candor, and Raena would be responsible for dealing with that in her own way.

She wouldn't fear something so silly.

Aven feared nothing.

When Aven reached the edge of Painters Lake, she held her satchels awkwardly. There was a bustle of thick, ruddy Edivan horsemen and stable hands loading up a long row of wagons. Aven counted nine wagons, five of them for carrying passengers and four for cargo. She resisted the urge to seek out familiar nobles of Candor, instead focusing on her task of finding the servant's wagon.

It was cold, even though summer was near. Aven tucked her black hair behind her ears and pulled her woven hat down to cover them. She thought of how blistering hot the deserts of Candor would feel. She might miss Ediva, in an odd way. It was the most beautiful of all the kingdoms, she supposed, with the picturesque snow-capped mountains and swaths of infinity trees. Aven stared through her clouded breaths at the reflection of the peaks in the shallow lake. She tried to remember the names of them, wishing she spoke Edivan better, like Allyn and Bell did. With a huff, she decided this journey would be her chance to learn more of the language.

"Bow to the King!" a man shouted from behind.

Aven turned quickly and dropped to her knees, muddying her woven grey dress. She felt the icy ground soaking through the fabric and chilling her legs. Peering up through her lashes, she watched King Micha approach on foot, surrounded by an entourage of nobles and guards. Among them were Sir Jonn, Allyn, Raena, and Bell. Aven fought the shiver that ran through her at the humiliating position she was in, bowing prostrate before the knights who would have served her only a few short weeks before. As if thinking the same thing, Raena's periwinkle eyes met Aven's, then darted away.

King Micha gave a short speech in Edivan, mentioning the names of the Candorians and gesturing to the caravan. Aven inferred through context that he was giving them a blessing for the mission and journey ahead.

"Fla pas na halum," Micha said, allowing a pause.

"Fla pas halamna," Aven echoed along with the serfs and peasants, beside her. She'd been told it roughly translated to 'joy from the Almighty of time'.

Micha gave a short bow and left, his royal guards following along. When he was out of sight, Sir Jonn bellowed a word in Edivan and the peasants began to rise to their feet. Aven did the same, remiss to see the dark stains on her skirts and the growing wet spots. Fortunately, her satchels were made of leather, otherwise the few clothing items and embroidery she'd packed would be soaked from sitting on the wet ground. She gathered them by the straps, her wavy black hair falling into her eyes.

"Does this mean you're taking the caravan?" a familiar, husky voice said from above.

Aven dropped to her knee immediately, back into the mud. "My Lord," she muttered, staring at Raena's darkened leather boots.

"Oh," Raena said, letting out a loud sigh, "please um, please stand up."

Aven spoke through her teeth, "You know I can't, my Lord."

"Right."

There was a brief pause, and Aven bit her lip, focusing on the little pool of dirt and half-melted snow between them. She could clearly picture Raena's furrowed brow of frustration. Around them, Aven heard the continuing bustle of peasants loading the caravan, and she thought she even heard Allyn's distinctive laugh in the near distance.

"Well," Raena mumbled, "you won't have to bow to me when we're in Candor. So, that will be nice."

Aven's tone gave away her displeasure, "If you say so, my Lord."

"Erm, all right," Raena's voice broke with a nervous laugh. "Well, Bell is here, to say goodbye. She'll want to…to say goodbye to you."

Aven nodded, feeling a swell in her chest at the mention of Bell. She was about to ask where the lady was when Raena blurted out a warning.

"Sir Jonn is coming."

Aven kept her eyes still fixated on the ground. She felt the cold seeping back into her skin through her wet skirts. She waited a moment, then watched the second set of boots appear alongside Raena's.

Sir Jonn spoke, but only to Raena, "They're ready to load, you ought to settle in. You'll be in that third wagon, and I'll be in the fourth with Allyn."

"My own wagon? Lucky me."

"Seemed the best choice, considering," Jonn said.

Aven's cheeks flushed with quiet rage that Jonn pretended she wasn't even there, like she were any ordinary peasant. He knew better.

As if Raena read those thoughts, she asked, "What about Aven? Where can my Duchess ride?"

Jonn grumbled something indistinct, then spoke louder, "The pages and horsemen are in that wagon there, and I think the handmaids and peasant women will have a wagon. I'll ask Elo, he's the lead horseman."

"Then she'll have a wagon to herself?" Raena asked.

Jonn said something quiet, again, and Aven could only hear his tone. She wasn't surprised that it sounded negative and condescending. When they were done whispering, Jonn walked away.

"I'm sorry about that," Raena said, "this is horseshite, honestly. I'll make sure you're comfortable in the caravan."

"It's fine—"

"It isn't. I hate it. I'm glad things will be normal again in Candor."

"I said, I'll be fine," Aven said, raising her voice.

Raena made a humming sound.

Aven resisted the temptation to look up into Raena's eyes and explain exactly why she would be absolutely fine and didn't need any help. She didn't want pity anymore, and she wasn't going to let the Candorians continue to pretend like she would be returned to her status among them. They were lying, and they knew it. Aven wasn't a duchess without a duchy, she was a pig farmer.

Someone called for Rowan.

"I have to go," Raena said, "will you at least look at me?"

Aven lifted her chin, peering around as she did for any signs of someone watching. She saw that everyone appeared to be occupied with loading the horses and heaving supply bags into wagons. Hesitantly, her eyes trained on Raena, who wore a sad expression.

All of the anger in Aven quelled at the sight. She felt a contorted sensation in her chest that turned to a pang of guilt. She had hurt Raena.

They communicated without words, a sustained gaze of knowing. Raena's face turned to something softer, yet apologetic, and Aven wondered if her own expression mirrored it. Aven soaked in how much change she saw in Raena. There was a change there from the woman she knew, and it wasn't just the strange look of Edivan clothes or the way Raena no longer wore the colors of Colby on her face and hair. In fact, if it weren't for the bronze crown and accouterments covering Micha, Aven might have mistaken Raena for the King at a distance.

"I'm glad you're coming to Candor," Raena said with finality.

Aven nodded, and lowered her face again. She stayed kneeled and watched as Raena's boots turned in the mud, then walked away.

CHAPTER 6
AVEN

No one hurts you more than the person you trust the most

Aven was indeed put into a wagon with peasant women, who were regularly tasked with cooking for the rest of the caravan when they made camp. Allyn and Raena tried to approach her several times the first few days to strike up a conversation. Aven busied herself, joining the other peasant women in labor, and fixating on tasks every time the knights were near.

She also laundered the men's clothes when they stopped in the afternoons. For the first week of travel, this was a freezing cold task. The rivers were rushing with glacier water from the Calam Mountains, headed to sea, and Aven's hands were numb after the first few sets of trousers. The Edivan women were hearty and laughed when she shivered. They remarked after her red hands, nodding to each other as they continued to wash. Aven could imagine their mockery, but couldn't help that she'd hailed from an entirely different realm.

"You'll be sweating when we get to Candor, though," Aven remarked, knowing they wouldn't understand.

Raena, Allyn, and Jonn often left their wagons to stand by the fire, resting their palms on the hilts of their swords, and engaging in 'men's talk'. The peasants didn't approach them, except to hand them food or ale. If Aven had to walk past, she made sure she held her head high. She could feel their eyes on her or their conversation lull in her presence, but she hoped they noticed how cold her lack of attention felt. Especially Raena.

On the eighth day they stopped for camp earlier than usual, and the knights gathered around the fire as soon as it was made. They were at the foothills of the Calam Mountains, and they would ascend the pass in the following days. Aven was gathering the dirty clothing to wash, standing near enough to the men where she could listen.

"Tomorrow'll be rough," Jonn said to the knights, "we oughta have a good time, tonight. Let the horsemen share the ale, and break out the kelpi."

Allyn groaned, "We didn't bring kelpi, did we? I'll be sick of it."

"Then give that to the horsemen," Jonn said with a laugh, "we'll have the ale."

Raena glanced at Aven, then back at Jonn. "Seems like we'll be sick in the morning, trying to ascend the mountain. Maybe we ought to celebrate once we reach the bottom on the other side?"

Jonn scoffed, "Rewards are part of leadin', Rowan. The men need motivation so you better learn how to pretend yer one of 'em, without imbibing too much. Make 'em your allies, then they'll work harder for ya. They'll enjoy a party before we sludge like beasts through piles of snow."

Aven spotted Raena shrugging, but the conversation seemed over. Jonn called for the peasants, instructing them to bring out the ale and kelpi. Aven scuttled down to the river, a fairly long walk.

She wished she could understand the Edivan women, who seemed distraught over something. As they washed, two of them argued, their voices growing agitated and fast. The conversation seemed to climax when Gena, the younger of the two women, shook out a tunic and threw

71

it onto the washboard, then stomped up the river bank and back into the trees. Aven looked at the others for hints of the problem, but they were all silent, scrubbing clothes with unexpressed anger.

Aven stayed as late as she could at the river, but when her joints were so numb, they wouldn't bend, she went up to warm herself and help with the cooking. There were a few fires going in a long row, and the women were busied around them. Some of the pages and a cluster of horsemen helped to unload food from the wagons and stoke the fires, but otherwise, the men were meandering between the two areas of camp. Aven could hear the men laughing and hollering around the knights' fire, indubitably the ale already flowing.

When a few hindquarters of froll were seared through, Aven took a platter out to serve the knights and horsemen. As she walked up, she was met with the distinctive scent of kelpi and the sardonic laughter of men who'd already indulged too much. Commoners weren't allowed to drink with noblemen in Ediva, but it seemed Sir Jonn was apt to choose which rules he followed. Aven followed the other womens' leads and set the prepared food atop a split log. She paused then to observe the men lounging around the fire. Most of them had pulled out the cloth and moss pads for sleeping and stacked them together. They sat on the beds and the ground, their boots warming around the fire. Everywhere were scattered goblets, plates of food, and wooden pieces for Watts, an Edivan game. Aven scanned the Edivan faces for paler skin and blonder hair, hoping to catch sight of Raena. Before she did, her eyes landed on Allyn. The mustached knight was further from the fire, standing shadowed under a tree. He was holding a horn of ale in one hand and gesturing with the other while he spoke to a peasant girl. Aven recognized the girl and thought her name was Dary, or Dany, perhaps. He reached out with his free hand and in a move that seemed to have no preamble, he grabbed the front of her dress and pulled her forward. She stumbled; her hands outstretched. When she fell into him, he laughed. Allyn's ale sloshed as he grabbed her around the waist and pushed her against a tree. Aven saw his hands drop to his belt and she turned her head in disgust to avoid seeing more.

Aven gathered her skirts and set to return to the peasants' wagons, when she heard the familiar voice of Sir Jonn. She would have passed, but heard a sentence that stopped her in her tracks.

"Gena, that's a beautiful name," Jonn was saying, "come on, Rowan. There's things ya can do with her."

Aven knew they must be somewhere nearby, in a pocket of the forest she hadn't seen, but now she was afraid to look. She kept her eyes set ahead on the path, listening with blood as cold as ice, frozen in her veins.

"No thanks, Sir Jonn," Raena mumbled.

"Really, lad?" Jonn slurred. "What're the men gonna think? You'll be th'only one alone t'night. Ya think we ever went to bed alone when I fought wif yer father? No, ya arse. She's gonna tell everyone the story of how you pleased her t'morrow. Get yer fingers wet, at least."

Aven heard a thud that sounded like a shove. Ringing filled her ears. A ball rose in the back of her throat but couldn't tell if it was the beginning of tears or vomit. Or both.

"Really, then?" Raena snapped, "So which is it, Jonn? Because now you want me to fuck a commoner, when for months you've been telling me I'd be beaten for it!"

There was venom in Raena's voice. Aven couldn't stay to hear the rest. The mention of her, as a commoner, being fucked.

Fuck a commoner.

Those words repeating in her head.

That's what she was. That's who she was.

A commoner. To be fucked.

Against her will, images of her and Raena together flashed through Aven's mind. Their kisses, their touches, their bodies intertwined. It had been tender and sweet when they made love, hadn't it? But now it was tainted in her memory, as if they'd both drank poison to drown them with lies. Their precious and sacred moments were reduced to the crudest statement Aven had never expected to hear from her lover's lips.

Aven didn't even realize she'd been running until she was far from the camp, down the only path that was familiar to her: the trail to the river where they'd washed the clothes. She gasped for breath, her lungs burning in the freezing night air. She was already so close she could hear the gush of water.

She stopped, catching her breath, the river ripping past a mere meter from her toes. A few more steps and she'd teeter off the bank. Aven wondered. Her anguish filled her up like a candle blown out, leaving darkness to overtake her. She thought to run into the icy water and let it sweep her away. She heard that the cold would kill you before the water filled your lungs. She imagined her body careening down the river, white and frozen, bludgeoned by rocks and wrinkled from soaking.

Aven shuddered and closed her eyes. She lifted her hands to her chest and felt it rise and sink. She let the dusk soak in. The steady chirping sounds and heady smells of the forest guided her breathing and her thoughts. She was aching from the inside out, and she couldn't control the pain. She knew if she didn't suffocate it, bleed it dry, it would hurt her beyond anything she could bear.

Thoughts of other nights with Raena came to her. Sleeping under the stars, high in the trees. Aven's rage built and she clenched her hands. She stared at the river and tried to imagine the tumbling waves were her anger, cast out and eaten by a fish or tossed against rocks, no longer inside her. Even sadness couldn't remain. There was no room inside Aven for such useless feelings. They couldn't hurt her if she silenced them. There was a little flare inside her chest, the tug of pain, warning her that she still hurt deeply. But Aven shook her head and willed the pang away.

"Stop it," Aven whispered, "this doesn't matter. This is senseless."

She was convinced. She had beaten the pain. She wouldn't let those memories back.

Aven let out a long sigh and cleared her mind. She was fine.

She was just fine.

Feeling suitably numb, Aven turned and walked up the path, destined for the peasants' wagons. She thought of the embroidery she could achieve alone in the wagon while the others were occupied with their debaucherous celebration a stone's throw away.

When Aven neared the wagons, it was dark enough that she could ignore the silhouettes dancing about in the firelight. She could pretend they were no one. The commoners she was growing familiar with and the knights she knew were fading into faceless shadows as she blocked them from her mind. She entered her wagon and pulled back the layers of curtains to keep out the cold.

Aven lit an oil lamp and settled onto her cot with two worn tunics and her bundle of threads. She set to her task, stitching them together to make one useful tunic. She supposed she had hoped to give it to Raena, but now perhaps she would stitch a desert mustelid, the sigil of House Lox. Allyn could use a new tunic, and then it wouldn't seem as if Aven was showing favoritism. As she stitched, she wondered if she might make a Candorian tunic for Jonn as well, though he didn't wear a sigil. Perhaps he would want to wear the colors and sigil of House Schinen he had once served. After all, when they returned to Candor his identity would be known. He might as well bear the crest so there was no doubt to where his loyalties still lie.

His loyalties to Henry Schinen. Aven's mind slipped back to that moment, back to the weight of Jonn's words. Perhaps it had been naive to expect that Henry and Jonn were men of honor. Or perhaps Aven's idea that honor extended to treating women with respect was true naivety.

She started when the curtains of the wagon were ripped open by a strong, hasty arm. Raena's golden head dipped in, and a broad smile spread across her face at the sight of Aven.

Against her will, Aven felt that familiar, warm pull in her heart return.

"You are in here," Raena whispered loudly, "I've been looking everywhere for you."

Aven's lips tightened. She wrapped the tunic around the needles and tucked it between her bedding furs. When she glanced up, Raena had shut the curtains and was closing the gap between them in a few short steps. Aven felt the well of her heart threatening to open wide, but she fought it, remembering the flow of the river carrying her longing away.

Raena stumbled, giggling, then dropped to her knees in front of Aven. "Everyone is at the fire, having quite a party."

"I know," Aven said, balling her hands in her lap.

Raena raised an eyebrow and placed her hand on Aven's knee. Their eyes locked, and Raena grinned wildly as if she were a wolf alone in a yent's yard about to partake in a feast. Raena's hand gathered Aven's skirt, pressing it higher.

"We can be alone for an hour, at least," Raena mumbled. Her words were slurred and the smell of alcohol on her breath was blatant as she leaned in toward Aven's neck to kiss it.

"Please," Aven started, struggling to find the right request.

"Mm," Raena murmured against Aven's throat, "I've missed you."

"Wait," Aven found her voice and pressed her hand to Raena's chest, giving a gentle push.

Raena rolled back to the balls of her feet, crouching on the floor. She peered up at Aven with a wounded expression. Raena blinked and her eyebrows fell, turning into an air of determination.

"Actually," Raena began, "there's something I want to ask you. Something important."

Aven rested her hands in her lap and steadied herself with a long breath. Her silence signaled encouragement to continue.

"All of the men are bedding women tonight," Raena said, "Jonn is paying attention, he told me I had to do it. He said the Edivans talk about me, they question…you know, a lot of men question why I'm different than them. It's not good for me."

Aven furrowed her brow. "I've never heard anyone question you."

"Well, you aren't around, when it's just the lot of us. Knights, guards, they always talk about their cocks and women they've been in."

"I see," Aven glanced away, staring at her needlework. "So, you talk about that, too, to blend in?"

Raena hiccupped, "If I'm the only man who doesn't bed a woman tonight, they'll think there's something wrong with me. It's dangerous for me."

Aven nodded.

"I wouldn't ask you if I didn't think I...I need your help."

Suddenly the weight of the air in the room seemed to tighten around Aven's body, as though pressing upon her and crushing her chest. Aven took great pain to breathe, her body laboring with the ache of her heart.

Perhaps Raena was tired of waiting for an answer, because she slumped forward, her chest against Aven's knees. Raena tried to kiss Aven's thighs through layers of skirts, and Aven quickly scooted to the side, separating them.

"Hold on," Aven said, gently holding Raena's face in her hands, "what exactly are you asking me? What do you want? Permission to bed another woman?"

"No," Raena snapped, "of course not."

"Really? Because that's what it seems like to me."

Raena fell back, her periwinkle eyes looking wounded in the dim lamplight.

"I want...would you be willing to..."

"Spit it out, Rae," Aven whispered the name.

Raena sighed, "I need the men to see us. To see me...with you. Maybe we could go behind the caravan and you could...I mean, we could make it look good. You know? Like I'm really putting my..." she gestured with her hands to pantomime, putting two fingers through a circle she made with her other hand and thrusting them in and out.

It took all of Aven's energy not to shove Rae onto the floor.

"I...see," Aven muttered.

77

"It doesn't need to be real; it just needs to look real. After they see it, they'll leave me alone. Maybe they'll leave us alone. Jonn will get off my back and they'll shut up about how I need to blend in with the others. I can be like the men in every way, except for this one thing. Afterward, maybe we can come back in here? Be alone together while they're sleeping? Could you do this…for me?"

Aven could feel her own expression betraying her. She didn't want to let on anything she'd heard, and she didn't want to share the hurts she'd felt over the past hour. But here was Raena, sitting a breath away, expecting answers and explanations that Aven couldn't share. Perhaps giving her body would be easier than her emotion.

Raena's hands were on Aven's thighs, and though they stared at one another in silence, Raena's confused expression wore away. Her eyes were alight with a wordless dare. Raena slid her hands higher until her thumbs touched the crease of Aven's hips. Something about the intimacy of the touch and how much Aven had craved it, yearned for it, alit a fire within her.

But not a fire of passion.

A fire of rage.

Aven shoved Raena's hands away. She stood to her feet. She towered over Raena, still crouched on the floor. Without needing to, Aven flattened her skirts and wiped her warm hands across her waist.

"Let me tell you something I should have told you back in Ediva," Aven snapped. "I might be in love with you, but that doesn't make me your property. You don't get to leave me sitting around with swine like I am a piece of trash you've discarded, or a bone you toss on the floor after a meal for a slave to clean up. I'm not that woman. If you want a woman like that, go find yourself another commoner to fuck in front of your friends. I almost wish you did come in here and ask permission to go find someone else."

"I'm sorry—"

"Did I seem like I was finished? I wasn't. I'm tired of waiting in my bed for you, every night. I'm tired of crying and hoping you'll show up. I'm tired of hearing women getting raped by your so-called friends and hoping you are going to do something about it. I'm tired of thinking that you'll be a different sort of man and be better than the rest of them, and then being disappointed every time. What should I have expected? What did I think? That you were coming in here tonight, to what? To make love to me, and tell me that you love me, and that you are going to stop pretending that you don't even know my name when the other knights are around? Well, I'm a dumb fussock then, aren't I?"

"No—"

"Because here you are, asking me to do something else for you. As if I haven't been doing everything you've asked me to do since I watched the Boens slaughter everyone else I loved and destroy all I had? How about you ask me how I feel? No? Okay then, how about we settle for making Sir Rowan look like he's getting his pintle wet behind the caravan?"

Aven hadn't realized she was near screaming until the final words left her lips. The silence that followed felt even louder, though that couldn't be true.

Aven's heart was racing and her head felt hot. Everything that had brewed inside her was out in the open. She felt out of control, as if she'd exploded, and her guts were spilled across the floor for anyone to see. For Raena to see.

Raena's face was more pale than usual, and her lips were tight. She stared at something beyond Aven, as though looking through. Aven resisted the urge to turn and see what it could be.

"I didn't mean to be hurtful," Raena muttered, her voice trembling and quiet.

"You didn't think that was hurtful?" Aven said.

"I'm not like the others. I'm different...I have to act like them. It's how I make myself safe. And I had to stay away from you before. I had to…or we were both in danger. I could have…we could have been executed."

Aven shook her head. "You're missing the point. It's not about the danger. You still have choices with who you are, with how you act. You are respected because you're a knight, and because you're a noble, but you refuse to extend that to anyone."

Raena's steely gaze broke and her cheeks began to darken and flush. "I think I need to go for a walk."

Aven had the urge to fall to her knees and pull Raena into her arms. She wanted to fall apart together, laying on the bed, forgetting everything outside the caravan. She wanted to say it was all right, she wasn't angry, everything was forgiven.

But that wouldn't be true.

And everything would go back to the way it was.

Sir Rowan, the knight, friend, and pal to all the men. Sir Rowan, laughing about slaying Boens and bedding women and ready to punch anyone who disrespected him in the jaw. And Aven, the commoner, the pig butcher's child—a worthless girl who got lucky and once ruled a duchy but had nothing, once more.

Raena avoided Aven's icy stare as she stood up and walked by.

Aven turned to watch her go and heard a familiar laugh from outside. When Raena pulled back the curtain flaps to step out of the caravan, Allyn was standing there. He was shirtless, his chest red, and his dark hair unruly.

Allyn smirked, "Up to it again, Ro? These peasants not good enough? I should've figured you'd be in 'ere."

"Fuck off," Raena muttered, stumbling out onto the steps.

"Didn't get any?" Allyn chuckled, "Did your sweet duchess say no? Let me talk to her."

Raena said something indistinct. It sounded like Allyn shoved past, then his head and shoulders appeared in the doorway, a salacious smile beneath his curled mustache.

"Evening, Aven," Allyn slurred. "Come on sweetie, you know these Edivan girls talk. They think Rowan here is a boy-fucker. Wouldn't you help prove them all wrong? You're a nice girl, it's the least you could do for Ro."

Aven felt a renewed lividity spreading through her bones. She couldn't speak. Against her will, a traitorous and hot tear broke free and rolled down her cheek.

Raena was pleading for Allyn to shut up from outside the wagon, but to no avail.

"Didn't he tell you our idea?" Allyn continued, staring at Aven, "Surely you didn't say no, it's brilliant! Come on, now, be a good lass. Come out back and put on a show with your knight here. I'll wait five minutes and then bring the boys to see it."

When Aven said nothing, Allyn leaned back and held open the curtain further so Aven could see him. He thrust his hips through the air, biting his lip as he pantomimed the sexual act.

Aven bit back the urge to vomit.

"Come on, then," Allyn repeated, still thrusting with bravado.

"Let's go," Raena shouted from behind him, snaking her arm under his shoulder and yanking him backward.

Allyn laughed, "What, you're not going to try to fuck me, then, are you? No thanks, Ro!"

Allyn's drunken laughter echoed into the night as Raena dragged him away.

The curtain flaps didn't fall shut completely, hung up somewhere to leave a gap, but only the darkness was visible through them.

The men's voices blended into the faraway sounds of the party at the campfire, and it seemed Aven finally had her peace. Alone.

She went to her bed and sat, picking up the needlepoint once again, but realizing her hands were shaking far too much and her mind was far too busy to resume the work. Instead, Aven held the needle and stared at the sharp point. She wondered if it would be enough to protect herself should either of them—or any other man—try to come for her in the night.

She sat like that, staring at the needle, until the sounds from the party began to die down. When a few of the Edivan handmaids stepped into the caravan, Aven blew out the candles so they wouldn't see the tears that had been streaming down her face. Not that they could ask questions, anyway.

Aven laid in the dark and listened to the others breathing, snoring, sound asleep and full of kelpi. Some part of her thought perhaps Raena would cool off and come back to apologize, perhaps after Allyn was passed out in the woods.

But when dawn broke and the sunlight began to leak into the caravan, Aven could have laughed at herself for holding onto her hopes. With a deep breath, she bolstered her heart, shoving her emotions deeper within as though locking them into a vault. A vault that she would not open again for Raena to see.

No, Aven resolved, she would not make that mistake again.

CHAPTER 7
AVEN

Going home, if any such place exists.

The caravan took the northern pass in two days. Aven was glad to be entering a warmer climate back into Candor, though a weight pressed on her chest. She hardly ate for days, telling herself she was too busy tending to tasks for the wagons.

The Edivan peasant women treated her differently, though she couldn't articulate how without understanding them. No one offered to translate for her.

Raena had been scarcer than ever, hidden away. Once they reached the farthest edge of the Calam Mountains and were out of the northern pines, Jonn called for another evening celebration. This time Aven didn't risk being found alone by either of the drunken knights; she found one of the cargo wagons more emptied than the others, and built herself a place behind the sacks of grain to hide. She waited until the kelpi and ale began to flow, biding her time at the busy cooking fires to prepare meals for the men. A group of women brought out an arm harp and a fawnskin drum, and when the music grew in volume the Edivans began to dance. Aven laughed as she moved through them, clapping along though she went the opposite way. Casting a glance over her shoulder to ensure no one watched, she slipped into the storage wagon unnoticed.

She spent the night there, behind the grains, and that wasn't the last time.

For a fortnight they traveled across the northernmost edge of the Candorian desert. It was cold, so close to the barren wastelands and the upper mountains that wrapped across the north like a lizard's tail. The sunsets were more orange and pink than anything Aven had ever seen, and mirages on the sand were plentiful in the afternoons. She tried to fixate on the beauty when she could find it, willing herself to try and fall back in love with Candor. She didn't think she would ever return to Ediva again.

Aven had to guess where they were traveling most of the time. The peasants couldn't tell her even if they knew. Though on the fifteenth day, Aven could tell they had turned to the southwest and there was a keep in the distance. The hills ahead were flattened, covered in scrub brush but no tall trees to obscure the view. Each time they crested a ridge there was another vast stretch of rolling fields to behold. Aven marveled at the way the plateaus were cut-away, as though the Almighty of earth had carved the edges with a shovel the size of a whole duchy.

When they were mere hours from the keep and were pressing onward into dusk, she assumed that it would provide their lodging for the night. Aven felt tightness in her chest at the thought of being inside an unknown noble's house.

Sir Jonn was riding his rouncey up and back beside the caravan. Unfortunately, Aven had chosen to walk beside her wagon, taking in the desert air and enjoying the heat. She tried to duck out of his view, but as if he could smell her apprehension, he motioned for her to come closer to his mounted position. Aven raised an eyebrow and walked off the path, dodging scrub brush and subconsciously searching for snakes.

Sir Jonn dismounted and stood beside his horse as she approached.

"What is it? We're far from the wagons. I'm afraid we'll lose them," Aven said.

Jonn's mouth tipped into a crooked grimace. Aven realized he'd been expecting a curtsy and some form of address. She rolled her shoulders back to stand firmer, facing him with boldness.

A moment passed with his mahogany eyes boring into her, then he huffed and glanced away.

"We'll catch up," Jonn grumbled, "I'll take you on my rouncey to the last wagon, at least."

Aven resisted the urge to cross her arms and demand his meaning for pulling her away. At dusk, in the desert, she was ever-mindful of the threat of snakes. She felt her brow tighten with a curious glare.

Sir Jonn sighed, "We're staying at House Lox, t'night. That's the keep ahead, we'll be there 'fore the moon hits. It's Allyn's House."

"I know where he heralds from. You forget I was raised in Candeo?"

"Certainly, I've not forgotten your parentage, Aven. Have you?"

At that Aven clenched her fists, staring into him. She was positive her eyes were alight with fire that had been burning since the first day she reached Ediva. Since the moment Sir Jonn pulled her aside in their "new kingdom" and explained that she was nothing but a commoner, and would be fortunate to get more than a peasant's treatment.

He was right. She was born from nothing. But she could still hate it.

"I don't enjoy telling you this, but Rowan begged me to speak with ya 'fore we reach Lox. It should be his own doin', but ya know how he can be."

"I do know precisely how he can be."

"Right, you do. He's shy, impulsive. He's also a bit paranoid, you've seen as much. I think we both know what I mean." Jonn raised his eyebrows with a meaningful pause.

Aven dipped her chin slightly.

"There's a lot at stake," Jonn continued, "he's terrified to return 'ere where he was exiled from, an' he was freed from the gaol. There's a risk any one of these dukes or lords will wanna turn against him, if they were loyal to your Zander. King Micha arranged the right lords, best he could.

He thinks he paved a way for Rowan to be here safe, but ya don't know anythin' for sure, can ya?"

Aven shook her head, and gave in to crossing her arms. "What are you getting at, Jonn? I want you to be direct. Especially as we stand here in the ice-cold desert, with our caravan fading down the road."

"Cheeky lass," Jonn mumbled, "Rowan needs ya out of his way."

"Is that so?"

"Indeed, and if ya think about it, you'll know it's so. Stop and think for a minute about what's ahead of him."

Aven dropped her arms and turned away, exasperated.

Jonn spoke louder, "Ya can't think the two of you will be…you're smarter than that, aren't ya? He's going to be close to the king, whoever that'll be next. He has to find a way to forge this pact with the Boens, or else we'll lose a kingdom. Ya understand that? It isn't a small thing we're fixin to do now. Candor can fall."

"Candor can burn!" Aven shouted. As the words left her mouth, she was shocked to hear them.

Jonn's face twisted into disgust. "Here I thought you'd want the best for him, and his home, if you loved him. Then I suppose ya can't be at his side, can ya? What kingdom is worth saving, in your eyes, if not Rowan's?"

"Perhaps none of them, if they refuse to change."

"Change?" Jonn asked, appearing for a moment he may be curious, then he shook his head. "If ya can't respect Candor, at least respect Rowan. He needs ya to leave him be. He can't be worryin about ya anymore."

Aven lifted her chin, "Are those his words?"

"They are. He was afraid to tell ya."

"Swear it."

Jonn scratched at his thick grey beard, "I don't have to. Swears are promises made to dukes and lords. I don't swear to common girls."

"Swear it on Lord Henry Schinen's life."

Aven stared into his eyes, not wavering.

Jonn chuckled and shook his head. "A'ight, fine. You want to break your heart, go on, then. I swear it. Rowan wants ya gone." He glanced after the caravan then mounted his horse. He reached behind him, offering a hand for Aven to climb onto the back of the rouncey.

She kept her arms folded, returning his offer with a steely glare. She hoped he wouldn't repeat himself because she couldn't be certain she would control her own words. Aven might scream or launch forward to claw at his eyes. No one could say how her rage would be released—especially her.

Jonn stiffened, reeling back when he caught a glimpse of Aven's rage. He grabbed the reins with both hands. "Fine then, die out here."

He kicked the sides of the rouncey and was off. Like a coward.

Aven gritted her teeth and sniffed in a sharp breath through her nostrils. The cold nip of the desert night chilled the burning flame of her anger. With her skin cooling fast, Aven shivered with a pang of regret. She might've tried to run after the caravan, but her last opportunity was fading further in the distance with each second. She tightened her furs around her shoulders and walked onward down the road, holding her head up. She was resolved not to be seen by Jonn again. She would stay far enough behind the caravan but seek shelter in Lox for the night.

After that, she couldn't know.

The steppes were casting tall shadows in the moonlight, like sleeping giants over the breaks in plateau. The ground appeared grey like dead flesh after sunset, and Aven felt more vulnerable and alone with each footstep. She felt a familiar craving for Raena, but shook it away. The torches of House Lox flickered, beckoning Aven toward the outer walls.

When Aven neared the guard post, she shuddered. Her feet ached from walking later into the night than she had in weeks, but she kept pressing on. A torch came down the guard's tower then began drifting toward her. She couldn't see who carried it, their shadow behind the flame. She ignored the brief pang of hope that it would be Raena, or that Raena might come bounding down the road, noticing she'd left the caravan and fearing her lost.

Instead, it was three men, standing back from her with the torch.

"That's far enough, miss," a stout one called out.

They kept hands on their swords as they stood, a few meters ahead of her. Aven could feel their eyes looking her over, even though she struggled to see them through the brightness of the torch.

"Ya know yer approachin' a keep?" another one asked.

Aven nodded, "Yes, House Lox. I was with the caravan from Ediva, but I stopped to relieve myself a while back, and they went on without me."

The stout one with the torch held it out as if trying to reach her face. "Ya don look Edivan. Ya don sound Edivan, ei'er."

"I'm not," Aven said, "I'm from Candeo. I'm a pig farmer in the citadel. I was displaced during the fight with the Boens and now I am trying to return home. The caravan was taking me back."

The stout one lowered the torch and laughed. With the light down, it illuminated their faces from beneath, and Aven could see them for the first time. She was surprised by how young their faces looked. Even covered in shadows, they couldn't have been older than fourteen, barely come-of-age. The two taller guards wore pads and tunics that stuck out beyond their shoulders, with sticks for arms poking out of the sides. The short one filled out his garb sideways, but it hung nearly to his knees. Aven's mind raced with the oddness of it all, trying to think of how to deal with them.

"You and e'ryone," the tallest of the boys said through a laugh, "let's all go to Candeo, an' march right up to the king, how about?"

Aven's brow tightened as they continued to laugh, seeming to egg each other on.

"Yea," the stout one giggled, "meybe we'll all go an' they'll make us lords."

Aven's patience was thin and her intimidation worn away, "Listen lads, I'm not apt to stand out in the sand waiting for my bones to freeze tonight. Will you give me shelter so I may be on my way in the morning or not?"

Their smirks fell away.

"A'ight ya can sleep in the field," the tallest one said, "there with the other peasants. But we'll take yer weapons. Search her, Char."

The quiet one called Char stepped forward, and the stout one came along to hold the torch. Char appeared embarrassed, his chin dipped and his eyes darting about, as he patted Aven's dress with random swats. Aven might have laughed, if she weren't so worn down and put out.

"Nothin," Char muttered, turning his back to her.

"Not even a dagger?" the tall one asked. Aven thought it a fair question, knowing she hadn't been searched thoroughly. She didn't have a dagger, but was starting to suspect that she should.

Char shook his head and made a scooping gesture, indicating for Aven to follow them. The three boys kept ahead on the road, and Aven gave them space. Char kept looking over his shoulder, as though he were afraid she'd transform into an assassin and slit all three of their throats. She wondered if he wasn't wrong to be wary, as they seemed particularly vulnerable for guards.

They reached the farthest outer wall, but the boys didn't try the main gate. Instead, they turned and walked along another footpath, leading along outside the brick structure. The wall was thick and curved, weaving with the uneven landscape. Aven wondered if they truly knew where they were taking her, as they stopped a few times and glanced about, shoving one another and pointing into the shadows.

Finally, they reached a corner of the wall and they broke away from it, out into an open field. Their path began to descend a hill, and Aven could see a concave of the field ahead, forming a desert bowl. There were asymmetrical shapes scattered in the divot, as if it were a platter of gems at a market. Aven couldn't make out the shadows at first, but when they drew nearer, she recognized crude camps. A few fires smoldered, one aflame, lighting the area and errant shadows moving through the bowl's center.

The three boys stopped, and the tall one gestured. "Ya see now?" he asked. "Go on ahead, join the others."

Aven glanced back at the bowl, then the boys' faces. "Your peasant camp is outside your walls?"

"Yea," he answered with a shrug.

"But, what about animals? Ruvians? You don't guard your peasants?"

He kicked at something in the dirt, "This works fine. Stronger peasants guard the outside, an' we can see this from our tower."

The stout one pointed toward the keep, "Ya, see? Our tower, right there. Ya'll be fine, lil' princess."

The boys glanced at one another with nervous expressions, as if confirming what they ought to do next, then started back up the path the way they'd came. Aven watched them go for a moment, then studied the peasant camp with incredulous wonder. She scanned from her vantage for any sign of protectors keeping night's watch or patrolling the edges, but saw only shapes moving in erratic patterns. She tried to pull a deep breath for strength, but the bite of the cold air fought with her lungs. It struck her as amusing how she could spend so long living in the dead cold of Ediva's mountains, and still be chilled by the desert night of Candor.

With no other choices and growing more exhausted by the second, Aven marched onward, down the slope and into the bowl. She wasn't surprised when she passed the first few people sleeping on the ground and no one had stopped her. They were fortunate she wasn't a bandit or a wolf. Aven continued deeper toward the nearest fire, treading carefully to avoid any dark places on the ground that may be a sleeping peasant. When she was nearly to the fireside, two men appeared from a shadow and approached her.

"Oy," one said in a rough tone, "speak Candorian?"

"Yes," Aven replied.

"Where ya from?"

Aven hesitated, unsure of the right answer, but thought to avoid what she'd said to the guards. "East Shore. The Boens killed everyone in my keep. I escaped and I'm trying to find a place to serve."

"Oh yea?" the second man said. "We got a lot of ya. But if ya weren't born in Candor, ya don't get to sleep by the fire."

Aven bristled, "I was born in Candor."

"Matter of fact?"

"Aye," she insisted, "my parents are pig farmers for the crown. My father's line served House Payton for a hundred years."

The two of them shared a look, then shrugged.

The first man smiled, "Good, jus' makin sure. Come on, we got space for a mite thing like you."

Aven tried to not think about the implication for everyone else, Edivans and alike, who were left to freeze at the outer edges of the camp. Then again, it seemed a harsh place regardless.

They showed her to a patch of dirt, sandwiched between two dark lumpy shadows that she assumed to be sleeping adults.

"Not much for furs left," the man said. "Ya hafta come early in the day an' claim 'em."

Aven wondered if she intended to return 'early in the day' to take up a better spot and better furs. She convinced herself she wouldn't want to, though she knew it might be her only option. She nodded to the man without a word, then laid down in the dirt.

Her feet were closest to the fire and she hoped it might keep her from freezing altogether. Otherwise, her body was ice cold above her knees. There were constant sounds—peasants coughing, babies crying, men roughing about. Instead of trying to sleep, she focused on all of the sounds, hearing each one. They were distractions and she welcomed them. As long as her focus stayed on the camp, the world beyond it would disappear until there was no Colby, no crown, and no Raena.

Somewhere between a child wailing and a mother's comforting words, Aven found sleep.

CHAPTER 8
BELL

Men are easy. Birds are superior.

There were two things that Bell loved deeply: Sir Finley and her war hawks.

The latter were brilliant, and the former was a stupid dolt. She watched as he sipped from a horn of kelpi, leaned back in his chair, conversing with Micha.

King Micha—now there was another idiot.

Though the evening meal had finished hours before, all nobles and councilors of Ediva lingered in the gathering room to sip on drinks and continue conversing. They would be done when Micha was done, and Micha wouldn't be done until he could sneak away from his religious councilors without fuss.

It was the same routine since they had arrived, more or less, though Allyn and Raena had been a part of it until a fortnight ago.

"More kelpi, my Lady?" a man asked.

Bell glanced to see him—another plump Edivan, skin covered in short fuzz like a doe's ear. "No, I've had enough."

She heard a familiar laugh and turned to catch Finn's eye across the room. How he managed to regain his spirits and still laugh after all he'd been tormented by in his short life seemed stupid, albeit wonderful. It was no surprise that Micha enjoyed his company; everyone else humored and patronized the King, but Finn's amusement was always genuine and ready to burst forth.

Bell sipped her last dredges of kelpi, cringing at the pulp.

Micha cleared his throat and stood, prompting all others to rise brusquely to their feet in response. "It is time for us to end the evening, I'm afraid."

Several nobles groaned a half-hearted mumble of solidarity, though Bell had seen them yawning most of the evening. Their energy waned, the same as hers had. Micha cast a glance in her direction, fast enough that she was sure it was unseen by others, but she caught his twinkling grey eyes all the same.

He was bold to invite her with that daring expression—but he'd been bolder.

As the nobles shuffled out, Bell was quick to excuse herself and weave to the front of the crowd. In the hallway she broke ahead and gathered her dress to walk swiftly. In a matter of minutes, she was in the ladies' wing chamber and had assembled a basket of seashells. They were nothing special in some parts of Boenaerya, but Edivans believed them blessed.

Bell rubbed a dollop of spiced scents on her chest and thighs for good measure before she returned to the hallway. She walked opposite the crowd, men still retreating from the gathering room and clambering toward their beds. No one questioned her direction as she neared closer to the King's royal wing, until she reached the first post of guards. Bell recognized the first, he was one of the few who spoke Candorian.

"Good evening, Lady Bell," the first guard sang. "You have another basket of shells, is it?"

"You know I do," Bell nodded.

"Go on up to the King, then. He may be asleep for the evening; his chamber guard will let you leave the shells."

Bell curtsied out of habit then ascended the stairs to the King's tower. As she passed the small windows she could look out and see the top dome of Castle Salish's center, painted and glimmering under the moonlight. The windows at the opposite side of the spindle faced the powerful mountains, dominating the foreign kingdom like ruling giants.

Bell passed open arches that led to the King's many additional rooms: negotiation hall, homage room, personal knight's quarters, and the chambers meant for his future wife and children. There were plenty of those, including a birthing room.

Near the top, Bell reached her destination, disappointed to find the guards accompanied by a gaggle of religious councilors engaged in conversation. She curtsied and waited.

"Ah, Lady of Candor," Weft stepped forward out from the group. His thick hair was curling around his face, shadowing it in the dark.

Bell suppressed a groan. "Pardon me, I've brought seashells for the King."

"It's rather late, don't you think?"

"Well, we were still feasting and drinking together only a few moments ago. Surely, he has not gone to sleep."

Weft pursed his lips, "I will inquire." He reached for the door but before his hand made contact, Micha's voice called through it for the "Lady of Candor".

The expressions on the other councilors' faces matched Weft's: disgust.

But that was the King's concern, not Bell's. She flashed them a sly smile as she moved past, carrying the basket of shells like a trophy. The men grumbled in Edivan, perhaps calling her a 'whore' or any other variety of colorful language. Bell held up her chin when she entered the King's quarters, closing the door behind her.

It was dark in the first chamber, and she jumped at the shadows. Any one of them could be Micha. She continued through, setting her basket on the floor. His "gift" was her token to allow her entry. She no longer needed it.

When she stepped into the second chamber, he was there.

Micha was a sight, visible in the moonlight. His tunic and top were removed, his bare chest glistening with sweat. He had a flowing wrap around his waist that hung to the floor.

Bell brought her hands to her stomach and eyed him from the archway. They beheld one another in a daring gaze.

"Did you bring me shells?" He asked, his voice low and husky.

"Yes, Your Majesty."

"Good," he replied, "but that's not all I require."

Bell fought a shudder. "Majesty, I have nothing else to give you."

Like a predator, he stalked toward her, light on his feet. His grey eyes bore into her with desire, and she would be helpless against it.

"You have something," he whispered, "and you may choose to give it, or I will take what I need."

"I cannot give you whatever you're wishing for, I'm afraid. I am a pure woman, expected to save my body for a Candorian Duke or Lord."

Micha reached out and with a swift, muscular arm, he grabbed Bell around the waist and jerked her toward him. She squealed, her hands instinctively slapping his chest to try and push the King back, but he became more determined. He grabbed both her arms and pinned them to her sides, then pulled her so close to his body that she could not maneuver.

"Your dukes will be honored to have a woman who has first-served her King."

Bell writhed and twisted in his grasp. "Don't touch me, I demand you let me go."

Micha's grip loosened, and he leaned back with downturned lips. "Do you want to go? I'm sorry, did I misunderstand, I—"

"No, Micha, honestly," Bell grumbled. "I don't mean it. For the hundredth time, I don't mean it when I tell you to let me go."

"Of course, of course, I know…"

His brows raised and he allowed a sheepish smile.

Bell sighed and relaxed, leaning in to rest her cheek on his naked chest. "Is it so difficult for you to enjoy the game of chasing and coercing me?"

"No, not at all. I enjoy it. I know it excites you."

"Mmm. It does."

"We can continue it, if you wish. I understand now."

Bell waited a second longer until she felt his arms soften completely, then she sprung free, breaking from his embrace. "Stay away, I'll scream for help!" she threatened, running toward the bed.

Micha broke into a broad grin. "No one will help you. I am the King."

With permission granted, he devoured her, playing the role of the tyrant. She was the willing victim, and that was exactly how she wanted it.

When they laid in his massive pillowed bed, sated, she pushed the blankets off where her body was still exposed to him.

"You don't have to be so hesitant with me," Bell said.

Micha drew a few short breaths. "I'll be more confident, next time. I still worry that I'm being too much. I can't help it. I don't want to hurt you."

Bell rolled toward him, kissing his bare chest. "But I want you to hurt me," she murmured, "that's what I keep explaining to you."

He grumbled an approval.

She stopped her kisses and brought her hands under her chin, looking up at him with bright eyes.

"What is it?" Micha asked.

"Nothing, only thinking."

"Well, what're you thinking about? Are you not satisfied?"

"I could be happier with more, I think," she purred, "but I'll wait for you to be ready."

"Hmm, I pleasured you and you rode me like a stallion. I think I'm choked dry."

Bell pouted, stroking his chest. "You know, a good king makes sure his people want for nothing. But I'm still longing."

Micha groaned but a smile teased the corners of his lips. "Well maybe I'm not a very good king. You wouldn't be alone in thinking so."

Bell shook her head, "They don't think that."

"The zealots do. The Stratera is their doctrine above the laws of the kingdom. It's not like Candor at all, I'm sure you can see that."

"You'll learn to settle their religious zeal, I've no doubt. You learned how to pleasure women, after all, and now you're not a naive mountain boy anymore. You're a wild lover. How many women have you pleasured the way I taught you? Twelve? Fifteen? Most men can't please even one."

Micha smirked. "But you're still my favorite of them all."

"Careful, King."

"There's nothing wrong with preferring you above the others. I can keep you as my lover as long as I please. Who will stop me? Weft? Vandy? The Boens?"

Bell chuckled. "You think I want to stay your lover when you have a wife and gaggle of little princes running about? I doubt your new wife will approve."

"I don't know her yet, but she'll listen to my requests."

"Oh, I was wrong. You really haven't learned much about women."

Micha rolled to his side, reaching for her. "Then teach me about you."

"Maybe."

He gripped her hips in his large hands and pulled her closer. "I think I am beginning to feel ready again. Would you like to inspect it for me?"

"I'm not here to answer every whim of yours," she quipped, then lowered her eyes to his growing manhood, "but I suppose it will be to my benefit."

"I thought so. I thought you said you 'wanted for more'."

With a smirk, Bell gripped his cock with both hands and pulled gently. He groaned at the sensation, and her smile broadened.

"I know what I want for," she said in a low murmur, "and I know you'll give it to me, won't you?"

He nodded, his eyes fluttering shut.

"You know, King, I've been thinking."

"What's that…"

Bell pushed him onto his back and she mounted him quickly, straddling his upper thighs. Her hands returned immediately and continued to stroke him where he was beginning to grow.

"There are things I'd like," she whispered, "especially if you are to be married and I'll be left to my own devices."

Micha squirmed. "I can't give you as much as you might think."

"Don't worry, I won't ask for the throne." She shifted forward and her center pressed against his. He grasped her hips, but when he tried to thrust, she knocked his hands away. The dominance caused him to noticeably shudder, but he said nothing, waiting for her command.

Bell continued to roll her hips in a manner both slow and soft, torturing him with the building pressure. "You know, I wasn't simply some pretty lady, waiting around for a man to fulfill me. Have you thought of that? Have you thought of who I was, before I was kidnapped from my keep?"

Micha nodded, struggling to catch his breath.

"I was allowed to train with the squires sometimes. I know a thing or two about…swords."

"Yes," Micha said through clenched teeth.

Bell leaned forward, adding more pressure. "Have I told you about my war hawks? They were wild, answering only to me. I tamed them. I taught them. I made them what they are. Does that remind you of someone? Perhaps one king who thought he could do whatever he wanted, but I made him my well-behaved pet, didn't I?"

Micha whimpered, "Yes. Please?"

"Please?"

"I want to be inside you."

Bell chuckled, "Oh, I know you do. Predictable. Let's see if I feel like you've earned it."

He lifted his back off the bed, but the moment he moved she lifted her hips and pulled away. Like a compass, he followed her. Bell gave a smirk and shook her head, and it was enough to remind Micha that in this game, he was the plaything.

Subdued, his body collapsed into the furs, and he slipped his hands under his back to pin them there.

"Mmm, that's a good boy," Bell praised. "Would you like to know what will get you my sheath around your sword?"

Micha sighed, stuttering an affirmation.

Bell leaned forward, her bare breasts grazing his muscular chest. Her lips brushed his ear as she whispered. "Give me command of your King's Troupe, so we may ride for Hawk's Keep and retrieve my birds."

Micha jerked his head back, his periwinkle eyes searching for hers. He stared for a moment, incredulous.

She stared back.

Micha's face twisted into a scowl. "I...how could I? My King's Troupe...Bell, you're joking."

Bell shook her head and drove her hips forward, bearing down on his manhood again.

Micha moaned, "That isn't fair. I cannot...I didn't even send members of my Troupe with the caravan to Candor."

"That was a caravan. I'm not asking for much. The Troupe is forty to fifty men? I won't take them all. I only want enough to protect me through Boenaerya and back home. I'll return with my birds."

"But what if they are ambushed? What if you choose to stay at Hawk's—"

"That's enough," Bell said. She reached down to grip his shaft and in a swift, familiar motion, she guided him to her core. In one instant, she enveloped him.

Micha tore his hands free and violently gripped the furs on either side of them.

Bell writhed agonizingly slow. "I shouldn't have to beg you for anything, should I? I'm taking good care of you, are you going to reward me?"

Micha took a short breath in then shut his eyes. He tensed for a moment, then let out the breath through narrow lips. "Yes. Yes, whatever you want."

Bell smirked and leaned in close. "Such a good boy," she whispered.

CHAPTER 9
BELL

Correction. Men are easy Finn is marvelous

She slept in her own room. It was a mountain of the fluffiest furs and feather pillows in the castle, she was certain. Being a lady sometimes had perks; she could flaunt her status for the small indulgences.

Micha's bed was hard and sparse of coverings.

Aven's was cold, but had enough woven blankets to be comfortable if you made it a cocoon.

Finn's was thick, firm, and slanted to keep blood flowing to his legs.

Bell slept in all of them—for different reasons—and preferred hers to any other. The only of her dear friends she had not slept beside was Raena, and that seemed fitting. Ever since the Boens had come and Raena had been imprisoned, she'd become too filled with her own self-righteousness to bear. Even Micha once mocked "Sir Rowan" for trying too hard to be perfect and amicable.

But Finn would never speak ill of Raena. Even if it was in jest. He was still stuck in that thirteen-year-old version of himself, the protective squire. It was as though Bell's father Sylas had asked Finn to keep Raena's secret yesterday, and not nearly ten years prior.

Bell loved the way Finn clung to things. She knew he would cling to her. That's why she went to his room at the first light of dawn, through the weaving halls to his chamber. The usual barons weren't in the hall, so Bell hoped he was present as she pushed open the door.

"Finnamin, it's me," she called from the outer sitting room.

"I'm being dressed!" His voice rang through the open archway.

Bell continued into the deepest room. When she passed the threshold, Finn tutted and shook his head. He was on the bed with two barons on either side. They were fastening his pants around his limp legs.

"You could have waited," Finn groaned.

"And miss out on staring at your bare-naked chest? Why would I voluntarily ruin my morning in such a way?"

"Though you insist on being lewd, I can assure you, my bare chest serves no sexual purpose."

Bell smirked as she took a seat on a painted resting stone. "It can, you just aren't as creative as I am."

"I'd prefer to kiss a horse than do whatever you're imagining."

Bell glanced at the barons, who were settling a wrap around Finn's lower half. He caught her eyes and spoke as if he read her thoughts.

"These two don't speak a lick of Candorian," he assured. "Want to see? Hey baron, Bell will suck your cock if you like. Don't be shy, go on, pull it out."

Bell giggled despite herself. The baron gave no reaction at all, continuing with his work.

"You're not wrong," Bell said. "I'd take that stocky one. Or should I say, he could take me."

"Disgusting."

"I rather like them, the fluffies."

Finn shook his head. The baron on the left held up a tunic, but Finn grabbed it to insist on donning it by himself. The baron to the right continued holding him upright as he slid the shirt over his head.

"I don't suppose I'll want to know the answer," Finn sighed, "but I suppose you're still doing that with the King?"

"Doing...?"

"That."

Bell laughed again. "You understand that saying the word isn't doing the word, Finners. But yes. I am still doing that. It's pleasant and satisfying."

"Good, I'm glad you're happy."

"That's actually related to why I came to speak with you."

Finn held up one hand and gestured to the barons. He set both palms together, like a slant roof. They nodded and one grabbed a thick roll of fabric from beside the bed, placing it behind Finn's back. Bell smoothed her skirts and fiddled with a loose string as she waited for the two helpers to finish and be excused. She knew they would wait beyond the door within earshot, but at least she and Finn would be given the perception of privacy.

When they were gone, she moved to the bed, lounging across it with her head beside his lap.

Before Finn could jest, she put her hand on his shoulder.

"Do you remember how the three of us were allowed to sleep together, some nights?" Bell said.

Finn nodded.

"My father never let me around boys. Any other boys, that is. He punched Cames for trying to take me into the woods."

"That's right, he hit him so hard, Cames vomited."

"All for trying to get me alone," Bell mumbled, "but father never cared if I was alone with you and Rowan."

Finn paused, swallowing audibly. "Do you resent that?"

"Why fucking would I?"

He smiled. "Because you wanted to roll with boys who would...boys like Cames. You missed those chances with the two of us."

"Hmm," Bell reached up and twirled the ties of his tunic. Her fingertips brushed over his chest. She thought about how any other man would take advantage of her in this position——if not minutes before.

"Was there something you wanted to tell me?" Finn asked softly.

103

"There was," Bell said, "I've asked Micha to give me men for a journey home. I'm going to fetch my birds, and hopefully…"

"What?"

"I need to warn father of the Boens."

"When are you leaving?"

"We hadn't decided. He only agreed to it last night," Bell paused, thinking. "I will ask him to send me tomorrow. I have waited too long already."

Finn's muscles tensed under his thin tunic. "Bell, this is a dangerous journey, and Lord Sylas knows of the Boens, I'm certain. He won't be unguarded."

"No one knows the danger as well as we do. He doesn't know that the Hornes will push the Boens into Candor, and Hawk's Keep will be the first footfall for their warriors after the mountains."

"You're not a war strategist."

Bell jerked her hand away but Finn grabbed for it in a swift motion, clutching her fingers.

"Listen to me, please. Bell, this is foolish. Rowan is already in Candeo by now for certain. Your father may even be there in the citadel, preparing to take the throne. That's where he should be, and surely if he's heard the news of Zander's execution, he would've ridden for the castle."

Bell scoffed. "He doesn't want to leave Hawk's Keep."

"He would, to save the kingdom."

"Then I'll hear of it, and I'll go to Candeo."

Finn's brow furrowed. "Why? Rowan, Allyn, and Jonn are already there. They will warn Sylas of the war to come. He can easily lead the kingdom toward peace. In fact, I'm certain that he alone is the only man who can do so, and save Candor from ruin. You should trust that Rowan will do what he promised and that Candor will be protected. Even if they do not ally with Ediva, they can defend the kingdom."

Bell pulled her hand again and this time tore it free from Finn's grasp. She propped up on her elbows and stared into his chestnut eyes with fervor. "I'm not asking your advice, Finn. I'm telling you as a courtesy.

I'm going home, and I'm getting my birds. It's got nothing to do with all of these…politics."

Finn grimaced and let out a short breath through his nostrils.

It was quiet, the air heavy between them. Bell watched him for a reply, but when none came, she relaxed into the bedding and put her hands on his forearm. She gently scratched her nails across his thick, smooth skin, appreciating how different he felt than Boeny Micha and the furry Edivan men she'd been with for the past few weeks. She wondered still how it would feel to go further with him. It was bittersweet the way she longed for Finn to ravage her, yet knew she loved him more because that was the very thing he would never do.

"What are you thinking?" Bell whispered.

"That you're leaving me behind. That you're leaving and you might not make it back. That it's a dangerous, horrible place, and we did everything to survive it, but you want to rush right out into it again. That we are safe here and can stay safe forever, but you can't simply accept it and live a free life."

Bell let out a sharp laugh. "Oh, Finley, that's tragic. You make it sound as though I'm throwing myself into the sea to swim to the Horne islands."

He scoffed.

"What if they were my babies? That's what they are, practically. What if I left my children in someone else's care? Would you fight me against fetching them, then?"

"I'm not fighting you. I know you're going to do it; your mind is already made-up."

Bell reached up and patted his cheek with her palm. "I'll come back; I promise. I can't stay away from you. Then we'll have real babies together. A dozen of them."

"If you think of a way to give yourself a baby without us doing that—_"

"I have!" Bell popped up to where she was sitting beside him and kissed his temple. "I know you're teasing me, but I honestly have. One of

105

my handmaids, Landa, speaks Candorian and she warned me of a way the practicers of Stratera will impregnate women with a man's seed. They have done it many times to control their bloodlines."

"That's…repulsive."

"Isn't it? Though sometimes the woman wants it."

He shook his head as if banishing the thought. "Why was she warning you?"

"She told me to sleep with leatherskin pants. They are too hard to take off without waking the woman. All of the noblewomen wear them to bed here. Landa also said never to drink anything brought to me before bed. She said the Stratera leaders will give a sleeping tonic that helps—"

"This is sickening. I can't listen to this."

"Of course, it is, but that's how they have done it for ages. Perhaps over a hundred years."

"And you…want that…done to you?" Finn raised his voice to a high-pitched shout.

"That exactly? Almighties, no. I was merely saying that they know how it can be done without any contact at all. I thought of you. Wouldn't that be what you want?" She put her fingertips at the nape of his neck and stroked his dark hair. "Think of it. We could have all sorts of little nobles running around, heirs to Hawk's Keep. Or if my father takes the throne, they will be our princes. They could rule Candor when we are old and wrinkled and ready to lay in the sun drinking ale all day. I can't imagine any man I would rather have such an indulgent life with."

Finn bore a crooked smile and glanced away.

"When I come back from my journey, let's speak of it. That's all I ask of you."

"Alright," Finn muttered, "I'll think about it when you're gone. I would love…I have always wanted children."

"I know." Bell leaned over to kiss his cheek, allowing her lips to linger. He was warmer than she expected, and his skin smelled salty like the sea. She wanted to tackle him into the blankets and lay on top of him the rest of the day, tangled together in their childish, stupid love.

He reached up and held her face close enough so he could whisper in her ear. "Don't leave without saying goodbye."

"I won't," Bell promised. With one last kiss to his cheek, she stood from the bed and walked to the archway. She was about to pass through it when he called to her, and she turned around with an eyebrow raised.

Finn cleared his throat. "I know we always said we don't belong to one another, and I never mind if you are with men who want to…do the things I prefer not to."

Bell smirked, "I know that. Are you changing your mind?"

"No," he said, drawing out the vowel, "but I was wondering if you plan to still be with Micha, when you return?"

Her smile fell and she sighed. "I don't think so. No. I've thought it should end."

"Because of me?"

"No, silly man. Because he will likely be wed to a furry mountain woman by the time I return, and his advisors will be watching his every move, therefore I don't much feel like being executed over some average cock."

"His cock is average? That's surprising."

"Isn't it? A shame, really, when he's so thick everywhere else."

Finn chortled. "I hate that I'm going to picture that now every time I see him. Thank you for ruining the entire King for me."

"It's my pleasure. Shall I send your barons back in to carry you around?"

He shrugged. "If you aren't keeping me company today, I'll go watch the commoners playing ball games in the field."

"I hope you enjoy it. Have a wonderful day, Finderbox."

He hated that nickname, she knew, so she rushed through the door before he could respond, stopping only to gesture the barons back toward his chamber.

CHAPTER 10
RAENA

A strange diacon

Walking through Candeo was surreal, at best.

It was a far different citadel than the one Raena had been to for the Knight's Trial, which could have been only a year ago but felt like twenty. Raena remembered the streets being filled with color, light, and people who had seemed content. She wasn't fooling herself; they hadn't been dancing and laughing with glee. There had been an element of fatigue among the peasants, as far as Raena remembered, but it was nothing at all like the city she traversed now.

Perhaps she was accustomed to the bright mosaics and tapestries of Ediva.

Everywhere she looked in the streets of Candeo was a depression hanging over the peasants and serfs like a filthy cloud. The children's faces were sunken, the criminals were shifty and desperate, the religious groups clung together to shake in fear like a cluster of roe in the marsh. Most of the city's quarters smelled of dung or rot.

The first day they'd entered the walls, Raena had been sick in her guts and her head ached. Four days had passed, and the sickening feeling gave way to numbness.

Sir Jonn had taken the lead and Raena was bustled away into knight's quarters within the easternmost wing of Candeo castle. Half of the time, there were no meals, no guards, or no handmaidens. Raena wondered how Aven was able to find food, wherever she was. Was it harder for a commoner? The idea of Aven scrounging for scraps somewhere made Raena's lip curl in a sour expression.

"Yea, it's awful, right?" Allyn grumbled. "Some hero's welcome. We have to fend for ourselves, apparently." It was again time for an evening meal, and no one had brought it around.

Raena shoved her elbow into his arm as they walked through the corridor. "You act like we haven't done the same for the past four days. Hopefully this time there will at least be something in the kitchen that isn't putrid."

"We're idiots," Allyn mumbled, "tomorrow, remind me not to wait for the servants to come round. Instead, we will assume the worst and go to the kitchens the minute we get in from the training grounds."

Raena shook her head. "We aren't training the guards tomorrow, remember? Jonn wants us to speak with your uncle about our battle strategies against the Boens, and we'll sit with the Candorian council to discuss their boring nonsense."

"It's not all boring nonsense, thank you, I spent quite a few days working on that chart of genealogy for the seven families before we left Ediva. I'll be pleased to finally have it reviewed by a true council of experts for accuracy."

"They aren't experts," Raena said, lowering her voice, "your family knows better than anyone, I'm certain. I'm surprised they won't bring your brothers from House Lox to perform the full review."

Allyn puffed up his chest, "Why would they need to? My research is sound. I know from memory enough to trace the heir to the throne."

"Oh? So, you want them to review it; Why then? Sounds like what you're after is adoration, not approval."

A brief moment of silence passed between them, accented only by their footsteps on the marble stones.

Allyn took a deep breath as though preparing for a winded reply, but they reached the lower level of the castle grounds and were within earshot of many peasants. Raena wrinkled her nose at the offending stench, though it seemed to linger in the air everywhere in Candor, it was aggressive nearest the servants' quarters.

"Ah, look," Allyn chuckled, "it's Pelunia." He nudged Raena and pointed at the Edivan girl, whose eyes were averted from them both.

"Aye, leave her alone."

Allyn paid no mind and called out, "Found yourself a worthy job then, Pelunia? Glad you're on the kitchen staff, and not out hammering shields in the desert sun all day, or butchering pigs."

"Settle down, quim," Raena grumbled, "she still can't understand you. Haven't you tormented her enough?"

"Tormented?" Allyn grinned. "She didn't seem to think my cock was torment. Unless perhaps she's tormented by how much she misses it." To accentuate his words, Allyn grabbed his manhood and gave it an upward squeeze in Pelunia's direction. She didn't react, but a few of the servant girls chuckled and turned away.

Without another word, Raena pushed through the gaggle of commoners to make her way to the door of the kitchen. She excused herself and squeezed in the threshold despite the waiting crowd. Inside the kitchen there was no distinction between the hungry folks and the staff, as the real staff had likely been pulled out to backfill Zander's defeated legions, along with the rest of Candor's peasants and laborers.

At the far end of the kitchen were a row of cauldrons over open flames that spanned along a long wall. There were more than a dozen, each broad and deep enough that a man might sit inside. It reminded Raena of horse troughs, not even suitable for human food. The kitchen smelled of spoiled onions or perhaps meat that had been out too long in the sun. Raena crinkled her nose and elbowed closer toward the cauldrons, grabbing for a deep wood chalice.

"Is this a stew?" she asked, indicating a cauldron with a grey liquid inside.

A rotund woman with rosacea turned to glance at the pot and gave a weak shrug, then turned back to chopping a fish head at the end of a table.

Raena scanned the busy room for Allyn, but didn't find his mustached face in the bustling lines of hungry peasants. Surely, he could fend for himself and get his own meal. Seeing the other cauldrons were quickly being emptied and scooped from, Raena stepped up for her chance before it was lost for the evening. She grabbed one of the long iron ladles and took two helpings from the cauldron into her chalice. At no point did she see a sign of meat or vegetable within the mix, though the chunk to the broth indicated some kind of viscous starch had been absorbed.

There were no utensils or bread to dip into the grey mixture, so Raena took her chalice, tucking in her elbows and moving toward the wall to exit.

"The giver has given unto us all," a tall man muttered, bowing as Raena passed.

She stopped, holding the steaming substance in front of her chest, and turned to look at him. He wore a hooded cloak that flopped over his brow, where scales had been painted. If Raena didn't know better from his tanned desert skin, she might think he was decorated like a man of East Shore.

"Excuse me?" Raena huffed, squaring her shoulders to his.

The man smiled and his dark eyes focused on the floor between them. "The giver will continue to bring us death. The Almighties will be certain."

"To which do you refer? The Almighties of Ediva? You look nothing like any follower of Libre I've ever seen."

He shook his head, but to which question? The sustained grin on his face would have been warm if it weren't for the hollow deadness in his eyes.

Behind her there was a clang, like metal ringing across solid stone, followed by a series of shouts. Raena couldn't look for the source before frantic bodies were pushing her from behind, shoving toward the doorway. She didn't wait to find out why, and busted through the commotion and out into the corridor. Peasants were spilling out of the kitchen, some of them covered in remnants of food. One woman emerged surrounded by a cluster of concerned young girls. She shook her hands and wailed as she walked, her skin to the wrists flecked with sizzling hot liquid against her raging red flesh. Raena flinched at the sight of the probable burns.

As if speaking aloud her silent prayer of hope, a low voice mumbled to Raena's right side.

"May the Almighties heal her wounds."

She didn't need to turn to know it was the same droning voice belonging to the odd tall man. Raena stood with her back to the wall, assessing the exit flow of people as if there would be more answers. She wasn't sure what questions she needed to ask.

"I don't believe in all that," Raena muttered.

He didn't say anything, and Raena thought perhaps he didn't know she was talking to him. Perhaps she wasn't.

The chaos was waning, and Raena wanted to enjoy her soup while it still had heat to it. She imagined it would coagulate when it went cold, based on the grotesque texture. With a huff and a shake of her head, she turned to walk toward the stairwells that would lead her back to the knights' quarters. She cleared the busy halls and broke away from the peasants. She rounded a corner and took a few steps when she recognized the steady thud of a second set of boots behind her own. Raena waited until she was further in the next shadow and turned quickly, careful not to slosh her soup.

"Why are you following me?" she snapped.

Raena was not surprised to see the tall man, standing as though caught.

"I have a message for you," he muttered, "I was waiting until we were alone."

Raena chuckled, shaking her head. "Let me guess? This is when you tell me how following the almighties of Libre is the path to finding my own redemption and fullness in life?"

He shook his head. "I'm sure that you believe we are only one thing. But I am here to tell you we are much more than that. We see things you would not understand. I am a diacon, one who gives."

Despite herself, Raena felt a shiver at his words. His eyes were shrouded in shadow from the protrusion of his cloak, yet she sensed them boring into her.

"For instance," he continued, "how did I know where to find you tonight? I knew that I was seeking you and the Almighties led me to where you were."

"Yeah, that's not hard to do," Raena heard her voice tremble against her will. "Anyone might know I would be in the kitchen. It's where all of us have to go to fetch our meals, since no one brings them regularly to the nobles and knights. Wouldn't anyone know to find me fetching a meal in the evening?"

He lowered his chin, but said nothing in response.

Raena waited a moment, then realized he wouldn't answer. "Will you stop following me if I listen to your message? I'm ready for peace tonight."

He nodded again, slowly. "I concede."

There was another uncomfortable pause. Raena was tempted to shout at him that he must hurry up, or she would draw her sword and slice him through. Something about his arrogance and stoicism was building masonry within her spirit. She balled her free fist and stared into his elongated face with a harsh scowl.

The diacon spoke as if singing a drawn-out song. "I know who you are, and who you pretend to be. You will pretend to be another. You escape from pain by denying the truth. The truth is what will build you, but the lies are destroying you from the inside."

Raena felt her stomach growing hot with boiling fury, like a fire of coals from her guts that spread up into her skull. She stepped closer, unsure what she might do next.

He didn't move. He wasn't afraid.

He should have been.

"You want to deny the heir," he said, "you don't want her to take the throne. But you cannot change who she is, even if that means you must find a way to love what you hate."

Raena saw red behind her eyes as she lunged forward, trying to grab his robe. Surprisingly, he swung back and rolled his shoulders to evade her grasp with unexpected precision. No doubt her periwinkle eyes were wide and alight. She felt only the sting of hot liquid against her other hand where the soup had finally sloshed out of the goblet and onto her bare skin.

Raena jerked her hand back as if to pretend she'd never wanted to grab him, at all. She felt her cheeks begin to redden. "I told you I don't believe your pathetic…lies."

Amusement twinkled in his eyes.

Without another word, Raena spun on her heel and fled up the stairs. She didn't hear his pursuit, and somehow knew that he wouldn't dare to follow.

CHAPTER 11
RAENA

Change of command

It was morning, and Raena fussed with her formal Candorian tunic and trousers. She had somehow forgotten how many ribbons there were to tie, and the order they had to be laced. It was made worse by the shake of her hands and she longed to reach for a goblet of ale to calm her nerves. But she'd resolved to quit dulling her senses with drink ever since the night Aven disappeared. She was desperate to stay sharp, in case she caught sight of her duchess somewhere in the citadel. And Raena was continually glancing out windows and scanning the open spaces every time she left the towers.

Her fingers slipped and a ribbon came loose again, forcing her to start the knot over for the tenth time.

"Fucking sod it," Raena mumbled, tugging at the material so hard it might've ripped. Then what would she have done?

Finn and Sylas always helped her with this part. She'd never mastered these fancy ties. Fortunately, in Hawk's Keep, formal occasions were once every few years. The last time Raena partook in one she and Finn hadn't been older than seventeen.

Raena could almost hear Sylas's voice in her mind as she fussed with her laces, "You need to practice blending into the company of men. You will one day leave my keep and be out in the kingdom. You will meet people who have never heard of Rowan the Squire, or Rowan the Knight. You will need to prove yourself as a boy every time. Finn and I'll stay with you every minute, to always vouch for you. But you need to think about how you behave outside these walls."

How right he had been.

If Sylas could be in Candeo now, perhaps he would be proud of the way Raena had "blended into the company of men". Though, she lamented, he might've disagreed with some of her latest actions.

Raena didn't have a reflective surface as she had become accustomed to. When she thought her laces were complete, she went down the hall to Lox's quarters. He was in the outer chamber of the ample nobleman's lodging, and a squire was holding a blade to his cheek.

"Ah Rowan," Allyn said stiffly, holding his jaw tight, "need a shave?"

"You know I don't."

"That's right, Boeny-face." Allyn pulled away from the squire's blade and gave a wink.

Raena stopped short of rolling her eyes. "I was hoping you could tell me if my tunic is proper? It's been a while since I was at a formal Candorian affair."

"You didn't sit at the Queen's feet and butter her ass?"

Raena pursed her lips.

The squire slipped the blade a few passes over Allyn's chin. It was quiet enough in the chamber that Raena could hear the scratches of his whiskers against the metal.

"Alright," Allyn scoffed, pushing the squire away, "let me take a look at my man, here. Don't you know not to keep a knight waiting? I am sure Sir Rowan has better things to do."

Raena stood taller as Allyn narrowed his eyes, judging the tunic for a silent moment.

Allyn tilted his head back and forth before speaking. "It doesn't look as though the bottom knot is over, then under. Is it under, then over?"

"Yes, over, then under."

"Are you sure? It looks the opposite."

"Yes, I'm certain. That's the one I was positive of."

Allyn shrugged. "It isn't beautiful, but it's correct. You could add more flourish to the laces with more confident knot-tying. Most squires learn that, but I suppose you didn't."

"We didn't go to castle functions often."

"It shows. What about your duchess, didn't she have you dress well for ceremony? She seems...put together."

Raena swallowed hard at the dismissive mention of Aven. "No. She...we were even less interested in pomp while in Colby. We laughed at it, in fact, the silliness and pretense of it all." Raena's mind flashed back to the garden in Colby where she first had a formal introduction to Duchess Aven. Aven had rolled her eyes at the stiffness of Raena's demeanor. It felt like years ago. She couldn't remember hearing Aven laugh like that again since the Boens came.

"You make it sound like you were ruling that duchy the same as she. Though I guess she must've needed a man to tell her how to get it done, eh?"

Raena flinched, but Allyn turned his back.

"If you don't mind, Rowan, I'm going to finish my shave. This squire is slow. I'll join you in the throne room once I'm done, if it happens anytime this season."

The squire gave no reaction to the insult, returning to his task of shaving the pompous knight. It didn't take more convincing for Raena to wordlessly exit the chamber. She made her way through the citadel, winding toward the throne room. The combination of her laces on the outside of her tunic and her breast bindings beneath it made for difficult breaths. If anything, she would have preferred to wear metal armor, despite the weight.

As she reached the upper halls, something lingered in the back of her mind. A nagging feeling, similar to knowing she'd drank old ale—the sensation that she had done something wrong. It caused an unwanted tickle through her spine, and Raena hoped to shake it before she was presented before the sitting King and his council.

Raena rounded the corner and was given a once-over by the guards, who said nothing as she passed the threshold into the throne room.

The throne room of Candeo was grand and elaborate; a stark contrast to the humble circular mosaic and brightness of the King's council and throne room in Ediva. The shimmering gold and streaks of harsh quorrilium damned Raena's eyes and made it difficult to focus on anyone in the crowd. It was a small huddle of nobles, legionnaires, and knights who had gathered. They parted in the center making a hallway-like opening that led directly to the throne at the farthest end of the room.

Raena had expected the flags to be for House Payton; emerald and gold. She was surprised to see the pale white and straw yellow of Lox, scattered around the walls. Of course, Duke Lox himself was now on the throne, albeit as an interim. Raena stared at him for a moment as she stepped forward, studying the way he slouched to the side. As she walked, she scanned those assembled, searching for her place in the lengthy rectangular room.

"Rowan," a voice whispered.

Raena glanced to see Sir Jonn. He was a pace in front of a group of nobles, off to the right side of the throne. Hastily, Raena bowed toward Duke Lox, then shuffled to the side to join alongside Jonn.

"Where's Allyn?" Jonn muttered.

"Getting a shave."

Jonn grunted in reply.

Duke Lox held one hand in front of his face, rolling a small object through his fingers and fixating on it. His lips reminded Raena of Allyn's, the way they curved downward at the edges and represented a perpetual grimace. His eyes were dark as night, almost too small for his broad face.

Also, like Allyn, he had a mustache, but it was trimmed tightly to conform under his nose.

"We shall commence when my nephew arrives," Duke Lox announced without taking his eyes away from his fingers.

A few of the nobles whispered among themselves, creating a dull murmur in the room.

"We have to approach this carefully," Jonn whispered. "Are you prepared to do as I say?"

Raena spoke through the corner of her mouth, "Approach what?"

Jonn was silent behind her shoulder.

Frustrated, Raena turned her head, "Can you give me better information for what you're asking? I don't know the meaning of this."

"This is your moment. It's best that I don't ruin it for you by telling you what to expect. All that I ask is that your reaction is genuine."

Raena felt a twisting in her gut. Something about the way that Jonn was keeping things from her teased at a reminder, as though she could sense pieces of a puzzle that had been orchestrated against her will. For a reason she couldn't place, she felt that ache in her chest that represented only one thing: Aven. She longed for the feeling of Aven's gentle hand slipping into hers, their fingers easing together and gifting Raena with peace and belonging. But instead, her body felt cold and untied, as though she were drifting out deeper into an unforgiving ocean.

A few mutters from the door drew her attention, and Raena turned to see Allyn. He was smug as he burst into the room with no reservation, as though he were the one about to flop into the throne and lay claim over the kingdom. Allyn didn't bow, but rather gave a nod of his head toward his uncle, the sitting King.

"Thank you, Sir Allyn, for joining us," Duke Lox proclaimed with a disgusted undertone.

The occupants of the room shuffled about quickly, moving into places that Raena assumed were designated. There were chairs along the outer walls, shadowed by gaudy gold columns. Some of the elderly nobles took their seats, and knights took post alongside them. Raena watched

Jonn out of her peripheral view, but he didn't budge. She felt exposed, as if she was front-and-center, as many of the other nobles and knights were out from the shadow of the throne.

When the room fell silent again, Duke Lox straightened himself to sit upright and spoke with a nasal tone.

"It has come time for us to evaluate who may be next to sit upon this throne. As you know, I am here to hold the place until the rightful heir may claim the kingdom. Now that my nephew has returned from Ediva, we know without a doubt that Queen Zarana and the alleged King Zander have both been executed. There is no question that House Payton will no longer rule Candor."

A few people murmured in the crowd, then were silenced as Duke Lox glared about.

"My nephew has told me that Pri—...King Zander attempted to produce an heir with the daughter of Lord Sylas, but was unable to form the marriage or consummate the attempt. There will be no child born of Zander, and therefore, the next eligible House will be nominated to take the throne, permanently."

One of the councilors beside Duke Lox bowed to scribe something on a scroll, rapidly taking ink to paper. Raena recognized him as Salor Grent, the councilor of affairs.

The duke continued, "My family has traced each line with care and preserved the records of each founder of Calamyta. The seven families are in disarray, just as Candor is in disarray. We have lost the great families of Candor, and now Payton, and thus Schinen. There remains only four, Lox, Galewind, Grent, and Archer. All of those remaining are scattered, their next heirs lost in Boenaerya or foreign kingdoms. My house is one of the few that remains intact, though the grounds of House Lox's paramount library will not be guarded against Boens any moreso than this capital. Archer, or Sylas, has fled the kingdom and will not return a traitor. His heir, Lady Islabell, may produce an heir from one of the noble families, and perhaps take the throne as queen until she can produce a male heir of her own. However, the other families are scattered, the burden is theirs to bring their worthy applicants before the council of Candor, the noble houses, and the consults of House Lox."

Raena glanced at Allyn and tried to gauge his reaction, but his face was stoic, as if he were still back in his room receiving a shave.

"I am told that there are many men who want to present their claim to the throne," Duke Lox sighed and rolled his eyes. "This is not a contest of wit or nomination. We are not brash and uncivilized, like the Edivans, going around to choose any mountain goat to wear the precious Black Crown."

A few men laughed, and Raena noted the distinctive absence of sound from Jonn, beside her.

Lox smirked at their approval, then resumed his glare. "Many of you have been among the noble families since before the Equinox War with Ediva. Perhaps you recognize someone here today, from long ago? There is a knight among us who I wonder if you recall? He was someone of great prowess and achievement, and he has returned after more than a dozen years in hiding. I have granted him refuge and pardoned him for the treason that Zarana accused. What's more, I have made him a knight to our rule. He will now be the personal knight of my wife, Duchess Adorna. But I ask again, who among us recognizes and remembers his name?" Lox held out his hand, gesturing to Sir Jonn.

Raena, beside him, fought the urge to step back and disappear into the crowd as every eye in the room turned toward them. Of course, they weren't staring at her, but it made her skin crawl just the same.

"Is that Sir Jonn?" a nobleman asked.

All at once the room erupted. Raena heard her father's name shouted, over and over, as everyone answered with who the knight in question had been sworn to. She clenched her fists, digging her nails into her palms, and focused on taking slow, deep breaths. It felt as though all the air in the room was rising up to wrap around her and choke out the air.

Lox waved his hands, silencing them. He let out a laugh that sounded disingenuous. "It is indeed Sir Jonn, the knight of Henry Schinen. Though

121

now he will be known as Jonn-Del Lox, as he serves my House. He was fortunate to have survived the Black Spring of Zarana's murders, and there is even more to tell you. I know he has many stories. I've asked him to give us a full account. But first there are a few things he has shared with me that are of the utmost importance. This is why I have asked you all here, to witness his testimony."

Jonn-Del rubbed his hands together as he stepped closer, waiting for permission. At the bow of Lox's head, Jonn-Del rushed forward toward the throne and turned to face the center mass of the crowd. He shifted his weight from one foot to the other as he spoke.

"Greetings to all of you. I thank Duke Lox from the bottom of my heart for pardoning me and welcoming me back to my beloved home of Candor. I have missed this place more than you could imagine. I am ready to give everything I have back to this kingdom and pledge to give my last dying breath to its defense."

Raena watched as Lox slumped deeper into his seat, presumably bored with Jonn-Del's speech already.

Jonn-Del paid no notice, puffing his chest the longer he continued. "For many years, you have probably all wondered why the Queen, Zarana Payton, chose to massacre every member of House Schinen and raze it to the ground. I am here to tell you that the answer to that is far less sinister or cunning than you likely believed. I'm told there are many theories, and all of them are colorful and exciting! Usually, some form of debauchery is featured. But sadly, the truth is the obvious thing. Of course, Zarana wanted to methodically eliminate each house from the Calamytan families that threatened her son's rule. She was mad. She wanted to kill every Schinen, and next would have gone down the line, for Archer, and Lox, and so on."

A few in the crowd gasped, but Jonn paid them no mind.

"I don't know what happened once I escaped her death-bringing guards, but I do clearly remember that night. Some of her guards were crying as they murdered the women and children. They hated the task she sent them to do, and I believe that's why they became careless as I hid in the shadows. They may have seen me lurking away and chosen to do nothing. That's the only explanation I have for why they let me escape." Jonn-Del paused, glancing around the room. He wet his lips and his eyes darkened to a somber expression. "They let me escape. Me, and one small child."

Jonn-Del paused again. This time, everyone in the room began speaking all at once. Their words rose to a roar of sound.

Raena's neck and back muscles were so tight they began to ache. She choked and tasted bile at the back of her throat, fearing for a split second that she might vomit all over herself and the floor. She gasped as a hand clapped onto her shoulder. Allyn's voice mumbled behind her, his words indistinct and faraway as though she were alone within a tunnel and he was outside of it. Raena gasped, trying not to be obvious, and fought the urge to put her hands on her knees.

Lox shouted, and everyone went quiet. "Almighties be damned, keep fucking quiet! You have all been far too rowdy for this day. How are we ever to get through it if you don't shut your mouths and listen! After this is done, we have many proceedings to get through. The next person who talks that isn't me or Jonn-Del will be dragged outside and kicked in the shin." He pointed to a guard, communicating the order.

"Thank you, Duke," Jonn-Del said. "Now, it wasn't easy to hide the child. I will tell you all more about it tonight. It's a marvelous story, and Duke Lox has agreed to give us a feast. I know you might be wondering if the child survived, and I assure you that they did."

Raena turned to Allyn, searching his face to see if he knew what was coming next. If they were leading up to execute her, she wanted to see it coming. She'd prepared all her life for the idea that she might be found out and executed, yet somehow now that it was closing in, she didn't feel ready.

Allyn's face was riddled with confusion. He caught Raena staring and raised an eyebrow.

"We have recently been reunited," Jonn-Del continued, "and today I want you to understand why this day is monumental. Surely, you will recognize every bit of Henry Schinen in his features and mannerisms."

Duke Lox stood from the throne and bumped Jonn-Del with his shoulder, prodding him to step aside. "Yes, this survivor. I assure you all that I have verified it for myself. Sir Jonn has risked his life riding through the Boen's country to return the knight, Sir Rowan. You may remember Rowan from the Knight's Trials, only a year or so ago, though it seems like half a century. He told us he was of Brande, distant cousin of Lord Sylas. Who would question that boy?"

Raena felt as every eye in the room settled on her, the heat of their stares cutting into her. All she could do was stand still, absorbing, and looking for a route of escape. With the number of guards, she would never make it.

"Rowan, come up here, won't you?" Duke Lox asked.

Raena's legs felt like quorrilium blocks had been sewn to her feet as she stepped. Obliging, she took her place beside the throne, where Lox's hand gestured, then she faced the others. The three of them; Raena, Lox, and Jonn-Del, at the scrutiny of every noble and common eye in the throne room.

"Now Rowan," Lox clapped a hand to her shoulder, "there was no bastard son of Brande, was there? Go on, you may tell everyone."

Raena tried to speak, but her tongue stuck to the roof of her mouth.

"He's been scared," Jonn-Del said. "Imagine, poor lad has run from the Queen's assassins since he was ten years old."

"Eight," Raena muttered, not certain if any sound came out.

Lox didn't acknowledge her. "No one thinks twice about a little squire among the gaggle of boys. That's right where they put this Boeny lad, in the mess of Lord Sylas's lot. I'll admit, I knew when I saw him at the Knight's Trial he must be related to Henry in some way. Just look at his face! It's like Henry Schinen raised from the dead!" Lox grabbed Raena's chin and squeezed.

"He performed well, I hear," Jonn-Del said, "so well that he was banished. Which was a great service to keep him from being found out. Zarana and Zander would have killed him without question."

"Which would've been a bloody shame," Lox said, laughing, "considering he is now the heir to the throne!"

Raena couldn't be sure she heard it right. There was a rush of white appearing behind her eyes. She knew if she didn't do something, she might faint. She reached out in both directions for stability, and Lox grabbed her by the elbow.

"Come on then, lad!" Lox shouted, pulling Raena backwards. "Take your place."

He lowered her into a chair, and Raena felt the dull sensation of falling leave her cloudy head. It was then she realized where she was sitting: the throne. Someone from the other side of her placed something thick and heavy against her skull. When they pulled their hands away, the weight of it settled.

Lox swung his arms with dramatics and paced the stone floors, "Dukes, duchesses, lords, ladies, knights, and all gathered. I present to you, his royal highness, heir to the throne, son of Lord Gavin Schinen, nephew to Lord Henry Schinen, His Majesty and now the rightful ruler of Candor! Prince Trevin Schinen."

CHAPTER 12
RAENA

Men with new names

"How the fuck am I the Prince?!"

Jonn-Del cringed as Raena threw a metal chalice across the room. It clattered against the wall and ricocheted to behind the bed.

"Quiet, Trevin," Jonn-Del warned, holding out his hands, "you're never alone now, even when we're in yer chamber—"

"This isn't my chamber. This is Zander's chamber. It's still covered in the colors of Payton. I've asked for three days to have it changed. I've asked for three days to speak to you, alone. What is wrong with you and the others, all of you? Why make me the prince at all if you're going to insist on ignoring me?"

"Sorry, I'd to tend to somethin' away from the citadel. I tried to make sure ya would be cared for while I was away. Also had to make sure no one would bother ya', though."

Raena slumped to the bed and put her head in her hands. "This is torture. Do you realize what you've done? I can't get a moment alone. I was already surrounded by men constantly, now I'm in the eyes of every member of this kingdom. How did you think I would navigate this? What was your plan, Jonn-Del?"

He moved briskly to the bed and took a seat beside her, leaning in close enough to whisper. "I'm sorry, but it was the best decision. No one will ever know about ya', not even now. I said to Duke Lox that ya were wounded in East Shore and yer body is marred all over, so ya bleed and ooze from wounds often. I said ya are shy, and embarrassed, and hate anyone to look at ya'. A virgin. He assured none would disturb yer privacy. I'm sure Allyn defended the story, he's a good lad with yer interests at heart, like me. Ya'll be safer now than you've ever been, ya know. No one would dare to harm a prince."

Raena ran her fingers through her hair. The act reminded her how she felt so unlike herself. Her blonde hair had grown past her ears in the style of Candorian men. She wished for it to be short like she'd worn it when she served Colby. She longed for everything to be the way it had been when she served Colby.

"Trust me," Jonn-Del murmured, "when've I done anything except protect ya? I've saved your life for this. I've never led ya astray. I've watched over ya every single moment, all the years since you were a baby. We are family. You're jus' like my own son. My own flesh and blood, Trevin."

"My flesh and blood is dead. My true family is at Hawk's Keep. My true family is in Ediva. My family is scattered across these forsaken kingdoms like a handful of oats thrown to the stables."

Jonn-Del put a hand on his chest. "That hurts. It burns me to hear ya say that. I understand if ya don't think much of me right now, but I don't believe ya mean it when ya say we're not family. Yer jus' angry, lad. It's all right. I think ya should apologize for that."

"Sorry, then," Raena didn't feel sorry in the slightest. "I'm not trying to be hurtful to you, but now my life is at risk more than it ever has been. I would've been safer disappearing in the shadows, or going back to Ediva. And I still don't understand what it is that you expect me to do, as the prince? Why did you tell them I was Trevin? Why did you convince

127

Lox? I've been alone with nothing to do but think of this for days, and I can't make any sense of it all. You should have told me before we went into that room. I almost…I nearly said—"

"That's simple. Ya had to be frightened and surprised so it would be obvious you weren't clamoring for the throne. If ya'd been confident and arrogant about it, anyone in the room would've questioned and said ya schemed it up. You looked the part. A lost, scared Schinen boy who feared revealing himself because he'd be executed by his father's enemies, after all. Or, rather, his uncle's enemies, I should say." Jonn-Del scratched his chin, thinking for a moment. In a quiet, reflective voice, he mumbled, "I wasn't trying to fool ya, but I knew you'd give yourself away. It had to be real. Yer not a great actor, if I'm honest."

"Well then if we're being honest, allow me to say your cunning ways feel like betrayal."

"I'd never betray you," Jonn-Del huffed, "I swore my life to you. Yer the only soul on this earth left I'd die to protect. Save for Duchess Lox, who I'm sworn to protect for duty. But you? I'd die for ya out of principle alone."

"Right," Raena paused, "you've said as much."

The tension between them was thick. Raena felt the weighty expectation; that she was supposed to thank or praise him for the loyalty he professed, but she refused to concede.

Raena thought of another topic to ease the pressure. "Duchess Lox…you'll be at their House from now on, then?"

"Soon, yeah. I asked the Duke and Duchess to stay in the citadel while yer gettin' accustomed to ruling. Once ya appoint a council and begin first decrees, they'll return to Lox and I'll accompany them."

Raena nodded, "I suppose you and Duke Lox want some say in who I appoint?"

"We could give ya advice, of course." Jonn-Del's eyes lit up.

"Right. And do you have advice for how I can handle the impending Boens? I'd like not to lose this kingdom before I've had a year to rule it if

I'm not going to be otherwise found out and executed. How about your advice for getting a semblance of an army together to defend us?"

"Ya have forty thousand men," Jonn-Del said, "nothin' near the army Zander had, but it'll replenish. They're scallions and young boys, but they'll train into warriors in time."

"Not enough time. We have to align with Ediva immediately."

Jonn-Del pursed his lips. "Appoint yer council, then think about Ediva and Micha. You cannot form an alliance without council vote—yer only a prince."

"Zarana did. She formed alliances however she chose."

"Zarana was a rightful queen with an heir. A male heir. But Zarana also broke our laws, and she was beheaded, a fate yer tryin' to avoid. I think you'll be wise to learn the laws and follow them precisely. Laws of Candor weren't made overnight, they were made by the kings before ya who learned from mistakes, so you won't have to. That's why all ya need is to study the laws and you'll know what to do. History will guide you better than your impulse."

Raena sighed. "I understand, but there are no laws for what to do in this case. What can history and laws teach us about Zander foolishly losing our armies? What can they teach me about negotiating with the Boens? When our ancestors ruled Calamyta, the Boens were farmers with sticks who traded freely. Now they are the deadliest warriors on this continent. You know as well as I do that if the Hornes come to collect their debts, they will push the desperate Boens into Candor, and I will not be able to defend us. No one will. The Boens will take this kingdom in a few nights of battle and we'll be wiped out of existence. I'm useless with forty thousand men, especially an army of boys. I either need an alliance now, or I need another hundred-forty-thousand with years to train them."

"They won't come to the desert in this heat. We will have until the dead of winter."

"Aye," Raena shrugged, "it doesn't matter when. I have to make an alliance. How can I do it?"

"Ya can be crowned king."

Raena flinched.

"You have to be king," Jonn-Del repeated, "there is a way. But it'll take longer than we have."

"What do you mean? Jonn-Del, stop giving me so many surprises. Be direct, I'm begging you. How can I trust you when you evade every question?" Raena's voice cracked as her frustration built from within.

"I won't," he said, "I'll tell you the plan in time. I've already set in motion what should be done to make you king. If you must press me, that's what I've been tending to the past few days. I had to go outside the citadel to meet a messenger whom I trust. Remember, I've been back in Candor many times since I took you to Hawk's Keep. I've eyes and ears in places that are safe—men I trust. One of them is taking a message for me back to Ediva. He is sending for Lady Islabell."

"Bell? Why? She has no reason to return to Candor."

Jonn-Del grimaced. "I know you won't like this, but promise me that you'll let the idea rest. Think about it for some time, a short time, if you can."

"Fine. Tell me."

"Yer friend, Lady Islabell, has been…intimate with Micha. They're not discreet, so ya likely know already. They're even less careful about keeping it a secret than you and the peasant girl."

Raena stiffened at the mention of Aven, but let it pass. "I was aware."

"Anyone in Castle Salish with two eyes and ears is aware," Jonn-Del sneered. "But I digress. King Micha is of yer complexion, he's Boeny, with purplish eyes and straw hair. There aren't many men fornicating with Lady Islabell carrying Boen traits. Probably jus' the one, in fact. So, it's an opportunity."

"I'd rather not—"

"Bell would do anything for ya, wouldn't she?" Jonn-Del snapped.

Raena rubbed her hands together, willing away the burning sensation of fear rising in her chest. "Of course, she's like a sister to me. But I don't care about what she and King Micha do, it's none of my business, and it's of no concern to you."

Jonn-Del waved his hands dismissively. "I don't care either about their sex, yer missing my point. It's a great opportunity, lad. Yer being short-sighted, but this is the way to solve your problem. Listen. My messenger will ask her to seduce him again and take his seed. When she's certain it's sown in her womb, she'll ask to return to Candor. She'll wed you immediately, before her belly swells. When the heir she produces is Boeny, no one will question—"

Raena leapt from the bed and paced the room.

"—that you are the father. With any luck, it'll be a boy. But either way, it'll be enough. You'll have your heir and it'll even look like ya."

Raena shook her head. Her mouth moved faster than her mind could catch up. "She will not do it. I will not do it. This will not happen, none of it. Have you already sent this messenger? Call him back. Call him back, at once."

"I cannot. He's across the desert by now, nearly to Hawk's Keep for sure. He's my most capable man and'll get there days faster than any other could. He'll even slip into Ediva without being noticed. If you're worried anyone will find out, I promise—"

"No. I'm not worried about anyone finding out." Raena snarled, "I will not do that. I will not subject Bell to that life. She deserves a choice. Your plan is no different from what Zander tried to do to her."

"How d'ya reckon?"

"How do I reckon? How do you not reckon! He took her from her home to force her to bear his children and make himself king. He made her do it against her will. Bell doesn't want or deserve to be forced into marrying men she doesn't love and forced to bear their children."

Jonn-Del laughed, throwing his head back. "Row—Trevin. Listen to yourself! 'A man she doesn't love'? Who gives a raging piss about love when ya are to be the King and Queen? I assure ya that in the history of Candor no woman ever loved her king. Ya know what she loves? Having a pillow under her arse and steamin' yent plopped into her mouth like

131

butter fat every morning. Having a nursemaid chase her little brats for her, and being free to roam about the countryside to gaze at the shirtless farmers plowing their crops. I assure ya, little Bell will enjoy being queen more than any other has, because she'll be married to a man she doesn't secretly hate."

"She'll grow to hate me. She will grow to hate the burden. And I'll hate myself for doing it to her. You don't know her like I do."

Jonn-Del shook his head. "You think you know her, but I know women. They are all alike. She will take to the throne."

Raena clenched her fists, feeling helpless. She couldn't stop what Jonn-Del had put into motion. She stepped to the window and peered out, glaring at the view below as though it could fix this mess. The prince's chamber was in a high tower, overlooking the forsaken arena where she had performed in the Knight's Trial. She remembered that day, fresh in her mind, yet it was like a dream she'd had about someone else. She could picture herself, out of her body. Sir Rowan was a different man than Prince Trevin, perhaps, and neither of them were Raena Schinen. But all of them were women. That's why there was nothing she could do about any of this. Raena's opinion didn't matter to Jonn-Del, because he knew she was another silly woman, didn't he? His words rang in her ears. They are all alike. She was expected to shut her mouth and accept his scheme, just as Bell was expected to.

Raena grabbed a lone, broad flower petal from the windowsill. Focusing on the arena, she ripped the petal into pieces while she spoke, her teeth clenched, her words punctuated and harsh. "I want to speak to Allyn. Please leave me. Send for him."

Jonn-Del scoffed audibly. "Now you're the one not telling me what you're up to."

"Then you should be accustomed to it."

She heard a shuffle and the scrape of his chair behind her, and Raena sighed with relief that he may actually leave without pushing her anger farther.

But he spoke again. "Don't do anything rash, Prince. Ya told me you would take a moment to consider this, and ya ought to. I told ya to rest with the idea. You got plenty to focus on with ruling and choosin' yer council. I'll help ya, and won't muck with whatever yer up to."

Raena spun to face him squarely, throwing the petal shards to the floor. "What do you think I am 'up to', exactly?"

"I have a clue."

"Then say it," she stepped forward, pointing to his chest. "I am tired of this. Everything is a puzzle with you. It's like you want me to drag your words out of you, by dropping me hints and alluding to every plan you've schemed up, and I'm always the last to know. Are you a coward, then? Are you afraid I'll put a stop to what you're conjuring? What is it?"

Jonn-Del backed away, raising his hands. "Settle down, Trevin. Yer guards'll hear ya. Have it your way, I wasn't gonna say anythin' because I don't mind what yer doin'. I know yer looking for that pig farmer girl. I know you've already asked Allyn to find her. He hasn't, by the way. She's been gone from Candeo for quite a while. He won't find her here, or in House Lox."

Raena raised both fists as if ready for a fight. She clutched the top of her tunic, letting out hard breaths through flaring nostrils.

"Come off it, I haven't done anything to her. She chose to leave after the way ya boys treated her. Another way I know ya—surprisingly—know nothin' about women. Ya both were shite toward her. She was a nice girl, a little innocent, maybe. I heard she ran from the caravan a few days after it happened, so by now she likely found occupancy as a serf. Perhaps even she's fled to West Twin, a lot of the peasants have."

Raena bit her tongue as the sting from his words made her body turn to ice and her anger was knocked out as if with a hammer. Her stomach whirled with revulsion and a hint of tears burned at the back of her eyes. She blinked. She was used to hiding her emotions away. She wouldn't dare to show weakness to Jonn-Del. She especially wouldn't show her affinity and love for Aven. But it didn't make them any less huge and real within her.

133

Jonn-Del shook his head and walked toward the door, muttering as he did. "You'll forget about her, trust me. I've loved many women, and once ya have another lover, the one before her slips from your memory. Soon, they are all the same in your mind. Maybe Bell will share yer bed, that'll take yer mind off it." He reached the door and disappeared into the darkness cast by the archway.

Raena blanched and wanted to shout after him. She wanted to chase him down, shake him, and demand more answers. She spun and grabbed the nearest object to her—the chair he'd been sitting in. With a barbaric yell from the depth of her chest, Raena flung the chair upward and kicked it in midair. Her hands ripped in the opposite direction from her foot, splitting the wood with a satisfying crack. Splintering shards flung outward and Raena cringed to avoid being cut as they ricocheted back toward her. The chair pieces bounced against the stone floor and walls, flung about the room.

Raena held one long piece in her hands. She screamed again and snapped it in half against her knee.

Of all the horseshite things Jonn-Del had said, the idea that Aven had simply disappeared without saying goodbye? No. Raena refused to accept it. She wouldn't give up on her search so easily.

Yet Raena couldn't bear the thought that perhaps Jonn-Del was telling the truth.

Fighting within herself, Raena eyed the pitcher of ale and goblets atop her serving table. With a tortured sigh, she kicked another piece of the chair away to clear her path. Before she could reason with herself, Raena realized she was pouring a drink. She gulped it down without pause and poured another.

CHAPTER 13
SYLAS

The Beast on the Wall

He was dreaming about being under the water again. The laughter of the Hornes was all around him, echoing inside the cigar-shaped boat, as it filled with salty sea. He fought against his chains and called to Isla, but her eyes were as hollow as the submerged ship.

They mocked him in their language. They mocked all of the "land-dwellers". As if being unable to breathe the water made them worthy of their torture.

When the water was to his chest and he was certain they were about to drown, the Horne leader called out for them to shut the hatches. The oarsmen kept on, sitting at the bottom of the boat, dragging their oars and propelling them forward. At the front was a window where the leader watched.

They skimmed through the sea, never underwater, never over. Sylas felt wrinkled and wet and his skin felt as though it might all fall off his bones like a peel.

"Sylas!" Isla was calling him. "Sylas!"

Not the dream Isla. The real Isla.

Sylas jolted up, rubbing his eyes. "What, what is it?"

"Lenon is coming."

He glanced around to get his bearings. That's when he remembered.

They had been brought to the Horne Islands, days—or perhaps weeks—before, and kept inside above-ground tunnels. The tunnels were damp and pitch black. They smelled of sweat and terra, as though the stones were men exerting themselves and Sylas lived in their armpits. None of them were bound, but there was simply nowhere to escape. The tunnels were the only inhabitable place on the forsaken islands, which were nothing more than giant rocks.

"Sylas, stand up," Isla urged.

A pair of strong hands gripped under his arms. Cames helped Sylas to his feet.

He rubbed the sleep from his eyes one more time, then stood as tall as he could muster. There was a warm light, far beyond them in the tunnel, and it was coming closer. At his feet, Isla and Sesca were fiddling with the lamps to start them.

The warm light came around the bend, and there was Lenon, the leader as far as they could tell. Behind him were six other Hornes, lanky and hunched in comparison. Lenon smiled, baring his teeth, and Sylas was instantly taken back to the moment on his ship.

"Good morn, Sylas," Lenon growled, "the sun is alive with the fire."

"Good morning, Lenon." Sylas bowed his head, as he had learned was expected.

Lenon held up the torch between them. "Would you like this? Take it. Make your fire. You heat your food."

Sylas reached for the torch. "Thank you. We have eaten raw fish for days. We do prefer to cook—er, 'heat' our food."

"Yes," Lenon said, "and I will bring you something special, now. Not from the sea. Now you have fire, you can eat. We set traps on the rocks for you."

He gestured behind him and muttered something in Hornish. Two of the tall men stepped forward, holding a long piece of leatherskin, Sylas though it must be from some large, furry sea creature. Atop the strip of leather were the usual cold, dead fish. But in the center was a sight that made Sylas retch: a gullfrog fully intact, with his head twisted as though broken. Beside him, four eggs, spotted with mud from their nest.

Sylas spoke through his fingers, "We…we do not eat creatures that are both of the air and the sea."

Lenon laughed, "None of you? What about him?"

Sylas followed the gesture to spot Davyn behind him, eyeing the leather's contents as though he were about to leap forward to eat it raw.

"I'm sorry," Sylas muttered, then addressed Lenon again, "we cannot cook or eat anything that can fly and swim. They evolved after Calamyta was formed, and they are unnatural. I will not prepare them."

"Ungrateful. That's your loss," Lenon sneered.

Sylas nodded, hoping the other Candorians from his ship wouldn't be too disappointed. It was only in Hawk's Keep that they followed the old religious rule about hybrid creatures.

Lenon grabbed the fish and held them out for the taking. Davyn and Cames took them. The Hornes wrapped the amphibian and eggs back into the leatherskin.

Lenon raised his hands in a shrug, "We will have to share these beasts with the others. They never complain."

Sylas raised an eyebrow. "Others? What others?"

"Oh, you will meet them. When the fire sun is highest, you will meet the others."

Sylas opened his mouth to question, but realized there was nothing he could think to ask. The two men shared a stoic stare for a moment. Then Lenon turned his back and walked out of the tunnel, followed by his band of Hornes.

"This isn't enough," Davyn was the first to complain, "this is less fish than they have brought us every day."

"The gullfrog was the rest," Sesca said. "We needed that meal."

Sylas held the torch out to Cames. "Use this to cook our fish. It may be less food, but it will taste better than what we've been enduring. Careful not to get the fire going or the oil in the flame. We don't want to smoke ourselves out."

"Should I go further out?" Cames asked, pointing toward the entrance of the tunnel.

Sylas shook his head. "It's too windy. If you lose that fire, we can't light it again."

Cames set to work in the dirt.

Sesca and Davyn stepped to either side of Sylas.

"I'm sorry," Sylas said, cutting them off, "I could not even prepare…that, for anyone to eat. We cannot." Looking beyond them, he could barely make out the faces of the other Candorian refugees in the dark, their expressions in shadow, but he could see enough to know they were displeased.

"I'm going to look out," Sylas muttered abruptly. He pulled his fur around his shoulders and made his way through the tunnel. The closer he got to the entrance, the louder the howl from the wind grew. By the time he reached the entrance, it was a dull roar.

The grey sky was thick with fog down around all of the rocky island. Their tunnel was so high on the rock that most days Sylas couldn't see the ocean below. He knew the Hornes must keep their ships there. The day the Hornes had brought them to the rocky cliff faces, he had seen land to the west. As they ascended a loose path up the island, struggling to make it up while the Hornes pressed them on, Sylas had cast several gazes to the coast. He imagined if he were a young man, Cames's age, he might have tried to leap into the icy water below and foolishly swim for East Shore. What then? Would being a prisoner of the Boens be any better than a prisoner of the Hornes?

Sylas huddled under his fur, the wind nipping at his skin. There was a mist coming off the ocean spray, even dozens of meters up. He was always wet and always cold. Perhaps soon he would grow scales and gills of his own.

"Aren't you going to eat?" Isla asked, behind him.

He turned to give her a half-smile. "There isn't enough. The Hornes will bring more fish tomorrow."

"We don't know that. Some days they have forgotten us."

"Or they ran out of scraps," Sylas muttered.

"Come back into the tunnel," Isla pleaded, "it's freezing here. What good will you be to us if you're ill?"

He shrugged, "Am I any good to you now, anyway? I can't save you."

Isla's eyes darkened. "You might. If the opportunity comes. We can't give up hope."

Sylas shook his head. "Go on back and have something to eat, love. I'll be there soon."

"Promise me you aren't going to do anything stupid."

"What would I do?"

She reached for his hand and took it between hers. "You frighten me when you get this way. Morose. You act like hope is lost."

"It is," Sylas muttered, "but that doesn't mean I'm going to fling myself off the rock."

"Hope is never lost."

He grumbled. There was no answer she would accept from him. He stared out into the fog, scanning for signs of any break in the clouds.

"Your fingernail is growing back," Isla whispered, "soon you'll have a new one."

"See? There is hope for some things. Hope for my finger."

Isla wrinkled her nose. "I'm going back. I can only stand so much of this cold. Please come with me?"

"I'll be there soon."

She squeezed his hand once more, then disappeared into the tunnel.

He didn't return soon. He let the wind whip against his face until his cheeks were numb. Candorians weren't meant for the sea, even though he'd always loved the water of the Western Founts near his home. If he lied to himself, he could pretend he was in the Calam Mountains, with the valley of the Western Founts below. Then if he jumped, he would likely die impaled on a pine below, instead of in a tomb of freezing ocean water.

Either way, wherever he thought about being, he imagined death.

Sylas wasn't sure how long he stayed at the tunnel's edge, but he heard voices coming from below. They were speaking Hornish. It sounded like blubbering to him, as though they were always talking underwater. He watched down the face of the island as a group of them appeared in the fog, coming up the paths between rocks.

"Sylas," Lenon called, peering up. He had a crooked smile.

Sylas didn't reply as the men drew closer, winding along the precarious terrain as if the slippery rocks were nothing. He thought of how he and his crew had nearly fallen to their deaths trying to traverse the same ground.

"I have a surprise for you now," Lenon said. He reached the tunnel's entrance and stood beside Sylas, towering over him. "Would you like to bring your people to see it? It isn't far."

"Do you want me to bring my people?"

Lenon squinted. "That is for you to decide. It will not make any difference."

"Then let me be blunt," Sylas stepped forward. "Are you planning to kill me? Because in that case, I don't want my people there. I will not subject them to witness it."

"Kill you? Not today." Lenon reached out a scaly hand and ruffled Sylas's long brown hair.

Sylas resisted the deep urge to clock the taller man in the jaw. Instead, he spun on his heel to go into the tunnel. When he returned to the entrance, Cames and Isla were on either side of him.

"This is all your people?" Lenon asked.

"The others don't need to go," Sylas replied.

With a nod, Lenon led them down the trail, moving much slower than Sylas knew he was capable of. They had gone a few meters when Lenon left the path, turning north.

"Where are we going?" Sylas called after him. The wind was ripping at him and it seemed to catch his voice. It was no surprise that Lenon didn't react and trudged on ahead.

Sylas, Isla, and Cames tucked their arms in tight and their shoulders high to fight the frigid breeze, but it was little to no use. They marched north, perpendicular to the ground, until Sylas was sure they would be lost without Lenon leading. If this was the Horne leader's way of taking them to their death, all he would have to do is simply run ahead. The three Candorians would be lost, freezing, and hypothermic by nightfall.

Then Lenon turned and pointed, wearing one of his crooked grins. Sylas was beginning to detest the constant state of amusement Lenon was in at the expense of their fragile lives.

Sylas sped up as much as he could while remaining careful on the wet surface. When he was a meter from Lenon, he turned his head to see the direction of the gesture. To Sylas's surprise, it was the opening of another tunnel. This one was wider than the one they'd been occupying, at least at the outside portal.

"The others," Lenon said, as if that were an explanation.

Sylas stopped to stare at him. "You want us to go in there?"

"Yes, we will all go."

"You first," Sylas said.

Lenon scoffed, but Sylas clenched his jaw in return. They stared one another down for a second, and then Lenon's smile broadened.

"Come on, you will like the others," Lenon said, then stepped into the tunnel.

Sylas glanced back to see that Isla and Cames were following, then entered the tunnel after Lenon.

As soon as they were deep enough that the wind died down, Sylas could hear voices from further ahead. They weren't carrying torches, and the light from behind was soon dwindling.

"We can't see in the dark," Sylas said.

Lenon's voice replied from somewhere ahead in the shadow. "Keep walking, there will be light."

If it weren't for the presence of voices ahead, Sylas would be sure they were marching toward execution. Perhaps not.

They must have rounded a corner, because all at once there was a bright orange light. Sylas shielded his eyes at first, then lowered his hand to take it in.

The tunnel opened to a chamber the size of a great room. It reminded Sylas of his banquet hall in Hawk's Keep. At the center were several poles standing freely with bright torches at the top. Around them in all directions were dozens of people. Most of them were men, by Sylas's assessment. Many were wearing styles of clothing he didn't recognize, but some were Candorians. They were arranged in circles, talking amongst themselves, as if in the middle of an afternoon picnic. After a moment, several sets of eyes settled on Sylas, taking him in.

"Who are they?" Isla asked from behind him.

Lenon held out his hands. "They are soon to be my army. Some of my army. There are many more of them in the other tunnels."

Sylas raised his eyebrows. "They are refugees, from the war with the Boens."

Lenon shrugged.

"But…" Isla gasped, "did you take them from East Shore?"

Lenon looked between the two of them. "I do not know where they call home. Most were captured by Boens. We asked the Boens for lands. That was the arrangement. The Boens didn't honor the arrangement. We had boats to move the Boens, so we used our boats to take more people."

"Take people. From East Shore?" Sylas asked.

"From anywhere we found them."

142

Sylas thought of how he and Isla had been taking refugees to the southernmost space between East Shore and East Twin for months. How many had they transported? Hundreds? They called the settlement "Haven", but perhaps it was doom. His stomach clenched at the thought. He may have delivered all those people right into the Hornes' waiting grasp.

"How many are there?" Sylas asked.

Lenon shrugged. "Enough for my army."

It was quiet between the few of them. The refugee "army" continued to chat, a few of them casting undisguised glares toward Lenon. The group was noticeably absent of children, the frail, or the elderly. Sylas tried not to think about what may have happened to them.

"What do you expect of them?" Isla asked.

"We will speak of that soon," Lenon said, then his pale eyes settled on Sylas. "You are a leader. You made your crew to give up their fight. You can make others listen. You will help me to make my army listen."

Sylas scoffed, chuckling. "What? You think I will lead an army, for you? You're…no."

Lenon shook his head. "You won't lead them. I will lead them. But you will make them follow me."

"They won't. No matter what I say to them, they will not fight their own people."

Lenon smiled, then pointed to Cames. "Come here, young boy."

Cames stepped forward. Lenon grabbed the young knight by the back of his neck and pulled his cheek to the wet, smooth wall.

"Can you draw?" Lenon asked.

Cames furrowed his brow. "Draw?"

Lenon reached for the narrow sword that dangled by his side. In a swift motion, he whipped it forward and sliced open Cames's belly.

"Bastard!" Sylas shouted, lunging forward. Before he could reach them, Lenon's sword was at his throat.

"Stay back," Lenon warned.

143

Sylas swallowed and held up his hands.

Cames was gripping his stomach as the blood began to flow.

"There," Lenon said, "now you have your paint. Can you draw?"

"Paint?" Cames groaned. "You want me to paint…with my blood?"

Lenon smirked, tapping the cave wall with his blade. "What else would we paint with?"

Sylas glanced again at the crowd in the rest of the chamber, somewhat shocked that none of them were leaping up to help. There were six Hornes and possibly a hundred men in that room. Yet the Hornes showed no awareness or fear of the refugees at all. How long had they been beating those people into submission? What had they done to terrorize all of them into not even attempting an uprising?

But then, where would they go? Into the water three hundred meters below?

Lenon was murmuring to Cames, not loud enough for the others to hear. Cames lifted his bloody hand and began. He made a few lines on the wall before he went back to his gut for more.

"Stop this," Sylas said, balling his fists.

"I will," Lenon replied, "when you can see what he draws."

Cames groaned again as he raised his hand, tracing out a few more lines.

Sylas glanced at Isla to see her mouth open in dismay and tears flooding her brown eyes. He was relieved she wasn't staring at him with disappointment. There's no telling what stupid thing he might try if he believed she was disappointed in him.

Lenon stepped back and waved his hands. "That is good. Good work, boy. You draw it very good."

Cames stumbled back, and Isla reached for him, pulling him into her arms. She inspected his wound, her hand over his to apply pressure.

"See this, Sylas?" Lenon said.

Sylas tore his eyes away from the sight of Cames's wound to where Lenon was directing his attention. "What? Why have you done this?"

144

"I needed to show you why you will make my armies listen. Do you see this creature on this wall? The boy has drawn it so well. If you do not make my armies listen then your friends will go swim in the sea with this. These are our friends."

Sylas stepped back to view the wall and the painting in Cames's blood. It was a humped creature, with four long paddle shaped limbs beneath it. Its tail was twice the length of its body, whipping around it. The head was on a thick neck, and reminiscent of a horse. The mouth was gaping, and bore plenty of teeth. At least, that was how Cames had made it appear.

Perhaps the most disturbing part of the drawing was not the beast at all, but how next to it, Cames had drawn a singular man. The man was only the size of the creature's head.

"You will come up with a plan," Lenon said, "or you will decide who we feed to the garons first."

CHAPTER 14
AVEN

Family by blood, but not by heart

As Aven trudged through the desert on foot, avoiding Ruvians, snakes, bandits, and leering men, she had hoped returning to her childhood home would be a warm occasion. She had pictured the faces of her six older brothers and their parents, smiling to see her safe and well after knowing Boenaerya was devastated by Boens. She had imagined being pulled into loving arms, fed the best ham from their pigs, and given a warm bed and regaled with stories of the years she had been away.

That hope was crushed the moment she stepped into the once-familiar hovel.

It was not only the fact that five of her brothers and her father had been sent away, and only Strand and her mother, Gailia, remained. It was the cold and apathetic way they greeted her, acting as though she'd gone to toss stones in the river and was back with muddied shoes as an inconvenience to them.

Aven's heart ached at their dismissal, but then she cursed herself for being so foolish to expect anything more. She decided she'd been wrong. She'd been wrong to put her desires first, to need her family to care for her, when clearly their lives had been shattered by the distant war and subsequent squalor state of Candor.

Within the first few minutes of her arrival, Strand and Gailia made it clear that Aven must pull her weight.

"There's nowhere for you to sleep," Gailia had said. "This hovel was small when you left, it's still small. And I won't take down your brothers' beds. They'll come back and expect to find everything as they left it. You want to stay here; you're going to help. No running off to the little library or hiding from the sun these days."

Aven cringed at the mention of her sickly childhood and her time inside the castle, but nodded.

That had been a fortnight ago; but every day was the same treatment from Strand and her mother.

In two weeks' time, neither of them asked how the nearly ten years had treated her. Surely Gailia knew that Aven's husband Eathon had died. Perhaps Gailia even knew that the people of Colby had perished under Aven's rule of the duchy.

Aven felt the emotional memory of coping with her mother's coldness come rushing back to her. It was as familiar as making a meat pie, after all. Aven reminded herself that her needs didn't matter, her voice wasn't welcome. She kept to her small corner in the hovel and didn't ask for help. When her sadness threatened to bubble out from within, she found excuses to retreat to the privy and silently gather herself by squeezing her hands, biting her lips, and focusing her attention elsewhere until the feelings subsided.

Strand noticed her frequent absences and brought it up when they were in the barn, readying for the fourteenth night of pig slaughtering together.

"Did you develop a stomach ailment?" Strand asked, inspecting his cleavers without glancing in Aven's direction.

"What do you mean?"

"When you were gone, all this time. Did you get something…you're always running to the privy. Are you pregnant, maybe?"

147

Aven gasped, "Almighties, no. And no, I...there's nothing wrong with my stomach. I don't think I'm using the privy more than any other woman."

Strand threw a questioning look over his shoulder, but Aven shrugged, with no words coming to mind that might insist otherwise. If another of her brothers had been there, perhaps she could have shared the emptiness and grief she felt.

But not with Strand. He was simple and rude on his best day.

Strand had stopped tying up the hog he was fussing with and stared, now adding a curious raise of his brow. "How did you manage to survive and get all the way back here, anyway?"

Aven balked, hesitating at Strand's sudden interest. Should she tell him about Ediva? Tell him the stories of Raena saving her life? How she'd hid underground with Lady Islabell from their own kingdom's soldiers? Or should she even explain where she had spent the past few days prior to her arrival: traveling through the desert alone, starving, afraid, hiding behind a merchant's cart? How she could have collapsed there in the sun and been left for dead, eaten by vultures, but she managed to dredge onward to Candeo. All for what? To be reunited with her brother and mother who, as far as she could tell, had little concern if she were alive or dead, in Candor or Ediva, a duchess or a serf.

"What do you mean?" Aven whispered.

Strand shrugged, "How did you get across the mountains and all?"

"Oh," Aven felt her heart sink, and she cursed herself for the disappointment. "I came on a caravan."

Strand had been satisfied enough with that response, as if it was a natural thing to survive an invasion and a war and simply hop on a caravan and ride over the mountains to another kingdom.

Aven hadn't needed the reminder of why Strand was her least-favorite brother, but she had been provided it. She groaned as she set to spreading out the thick chains that would soon hoist the pigs for butchering. While she worked, her mind drifted to how badly she wished any one of her other family members would surprise them all and walk through the door of the barn. Faer was her favorite, and he was assigned to the legions defending Candor nearest the Scablands now. Gregor and Tennel were guards outside House Grent. Davyn and C'olon had been sent to East Twin to escort prisoners. The irony was not lost on Aven that her family was taken from her in East Shore by the Boen War, and her family in Candeo was ripped apart by the Boen War. Though really if she blamed anyone, it was Zander for conscripting every able-bodied man of Candor and drying up his well of armies.

Everyone, except arrogant Strand. He'd been left behind to ensure the quota of meat was met for the crown.

"They are growing bolder," Strand explained, bent over a piece of hide. He slid his blade across it, sharpening with expert precision.

"The cleavers?" Aven asked, ripped away from her thoughts abruptly.

They were alone in the pen, in the back room where they did most of the butchering. The air was hot and thick, even in the middle of the night, but not hot enough to spoil the freshly sliced meat before they could bury it in the cool underground.

Strand shook his head. "No, the gangs. They've been hell since the war, but now they will risk their lives to get to our meat stores. We are going to have to ask the crown for more guards."

Aven glanced at the entrance of the pen where a gangly, pimply boy of fifteen was holding a single spear. "The crown has given us what they have to spare. Clearly, they are light on defenders for our farm."

"We still have to ask. Not much else we can do, unless we want to sit here and wait for them to take everything we have."

"If they do, then what? We'll tell the crown the truth, we were overwhelmed. We can't provide meat if we're under attack."

Strand grimaced and beat the leather harder. "There's no excuse. We'll be beaten in front of the other farmers and left in the sun for a day. They'll make an example of us, they did it to Braedan in the spring."

Aven stared down at the cut of bacon she was slicing through, taking a moment to consider his words.

"You have noble friends, don't you?" Strand grumbled.

"Hardly."

"Well, see if any of them want to do you any favors after the years you lived among them. Get after them to send us more guards."

Aven shrugged, swallowing her next words. She wouldn't explain to her brother what she didn't need to.

He hadn't changed much on the inside; he was still stubborn and curt as ever. That had been the reason they had never been able to come to terms or see eye-to-eye. When they were children, Strand took every opportunity to tell Aven he hated her for not being a "brother", though he had five of those to choose from. It seemed he had never forgiven her for being born a girl.

The last time she had seen him, they were both awkward teenagers. He was still lanky and thin now, but he wore a thick black beard and kept his hair long and tied behind his head. He had decorated his skin with tattoos to honor Libre, the religion of Candor. Many of them were painted with gold and brown to represent the season of summer and the plentiful harvests. Aven tried not to stare at the way they wrapped around his neck and disappeared under his scruffy hair, as if a hand trickled around his throat.

The rest of the night they spent in silence, making cuts of the pig before sunrise. At random intervals, Aven heard screams and shouts in the distance, occasionally the clang of blades. They made her jump even though they had permeated the background of Candeo for over fifteen days.

In the morning she wandered the farm fields inside the curtain of Candeo Castle. Once or twice, she passed dark patches in the desert sand that appeared to be blood, not yet dried by the rising sun. It might have been from butchering, or something more sinister. She supposed the bandits were closing in, and Strand was right. Even where she wanted to be safe, there was always another threat looming around the corner. Aven longed to simply rest and not jolt awake with panic every night. She longed to walk without keeping a dagger in her belt and casting fearful glances over her shoulder with every few steps.

Between the curtain and the towers, she passed the old peasant door that was so familiar it was like rediscovering a lost childhood toy. That had been her way to enter the castle when she was a tiny, curious girl. She could picture every step beyond it perfectly—the stairwell that wound up, through the wings, eventually reaching the Queen's private library. She tried to focus on the memories to see if she would feel something, anything at all. She searched inside herself. Had she been excited to read in the library? Had she been sad when she visited and the Queen was too busy to chat with her? Had she been frightened when Zander had teased and pestered her in the hallways? Could she remember laughing, crying, feeling joy? Aven knew the memories were there, but she was seeing them through a fog, layers and layers deep. Aven stared for a long moment at the door, willing herself to feel anything at all, but finding numbness was all that filled her. She wondered if she could bring up the good pieces of her feelings if she walked through that door. Perhaps then she could cling to her best memories of Zarana. Or would bringing her past back cause her to unravel everything else she'd buried and bring a flood of pain and rage she couldn't control?

"Get on then, peasant," an old man grumbled. He was wearing a leather tunic as if he were a king's guard, but held no weapon.

Aven jolted at his voice. She muttered an apology and continued on as he directed. She found the other edge of the wall and took the trail toward the royal stables. As soon as she saw the knight's training grounds ahead, her eyes scanned for pale skin and bright straw hair. Though she believed it unlikely that Raena would be up so early in the day, she held some shred of hope. Her heart raced against her will at the prospect. After all, knights meant Raena; or at least, the possibility of Raena.

A few knights were clambering about, jostling with one another and sharpening their weapons. As Aven approached the edge of the training yard, one of the elder knights charged toward her, holding a sword at his side.

"You, peasant," he shouted, "don't come any closer. If this is a trick or you were sent as bait, you best turn back. We'll slice you up."

Aven stopped in her tracks and raised her open palms toward him. "It's no trap, I'm here alone. I'm looking for someone, sir."

The knight grunted. "Alright, stay there. Who are you after? Give us your message and then back to the pig pens with you."

"A few men returned to Candor by caravan. They've been back a fortnight. One is Sir Allyn of Lox, the other is Sir Rowan of Hawk's Keep. Do you know them?"

The knight laughed, "Allyn and Rowan, that's who you're after? Cheeky girl, aren't ya?"

The change in his tone made the hair stand up on the back of Aven's neck. She took a slow step back.

"I know them well, and they will be interested in my whereabouts. I need you to tell them I've been here, please."

His laugh grew in volume, this time his eyes narrowing as he looked her up and down. "Those boys have been good to you, have they? You're looking for more from the young lads? Tell me sweetie, have you had a man with hair on his chest yet?"

Aven grimaced. Her palms began to sweat and she glanced to see who else was around, becoming all too aware of the sense that she was alone with this leering man.

It wasn't anything she hadn't faced before.

"I've been with men you would regret reckoning with," Aven snapped, "including my husband, who is twice your size and a duke of a noble house. I am a duchess, in fact, and I do not take kindly to your vulgarity. So, I remind you to watch your tongue."

He scoffed, his dark eyes sizing her up. "Settle down, then. I suppose you talk like a lady. My mistake, but you're dressed like a peasant, how was I to know?"

"Perhaps you shouldn't judge anyone, considering the state of the kingdom. I dress this way to move freely without being assaulted by the

Ruvians, the gangs, or the bandits. I suggest you try it if you've run into trouble."

"Aye," the knight said, "sound advice. Thank you, m'lady."

"You're welcome. Now, you will deliver my message, won't you? That's Sir Allyn and Sir Rowan. I wish to speak with them." She thought to tell the location of her hovel, but realized that would betray her identity as a pig farmer to the knight. "I—I wish them to meet me here, this time tomorrow. I will return at sunrise."

The knight balked.

"Is there something the matter, sir?"

He shook his head. "Don't get your hopes up, but I swear on the crown I'll deliver your message. What name ought I give them? They know you by it?"

"Yes. I am Duchess Avenna. They know me well."

His eyes widened with recognition and he bowed his head without adding another word.

Aven knew better than to press further with a crude bloke the likes of this one, and she made a hasty retreat back the way she came. She was rounding a corner at the curtain's edge when she saw the farm fields ahead.

Though they were alight with flames.

She heard the shouts and grunts of men locked in a violent battle, and her mind ripped her back in time. Her feet were glued to the spot as she was forced to remember it all as though it were happening again.

The Boens.

The Hornes.

Their rise from the ground. Their advance from the coast.

House Colby, burning from the inside out.

Everyone she'd loved in East Shore, suffering and screaming for their last breaths in the rising flames. Had they been slaughtered quick at the hands of the brutal Hornes? Or had they burned alive, feeling the air suffocate in the heat though their lungs melted within them?

"Stop it," Aven muttered. "Stop it, now." She clenched her teeth and her fists, gripping and releasing them, again and again.

With a few rapid breaths, she shoved the memories down and trapped them in. Back to the center of herself, tucked within the shields, held tight and locked away.

That was all it took to renew her strength, and Aven bolted forward, straight to the fire. She grabbed her skirts and held them as her feet pounded across the sand. Aven passed through the arches that divided the inner grounds with the servant's farms. It was then she could see the fires for what they truly were; centered on two hovels, away from her family.

A dozen men were running around the outside, trying to toss pitiful buckets of water in vain.

Another half dozen were scrambling with a pack of dark hooded bandits, further beyond in a patch of waist-high grain. The bandits were wielding shortswords and appeared to be advancing easily against the clumsy farmers holding shovels and sticks. A gangly farmer reached for a rock and hurled it. His awkward motion made Aven recognize him as her brother immediately, even from half a furlong away.

She felt her lungs burn and her sides ache as she sprinted with fervor. If the bandits made it beyond the first line of defense, the others would be too overwhelmed by the fires to see them coming.

Aven stumbled once, careening forward, but managed to stay upright. She passed a few families, watching from the safety of the footpath, staring with wide eyes at the commotion. When she was within earshot of the farmers weakly dousing the flames, she shouted with all her might.

"The bandits! Leave the hovels!" Aven cried.

A few glanced at her over their shoulders, then carried on with filling buckets from troughs.

"Look in the field!" She screamed, gesturing, "They're coming!"

One of the young men—perhaps a boy—followed her wild movements then jumped. He began to shout, grabbing the others by the arms and shoulders.

Aven was still running, but changed direction to continue onward to the field. Her momentary distraction of watching the farmers had caused her to lose sight of those fighting the bandits. Now as she scanned the grain patch ahead, she saw fewer men than she'd expected. Some had to be on the ground.

But Strand's gangly form was still upright, and he was flanked by two bandits in dark hoods. They were swinging wildly and he would be overtaken in a heartbeat, for certain.

Her breath was loud, but there was a growing ringing in her ears. She felt her senses dulling, the edges of her vision turning white. She feared her legs may give out, or her gasps for air may collapse her lungs. She tried to think of a time she had run so fast, but her mind couldn't focus on anything except pumping blood to her thighs.

She was a few dozen steps from the fight when she saw it. A bandit raised his blade high into the air, and Strand's long arms were reaching toward the other. He was diverted, twisting in the wrong direction. Aven heard a scream as the blade came slashing down, and Strand collapsed beneath it.

She realized the scream was her own.

Aven bolted on, renewed somehow, but the bandits were charging as well.

The first line of farmers had all fallen, Strand the last of them. With no one in their way, the bandits raged toward the farm hovels, intent on whatever raid they had chosen for this mission.

She couldn't fight them. She had no weapon. Yet there she was, bounding directly toward them, ready to collide like two children in a play yard.

She could see them now and make out their appearance. They were Ruvians, it seemed, their skin painted in symbols of the terra and nature. They wore thick hoods but remained bare-chested, to showcase the long scars across their chests. They were wild and unrestrained, covered in furs and bones of the animals, or perhaps humans, they had killed.

Aven let out a choked yell when they were within a dozen meters, and she did the only thing she could think to do: tuck her body and roll to the ground. Within half a second, the grain folded over her, collapsing partially over her crumbled frame.

The footsteps were pounding in the dry earth, like horses' hooves. She listened as they clambered by and seemed to pass. Without wasting a moment, Aven was up again and running toward the place she had last seen her brother, parting the grain wildly with both hands in search of him.

There were familiar clangs of metal behind her, and Aven knew the other farmers must be engaging with the Ruvians, but they weren't her problem anymore.

Her fingertips brushed over a wet stalk and she glanced at it, surprised by the sensation.

Blood.

She whipped her head up to see a smattering of red across the golden grain, and Aven traced it toward an origin point. In a few leaps, she was there, and saw the stalks given away. It reminded her of a stag's down. Her brother laid in a heap on his side, his legs spread wide. His grey tunic was brown at the shoulders, and Aven couldn't remember if it had been that color before.

With a quick glance backward to ensure no bandit had turned to pursue her, she fell to her knees.

"Strand," she tried to say but the name caught with a choke in her throat. Aven grabbed his arm and pushed, heaving him over to his back.

His eyes were closed, but he appeared to be breathing. At first glance, she couldn't see a wound.

"Strand," she said again, "can you hear me? It's Aven. Wake up, please."

She pressed his shoulders, shaking them.

He let out a groan.

That was when she saw more blood on the ground, pooling in the dirt under his skull. She pushed his shoulders again, rolling him further, revealing a gash on the back of his head. The blood was flowing, but he hadn't lost much as far as she could reckon.

Aven grabbed the sash from her simple dress and ripped it from her waist, bundling it to hold firmly against his head.

"Strand, can you walk?"

He groaned again, intelligible this time. "No. Yea."

"Come on, we have to get out of here. The Ruvians will bring more."

"Gailia?"

Aven's heart plummeted. She jolted to her feet and scanned the farms. The fires had formed a wall of black smoke, and somewhere beyond it was their hovel, and their mother inside it.

"We have to hurry," she said, reaching for his hand, "we have to get her out of there."

"The bandits won't try more than one hovel," he said. "They'll raid one and then run before the guards assemble to fight them."

"Come on, let's make sure it's not ours they try then."

Strand held the sash to the back of his head and wobbled to his feet. His steps were awkward like a foal taking its first few, but he managed to lurch through the field.

As they trudged ahead, Aven kept her eyes glued to the mess of raiding bandits. It reminded her so much of the stories she'd heard from her people when she had been duchess of Colby. "The Hornes take us by surprise" they'd told her. "They rush in without fear", "they always have the upper hand", "we couldn't save our sisters from their raiding party". She'd heard every story but had become numb after the years. How could she allow herself to feel the pain and suffering of every poor soul who lost their loved ones to brutal and cowardly warmongers? Now it was a flood of those repressed emotions as she had a scene to paint into the stories she'd only imagined. Before her was the real telling of it all, the bandits throwing humble farmers to the ground as if they were straw dolls and taking what they wanted. When she saw two of the bandits grab a girl,

157

perhaps no older than Aven had been when she was attacked, she turned her head to focus on the horizon.

Strand hobbled slower than she wanted, but at least they were getting farther from the commotion. In a minute they were through the smoke and saw their pig field, the wood fence wrapping around its border. At the center, their stone and plank hovel. The windows were covered to keep the inside dark and cool. There was no sign of trouble, but they continued to jog all the same.

The usual guards were nowhere to be seen, likely either abandoned their post in fear of being slaughtered, or perhaps they did the brave thing and rushed into the fight. Aven somehow doubted it was the latter.

Strand burst through the door. "Gailia?"

Their mother was there in an instant, wearing a disgruntled glare. "What is it? Quiet down."

"Bandits," Strand explained.

Aven slammed the door and grabbed for their table to blockade it shut. "Come on, help me."

"Don't wedge it," Strand said, helping with the table, "they'll try to start a fire and smoke us out if they come for us. We'll need to escape."

Aven nodded. "Come on, we'll hide in the loft then. If they come looking, they might not see us."

Gailia shook her head with her eyebrows raised and mouth hanging open. "The bandits got past the guards?"

"Aye," Strand snapped, "you know those lousy guards didn't fight worth shite. They ran away like pissants, no doubt."

"Give them mercy, they are mostly children themselves. Think of your brothers, out there—"

"We haven't time," Aven interrupted, "get into the loft, please."

Gailia scoffed, but turned to climb the ladder as she was told.

The three of them scrambled into the tiny loft that had been a bed for Aven's parents, and now belonged to Gailia alone.

CHAPTER 15
AVEN

No one left to turn to...and even then, it's too late

In the morning she returned to the knights' proving grounds.

Her face fell when she saw him, but she sucked in a breath and forced a smile. After all, any response to her request was positive, even if it wasn't the knight she truly wanted to see.

"Aven, my dear," Allyn Lox said with a cold smile. He stretched out his arms for her and pulled her into an awkward embrace.

She pulled back before it could linger.

"Glad to see she wasn't lying, then," the burly knight from the day before grumbled. He seemed to need to see for himself that the message hadn't been a farce.

"Come on, this is my friend. A duchess, no less," Allyn scolded.

The knight shook his head with a cluck and then left them to talk alone.

"Thank you for coming," Aven said. "I am sure you are busy tending with many other things now that we are back in Candeo. I am afraid I saw no other choice but to contact you."

Allyn waved his hands. "No, no. Don't make excuses. Listen, I know that things in Ediva were hard for you. It was strange for all of us, being in that foreign land. And I'm sure we couldn't have done anything more for you than we tried to do. Rowan, especially."

Aven opened her mouth to utter a protest, but he pressed on.

"I was quite disappointed when you left the caravan. I didn't even know about it, at first! I thought everything was great, and was getting better for you. Honestly, I thought you'd be ecstatic to return to Candeo and be treated as a noble once again. After all, a duchess of East Shore surely has to be recognized as…something in Candor, I suppose? So, I had no idea you were feeling so distraught. I suppose that's all Rowan, though. He's quite a horse's ass."

Aven wrung her hands together. "How is he?"

"How is…Rowan? You still care for that stupid bastard, do you?"

She glanced away, focusing on a sound in the distance for a moment.

Allyn let out a laugh. "Ah, I suppose you do. Well, first true love and all that, eh? He's fine. He has some news, but I'll let you find that out for yourself."

Aven raised an eyebrow to that.

"Don't worry about it. Don't fuss. You've got nothing to worry about. None of us do, now."

"No, Allyn, that isn't right. There is plenty to worry about. The kingdom is falling into chaos since Queen Zarana was executed and the legions fell. Without the armies, gangs and Ruvians rule the open spaces. They might not be bold enough to enter the curtains of Candeo, but they ransack every village and farm outside the walls. Surely you—"

"Yea, of course. I mean, I know that's happening. We sit through plenty of council meetings to hear about it, every day. But it will wear off. They will get tired of being beaten back by our guards and they'll dissipate."

"Your guards?" Aven chuckled dryly. "What guards? There are no guards. There are boys who haven't yet grown body hair and men teetering on the end of their days. They have blacksmith hammers and shovels for weapons, if they're lucky. Have you seen these so-called guards? The best of them have been sent to the outer edges of Candor to guard the foothills of Calam—"

"Alright, that's enough," Allyn balked. "I don't need a war strategy lesson. I get enough of that. Is that why you brought me here? To complain about the state of our guards? We are doing the best we can. Everything will calm down in a fortnight or two."

"No, that's not exactly why I asked you here. Though, I suppose it is relevant."

Allyn raised an eyebrow. "Go on."

"My family is in danger. We have not been able to defend our farm, and we must supply our pigs to the crown. My brother and I cannot meet the quota for summer, due to the bandit attacks. Also, my other five brothers have been sent away to defend from Boens."

Allyn shrugged. "Well, the Boens won't attack, we know that now. We are stopping the Boens, and by winter we can draw back the forces. Your brothers will be home then."

"We cannot wait until winter. If my family does not make our quota this summer, my brother and I will be beaten and hung in the fields."

"For fuck's sake, what?"

She gave a slight nod, focusing on him with her hazel eyes.

Allyn pulled at the corner of his mustache. "Well, that's…that's truly barbaric. Who is doing this? I can have them flogged for it."

"You might hope to do so, but this is the way it's been for years. You aren't going to change the way the serfs are treated by flogging someone. These are the crown's tax keepers and sheriffs; this is the way they run things."

"Well, I assumed they kept order and discipline, but that's counterproductive."

Aven rolled her eyes. "I want your help, please. I don't want violence. But perhaps you can talk to the sheriffs and beseech them to ease up on the farmers until the bandits are pulled back. We don't have the ability to fight raids and attacks while butchering pigs at this rate. My brother Strand says we are producing but a quarter of the meat we have in years past. Which, when you think of it, is still impressive, considering that six of my brothers and my father have all been sent to guard other houses and the passes."

Allyn nodded. "That's impressive, yea. Listen, how about if you come stay in the castle for a while? I am sure it will be no trouble. We have a lot of vacant chambers since the legions were taken. There are soldiers' quarters. They aren't luxurious but they are safe. I'd have enough for the three of you."

"No, my mother would never agree to it. She is too proud. She was too proud to leave Candor and join me in East Shore, though I sent for them every year."

"That's stupid of her. I apologize, but she sounds foolish."

"I understand, but that is her way. She believes in Libre firmly, and listens to the diacons. They have told her that everyone has a place and she believes her place is the farm."

Allyn grimaced, shaking his head. "Ah, I should have known it was religion. There is nothing more toxic or stupid than religion."

Aven remembered him saying as much to her in Ediva. She bit her tongue and swallowed her response.

"Alright," Allyn sighed, "I'll think of another solution. Will you show me to your hovel? I will go speak with—with Rowan. Tomorrow at this time, I will come with a solution. Perhaps he'll want to come along."

At the thought of Raena coming, Aven suppressed a smile. She shouldn't feel such warmth, but she couldn't control the way her stomach tickled at the mere mention of Raena's presence.

They walked together along the path, chatting. Allyn asked polite questions about how pigs were butchered and how the meat was preserved despite the summer heat. Aven was happy to answer to fill the silence, though she knew it interested neither of them. When they exited the citadel's curtain and entered the fields, Aven asked how Allyn was settling back into the castle.

"It's boring to be here," he muttered, "I am looking forward to going home. As soon as I finish transcribing the noble lines and documenting the succession, I can return to House Lox. My uncles and cousins have work for me there."

"So, that's what your day consists of? Transcribing the successions to the crown?"

"Aye. There is a new line, now. The nobles want to understand who will be next, if this prince is executed."

Aven raised an eyebrow. "There's a prince, now? Forgive me, I am sheltered from information on the farm, I suppose. The last I knew, it was your uncle on the throne."

Allyn made a strange noise, something between a cough and a groan. "Yes, there's a prince. I'll have to tell you more tomorrow, it's quite a story."

"I look forward to hearing it. We haven't time now, I suppose." She lifted her hands and gestured to the hovel, showing him they had arrived as if it were a destination worth noting.

"This is it? Easy enough to remember."

"I could invite you in—"

"No need," he said, "I will return tomorrow. Perhaps we can have tea together then. Will you be safe enough in the meantime?"

She felt the heaviness of his gaze, as though he cared deeper for her than he would let on. The weight of it caused her skin to crawl. Without intending to, her mind flashed back to the memories of him, drunk, groping the Edivan servant girls by the dim light of the campfire. Her stomach churned and she glanced away from his brown eyes.

"I will, thank you," Aven muttered.

Satisfied, Allyn said his goodbye with a warm smile.

When Aven entered the hovel, Gailia was rolling a simple dough and Strand was sprawled out on the floor, in the corner.

"Don't wake your brother," Gailia muttered. "He's tired from butchering. He deserves a rest."

163

Aven resisted the urge to point out that she was well-aware, as she had been right alongside him, slaughtering and butchering just as many.

"May I help with the meal?" Aven whispered.

"No, but you can clean. This place was tidier when I had seven men living in it, somehow. It's amazing how much mess piles up. Though I suppose C'olon was always the one keeping clean house."

Aven nodded and obliged, picking up. Her mother's mood was sour, and Aven played out the words she wanted to say over and over in her head, trying to choose them. Without a doubt, Gailia would be angry, but delaying news didn't lessen the chances of her emotional reaction.

"Here, taste this," Gailia grumbled, setting a handful of dried brong nuts on the table.

The break in silence gave Aven courage. "Strand and I have been talking about the bandit attacks. We decided that something needs to be done. I've implored a knight to help us. He was with me in Boenaerya and he is a friend."

Gailia flung down the dough with an intentional thud against the cutting board. "It's East Shore."

"Pardon?"

"That kingdom is East Shore. You should know it, you lived there. We do not honor the Boens by giving them a land. We do not give them a named place, not in Candor."

Aven balked, her mouth going dry. "Aye—"

"And we don't need any handout from your friends. Just as I never needed them, nor your other help. I don't need anything from you, daughter, except you to pull your weight on this farm. You can help best by speeding up the slaughter so your brother isn't so beaten down and exhausted. He's doing everything here, and if you can't catch up, he's the one who will be strung up along the wall."

Aven pursed her lips, filled with insults she wanted to fire off. But what good would it do?

"If your brother wants to hear from this knight, so be it. I have the king's guards outside my door. That's good enough."

164

"Mother. You saw what they did yesterday. Those guards ran at the first sign of trouble."

Gailia grunted and slapped down the dough again.

Aven glanced at Strand to confirm he was undisturbed by the mild commotion.

"Talk to your brother then," Gailia said, "it seems no one wants to respect my wishes for this household. No different than it's ever been."

Aven grimaced. There was no talking sense to her mother in such a mood. She returned to scrubbing the surfaces with a rag, hoping that Strand would make the case she'd been unable to.

That afternoon Aven took as long a nap as she was allowed before her brother woke her to go out into the pens for another slaughter. As they walked by the light of the moon and an oil lamp, she heard a rhythmic wailing from the direction of the adjacent farm.

"What's that about?" she whispered, sidling up to Strand.

"Braedan's wife has been crying all day. One of their boys was killed."

Aven felt her chest go ice cold. "Their boys? Their children are...young."

"Aye, he wasn't yet eight, I think."

An image of a young lad flashed in her mind's eye. She tried to remember if it was Braedan's son she was picturing, but realized it was the face of Cam, Eathon's youngest brother. Her heart ached with that familiar pulse, pulling her to the past, suckling at the grief she pushed down. Aven shoved it deeper, flinching away the notion. She was tempted to ask how the boy had been killed, but couldn't trust herself to hear it without conjuring up feelings she wouldn't want to deal with.

They carried on in silence to the pig pens. Aven did her best to work faster, thinking about Gailia's words. There was no way she and Strand could ever catch up to the quota, but she would be damned if she didn't give it her all.

Strand hoisted the pigs up with the chains and leather lofts to keep them from squirming. Aven stepped in with the thinnest blade and

165

readied to slide into the first pig, who was lounging with his legs spread, unaware that his life had mere seconds remaining.

Strand grinned, his pale tattoo stretching at his jawline. "Remember when you arrived, the first night you could barely stomach to watch me slice the pigs? Now you do it as though it's nothing at all."

Aven pursed her lips. "It's what I have to do."

He chuckled and grabbed the pig's hind legs, holding them steady. "Ready when you are."

Aven stepped forward and with a practiced methodology, she struck the animal's inner thigh. Her knife cut through like butter, ripping the femoral artery wide open. The crimson blood gushed into the pig's underbelly, then poured to the floor. The pig squealed and kicked at the pain, but Aven was numb to it now, like so many other things.

"Next one?" Strand said, stepping down the line.

Despite the squealing of the animal beside it, bleeding out toward a rapid death, the next pig was calm and composed as though enjoying a leisurely nap.

Aven wiped her blade on the thin material of her skirts, and readied for the next execution.

They continued on this way until ten pigs were at peace, slung up from the ceiling of the pen and ready to be butchered. Strand didn't need to say a word when he went to the wall and took down a cleaver and a long blade for skinning. He handed the latter to Aven. Her hazel eyes met his brown ones for a moment and she gave a slight smile.

They may not have been to get along in any other matters, but at least they could manage to close their mouths enough to work alongside each other.

Through the night they tirelessly separated the cuts, broke away bone, filleted the flesh, and buried the finished slabs of meat into the ground.

It was nearly sunrise when they had one pig remaining. Aven's arms, dress, and maybe the rest of her were covered in thick blood. She had no doubt she smelled of rot and death. Her shoulders burned from exerting the muscles by raising her arms to slice above her head. She was hungry and sore but yearned for nothing more badly than sleep.

With heavy sighs, they eyed the final pig.

"We might make do with a few large cuts on this one," Strand suggested, "I haven't much energy left, and you look as bad as I feel."

"Yes, please."

He nodded and raised the cleaver when the sound of something banging against the side of the pen startled them both. Aven jerked toward the entrance to see the darting form of a Ruvian rush across the threshold.

"Bandits," she whispered, reaching for a scythe and the fillet blade.

"No, take this," Strand said. He grabbed a thick pole, one meter long, and traded it for the fillet knife.

Both of them armed with blades, Strand and Aven tiptoed toward the exit of the pen, creeping as silent as possible. Aven heard her heart pounding in her ears. Her mouth tasted of metal—the familiar rush of adrenaline filling her.

There were a few voices outside whispering low. By her estimation, there were at least three men. Ruvians weren't known for starting a fight they couldn't win, but they'd grown desperate and hungry along with the rest of Candor.

Strand stepped ahead of her, putting himself first in harm's way. She could see around his narrow shoulders to the orange hue of the sunrise reflecting off the pale ground.

In the dim light, a shadow emerged. The Ruvian was short, thick, and muscular. Aven shuddered at the sight of a pike in his hand, tightening her grip on the scythe's handle. But when the light caught the Ruvian's face Aven realized that it was no man after all. The delicate features were shadowed by the woman's hood, her angular face portraying a desperate but determined expression.

"Listen," the Ruvian growled from under her hood, her pale eyes obscured. "We can make this easy. I've got a hungry family."

167

Aven leaned closer to Strand's back and peered out of the door. Outside the pen were a few more Ruvians. They were huddled together, holding crude weapons, but no larger than children. Aven spotted one looking back at her with fear in his eyes. His hair was matted beneath his hood as though he'd never been bathed.

Strand glanced as well, then focused back on the Ruvian in the doorway. "What are you after?"

"Just enough food. That's all."

"How much is 'enough'?" Strand protested.

The stocky Ruvian's hands twisted along the pike's hilt, as if demonstrating her strength. "Get out of my way and I'll decide for myself. If you don't—I'll kill you both."

Strand balked. "This is the King's farm. These are the King's meats. If you take them, expect the wrath of the Kingsguard on—"

"What Kingsguard?" The Ruvian scoffed. "They've all gone to the Calam Mountains. Stop playing, and shut up. You know what's good for you. I'm twice your size, mate."

Aven saw the muscles in Strand's shoulders tense at the insult. Aven had heard rumors that the leaders of Ruvians were warrior women; girls who were trained from birth in fighting and killing. She had no doubt that this woman before them probably had been slitting throats since childhood. She likely could kill them both, and would if they didn't quickly step aside.

"Strand," Aven whispered, and placed one hand gently on his elbow.

"That's right, Strand," the Ruvian mocked. "Listen to your girl, there. She doesn't want to die over some meat today."

"And we'll be beaten if we can't give our meat to the crown," Strand insisted.

He continued to talk, explaining how critical it was that they meet their quota. But Aven knew his words were in vain, she had seen enough bloodshed to know what was coming next. The Ruvian's eyes darted about anxiously, shuffling back and forth on light feet, preparing to strike.

168

Aven tried to grab for Strand, to pull him backward into the pen with her, but she couldn't get a grip on his shirt while holding the scythe.

The Ruvian wasn't speaking. She was focused on Strand's face with an intentioned stare. She lifted her pike.

"No, stop!" Aven cried, screaming out from behind her brother.

The dull end of the Ruvian's pike came down first, whistling through the air in a well-aimed swing. Strand raised his arm in a feeble counter to block the wooden shaft, stepping in. The iron end barely missed contact. He shouted as he collided against the Ruvian's chest, knocking her back a few steps. Strand whipped his fillet knife back and forth, slicing the air with a whirring sound. The Ruvian lifted her arms and dodged the reckless blade.

When he stepped closer, the Ruvian went wide. Flanking him, the Ruvian pushed Strand with her free arm, knocking him sideways into the hay.

With both of them free of the pen's doorway, Aven bolted forward with her staff, practically throwing it with her weaker hand. Without much momentum, the end of the staff seemed to bounce off the Ruvian's ribs with no effect at all.

Strand jumped up, stood, and lunged for the Ruvian with his knife. But there was too much space between them. The Ruvian spun and her heavy pike connected with Strand's arm, landing with a sickening thud.

Strand screamed and dropped again, this time to his knees. He grabbed his arm and sputtered in pain. Somehow, he managed to maintain his grip on the blade, though the top portion of his arm bent slightly outward at an unreal angle.

The Ruvian lifted the pike high above her head and readied for a final blow.

"No!" Aven screamed. "Don't kill him!"

But the Ruvian was fixated. Her pale, shadowed eyes were locked in on Strand's moaning and prostrate frame. The Ruvian stepped forward and her momentum engaged, as though she were out behind a woodshed taking an ax to a few logs of pine.

169

Aven shouted again with no distinct words or language. Time seemed to stop as the Ruvian's pike came careening down. It shimmered in the early morning light, a blur of metal and wood extending from her thick arms.

The sound it made as it met Strand's skull. The echo of iron on bone. The sick, twisted crack as the Ruvian rolled the weapon to pop it free from its landing place.

Strand didn't even choke.

In that instant, he went silent. All of the air was silent.

Strand's body remained upright for a moment, as though refusing to accept that his death had come. Then all at once, his long frame toppled to the side.

Aven saw the side of his head caved in, her brother's blood and brains exposed, facing up toward the purple dawn.

The Ruvian sighed, catching her breath with a heaving chest.

Aven dropped the staff in one hand and with her scythe she ran forward. Everything inside her turned to white and red, as though the world had been painted in blood and skin she must cleanse from existence.

She screamed again, but this was a guttural scream of rage. The Ruvian's eyebrows raised with surprise as Aven reached her and slashed the scythe across her chest, making an easy slice. She readied the blade again but the Ruvian's fist hit her hard in the stomach, knocking her back. She looked down for a moment and tried to catch her breath but all the air had left her lungs. Desperate, Aven gasped.

The Ruvian kicked her hand, sending the scythe flying and clanging against the side of the pig pen. She took two steps and wrapped bulky arms around her, forcing Aven to spin until the Ruvian held her from behind. Aven struggled, whipping her arms, kicking her legs in protest. Desperate, Aven tried to remember anything she'd ever been taught about how to escape such a grip.

The Ruvian breathed hard against the back of Aven's neck; she smelled of stag hides, ale, and molding earth. The Ruvian dropped the pike and tightened one arm across Aven's waist, the other around her neck. Aven tried to yank her arms free while her eyes scanned for a weapon she might reach. With each flail, the Ruvian's grip on her neck tightened, threatening to steal her breath.

"That's enough now, isn't it?" she whispered against Aven's temple.

The strong woman's arms and the huskiness of her voice reminded Aven for a split second of Raena. The horrifying thought gave Aven a shudder. Instead of security in the embrace, this was death, coming for her. Aven cursed herself, disgusted, and tried to fall forward to escape.

Aven's vision began to blur as the grip on her neck squeezed harder, and she stopped flailing, forcing her body to be still. It worked, and the Ruvian loosened her hand enough that Aven could breathe for a moment.

"I can't have you running off to get your guards," the Ruvian sneered, "come on and wait with me inside the pens. Go nicely, and I won't slit your throat."

Aven nodded.

"Promise, you won't run?"

Aven's throat was sore, but she croaked out the words, "I won't run."

"Good girl," the Ruvian's grip around her neck loosened. She pushed Aven forward to the pen door, keeping one hand grasped around Aven's arm. She shouted at the young Ruvians, "Oi, you stay here and yell for me if anyone comes. I'll be collecting up the meats inside."

The children—and now Aven could see they were all definitely children—gazed back with wide eyes, saying nothing. If they were shocked by watching their mother murder a man in cold blood, they weren't showing it.

The Ruvian pressed herself into Aven's back and they walked, still gripping her arm tight enough to bruise as they entered the pig pen together. Aven wanted to vomit from fear. Would this woman kill her? Would this woman…rape her? Aven wasn't sure that was even possible, but something was sickeningly familiar about the sensation she felt with the Ruvian's eyes on her body. She wanted to think of this brute being

171

poisoned and the satisfaction of watching her eyes turn red and her face turn blue, the way Zander's life had been choked out of him from the inside.

She could imagine she was somewhere else. That was the way to escape it. That was the way to forget.

They didn't go toward the hanging meat, and that's when Aven knew she was in trouble. The momentary relief she had felt eroded into immediate panic. But before Aven could whip around to run, the Ruvian shoved Aven down into an empty pig pen.

She crawled toward the wall with haste but had barely made it a meter when she felt an explosive thud against her side, the Ruvian's foot connecting with her ribs. Aven was sure she heard and felt a crack when the foot connected a second time. In rapid succession, the Ruvian kicked, and it sent Aven tumbling against the wooden wall of the pen.

When she rolled to her back in the straw, the kicking stopped. Aven heard groans and whimpers, and realized they were coming from her. Aven's eyes were clenched tight, but she peeked them open enough to see the strong Ruvian towering over her. The woman was glistening with sweat, catching her breath, her fists raised over to the front of her chest. Aven couldn't move. She wasn't even sure if she was breathing at all, or if her lungs had been pierced through by her broken ribs.

The Ruvian leaned down and grabbed the front of Aven's dress, yanking her up off the ground.

"Please…" Aven gasped.

"Please what?" The Ruvian mocked, "I'm not stupid. I can't have you getting back up. It'll take me time to carry this food. You're going to lie here, nice and quiet."

Aven didn't know she had the capacity to feel more afraid. In fact, she couldn't. All she could do was make peace with the fate that awaited her.

Then the Ruvian brought both hands to Aven's neck.

When the Ruvian squeezed, Aven knew her fate. Death. She was going to die, here in this forsaken pig shite and hay. She had survived a war, a hostile kingdom, traveling across Boen-infested land, for what? To be killed over a few slabs of meat.

She kicked her legs, but couldn't stretch them high enough or hard enough to do anything to injure the powerful warrior above her. Aven grabbed and clawed at the thick fingers around her throat, scratching, feeling them tighten in response.

Tears formed in her eyes.

Everything around her was fading.

But Aven's mind began to drift. Her thoughts took her to a faraway place. She thought of picking berries in East Shore when she had first arrived as Eathon's betrothed. She thought of laughing in the fields as they collected the harvest. She thought of the way that Eathon's younger brothers had all taken a liking to her from the beginning, and the way they always wanted to play with her as though she were a child and not a lady-in-waiting who had come-of-age.

She felt the Ruvian's breath and sensed her leaning closer, but Aven wasn't there anymore. She was at the edge of the ocean, gazing out to watch the Colby fishing boats. She was thinking about how to stop the Hornes from taking their people by surprise. She was slipping her hand into Raena's and they were staring out at the sea together. She was getting lost in Raena's periwinkle eyes. She was listening to the waves and thinking a storm may be on the horizon.

"Now now, lass," an arrogant, familiar voice said from far behind them. "I love to choke a woman now and then, too. But you've got to at least give her a kiss first."

CHAPTER 16
AVEN

Butchering a pig

Allyn's sword had been so quick that Aven didn't register what had happened until it was over.

She was still on her back in the pig pen. She wretched and gasped for air, her throat burning. The Ruvian's face was staring up at her, lying beside her on the straw. The warrior's eyes and mouth were locked wide open with her hood still on, covering her thick braided hair, and the blood began to ooze from her severed neck.

"Ugh," Allyn groaned, "I hate when I get the angle wrong. Do you see? Disgusting."

Aven's hands rubbed her neck trying to will the air through it as she choked. Through watery eyes, she managed to stare up at the knight who'd saved her life. Allyn was pointing to a trail of blood splattered across his bright yellow pants.

"Well, these are ruined," Allyn said.

Aven felt the urge to cry in relief or perhaps anguish. With all her might, Aven rolled to her side and raised her battered body off the ground. She hunched over, holding her ribs. "Thank you," she croaked.

"Yes well, I'm sorry for the poor sap outside that I didn't come a few minutes earlier. However, you did say sunrise, and I am here when we agreed. Lucky for you."

"That poor sap…that's my brother, Strand."

Allyn tilted his head, his brows furrowing in a pantomime of empathy. "Aw, Aven. I am so dreadfully sorry. What a shame."

"It's alright," she muttered. "Thank you."

"Aye, those Ruvians are worse than I thought. What kind of cocky fussock comes busting into the prince's farms and swings a pike around, killing peasants? This is the worst I've ever seen Candor; I swear of it."

"Yes, I hate to say, but I told you it was this way."

Allyn balked. "Well, I assumed it was bad, as you said, but this is unfathomable. The audacity of it. There are guards wandering about everywhere. Truly there's nothing more to be done, we can't stop fools who are willing to risk death over a little meat, can we?"

Aven bit her tongue. She took another moment to look over herself, brushing away dirt on her dress as if she could wipe away the feeling of disgust that washed through her.

"Ah, I'm sorry," Allyn pandered, "I will have someone come to collect your brother's body and put him to rest. What else may I do?"

"I suppose it doesn't matter now. He's gone, there isn't much left to protect. My mother and I—"

"You and your mother will be protected. I swear of it."

Aven held her breath.

Allyn pulled at his mustache with one hand, and reached out with the other, beckoning her. "I'll take you into your hovel, if you like. Let me walk with you. Can you walk at all?"

Aven nodded, taking a few shaky steps to prove it. "I'll need…I think my ribs are broken."

"I've had broken ribs before. Nothing you can do about it. Wrap something tight around your chest and try not to move a lot."

Aven flinched at the idea, immediately overwhelmed with the weight of her responsibilities on the farm. "My mother can wrap me up."

"Alright, then go on, and I'll get a few men to help me tend to this body and your brother."

Aven lifted her chin and eyed him for a moment, then conceded. She left the pen with her shoulders low, taking short steps and painfully slow breaths. She dreaded the sight of Strand's body on the ground. Yet when she walked into the fields, it surprised her what struck her. It wasn't her brother's still-unmoving frame crumbled in the grass, but rather the sight of the panic-stricken Ruvian children. They were like tiny dolls, unsure how to move or where to go. For some reason Aven expected they would have scattered, but they clung to one another with wide eyes like does watching the forest burn.

"Go on back to your camp," Aven said, "your mother isn't…she won't be coming along. Go home."

They stared at her and Aven wondered if they even understood.

She was unable to think of anything else to do for them, and so she continued on. She didn't look back as she reached the hovel.

———————————

Gailia mourned for days.

Allyn secured a barn within the castle curtain where Aven and Gailia could take their pigs and live in safety. It was bare of amenities and required them to sleep among the animals, but it was free of bandit attacks. At least, it would be until the Ruvians or the gangs became bold enough to start penetrating the curtain, which Aven assumed would be their next approach. After all, the farmers were being driven out so fast, perhaps soon there would be no harvests or meats left in the stockyards for the raids.

Gailia refused to stay in the barn the first three nights, attesting that she belonged in the hovel and wouldn't take a "hand out" from Aven or her friends.

After the third night, Braedan's hovel was attacked by bandits and burned to the ground. He and his wife stood outside and watched, their

176

two remaining children in their arms. That had finally broken through Gailia's resolve. In the fourth night, she snuck into the barn after dark and slept on a pile of hay and hides.

Gailia was gone by sunrise.

After those four nights, Aven was healed enough to try butchering again. She had to drag the pigs and slaughter them on the ground to keep from reinjuring her tightly-bound ribs. After a few more nights, she stopped noticing the pain. She slept a few hours before dawn if she could manage. She awoke often in a panic, her breathing labored and heart pounding before she opened her eyes. She regularly found her hands on her throat, pulling at the ghosts of the Ruvian's fingers. Other times, she thought she heard Strand's voice. In those dreams, she sobbed, but no true tears would come when Aven was awake.

They had a funeral for him out in the fields. Allyn was true to his promise. It was an honorable goodbye for a reliable, if stubborn, man. Aven hated to see Strand's body buried into the earth. All she could think as they covered him in soil was how the Boens may be deep under the ground if they ever found a way past the rocks beneath the Calam mountains.

But the Boens were a long way off. The Ruvians and gangs were ever-present.

Every man and beast outside the curtain of the castle was under threat, and it wasn't a matter of if, but a matter of when they would be killed.

"Can you bring others into the walls?" Aven asked Allyn after the funeral.

"It was hard enough for me to secure this shelter for you and your mom," he replied.

"What do you mean by that? Surely it wasn't any trouble for you to put me into an empty barn."

Allyn twirled his mustache, appearing thoughtful for a second. "It wasn't exactly an empty barn before. I don't want you to feel guilty for it, so I am sorry to tell you."

Aven's jaw dropped. "You told me there had been no one there. What happened to the people who lived in it before?"

He shrugged. "I don't rightly know, to be honest. I told a few sheriffs to find a place for you and they brought me to the barn. There were still some effects, personal things. A few beds. I had those taken out before I showed you to it."

Aven felt her blood heating, rushing down from her cheeks with a wave of simmering anger. She folded it away. Allyn wouldn't appreciate her emotions if she showed them.

"It's alright," he assured, "I'm sure they are also safe. Probably put up in another servant's house within the walls. There's no problem with where you are, it's the right place for you and your mother. It's better too, that I can keep an eye on you."

"Thank you," Aven muttered.

"Of course. It's no problem at all."

The anger that built inside her gave way to boldness. "Is there any chance I may see Rowan soon?"

Allyn's lips curled downward. "I did tell you that we would talk about him, didn't I?"

Aven nodded.

He glanced around as if to see who else was nearby. The other farmers were lingering around the burial site, consoling Gailia and talking amongst themselves.

Satisfied, Allyn leaned in to whisper. "I thought perhaps you would have heard by now, about the new Prince?"

"Only what you told me. There has been no talk of royalty here among peasants." Aven gestured to the grave. "I am sure you can see why we are a bit preoccupied with our own concerns."

"Right, of course." Allyn rubbed at his bare chin. "I don't mean to diminish. It's just rather a large to-do, honestly."

"Can you explain, please?"

"Your patience is thin, I understand. I am trying to tell you this in a way that…I want to protect her."

178

Aven bristled. "Who do you mean? What do you mean by her?"

Allyn tilted his head and narrowed his eyes. "You know who I mean. You and I, Jonn-Del, we know the truth. We have to protect her and who she is. But it is much more complicated now. I fear that Jonn-Del has overplayed his hand by trying to change who she is again."

"Who is Jonn-Del, you mean Sir Jonn?"

"Aye, he is Jonn-Del now. I forget there is so much that you simply do not know. My apologies."

Aven shook her head. "Enough, tell me what has happened to Rowan. Please."

Allyn scoffed. "Alright. Be crass about it." He leaned in again, so close that his breath was against her cheek when he spoke. "Word spread that Queen Zarana pushed for Trevin Schinen to take the throne. Everyone knew that's who was expected after what she said. The long and short of it is, Jonn-Del asserted that Rowan was actually Trevin Schinen, escaped from House Schinen after the slaughter. He attested to it, and my uncle the duke accepted it. Our boy Rowan has been sitting on the throne as Prince Trevin for a bit. I'm surprised you didn't hear of it, but then again, he hasn't done much to address the people or even be seen by the peasants."

Aven felt the blood drain from her face. She felt her body go ice cold and she opened her mouth to speak, but the words wouldn't come.

"Now you see it," Allyn whispered, "why I said it's worth protecting. He has been secluded, hiding in the royal chambers and coming out only to sign decrees or meet with the council. I think he believes if anyone sees him, they'll know his secret. There's no chance he would risk being seen out in the open."

"But he'll still see you? You can talk to him?"

Allyn shrugged. "I suppose. Though I'm not sure I prefer to. He is fretting over what to do about the impending Boen attack. It won't be long and he'll lose the kingdom, I fear."

Aven tried to swallow and found her throat much too dry. "I need to find a way to see him. I need to talk to him. There has to be a way that we can—"

"He won't see you," Allyn snapped.

Aven didn't want to believe it. Something in the tone and the look of Allyn's eyes reminded her of the day when Jonn had said the same thing. It felt empty, so finite. How were they both so certain of Raena's feelings? Unless they were both liars.

"I'll talk to him," Allyn said, softer. "I'll ask him if he is willing. I know your intentions are good, and maybe you can work some sense back into his mind. He needs to be pulled out of this spell and realize that he can leave the tower once in a while."

Aven nodded, at a loss for what else to say.

"I'll be back with an answer for you," Allyn said. He turned to leave, then stopped himself, coming back and reaching out his arms. "I'm sorry, you've been through so much."

Though it felt painfully wrong, Aven was sure she had little choice. She stepped into the uncomfortable embrace, allowing the taller knight to wrap his arms around her for a moment. She felt the cold metal of his steel breastplate against her cheek, and hated to admit that it made her long for Raena. She tried to pull back, but he clung on for a final squeeze, rubbing his hands across her back. Aven could smell the hint of ale on his breath and she wondered if it was always present in his daily life. With obvious hesitation, he finally pulled away.

Aven muttered "thank you" and resisted the urge to grimace.

When Allyn was gone the funeral began to disperse. Gailia and Aven went back to the hovel and began to go through Strand's possessions, choosing what to keep. He'd had so little of his own things. Aven was surprised when she came across a book among his clothes, tucked away from view. At first, she thought it must have belonged to Faer; he was always talking about imaginative tales. But then she recognized the shirt as one Strand had worn a few days before death, and she knew the book had been hidden by him without a doubt. The title was Winter Nights on

180

the Rocks of Horne Island. Aven gently turned the pages, admiring the art. It was a myth about creatures fighting over the people of Calamyta. Great beasts, hawks, and sea creatures. The creatures were called dunnes in the caption, but were described very much like garons. The drawings appeared like garons as well, though the sizes were disproportionate. A single beast was larger than twenty men. Fighting the garons were the war hawks, also so large it was unrealistic. At the end of the story, amphibious birds attacked both creatures with fire breath.

As Aven turned the pages and thought of the imagination and excitement wrapped into such a story, she felt herself begin to cry. Strand had been such a simple, reserved man. He had never shown interest in creative or outlandish thoughts, yet here was a book filled to the brim with wondrous stories. Aven wiped her tears, wishing she had known more, and realizing it was the first time she'd been able to cry.

"What's that, then?" Gailia said, wiping her hands dry with a rag as she stepped closer.

"It's a book. Have you ever seen it before?"

"No. The boys sometimes tried to read. I think C'olon and Gregor can read alright, but Strand never could."

Aven shook her head, willing away her anguish. "Maybe he learned."

Gailia shrugged, reaching for a pile of Strand's tunics. "I am going to give these to Braedan if it's alright with you. Almighties know he lost everything he ever had in that fire. He is a bit bigger than your brother was, but he can cut the sleeves if these are too small."

"Please tell him that I'll help him sew them, if he finds they don't fit."

"Aye."

Gailia was nearly to the door when Aven stood and called her back.

"I am going to leave for the barn. Will you join me to sleep there tonight? I worry about you here alone."

Gailia pursed her lips but then nodded.

Aven forced a smile. "Good, I'll pack these things and take them with me, if you don't mind. I don't want to leave anything else here, in case the hovel is raided in the night."

"Take that jumpy pig with you. The one that's been sniffing around."

Aven raised an eyebrow. "The stray one?"

"Aye," Gailia mumbled, "he must have run loose from one of the farms, I think. If you find him tonight, take him to the barn."

"He might have disease—"

"Slaughter him quick, then. We have a quota to meet. With or without your brother, we have to do it."

Aven furrowed her brows but didn't protest. She was certain the quota no longer was expected, but her mother was resolved.

Without another word, Gailia left the hovel.

Aven took care to gather Strand's things into a satchel and wore it on her back, including the book. She stopped by the pen to take an extra butchering knife. There were two thick stains of blood from the Ruvian; one where the woman's body had bled and a smaller one where her head had landed, half a meter away. If anything could be said for Allyn, he was absolutely deadly with a sword. Aven noticed her hands were shaking and she wiped them on her skirt.

When she stepped out of the pen, she heard the sound of iron smashing against bone. Unwillingly, it played in her head, over and over. Aven clenched her eyes shut and took a few hard, long breaths. She listened, desperate to focus on anything real to pull her out of the memory that swirled around her, unwanted. A bird, singing far away, brought relief. Aven echoed its song by whistling lowly, thinking of the bird and nothing else, until she had composure enough to open her eyes and walk once more.

The sun had begun to set when Aven found the jumpy pig. It was a scrawny thing with a bug-eye. She talked softly until she was close enough to loop a rope around its neck. Then she lured it with a sweetroot back to her barn. She half-dragged the scrawny thing and strung it up on chains with haste, not wanting to risk taking it around the others. Within a few minutes, she had her blade at the inside of his thigh, slicing his femoral artery clean through.

When he bled out, she thought of making a comment aloud but realized there would be no one to hear it.

She was so absorbed in butchering the little pig and working to get meat from his wilted body that she didn't realize Gailia had never come to the barn. It must have been at least midnight, and Aven felt a wave of panic jolt through her.

"There's nothing anyone can do about it tonight, so you best be alive, you stubborn ass," Aven muttered to herself. She slammed the hindquarter down against the butchering table, flesh splattering against the wood.

Sloppily, she tossed the meat in the stone box, letting exhaustion and annoyance get the best of her. When she rinsed in the basin, Aven splashed the cool water on her face and groaned into her hands. The well of emotion within her tapped at her resolve, threatening to demand her attention, but she slapped her face and shook it away.

As she removed the butcher clothes, she took care not to pull her sides where her ribs were still tender. She was getting used to working around them, favoring them while they healed. Now that her tasks of butchering and cleaning up were complete, Aven had nothing to focus on except how alone and exposed she felt in that barn. She eyed her bed and a shudder ran through her, waves of fear she'd felt in the past coming back for no explicable reason.

As if on cue, there was a sound outside. Far in the distance, perhaps, but it was something between a howl and a wail. When the cry was joined by men's shouts, Aven's mind was made up. Aven grabbed a butcher knife and ran toward her bed, as if the hides over her could protect her from the horrors of the night. She wrapped them tightly around herself, the butcher knife tucked between her body and the barn's wall.

For longer than she wanted to be, she was wide awake. Thinking of Strand's mythical book. Thinking of Gailia. Wondering if she had noticed anything strange when she'd been out chasing the jumpy pig. Had she seen Gailia? Had she seen signs of trouble? Was Braedan out in the fields? Aven replayed the evening a few times in her mind, searching for clues of where her mother might have gone off to. When she had envisioned it, a dozen times, sleep overtook her.

———————————

There was a soft pull. Gentle. Then a cool breeze.

There was warm breath. The opposite sensation.

Her body was cold, but her face was being warmed.

Something smelled familiar. It was the scent of ale; sweet, but sickening.

Then a weight pressing down on her chest. The sensation of being suffocated.

Aven knew what this was. Aven knew the feeling of a man on top of her.

She knew it as it roused her from sleep and she realized it was not a dream, but a real man, here in her bed.

His hands were roving but without urgency. There was a tenderness to his touch as if this were something he believed was wanted.

Aven recoiled, pushing his chest. Her eyes flew open and she scooted away, out from under his weight. His leg still pinned hers.

"It's all—" he began, but was stopped by her elbow to his mouth.

She pushed back once more and found her back against the wall. There was nowhere else to go.

He scooted after her, his hands finding her waist. He gathered her skirt, teasing it higher. His dark shadow was leaning in. He buried his head in her neck, inhaling deeply.

Aven felt the knife against her back, laid along the wall. She kept one hand pressing his chest with futility but snaked the other arm behind her. Her fingertips brushed over the handle, and she twisted, trying to reach higher.

He was murmuring something indistinct against her skin. Rough facial hair scratched across Aven's jaw.

He reached down between their bodies, the back of his hand grazing her thighs as he freed himself from his trousers.

His body rolled forward, fully pressing on top of her again. He laid flat over her, kissing her throat.

Aven felt three things at the exact same time.

The handle of the knife against her palm.

The hot air from his mouth as he cried out in pain.

And the bristle of his mustache against her neck.

"Aven!" He screamed, into her ear.

Everything stopped.

She let go of the knife and dropped it into the hay as if she could erase what she had done. As if she could go back in time to one second before.

She felt a hot gush of liquid against her skirts, soaking through so fast it coated her thighs.

"Help me!" Allyn cried. He rolled to his back and even in the darkness she could see him now.

"I—I didn't see your face," Aven said. She stared as he pressed his hands firmly to his thigh. His femoral artery.

Something flashed in Aven's mind. A vision of the pigs. A vision of the Ruvian in her pen. A vision of Zander, in the Queen's library.

She thought of reaching out to help him stop the bleeding. She thought of where she would apply pressure.

"What did you do?" Allyn shouted back. Then he repeated it, screaming.

Aven sat up, observing him. She could perhaps put her knee at the inside of his bleeding leg, at the junction of his hip, and her weight might stop the bleeding. She could call for help. She could.

But her eyes roamed over him, now adjusted to the dim moonlight from the barn door.

He was in his knight's undertunic and loose riding trousers. He appeared freshly bathed and shaven. And his manhood was out.

Allyn had planned this. He had planned to take her.

She thought of the Edivan women.

The Edivan women around the campfire.

Unable—or too afraid—to resist his groping advances.

"Aven, help me," he wailed, his voice growing weaker.

Aven was frozen to the spot. Her eyes trained on him.

Allyn of Lox. Man of the library. Allyn of Lox. Competed in the Knight's Trial. Allyn of Lox. There at Queen Zarana and King Zander's trial. With them in the forests of Boenaerya as they fled the Boens. Helping Raena and Barton through the wild.

And Allyn of Lox. Selfish, arrogant, and ready to shove anyone aside for his own gain at any opportunity.

He was like all the others, wasn't he?

"Aven…" he murmured. He rolled to his back, his breaths turning shallow. With one hand, he reached for her in the dark.

Aven took his hand and held it between hers, resting it in her lap.

"Help me," Allyn said, a final desperate plea.

Aven searched her memory for the prayers of Libre, but couldn't recall. Knowing their time was limited, she recited the only thing that came to mind.

"Your body is a chalice, but it is the water that quenches thirst. Your body is the tree, but it is the fruit that provides the life. Your body is a vessel, but it is only to carry your true self. Your soul is the water. Your soul is the fruit. Your soul is your true self. The Creator has a new vessel for your soul. We know not the vessel. Go forth to your new adventure."

She listened.

All was quiet.

Not even the sound of his breath. His hand was limp in hers.

Aven felt a flood of panic when the reality seeped in. She was a peasant—she had once been a duchess, but by birth she was a peasant. She had killed a nobleman and left him to bleed out on the floor of a barn.

186

Surely, they would hang her. Without a doubt, she would be dead by sunrise.

When she heard footsteps and the door easing open Aven leapt up, dropping the dead man's hand.

"Who is it?" She called out to the darkness.

The door was half open and in the moonlight was a silhouette of a man. His shoulders were broad and he stood tall, his frame filling the space.

Aven couldn't see him well enough, but the way he stood there told her that he was taking in the sight of Allyn's dead body.

If only she'd had a few minutes, she might have butchered him. She might have cut his limbs and buried him in the stone boxes with the rest of the meat. She might have hidden him away from view and bought herself time.

Or she might have damned herself more when they found the body.

"I can explain," she said to the stranger, raising her hands, "it was an accident. He...he accosted me."

"He accosted you?"

That voice.

Aven would know that voice anywhere.

Though her heart had been through enough already in one night, it still had the energy to explode within her chest. A swelling filled her insides and she choked back a sensation so strong it threatened to burst her.

"Rowan," Aven whispered.

CHAPTER 17
AVEN

Tragedy and fear make friends out of enemies

Raena stepped into the barn and shut the door behind her. In a few steps she crossed the space and kneeled beside Allyn's body, studying it. Aven returned to sitting on the edge of her bedding, tucking her knees beneath her.

Aven could see the outline of Raena's face now, and she knew that Raena could see everything as clear as if it were daylight.

Raena shook her head, her periwinkle eyes trained on Allyn. "He told me… he—he told me to follow him."

Aven gasped for breath, finding her lungs impossible to fill.

"What happened?" Raena asked, doubt edged in her tone.

"I—I was sleeping. I had seen him earlier today. He hugged me, I think it must have…he must have gotten an idea from it. I woke up to him in my bed. I swear I didn't know it was him. I thought he was a bandit, maybe. I don't know. I hardly thought about it. I just knew where to train my knife."

Raena's gaze snapped up. "Where is the knife? Show it to me."

Aven dug into the hides and found the knife, then handed it over.

Raena held the object and turned it over in her hands. "A butchering knife, is it? This doesn't look like a weapon for fighting that I've seen."

"Yes, it's…I used it for the pigs. It was my brother's."

Raena stared. "Where is your brother? Is he going to come here?"

"No…he's dead."

"Almighty's breath. Everyone is fucking dead."

Aven's chest clenched.

It was quiet for a moment. Raena stared down at Allyn again, as if she hadn't accepted his death as reality the first time. As if she were trying to will him back into life through her mind's power alone. Aven couldn't help but think about how Raena was near and it was a relief coated with fear and tension. She wanted to ask why now, and why here, and why everything had been the way it was.

"I don't understand it," Raena muttered. "he told me that he found you. He said you were safe and he'd brought you out from the pig fields to this barn. He told me at sunset we would go to see you and sneak out in the dark so Jonn-Del wouldn't follow. He came to my room and fetched me, but then…he sped away. I lost track of him in the street. But I knew where the barn was. Why…why would he do that?"

Aven grimaced.

"Did he say anything?" Raena asked. Her bluish eyes settled on Aven's. For the first moment since Raena entered the barn, they were fixated on one another.

Aven's face turned sour and she felt a painful ball rise in her chest. "Did he say anything? What more do you wish for me to explain to you, Raena? Which part of this are you struggling to comprehend?"

Raena shook her head, raising her hands. If she hadn't been sitting, she might have stumbled back.

"Do you not see that his cock is exposed? Are you missing the part where he came into my bed and pulled himself out of his trousers while forcibly laying on top of me? Do I need to explain to you what would have transpired if I had not had a knife and defended myself?"

"Alright, alright," Raena muttered. "Almighty's breath, I'm sorry."

"You are? You're sorry? Which part are you sorry for, precisely?"

Raena shrank, her shoulders slumping. She settled back onto her bum. "I'm…"

"Which part are you sorry for?"

"Um, which part would you…well, the part you're the most angry about."

Aven could have screamed if it weren't for fear of alerting someone else to the presence of a dead knight's body. She folded her arms and stared at Raena for a long moment.

Raena raised her eyebrows. "I was just a bit confused, I think. It seemed like he wouldn't have wanted to lead me here if he was planning to do…that."

"Really? Why don't you think that through for a moment, you dolt. I think that makes perfect sense, actually. What better way to finally get through your little pissing contests than to let you 'catch him' fucking your girl?"

"Well, if you didn't want it…"

"Do you think Allyn Lox is—was the sort of man who went around thinking perhaps a woman didn't 'want it'? No."

Raena glanced down. "He was a real dollop of shite. Though he was a great knight."

"It takes more than swords to be a great anything. When will all of you realize that?"

"What do you think you'll do with his body?"

Aven clenched her fists and resisted the urge to swing. "What will I do? So, you plan to what? Forget you ever saw this? Go back to your castle? Go be a fucking prince, then."

"No, no, I mean I'll help you. I can…maybe I can leave him near the pub. He loved to drink; it could look like a fight with a gang if I set him up in a street behind the place."

"You can't drag a dead knight through the streets. You're the Prince now, so I'm told."

Raena shrugged sheepishly.

Aven felt the walls inside her snap and collapse. Everything buried within her overflowed and all she felt was boiling anger rising up from the rubble. "You know what? I think I do want to hear that apology. I want you to tell me you're sorry for all of it, actually. I want you to say you're sorry for letting them shove me into a filthy disgusting room in the bollocks in Ediva. I want you to be sorry for every night I couldn't sleep because I heard a woman being beaten by her husband. I want you to be sorry for never coming to see me unless you wanted to fuck me and then disappearing. I want you to be sorry for acting like I was nothing to you in front of Sir Jonn and Sir Allyn and always trying to impress them and show off. I want you to be very fucking sorry for that charade you staged in the caravan, trying to make Allyn and his peasant girls catch you in the act, like you're an animal. You disgust me."

"I wasn't—"

"I'm not finished, Raena! I want you to be sorry for shedding me off and not having the courage to say it to my face. Be sorry for being such a coward and sending Jonn to tell me to leave. Be sorry for leaving me in Lox to sleep out where wolves or Ruvians could have taken me. Be sorry for ignoring my requests for you and sending Allyn out to speak with me. I want you to be sorry for never coming when I sent for you, and the way it's made me feel worthless. You had better be sorry for that. And now, finally, whatever the fuck this is? You interrogating me as if I have done something wrong when your arsehole friend just tried to rape me in my sleep? That's the thing I hope you're truly sorry for. But it's exactly what I should expect from you, isn't it?"

Raena clenched her jaw, the muscles rippling in her cheeks.

Aven didn't care if that was harsh. She didn't care if it hurt. She didn't regret a single word of it.

The quiet between them was almost worse than the vile string of insults that Aven was bracing herself to expect. But the insults didn't come.

"I can't…" Raena began, then swallowed. "I can't take back what I've done wrong to you. Some of it you are very right about. I see what you're saying, and I treated you…I've been stupid."

"Quite."

Raena raised one hand. "But some of the things you're accusing me of, I did not do. I didn't have Jonn send you away. I didn't ignore your requests for me. Until today, I have been searching everywhere for you. I forbade Allyn from leaving Candeo until he found you. He's been begging to go back to Lox for weeks, and I insisted that he stay and look for you. I commanded him to do it, even."

Aven bristled. "So that's one thing I was wrong about."

"Yes, and you're right…you're right about the rest. I am ashamed to admit it. But I am being honest with you."

Despite herself, Aven felt tears coming to her eyes. It seemed that letting out any of the emotion stuffed deep within allowed all of it to escape indiscriminately. She wiped it away, not wanting Raena to see or misunderstand.

"I…there's so much that I need to tell you," Raena continued, "I haven't been able to explain it all. There have been so many moments that I needed you. I needed your guidance. I need it now. I feel like I don't know what I'm doing without you."

"I have been here all along."

"Where? In this barn?"

"At my family's farm. In the hovel. Until a few days ago when Allyn brought me here."

Raena lifted her chin. "Ah. Somehow…I should have known that, shouldn't I?"

Aven couldn't reply. The tears grew thick in the back of her eyes, her throat filling with water.

"I am sorry," Raena said with sincerity. "I am so sorry. I never thought I was brilliant by any means, but I should have been smart enough to keep you and protect you. I promised you that you would be safe and I let you…if I would have lost you…"

"You're lucky you didn't. My spirit would have returned from the afterlife and cut your throat."

Raena chuckled. "That's from the legend of Logan, is it not? She does that to all her lovers."

"Yes, I'm surprised you know it."

Raena's laugh turned to a soft smile, caught on her lips, and the tension from the air began to melt. They shared a look between them.

"May I...may I touch you?" Raena asked. She extended her hand.

Aven returned the gesture and their hands met. They held each other's fingers for a moment, hovering above the top of Allyn's dead body. The crudeness of the moment wasn't lost on Aven, but she felt such relief at the simple connection between the two of them.

"We have to do something about this body." Raena whispered.

"I know. Don't think that I am done being angry with you."

"Oh, I've no doubt about that. I know you will be angry with me for as long as I deserve, which could be years. I will keep on trying to earn back your favor."

Aven rolled her eyes. They let go of each other's hands and focused together on the corpse.

"What if we burn down the entire barn?" Raena asked.

"You would risk setting fire inside the curtain? It's summer, Rae. You might not be able to stop the flames from overtaking every building this side of the citadel. There are dozens of dry barns here and servant's quarters."

"Aye, right."

"We could put his body under the meat, in the cart. I have plenty of pigs done butchering. When I take the cart out in the morning, no one will notice. I could go out to the farms and find a field to leave him. It would look like he'd been attacked by bandits."

"He doesn't look attacked at all, though. Allyn would have fought to the death. No one would believe that he was taken by a bandit and sliced so cleanly in the leg. They would've had to beat him with something until he couldn't stand before he would be relenting to a wound like that."

"Right," Aven whispered.

Their eyes met and a wordless thought passed between them both.

Raena glanced around the barn. "Right."

Another moment, and Aven swore they were thinking the exact same thing.

Raena stood, brushing her hands over her thighs. "Do you have some of those things that you hoist up the pigs with? Something…a rope, maybe?"

"We have chains and shackles that go around their ankles." Aven stood as well, knowing exactly what was coming next. She walked to the butcher's table and began to ready the space, same as she would for any slaughter.

"Okay, what about weapons? Do you have swords, anything like that?"

"Besides cleavers and fillet tools? I have a few shovels and a pitchfork for the hay."

Raena slid her arms under Allyn's body and bent her knees. In a swift motion, she hoisted the man onto her shoulders. It reminded Aven of Strand lifting the small pigs.

Aven opened the shackles and held them out.

"Put something soft on those," Raena said, "if his wrists are bruised, they'll know he was strung up."

Aven muttered "Ah," as if that were some kind of obvious knowledge she would be expected to know. The reality of making a murder look like the results of a bandit attack was not something she'd ever contemplated.

But Raena seemed to be filled with confidence that she knew precisely what to do. "He needs to be upright so the blood trickles down. He also needs to be moving, so it looks like he was fighting all along. Do you think you can push his body while I strike him?"

Aven nodded. She grabbed two rags from the knife cleaning pile and tossed them to Raena.

Raena put the rags around Allyn's wrists as she attached the shackles.

194

Aven went to the wall and grabbed the chain reel, turning the crank to raise him. She was surprised how easy it was, though she supposed she had grown used to hogs at least twice a man's weight.

There was a distinct smell of death in the air as the body lifted from the ground. It was not unlike a butchered pig, when a slip of the blade opened the intestines and the contents spilled. Aven resisted the urge to pull her dress over her nose to block the smell.

Raena grabbed a cleaver in one hand and a shovel in the other. "Right, this shouldn't take much. A few blows ought to do it."

Aven felt the contents of her stomach rising to her throat, but she trudged on. With a heavy sigh, she gave Allyn's back a push, then stepped out of the way as he swung from the chain, dangling a hand's width over the floor.

Raena swung, striking at his arms, then his legs. She bent low, then high, darting about. If Aven couldn't see her "opponent" she might have thought Raena was engaged in a real fight.

It was repulsive.

Aven choked back the urge to vomit, retching a few times and turning away to regain her composure before she gave him another push.

Blood seemed to seep unnaturally from Allyn's dead flesh, but Raena stepped back and viewed it with eyebrows raised in satisfaction.

"I think that's convincing enough," Raena said. "Let's put him in the cart. We have a few hours before sunrise."

Aven nodded and went to lower the reel.

"I'll have to go soon, I'm afraid."

Aven didn't look over her shoulder. "Oh?"

"Yes, they might not notice Allyn is gone for a day or two. But they'll be looking for me, if they aren't already. Jonn-Del especially notices when I leave the castle."

Aven nodded. "Yea, I'm sure it's something for the prince to be outside in the dead of night."

Raena grabbed a hide from the ground and wrapped it around Allyn as she lifted him. She unshackled his wrists and carried him to the cart.

Aven thought of cleaning up the blood, but realized there were plenty of spots for pig's blood already. She would change her dress, at least, still soaked in red.

"Do you need anything more?" Raena asked.

Their eyes met, and it was another tense exchange, but there was a softness in Raena's expression. A fondness, perhaps. It was like seeing a memory come to life. This wasn't the Raena from Ediva. It wasn't even the Raena from Boenaerya where they made their escape. This was the Raena who joined House Colby, who swore to protect her duchess, who asked at their first meal if they ought to feed one another.

This was her knight.

Aven walked forward as though her legs propelled her, floating through the air. She felt weightless, almost controlled by a spell.

Raena dipped her chin and raised her shoulders, standing taller, poising herself.

When Aven was one step away she stopped and gazed up into those stormy blue eyes. Their closeness was terrifying and perfect and necessary and it ached. It ached deep within her. Aven wished she could reach out and rip away everything that had hurt her, but she saw it had hurt Raena, perhaps even as much.

It was Raena who reached out first. Her hand found Aven's cheek and cupped it like a delicate piece of treasure. Her other arm tentatively snaked around Aven's waist. They stayed there, Raena holding her, Aven's arms hanging at her sides.

"I meant it," Raena whispered. "I am so sorry. How can I show you?"

"I know you are. You don't have to do anything more. I know you felt you didn't have a choice."

Raena's eyes dropped. "Some of the things...I had a choice."

"Fair enough, you did. But I understand you. That's what you forget. You forget that I see you for what you are. I know you are good, Rae. I know you want what's best for the people you love and your kingdom."

Raena shook her head, averting her gaze.

196

Slow and tender, Aven reached up and traced her fingertips along Raena's neck and into her short golden hair. She scraped her nails there, rubbing them over Raena's scalp. It was enough to soften the prince, and her eyes fluttered shut.

Aven spoke tenderly as though soothing a frightened cub. "I know you are good. You've been pushed into places where you're scared. You've been backed into corners. This kingdom isn't kind to us, Rae. It isn't kind to you. You've lived in fear for so long, it's all you know. Even when things are alright, you're afraid. You are always searching for a way to keep yourself safe, and that's alright."

"Except with you," Raena whispered. "I am always safe with you. I can't believe I hurt you so badly."

"I'll heal. I'll recover. Everything can heal, even you."

Raena's eyes snapped open. "Me? You didn't hurt me."

"I am sure I did," Aven whispered, gentle and soft, "it's alright. I know you are afraid of being left alone. I know it hurts; you don't have to say it."

The air between them filled with tension as Raena pulled back for a moment. Her brows twisted together with confusion, and she opened her mouth to breathe something of a protest.

Aven held steady, her fingertips continuing their soothing pattern on the back of Raena's neck. She stared, her hazel eyes firm, refusing to relent or admit she may be wrong.

Raena took a deep breath, then eased, her chest falling. "You know the things I never reveal. I don't know how you see what's in my heart, but you find it. You're the only one who can read my thoughts."

The admission caused Aven to lean in close and rest her cheek on Raena's chest. The tunic's leather was smooth against her face. Aven recognized the smell of Raena instantly and closed her eyes to become lost in it. Raena's arms wrapped tightly around her and held her as though they should never let go again.

They stayed like that, neither of them daring to move except for the smallest brush of their hands across one another's skin.

After what felt like an eternity yet never enough, Raena kissed Aven's forehead and stepped back.

"I have to go, but I will be back. Tonight, I will come here at sunset."

Aven nodded, not allowing herself to feel hope. She would wait until they were reunited to feel anything at all again.

Raena sighed and kissed her cheek. "It's hard to say goodbye to you, even if only for a few hours."

"I know," Aven mumbled.

"Will you be here? Will you be here at sunset?"

Aven nodded.

"Good. I will come and bring you into the castle with me. Jonn-Del be damned. I am the prince, now. He made me the prince. He cannot take it away without being put to death for hiding who I was. He will be executed right alongside me. He won't dare stop me."

Aven raised her eyebrow at the bold notion, but thought to wait until the evening to discuss it at length. She was suddenly preoccupied with the task ahead of sneaking Allyn's body out to the fields, undetected.

"I'll see you tonight," Raena said once more. She paused and stared at Aven's lips for a moment as though debating with herself if she would be allowed to press her own against them.

Aven gave no indication, merely held steady and waited.

Seeming to decide, Raena turned for the door of the barn, leaving Aven alone with the dead Allyn Lox and a few dozen cold cuts of pig's meat.

With a sigh, Aven set to work loading the meat over the corpse.

CHAPTER 18
BELL

Hawk's Keep is the most brilliant symbol of Candor's strength

The ride down the Calam Mountains had been rapid, and they reached the Western Founts faster than anyone in the party had anticipated.

"That's what happens when you choose to bring me along," Bell teased.

The dozen Kingsguards scoffed at that. They appreciated most of her jokes and ribbing, but seemed to grow tired of her mocking them. Bell noticed they perceived everything as mocking, the past few days.

When they reached the Founts, Bell realized it felt quiet, as if there was a presence missing from the pines. The outer edge of the foothills wasn't familiar to her, but the Kingsguards assured her they were on the right path as they wove through.

They camped one night in the pines before they made the final stretch. There in the distance, Bell saw her home. Hawk's Keep.

The walls seemed smaller than she remembered, as though it had shrunk in her absence. Surely, she had not been away so long that she didn't recognize the home she had been born inside, grown to womanhood, and then rushed away from. It had been but one year and even the air surrounding the keep appeared changed.

Bell began to search the trees overhead as they rode on.

The Edivans hardly spoke Candorian, save for one: Bothell.

"How're you looking?" he asked, riding up alongside her.

Bell's brow furrowed. "Do you mean 'where'?"

Bothell grunted.

"Perhaps you mean 'why'," she mused, "at any rate, I am looking for my hawks. That is why we are here, after all. They may be in the trees. At times, they would wander away from the nests if food was scarce. If no one has been tending or training them, as I did, they might be in search of rodents to scrounge up. They are also curious."

"Aye," Bothell replied.

Bell had no idea if he truly understood. Their communication was broken, at best. When they started the ride, Bothell had tried to diligently repeat every word she said in Edivan to the others. Once they reached the lower boundary of the Calam Mountains and began the laborious climb, he grew tired of playing translator and ignored her rhetoric.

"You see the outer edge of the keep? The farthest west?" Bell pointed.

"Aye," Bothell said again.

"That is the edge we should approach. If we ride to that corner, they will spot us with the guard post. Those are the keenest eyes. The men there will know it is me even before we are within shouting distance. That way they won't fire an arrow or send a party to halt us. My father wouldn't send men to strike us down unless he suspected an invasion."

Though he was sitting beyond her peripheral view, Bell had a sense that Bothell was rolling his eyes. He was a thick, hairy mountain man. Even hairier than a few of the Edivan men she had seen; Bothell's beard seemed to wrap around his neck and disappear into his collar. He wasn't the sort of man she usually bedded, but curiosity lingered in her. She thought it might be worthwhile to slip into his tent one evening, if only for the novelty of discovering where else his thick, curly hair covered. In her experience, the best Edivan lovers were the gruffest, and Bothell certainly met that description.

Unfortunately, he also smelled horrific, as if he had fought his way out of an animal's rear end. That had deterred Bell from pursuing her interest with him. If anything, she was longing for Micha. It had been days and nights alone.

There was a lady-in-waiting in Hawk's Keep named Hana who she hoped to see. Before she was taken by Zander, she and Hana had been bedfellows, and no one had noticed or cared. That was the best part about bedding women; everyone assumed it was innocent, especially for someone like Bell who was so aggressively flirtatious with men. Bell hoped that Hana had managed not to be married off to some stupid noble, because she was frequently miserable and depressed at the burden of being a lady-in-waiting. Being miserable apparently made Hana desperate for consolation, praise, and "marriage practice" as they liked to call it. Of course, Bell was happy to oblige and would do so tonight if she had the chance. She felt a quiver between her thighs at the images of her and Hana that sprang to mind.

"There," Bothell muttered, pointing a thick fist toward the sky.

Bell glanced up to see a goggin flying overhead, swooping between two pines. "Yes? That's a goggin. They are scavengers. Don't leave any food out, they'll find it."

"Yours?"

"Mine? My bird? No. My birds are called hawks, and they are at least two meters larger than goggins. In fact, they may have grown now. A proper war hawk, when cared for properly, can be a full four meters wide in total. That goggin was no bigger than an average…listen, would it help if I showed you, like this?" Bell held up her hands wide at her sides, simulating wings.

Bothell shrugged.

"Alright, imagine this length? This is a goggin. Now give me your hand?"

Bothell understood, reaching out his arm. Bell took his fingers and clung to them, then lifted her arms once more.

"This wide? This is how large my war hawks are. Or at least, it's how large they should be. I haven't seen them in a year."

Bothell nodded and put his hand back on the reins of his brusky horse.

Bell furrowed her brow and continued to watch the sky, allowing Bothell to lead their party around to the western edge that she had indicated. He kept them in a wide pattern, giving plenty of notice to the out lookers of Hawk's Keep, but Bell knew her father's men had likely spotted them when they came down the mountain, at least a full day before.

As they cleared the pines, Bell speculated aloud. "Hmm, it's odd that my father has sent no one to meet us yet."

"How?" Bothell asked.

"You mean 'why'. It's odd because they should be excited for my arrival, and they would have seen us coming. There should be a greeting party setting out from the western gate, but it's still up."

"Why?"

Bell sighed. "I don't know why you're asking that, but I'll guess. You want to know why the gate would be up? It isn't because they are under siege or attack, in that case they would raise the colors. No, perhaps they are busy with guests. Perhaps there is some event taking place that has them indisposed. We'll enter and my mother will see us to quarters until they are ready to meet us."

Even as she said it, Bell was filled with a sense of dread. She couldn't explain it to Bothell—and he wouldn't understand it fully—but there was something ominous and wrong about the keep they were approaching.

When they came to the edge of the gate where it would have opened to them, Bell stopped her brusky. The men stopped in kind, looking at her with expectant gazes.

"They ought to open it now," Bell whispered.

She gazed up at the walls, high and dark. She scanned the parapets for marching soldiers, legionnaires, guards, horsemen, or rangers. All she saw were the stones and flags at the top of the walls.

"No people," Bothell said.

Bell whipped around to shoot him a nasty glare. "Of course, there are people. My father would not abandon his keep."

Bothell shrugged and held up his hand as if to insinuate that abandoning was exactly what Lord Sylas had done.

Bell shook her head, scanning in all directions for signs of life. That was when she realized the other elements that were missing, the pieces of their noble house that were so much part of her reality before, she had forgotten to take note of their absence. "Where are the farmers? The peasants...where are all of the workers?"

Fortunately, Bothell had the good sense to not engage and attempt to reply to this question because Bell wouldn't have been able to extend any kindness.

As though they sensed her anguish, there was a cry overhead.

The screech was a familiar sound. Bell felt her heart race and a plummeting sensation spread through her stomach. She snapped her mahogany eyes toward the sky and scanned against the bright glare of the midday sun.

Their magnificent silhouettes raced overhead, churning and dancing around one another. There were four of them, and they were indeed larger than Bell remembered. No doubt they had grown in a year. She was expecting them to be an arm's length but it was obvious by the span of their wings that they were large enough to lift a man into the air.

She had trained them to do so.

There were three males and one female circling. Only the female made calls, and she was screeching again as if to say hello.

The fifth bird, another female, was not among them.

"Hawk," Bothell said, his mouth catching up.

"Yes," Bell whispered in awe, "those are my hawks. Those are the birds we are here for."

"Big."

"They are so very big."

Something tugged at Bell's heart—a little gift she had kept inside begging to be unwrapped. She realized the power that she had yearned for was right in front of her. As she watched, the birds shifted. The female started first, her golden eyes training on the Kingsguards, then she tucked her head and dived. As she descended toward them, she reached with her talons, extending them forward.

She was a smart bird. She was swooping straight toward the smallest of the Kingsguards. He raised his sword overhead and cowered, covering his face with his free arm.

The hawk dove until she was less than a meter above, then coasted onward before flapping her massive wings to rise again.

The Kingsguards were shaken, shouting and jolting on the backs of their bruskies.

"She'll do that again and again," Bell said, loud enough for Bothell to hear her over the other men's cries.

"Stop!" Bothell responded, pointing at the sky. He repeated something in Edivan, likely a command.

The hawk was readying for another dive.

Bell removed her riding gloves and with a heavy sigh she clapped her hands together then rubbed her palms.

The bird didn't respond.

Bell repeated the action. This time, the hawk changed course. She swooped higher above, then turned, and flew to a perch high in a pine tree. Her yellow eyes were trained on Bell as she sat. The other three birds joined her. Bell remembered the males being interested in the female's leadership, but not so excessively that they copied her the way they were now.

"She's the Queen," Bell remarked.

"Queen."

Bell shook her head. "No, no. That's not how I meant that. Though it occurs to me I never had anything to call them. Perhaps I ought to give them names? Especially if we are to take them all the way back to Ediva."

Bothell shrugged, his eyes not leaving the perches above.

A fire rose within Bell as she gazed at them. Her heart felt full. She thought of Micha and how happy she would be to show him the birds. If he wasn't too busy caring for his new wife and planning for filthy babies, that is.

"We shouldn't try to go into the keep," Bell said, surprised at the coolness of her own voice. "If my father's people are gone it may be occupied by Ruvians. Or perhaps another enemy. Maybe the Boens have already been here."

Bothell shuffled. "Where?"

She ignored his question, tiring of explaining everything for once. Bell realized they would need to enter the keep so she could fetch her things. She had so much there, including her training gloves that would keep the hawks close as they returned. The risk otherwise that the birds might fly away at a sign of trouble or viable prey was too great.

She motioned for Bothell's attention, waving to him until he glanced her direction, peeling his grey eyes away from the sky.

"Send one of your men to the upper parapet. The top of the wall? He can look into the keep and if it is safe, we will enter."

"Ruvians?"

"I've changed my mind," Bell snapped. "There are things I need from inside the keep. Send him now and we will be out of there before nightfall. I'll show you a place that your man can get through the wall, a small passage. You will need to show him how to open the goat gate to let us in. The horses won't fit, but we can crawl through."

Bothell nodded and began speaking in Edivan to the smallest Kingsguard. Bell wondered if he was relaying her message correctly, but she had to assume they would understand enough to execute her plan. As they talked and stared at the walls, she lost herself gazing up to the sky. The birds had begun to fly again.

"I'm so happy to see you," she murmured.

Hawk's Keep had been a lively, prosperous place.

Even in the battles with Ediva, referred to as the Equinox, Hawk's Keep had never been breached. Bell learned as a lady-in-waiting that Hawk's Keep was considered the center of the world for hundreds of years. The Calamytans taught that whoever held the keep would have the token strategic piece to defend and win all conflicts. But the Equinox had proven that to be false, since it was a stalemate between Candor, Ediva, and the respectful allies.

But now who would hold the power of the keep?

Bell expected to see signs of life. She thought perhaps there would be bodies, or discarded belongings; remnants of people who had spent their every moment within those walls.

She scanned the interior of the courtyard to see nothing but a field, covered in grass. There were slats in the ground where hitching posts had been attached. There were grooves where carts had been rolled for the peasants' market. There was an anvil where the smiths had worked to display and sell their tools.

But it was empty and void of that familiar buzz, that vibrance that spoke of humanity.

Hawk's Keep was truly abandoned.

Bell longed to hold herself together. She stood at the center of the courtyard; a lone woman surrounded by the dozen burly, hairy Edivan Kingsguards. She was like Queen, the hawk, a leader of men. They beat with the same heart.

And Bell's was broken.

She felt the sob start in her throat and then it welled up with such power to the surface that it exploded out of her in a wail. Bell dropped to her knees, her dress meeting the grass with force.

The Kingsguards were shifting around her. Some stared openly, the others appeared to busy themselves with wandering the yard. Their energy was awkward, but Bell could not maintain her composure for the sake of their comfort.

The words she screamed were unintelligible curses. She felt no tears, but they wanted to come. All of the liquid from her body seemed to rise to her throat, coating her mouth with water. Her next wail was caught in a choke and she gurgled, then coughed through it.

Everything filled her mind.

Separating from her 'brothers'. Being ripped from her parents. Being ripped from her home. Finding Finn, face down, trampled by horses, his legs so destroyed and crushed that the bones were practically flattened. Dragging his body to safety, time and time again. Believing he would never wake. And now to return and see her father's marvelous keep in ruin, left to be taken by whoever came upon it and welcomed themselves inside? The very next stray Ruvian might as well declare himself Lord of Hawk's Keep. That is, if they could find enough followers to till the land and farm from the earth and fish from the lakes.

Bell let another round of sobs leave her.

She felt the tear, deep inside her body, of sadness giving way to rage. She wanted to wait within that keep for days or seasons or years. Whatever it took until some pissant tried to take it from her family's care. Then she would slit them into pieces and feed their flesh to her birds.

"Help?" Bothell said beside her.

207

Bell turned to see he had lowered to a squat and was studying her intently. She sucked in air to end her sobbing, and without giving it a thought, she reached for him. He gave her back a quick pat with his burly hand. In response, she tumbled forward into his arms.

Bothell stumbled but caught himself and her, staying upright. He tensed at their contact, then released a breath.

Bell was surrounded in his disgusting stench. Somehow it was both repulsive and comforting all at once. She murmured into his thick, hair neck. "Will you enter the noble's quarters and bathe with me?"

He tensed, his shoulders flexing under her cheek. He said nothing in response, but Bell knew by his reaction that he understood. She also knew that he would comply. He was a simple, brawny man, and simple men would never decline her. And simple men were good for the kinds of things she enjoyed doing.

They stayed there in the dirt for a few moments, hawks circling overhead, until Bell finally rose to take his hand and lead him into the keep.

CHAPTER 19
BELL

I think of nothing else

The small party moved fast together. The only thing that slowed them was caring for the birds and convincing them to follow over the mountains. Without trees for them to perch at the peak, the hawks had been uneasy. But Bell had her training gloves and an abundance of yent meat to entice them and she kept them close.

At night she bedded Bothell without regard for the other mens' opinions, and she was certain they'd had them. The Edivans kept loose camps with tents spread wide, except in the mountains where they were comfortable being closer together. In the mountains she was sure to express her pleasure even louder for their benefit. Bothell was puffed up with pride and likely unbearable to the others for the duration of the journey.

When they returned to Ediva, House Salish was bustling. It was quite unlike the castle it had been a fortnight before. There were two or threefold more mountain peoples about, fluttering in preparations.

Bell ignored them and hastened to return her brusky to the stables and find a place to anchor her hawks in their new home. She could tell they were apprehensive by the way they kept diving and swooping in the trees, over a furlong beyond the castle's outer curtain. It was cold and the forests were sparse. But they would adjust to the new climate, Bell was positive.

When she found a stableman who spoke her tongue, she informed him that she would need a shelter for her birds by nightfall, and he must move the horses out, if necessary.

With that task underway, Bell rushed into the castle on a search with determination. She was filthy from the journey and felt as if she stank as badly as Bothell by now. But she could not spare another moment to bathe.

She darted through the hallways to the upper levels, past her own chamber and into the noble's quarters. The door to what had once been Raena's chamber was open and Bell glanced in, surprised to see it was occupied again by Edivans. She continued on to a closed door and pressed, pleased when it gave way, unlocked.

He was there, on a chair, in the center of the boudoir. There was a scroll in his hands that he was scowling over, but his brown eyes jolted up at the intrusion.

Bell rushed to close the gap and fell against him, draping herself over his lap and cushioning her head against his chest.

"Oof," he grunted, "you know my legs have been crushed once, that doesn't mean they will tolerate abuse from you." He tossed the scroll to the floor and wrapped his arms around her shoulders.

"I'm trying to see if I can crush them back into life." She murmured against his chest.

Finn tilted his chin down to kiss the top of her head, then recoiled. "You certainly smell like you have just returned from…a journey."

"And you smell like paradise. Is all you do here lay around and bathe and accept a showering of flowers and spices? I swear, if I heated you over a fire, I could eat you."

"That wouldn't be a bad way to die."

Bell nestled further into his chest, pleased with how his soft undershirt felt against her cheek. "I missed you every minute I was gone."

"How about your birds? Did you find them?"

"Oh yes, they are grumpy with this wintry place. I can tell they hate it here."

"That's concerning. This is the hottest spell we've had since arriving here. It's surely going to get much colder and the snow will cover everything."

"They'll adapt."

Finn sighed, rubbing circles on her back. For a moment they were both quiet and content. There were sounds outside the room, clangs and shouts beyond the window, a ruckus of peasants busy at work.

It reminded Bell of how different everything was. "Why are there so many people here? I practically had to fight my way through The Womb to get into this wing."

Finn nodded. "Ah, the King has been quite busy while you were away. He's chosen his bride and called the whole kingdom here for his wedding."

Though Bell was in the arms of the man she loved, she felt an odd tugging sensation inside her chest. A pang of something unwanted.

Finn leaned in, suspicion in his eyes. He scanned Bell's face for a moment, furrowing his thick, dark brows.

Bell's eyes darted away. She thought of something else to talk about, anything at all, but the topic of Micha's wedding repeated in her mind as if it were a knot caught in a sewing spindle.

"Are you alright?" Finn whispered.

"Of course," Bell said.

"I know...I know you've become fond of him. There's nothing wrong with that."

"Why would there be? But I am not any fonder of him than I am of anyone. Any other man, that is. Except for you."

Finn smirked. "Well, I am flattered with that distinction, but I don't believe you. I know you've enjoyed being in his bed. You don't have to

211

make it sound alright for my benefit. You know it doesn't bother me if you choose to—"

"Can we talk about something else? This isn't a topic we need to repeat. I already know how you feel, and I know how I feel, and you know how I feel. It seems the only person who doesn't know how I feel about this is Micha, the very fussock who ought to figure it out."

Finn nodded. "That's fair."

Bell shook her head, unable to continue.

After he cleared his throat, Finn shrugged. "Did you…did you see your father?"

The question hit Bell as though it were a slap across her face. Her body tensed and she willed it again to relax before her companion would take notice. He always noticed, but Finn didn't appear shaken by it.

She was off guard. She hadn't planned for what to say.

But there were his expectant, almost-hopeful brown eyes. He had no hesitation to ask her, did he? He had no idea who or what would be at Hawk's Keep, just as Bell had.

"Yes," Bell said, "he looked strong. He's recovered well from the gaol."

Finn's confusion broke into a smile. "Oh, I'm so glad. And your mother?"

"Yes, she's also well. She wanted me to stay. Of course, I could not."

"Did they ask after me? Had they seen Rowan pass through?"

Rowan. The lie was building. But Bell shook her head. "They were concerned with the state of things. I didn't tell them much except that you were here and Rowan was in Candeo. That was all they cared to hear. The keep is very guarded and built up with forces in preparation. You know it will be the first line of defense for Candor against the Boens. My father is ready to put up a great fight. I have no doubt he'll stop them all."

Finn's smile faded. "Well, that's something. That's good to hear that they are well. I wish I were there. I should be there, to help defend Hawk's Keep. Perhaps I will ask—"

"Finley, you can't defend a shadow from the sun. What good would you be in a battle against the Boens? Don't throw yourself into death out of obligation, please. There is much for you to do."

He grimaced. "I have plenty of usefulness. I am still great with a sword. I can be strapped to a horse, at the very least."

Bell leaned in and placed a gentle kiss on his rough cheek. "I need you here. Micha needs your insight on Candor. You and I need to anchor our kingdom to Ediva. We can keep peace between our two nations. That is a thousand times more critical than you swinging a sword while your legs are tied together."

"You're right, I'm sure."

Bell grinned. "Of course, I'm right. Now, I am tired from the journey. May I sleep in your bed?"

"I believe we will be expected for the wedding festivities. They have lasted every night, but they continue another three."

"Then let me sleep until we must leave."

"Fair enough, I'll wake you."

With a warm smile, Bell pulled the blankets around her and helped Finn to settle in beside her. When he was comfortable, she laid her head on his chest. With the sound of his breathing and the feeling of his chest rising, she fell quickly to sleep.

———

Edivan weddings were apparently festivals of religious symbology that ran seven days. Each day was another gift to another Almighty that required new rules and expectations. Bell was thankful that she had missed at least four of these ceremonies, but wished she could have also missed the final three.

The first night Bell arrived back, the theme was Sea. At least there had been a delicious feast with food from the ocean, so plentiful she'd been nearly sick from it. She had avoided Micha with deliberate success, noticing that he tried to approach her more than once but she evaded him in the banquet room.

The following night was a very different affair. Their homage was to the creator and keeper of "light", an ambiguous being. Bell had little tolerance or understanding for their beliefs—or any, for that matter—and reckoned worshipping the creator of the sun would have been more logical.

The festivities were outdoors and aimed to last all night. Once she partook in the feast, Bell slipped away toward the stables. At the annex of the buildings, beyond where the bruskies were kept, was the perch and shelter for her hawks. When she entered the gate, Queen flew down to join her from somewhere in the shadows above. Bell took a seat on a stone bench in the yard among poles and nests, freshly crafted at her request by the King's laborers. In less than a minute, all four birds had found places to rest a few meters overhead, at one perch or another. In the silence and moonlight, they settled, dwelling together.

The peace was broken by the approach of a stranger opening the gate with a squeak. The birds raised their wings: a threat, their predatory eyes trained on the span behind Bell.

She rose and turned, knowing who it was before she saw his straw hair and rosy cheeks in the pale light.

Micha raised his hands, stopping. "Whoa, they won't attack me, will they?"

Bell folded her arms. "Only if I ask them not to."

"I see," he muttered, "I was hoping we could talk?"

"About what? Your new bride?"

His blue eyes darted between the hawks, but he lowered his arms. "May I sit with you?"

Bell sighed. She held up one hand and pinched her fingers together, mimicking a beak, then turned it toward the ground and clicked her tongue. Queen flapped her wings, giving a long squawk, then settled. All four birds turned their beaks downward, though replying in-kind to Bell's command.

"Thank you," Micha said. He took a seat on a sturdy straw bale facing Bell, who returned to her seat.

"No need to thank me," she snapped, "I am simply saving my hawks from being put to death after they attack a king."

Micha balked. "Is there something the matter?"

"No. Why would there be?"

"Well, that's why I'm asking. The day you left, you were warm and…now you return and you haven't even said hello, or congratulated me, or—"

"Oh, I ought to congratulate you? Is that what you need? Then congratulations, Majesty. Your new bride seems plain and ordinary and perfectly ready to bear your manly fruits of hairy little mountain lords."

His eyes narrowed. "That's your Queen you're speaking ill of."

"She's not, actually. You executed my Queen. And even if I were a Lady of Ediva, she's not yet your bride until when, tomorrow? Is that when your wretched and dull ceremony finally ends?"

For a moment he appeared filled with rage, boiling inside him. His jaw was tight and his stare was cold, focused on her with intensity. Then, it broke. In an instant his features loosened and Micha let out a soft laugh.

"Yea," he scoffed, "yea, the whole thing is dull. I'm sick to death of it. If I have to eat one more feast, I might die from my stomach bursting."

"Hmm," Bell said.

"And you're right, she is plain. Perhaps the plainest girl I've ever seen. But she certainly won't be unfaithful, and her father is an honorable duke. They are one of the most esteemed and generous families in my kingdom."

There was a pause between them. The weight of it settled.

Micha's blue eyes found hers with intention. "Is that what's bothering you, that I am marrying someone else?"

She threw up her hands. "You would think I want to be married? To anyone? After what I've been through, that's absurd. I'd laugh if I weren't so disgusted."

"Maybe you don't want to marry me, of course." His brow furrowed as if his thoughts didn't match his words.

"We talked about this before I left, I'm surprised you don't remember. Do you think you're so worthwhile that any woman would sacrifice her desires to stay with you? I could still fuck you, if I chose."

He glanced about. "Please, Bell."

"What? There's no one here. My hawks would alert me if anyone approached. They were watching you the moment you wandered away from the feast. I saw them, on alert. I knew someone was coming."

He sighed with relief, then gazed upward for the birds. "They are beautiful. This is the first time I've been here. I hope that these perches were built to your satisfaction?"

"Yes, they are suitable. I may train the birds here."

"You told me there were five?" Micha raised an eyebrow.

"There were."

He nodded, studying her face for a moment. In the absence of clarification, he stood and rubbed his hands together. "Well, I hope that…I mean to say, I am not officially married, until tomorrow. Tonight is only a celebration but it is a means to an end."

"What are you saying? I already congratulated you."

He rubbed at his chin, a nervous smile curving the edge of his thin lips. "Right, you did. I mean that, if you wanted to bring me seashells tonight, especially since it's the celebration of the sea…"

Bell's face contorted with dismay.

Micha shrugged. A blush began at his neck. The sight of his pink skin spreading like a dam breaking gave Bell pause. She opened her mouth to ridicule him, then thought better of it.

"Probably best that we don't," Micha mumbled after a moment.

"I reckon so."

He nodded once, biting his lip.

"Perhaps you'll grow to love her," Bell said.

"Perhaps? And perhaps I'll grow to admire and follow the Almighties. I suppose anything is possible."

216

Bell smiled, tilting her head. "You're the King. You'll learn to love your role, and all that it entails. You'll learn to love the reasons for your power. All men do."

"And women don't? Isn't this what the hawks are for you, power?"

She bristled, chuckling it off. "You may see them as power. I see much more than that."

"Then maybe I'm capable of caring about more than power, too."

"Hmm," Bell said for the second time.

"I don't understand you. Everything you want is yours. You have your hawks. You have a refuge. You are given every desire you please."

"That seems like everything, to you? Surely you've noticed how I was taken from my family and now I'm forced to stay among strangers and adhere to your odd traditions."

Micha snorted. "No one is forcing you to do anything."

"No? You're keeping me here as bait. A concomitant thing. That's all I am. Leverage, so you don't lose favor with my kingdom. How does that sound?"

"You have freedom," he snapped, "you have every freedom. I will not punish you if you leave. I will not do anything to you. If you want to go and roam free, then you may. To be honest, part of me was surprised that you returned from Hawk's Keep at all. Though my men told me the state of it, and then I realized why you didn't stay."

Bell felt the tenderness of her wound reopening. She grimaced her eyes shut, biting back the sharp feeling in the back of her throat.

Micha seemed to take no notice. "I wouldn't have blamed you if you found another place to reside in Candor, though my messages from Sir Jonn tell me it is a lawless place of ruin, now. Despite their best efforts to install a king."

Bell swallowed, finding her voice return. "My father will stake his claim on that throne. He would not have left his keep if it were not for good reason."

"Perhaps," Micha muttered.

"You don't know him. Do not pretend that you do."

217

"I'm not pretending anything. I simply know that he has not been seen for a few seasons. I am concerned about his wellbeing."

Bell clenched her fists. "Why? Because you worry about how Candor will be ruled, to protect your interests?"

"No, because I know you love your father and because I...I care about you."

Bell rose from her chair and stomped across the frozen ground to where he sat, towering over him. For a moment, she stared in his eyes, tempted to strike him. Tempted to scream at him. Tempted to kiss him, there in the open moonlight.

He only stared back, his expression gentle and receptive.

She let out a long breath through her nostrils. "If you care about me, you will find somewhere else for me. I want peace. I want to be away from you and your new bride. I want to be somewhere that I can matter. You understand I was a Lady of Hawk's Keep? The keeper of warhawks. The daughter of Sylas. An heir to the Archer bloodline. That meant something, where I was from. That mattered. I was ready to take charge of my father's house and to lead his people. He had some of the greatest knights in all of Candor under his command. He provided warriors for the throne, fish from the Western Founts, and lumber from pines at the foothills of the Calam Mountains. All of that was due to belong to me, and my husband. And that's another thing. My father would allow me to choose any man, and to choose one of my same status, so we could lead Hawk's Keep without conflict of rule. Not a prince. Not a king. But a lord or a knight."

Something flickered in Micha's blue eyes and he glanced away.

"I have one," Bell said, leaning closer, "I chose a man. And my father gave his blessing. It is a pact that we made."

"Wh—who is he?" Micha stammered, flinching.

"Does it matter? Why would it?"

Micha pounded one fist into his open hand. "It's Rowan, isn't it? I have seen—"

"No," Bell said flatly, crossing her arms. "Rowan's heart is taken. And he is more of a brother to me than anything. Rowan and I always

218

saw each other as friends, as siblings, from the day he came to us as a squire. He is an idiot, but I suppose you all are."

"Then who is it?"

"Finn."

Micha nodded, opening his mouth, then closing it again. He seemed to mimic a face of understanding, but then his brow furrowed. "I am sorry if this is…it's none of my business. But Finn…"

Bell said nothing, taking a few steps to return to her seat atop the stone. She folded her hands on her lap and then raised an eyebrow expectantly at the King.

"We have a word for it, here," Micha continued, "in Edivan it's huptig. I don't know what it would mean in Candorian, but it's someone who…"

"I'm sure you can think of a way to describe it. But you're right, it's none of your business. And frankly, I will not confirm anything about Finn which would condemn him to you."

Micha shook his head. "Why would that condemn him? It is an honor to be a huptig. They are chosen to be diacons and teachers of the Almighties. They have no loyalties to husbands, wives, or children. They are given duties as our advisors and spiritual leaders. In fact, I have thought of asking Finn if he would ever want this honor, though I know he isn't passionate about Stratera."

"He is more interested than you and I, but that isn't saying much."

Micha chuckled.

"Anyway," Bell sighed, "he knows that I chose him. He knows that I love him. If he ever decides to have me for a wife, then he is the only man I would want for a husband. Otherwise, you lot be damned. I would rather die an old barren woman in my House with my birds and leave my successor up for debate."

"Your father would surely be disappointed."

"Well, my father was too busy at war with your kingdom to produce additional heirs to run his keep. So, I suppose he couldn't be too disappointed."

Micha pursed his lips, then looked back toward the feast. "I ought to return. They have probably already started to panic that I've been abducted."

"Is abduction part of the ceremony?"

He shrugged. "There is a part where the betrothed are expected to sneak away together before the seventh and final night...but suffice to say, it hasn't happened for us."

Bell smirked. "You aren't deflowering your bride in the bushes, then?"

"It turns out, I am not."

"What a shame. You have so much to offer. I suppose she will find out soon enough."

He smiled. For a moment they looked at one another, coy and matching grins on both their faces, threatening to give away all that was unspoken.

Micha rose, wiping his hands on his trousers. "It was a pleasure to speak with you, Lady Islabell. I hope to see you tomorrow night at the final celebration."

As though waving goodbye, the hawks above stirred. Their wings flapping a few times with a whooshing sound through the air. Micha scanned above for them as he walked out of the yard and out of the gate he had entered by.

When he was well beyond the steps, Bell raised one arm: a signal.

CHAPTER 20
BELL

New prince, same tired and selfish ideas.

It was the final night of King Micha's wedding celebration, and Bell was drunk on kelpi.

"In retrospect, drinking tonight was a terrible idea." Finn said. He sat beside her, propped up in his silver chair with his barons nearby.

"You're wrong. Every night we drink here is a good idea!" Bell shouted back.

As they sat, a procession passed through the circular, wheel-spoke streets. At every angle there seemed to be another droning chant from the diacons and followers of Stratera, covered in hooded robes with their peeking-out faces painted in white chalk from rock dust.

Finn shook his head. "This entire affair is terrifying. Death? Who ends a marriage party with death? I might be pissing myself. I wouldn't be able to tell, but I definitely might be pissing myself."

"Seven Almighties," Bell said, "the seventh is death."

"Right, I just didn't expect them to take it so literally."

Bell smirked, thinking that it would be literal if they killed someone. The new bride would be a welcome candidate. She thought to say it, but there were too many ears around them. Blasphemy and threatening the new queen wouldn't be taken lightly, in any kingdom.

"Did you know they are shooting fire into the sky at the end?" Finn asked.

"What does that have to do with death?"

Finn shrugged. "I don't think everything is to do with the Almighties. Maybe that part is only for fun."

"I see," Bell murmured. She scanned the street ahead. Beyond the front of the procession was a large group of Edivan spiritual advisors. She recognized Weft among them. She knew it was likely that Micha stood somewhere in the group.

"I'll return in a moment," Bell said, rushing to cross the streets at a break in the parade.

"Ah, fine," Finn called after her, "I suppose I'll sit here alone and wait, then?"

She cast a playful glance over her shoulder at him, catching sight of his own smirk.

When she reached the grouping of advisors, they wore stony expressions, eyeing her with no warmth.

"Excuse me," she muttered. She bowed her head and stepped toward the group. For a moment they stared at her with plain faces. But with visible hesitation and disdain, they stepped aside, allowing space for Bell to move through the crack in the crowd like water through rocks.

The final few parted and Bell saw him at the center. He wore a dark robe, more elaborate than the others, with multiple layers of thick velvety fabric gathered to his shoulders. His face was painted in a pale chalk, though it hardly showed over his naturally light skin. His tufts of blonde hair protruded, distinguishing him.

But Bell was surprised to see a matching group of similar complexions, with identical tufts of blonde all their own. She was still taking in their unfamiliar faces when he addressed her.

"Lady Islabell," Micha said. There was an audible shake of nerves to his tone.

"Majesty," Bell replied, bowing low to pantomime respect.

He gave a dip of his chin in response. "I trust you are enjoying the procession?"

Bell nodded, righting herself. She looked into his blue eyes and fought the urge to smirk. "It's…wonderful. What a pleasant end to these beautiful festivities."

Micha raised an eyebrow: a warning.

Bell continued. "I wanted to congratulate you, Majesty. Your bride is lovely. What a handsome pair the two of you will make."

"Thank you," Micha stated coldly. He turned to wave to the others at his side. "Allow me to introduce my family. I realize you have not yet met. Mother, father, this is Lady Islabell of Candor. She is heir to Hawk's Keep, daughter of Lord Sylas. She has taken refuge in Ediva since the Boen invasion, and is now my advisor on how to navigate this unprecedented way forward between our kingdoms."

Bell studied the man and woman he addressed. The woman was every bit as Boeny as Micha, with thick straw hair braided around her face to form a wreath. Her eyes were periwinkle, with tired lines in all directions. The man, in contrast, was plainly Edivan. He was stout and thick. He wore the ceremonial robe and the chalk on his face was clinging to a thick beard; hair that Micha lacked.

Micha gestured to them. "This is my father, Duke Micha Tymen. This is my mother, Duchess Alura Tymen."

Bell bowed again. "It's a pleasure to meet you both."

"These are my brothers," Micha held his hand toward three boys, "Lord Foulon, Lord Thibert, and Jule, a squire. These are my sisters, Lady Tanya, Lady Vana, and lady-in-waiting Vioria."

"A beautiful family," Bell said. Her eyes passed over all six of them, and she marveled at the age gap. Vioria appeared somewhere between the stages of walking and learning to talk. The lords and ladies had been given their titles generously, as coming-of-age was after thirteen in Candor, and Bell doubted Lady Vana was older than seven.

"Thank you," Duchess Alura answered.

"King Micha," Bell said, "where is your bride?"

His eyes widened and he glanced to his parents, though they did not seem to notice, fixated on the parade. "Um, I forget you are not familiar with the wedding tradition. Tonight is the final stage of the homage to our Almighties. The seventh Almighty is death. We celebrate death tonight by embracing the end of our lives before marriage. Pearl Salish will be brought on a pyre and it will be set aflame. If she survives, she is allowed to wed me."

Bell chuckled despite herself, hiding it behind her hand, and earning a skeptical gaze from Alura.

"I'm only teasing," Micha blurted, "of course, we don't kill anyone. We have a symbolic death of ourselves. Pearl and I will join each other atop a pyre, and be surrounded by dancers in red costume, to represent the flames."

"How lovely. I cannot wait to see it."

Micha hummed to himself; his lips tight.

"Well," Bell said, "Majesty, congratulations. I am sure you will be eager to produce an heir and begin your new life."

Micha's discomfort was visible. He shifted from one foot to the other, opening his mouth as if to stop her.

Bell felt the warm buzz of kelpi strong as ever in her veins. "You'll have your new bride, your seven children, you can live in spiritual harmony under strict Stratera. You may rule Ediva forever in the greatest of days. Why wouldn't you, the Boens are not about to lay waste to your cities and keeps."

Duke Tymen and Duchess Alura were fixated on Bell now, their attention fully drawn away from the ceremonies. With harsh and confused faces, they looked to Micha, deferring to his role as King.

Micha stepped forward briskly, touching his fingertips to Bell's elbow. He spoke in an icy whisper. "My Lady, I've forgotten that you have messages. They arrived today from Sir Jonn, in Candor. Perhaps you and I ought to speak, alone."

Bell couldn't help the laughter that rolled out of her. He was so anxious; she could see it. She pitied him for this unwanted life. But she also wanted to watch him suffer.

"Mother, father, I will return shortly," Micha explained. He gestured for Bell to lead away from the others.

She ignored the direction he intended, choosing instead to return to where she had been a moment before, alongside Finn. She took her seat, the two Candorians positioned at the edge of the road to enjoy the procession.

Micha muttered a greeting to Finn. "Are you sure this is where you want to do this? We are somewhat exposed."

Bell shrugged. "That depends. Are the messages going to put Candor at risk? Do they threaten our kingdom?"

Micha shook his head. "Of course not. Then I wouldn't have told you there was any message at all, where others might hear."

"Then tell us," Bell insisted.

"What's this now?" Finn said, leaning forward.

Micha cleared his throat, moving to where he was standing closely between their two seats. He leaned in, lowering his voice. "A message returned from Candor, today. Sir Jonn sent it. It regards the state of your kingdom and the chances they will be able to find a resolution with the Boens before winter."

Bell and Finn shared a look. Bell felt something inside her twist, but she subdued it.

"Things have changed significantly," Micha continued, "it would seem your man Rowan has been named crown Prince of Candor."

"What?" Finn and Bell both gasped.

225

"That's not possible," Bell blurted, "he is not...he is not in-line for the throne. He's a bastard, and his father Brande was not even in-line among the first seven families."

Micha shook his head. "Sir Jonn's message claims that Rowan was concealing his true identity. That he was young Lord Trevin Schinen."

Bell was stunned into silence, her mind racing.

"He had to hide while Zarana was alive," Micha said, "but with her execution, he no longer had to pretend. I knew that Jonn had a secret regarding Rowan, but I was not certain of the full extent of it."

"Aye," Finn whispered, "he would've been in danger if she'd known."

"I suspect she did know," Micha said, "I suspect that's why his name was the last thing she said before her execution. But at any rate, it won't matter now, and we'll never know. The important thing is that Row— Trevin needs to become king. And fast. We've only two seasons for him to declare a treaty with the Boens. You must understand more about this than I, but Sir Jonn insists that there is a solution involving his heir."

Bell nodded. "Becoming king. It's not that different than Ediva. Your spiritual advisors insist you produce heirs for legitimacy. In Candor, especially if the bloodline on the throne changes to the next successor, you must produce an heir before being made king. It has been that way ever since King Chorl Candor was barren and tried to give the throne to his wife, who had no claim."

Finn shook his head. "I think you've got it wrong. That wasn't when the law was made, it was before that. It was one of the first laws of the kingdom."

Micha raised his hands. "I have a wedding to get back to. Can the two of you argue your history after I've delivered my message?"

"We can argue all night. Can you wait until tomorrow?" Finn asked.

"No," Micha said flatly.

Seeing he wouldn't humor them, Bell and Finn nodded for the King to go on.

Micha sighed. "The messenger didn't explain why, but he said it is critical that…Bell—Lady Islabell, you must be the one to marry Prince Trevin."

Bell crossed her arms.

"That sounds…unlikely," Finn said.

"I cannot glean more," Micha explained, "it was a verbal message. I wish that I were able to speak to Sir Jonn in-person and find what he means by this, but all I can do is send you to Candor upon his request."

"No," Bell stated. She leaned back further, her arms tightening across her chest.

"What—what do you mean?"

"I mean, no."

"To which part?"

"All of it," Bell snapped. "I will not return to Candor. I will not marry Rowan. I will not do any of it."

Micha's nostrils flared. "My Lady, it is not your prerogative—"

"Are you not aware that I have been through this once before? Do you not know that another bloody worthless prince tried to force me to marry him, but a few months ago? What happened to him? You poisoned him, in front of all your nobles. He tried to kidnap me and take me against my will. You might think that I make a fine prize for Candor, but I am not a piece of fish to be passed between mouths and fed to greedy men. There are plenty of other ladies and women. Why am I the one who is fought over?"

Micha leaned in, speaking in a hushed tone. "I remind you that I am King, and he is the prince. You will not speak so insubordinately to me, or deny the orders that he sends to you."

"What are you going to do, execute me too?"

Micha's blue eyes darkened.

Bell squinted at him, mimicking, then a smirk spread to the corners of her mouth.

"You're drunk," Micha muttered.

227

Finn raised a shaky hand. "She is. Forgive her, Majesty. She's had too much kelpi."

"No," Bell snapped, "don't you dare try to belittle me. Kelpi or not, I deserve to speak."

"I won't execute you," Micha said, "but you could disappear. You do not treat a king the way you have tonight. You will not speak to me this way again."

"Then silence me, King."

Micha's cheeks began to redden. He leaned in so he was close enough to whisper where only she could hear. "If you threaten me, if you undermine me, I will have no choice. Please do not put me in that position."

"Then don't ship me off like property where my only future is birthing arrogant little princes until I slit my own throat."

When Micha pulled away, Bell could see the horror and fear in Finn's face.

Micha's blue eyes softened. "It's a shame that you cannot see past your own interests to find the greater good. If you do right by your prince, Trevin, and labor him an heir, he will become the King? That's how you can manage to join him in a pact with the Boens? You would be heralded for a dozen generations if you spun that story into your own heroic sacrifice. You would be the Mother of Candor."

Bell scoffed. "Women of Candor receive no accolades. Even Zarana's legacy of terror will crumble and fade by the end of our lifetimes. She will be forgotten and Zander's story will outlive us all. I'd be running into the same fate."

Micha stared at her, blinking slow. "It sounds as though you are saying you would be a queen like her, merciless, cold…"

There was a rise in a chanting song, somber in tone, from beyond the procession.

Micha shook his head. "I need to go. It is nearly time."

"Best wishes, then," Bell snapped.

Finn's response was more genuine. "Hope the ceremony is exciting!"

Micha shrugged toward them both, then turned and walked away. When he was beyond earshot and disappeared into the group of his advisors, Bell reached for another jar of kelpi. Finn tried to smack it from her hand, but she was beyond his grasp.

"That's gotten you into enough trouble tonight, hasn't it?" Finn grumbled.

"Trouble? I don't see myself in any trouble."

"You are. You might have…bonded with the King, but he's still a king. And we are still foreigners in this land with little recourse."

"And you think there's any guarantee of our safety, whether or not I speak my mind? If the Boens attack Candor, then our countrymen are at war. What will we be? Sitting like sheep waiting for slaughter. In a few months' time, we'll be dead, either way."

"Then why don't we return?" Finn asked. "Let's go home. Rowan isn't going to force you to marry him. Maybe he was asking, as a favor, but he wouldn't do that to you, or to anyone. Why don't we go to Candeo and ask him what his intentions are, face-to-face?"

Bell rolled her eyes. "He won't send us both. He'll keep you here."

"Oh," Finn said, his face falling with a thoughtful sadness.

"Can we forget about this, tonight?" Bell asked.

In front of them, the procession had risen to heightened levels, with the costumed participants climbing atop a massive stone pyre at the center of the street's intersection. The red-robed actors were coming forward, symbolizing fire and flames. It was more impressive than Bell had expected from Micha's bland description. On all edges of the crowd, drummers pounded booming leather-skin instruments, bringing the noise level higher with the anticipation of the grand event.

Finn rubbed his hands together and reached for his own jar of kelpi. He lifted it toward Bell with a smirk. "Forgetting our worries? It's what we're best at."

Soon the dizzy spell of drink and the crowd would win her over, and Bell would be carried to her chamber by a respectful guard.

———————

With the morning came a solid headache, a few trips to the chamber pot, and unwanted sunlight trickling in. Bell called for an Edivan handmaid to run her a bath. It was too hot, then too cold, and she finally stopped trying to communicate at all.

She was in the water until late in the mid-morning, hoping that most of the kingdom was in the same predicament. After all, if the King's wedding wasn't an excuse to imbibe too much, was there ever going to be one at all?

Bell heard footsteps in her chamber and assumed it was the handmaid. She sunk deeper into the water.

"Fjun," Bell called, saying the word for 'hot'. "Fjun, please."

"What exactly would you like a 'hot' of?"

She whipped her head at the sound of his voice.

Micha stood, bashfully blushing, wearing his full king's robe and crown. He was covered in color—threads woven in elaborate patterns and images to represent mountains, sky, sunsets, the sea, and perhaps fire. He was a decoration and he looked majestic and beautiful.

Bell shook her head. "You certainly shouldn't be in my chambers. Especially while I'm like this."

"Yes, well, I seem to find myself always seeing you when I am not supposed to. And I also seem to find myself always with information I must give you. Hopefully this will be the final time."

"Oh, hopefully?"

Micha sighed. He walked around the stone tub to the front where they could face one another more easily. His hands were folded in front of him, and Bell raised an eyebrow at the sight, giving him a mischievous glance.

"I have come up with a solution for you," Micha said, stone-faced. "You likely know I cannot send Sir Finley back to your kingdom. I am willing to send you, if you wish, but you said that is not what you desire. However, you'd had a bit of kelpi last night. Is that still your wish, today?"

"It is."

"Well, I thought as much. There is also the matter of your hawks. I do not have many places you may continue to keep them. They make the stablemen nervous, and they have spooked the horses more than once."

"No one told me as much."

"No, I don't imagine they would." Micha turned and glanced out the window, scanning the sky as if he would spot the birds in question. "I would like to propose another option to you. Along the coast of Ediva we have four islands, the Sandles. They are habitable, though cold. The Hornes never touch them. We have built temples on them, which have sat for perhaps a thousand years. Once a year, we take offerings to leave for the Almighties. There are some diacons who live on one of the islands, keeping up the temple and praying. But one has been empty for some time."

Bell scooped the water and poured it onto her shoulder, letting it drip across her back. She caught him glancing back at her, then he tried to pretend he was occupied elsewhere.

"I, uhm," he cleared his throat, "I think you could stay there. As long as you like, actually. You and Finley could take the hawks and be free to live in the temples. I can send you with a few people. A healer, a cook, a fisher. You would have what you need."

"It sounds too good to be true."

He looked at her, focusing on her dark eyes as if locked on a target. "Perhaps you should trust me, then. I don't want harm to come to you. I also hate that you feel like a prisoner here. Just because I need to worry about what is right for my kingdom doesn't mean that I don't care about your desires and wishes."

"Oh, my desires?" Keeping her eyes trained on him, she reached into the bath and slid a wet hand up her opposite arm to her shoulder. At her neck, she paused, tilting her head and stretching while she let out a purposeful sigh.

Micha shook his head. "I'm not…Bell, I'm not here for this."

"For what? To watch me bathe? It certainly seems like you are."

"I, no. I am not. I'm here to talk to you about the…island."

Bell smirked. She was between him and the door, and it was too lovely an opportunity to pass up. She gripped the sides of the bathing pool and pulled herself up. She rose above the water, her shoulders, then her breasts, then her stomach. Micha's eyes widened but he didn't look away this time. Bell stood, and the water was at her knees, all of her dripping wet skin exposed to him.

He pursed his lips, feigning an angry face. But his body betrayed him, and she could see how aroused he was even through his regal tunic.

"I best go," Micha muttered.

"Must you? Well, at least fetch me a drying robe, will you please? No one is coming in to help me and I don't want to walk around with wet feet. I may fall."

Micha followed her gesture and handed her a robe with haste. Redness began to pool at his neck and trickle up to his ears.

Bell wanted to laugh, but she held it in. He was so adorable and helpless. What would the people of Ediva say if they knew their mighty King lacked the self-control to deny his eyes a feast of his lover's body?

"I ought to go," Micha said.

"You already said that, yet you're still here."

"Yes. Erm. Yes." He took one step, then paused to gape at her again.

Bell stepped from the bath onto the stone, making a show of draping her drying robe over her as slowly as possible, and leaving it open around her chest.

"You can tell me your decision, as soon as you like."

Her smile broadened. "I think I would like your island. I will ask Finn what he thinks. We have always loved the water, and used to swim in the Western Founts. Could we swim near your island, or is the water too cold?"

"It's cold, but you can adapt. The diacons who inhabit a few of the other islands swim as part of their ritual, to pay homage to the Almighty of water."

"Will I get to say goodbye to you?"

Micha covered his mouth, rubbing his hand softly across his lips. "Perhaps not now. But soon. I will find a way for us to say…a proper goodbye."

"Then I suppose I shouldn't say it to you now?"

"No," he muttered, shaking his head. "No, I will say…I'll see you soon."

"Yes, Majesty, I'll see you soon." Bell curtsied low, allowing her robe to fall open off her shoulders. She glanced up in time to see Micha bite his lip, pausing to stare, then he shuddered. With a shake of his head, he bowed in response, then briskly walked out of her chamber. She watched him go, delighting in the sight of the scarlet blush covering his neck all the way to the roots of his golden hair.

CHAPTER 21
RAENA

A weak proposal

Aven had hidden the body.

She had taken it to the outer edges of the farms, a place familiar to her that Raena didn't know by description. When she returned, she appeared wrecked, muddy, and beaten down more than Raena had ever seen. But Raena kept her promise and brought Aven into the castle, to safely live among the nobles, where she belonged.

For nine days Aven had been officially in the castle as Raena's "East Shore advisor". She might have bathed away the pig farm stench, and donned noblewoman's dresses, but her eyes never lost that shadow of defeat. Raena studied the face of her former lover, gazing at her across the table while they ate, in silence.

It had been Raena's idea that they dine together in the king's guest-receiving room. But as the moments of silence ticked by, she began to wonder if it had been a mistake. They had not said more than a few words to one another since that night in the barn. It seemed Aven had unearthed a well of pain that overflowed with honest, raw emotion, and drowned Raena with it. Then Aven snapped herself together and pulled the lid over her heart, closing it once again to the world. Aven appeared cold and composed ever since, projecting an air that nothing at all could phase her.

Though her downtrodden eyes said otherwise.

"Do you like your room?" Raena asked.

Aven was taking a bite of pearled groul. She set her hand at her side and continued to chew, glancing up as she did. The silence lasted so long, Raena started to wonder if Aven had even heard the question.

But Aven swallowed, cleared her throat, and spoke. "I'm not sure how to answer that, Majesty."

Raena bristled. "How about the truth?"

"Does anyone speak honestly to a prince?"

Raena reached for a loaf of butter yeast and squished it, thinking while the pastry collapsed in her hand.

Aven continued in a soft tone, "I'm no longer your equal."

"You were above me. You weren't my equal before, you were above me. But I know you treated me with respect and dignity, so of course I will extend you the same."

"Respect for me isn't the question. Thank you for treating me well, but the kingdom is the true problem."

Raena grimaced and pulled a handful of butter yeast out from the loaf. She extended her arm toward Aven, wordlessly offering the staple. Aven glanced at it, grimacing either at the yeast or at Raena's gesture, it was difficult to determine which. Then, as though taking poison from an enemy, Aven leaned forward and opened her mouth to accept the bite. When she chewed the butter yeast, she avoided Raena's eyes.

It left an ache in Raena's chest, as though a piece of her own heart had gone cold via contagious magic.

"Thank you," Aven mumbled.

"Please," Raena said, caring to make her tone warm, "what is this truth you wish to tell me? I value your perspective above all others."

Aven nodded, her shoulders relaxing. "I will be honest. Your kingdom is…I'm not exaggerating when I say that it's dismal. You seem to have an idea but I don't believe you actually know how terrible it is outside these towers. Your peasants are being raped, robbed, and beaten to death every day. Your serfs are not faring much better. The knights are corrupt. The guards are children. Ruvians have control of food supply in all directions. Your armies are filled with elderly and ill men unfit to fight. Yet they could hold back some of these raids and defend the roads and farms. Instead? They are dying in the desert waiting for a Boen invasion that may or may not happen, and they wouldn't be able to stop it if it did."

Raena opened her mouth to respond, but Aven held up a finger in protest.

"You're the Prince. You have advisors. Are they recommending that you fill your armies with farmers and old men and send them to fend for themselves in the open desert? How long do they expect men to live in camps? And surely they do not have food supply if you hardly have any within your keeps and citadel."

Raena's cheeks began to redden. "They gave me several options, and I chose to focus on the most imminent threat. Without a treaty, the Boens will take our kingdom."

"And why can't you offer a treaty?"

"Only a king can."

Aven squinted. "Name yourself king."

"If I do that, I'll be put to death."

"Zander did it, and his people didn't put him to death."

Raena gazed into her goblet of ale for a moment, pursing her lips.

"What?" Aven asked. "What are you not saying?"

"I have already gained scrutiny from powerful men for posing as one person and then revealing myself to be another. I have been…advised not to break another law. There are plenty of enemies to Candor who may be to blame for an accident that befalls me. As you and I know, this kingdom can be a dangerous place where even a knight can disappear." At the mention of a knight, Raena's eyes settled on Aven's with a weighted stare. The meaning of her words were not unnoticed.

"Then if you cannot force a treaty, pull your armies back to defend your fortresses. You'll never outnumber the Boens, but at least you can have prepared men. Leave them in garrison to bolster and rebuild what you've lost. Train them and feed them so you have their strength in bodies and their will to fight."

Raena sighed. "How did this meal turn into a war strategy discussion?"

"You need to stop the Ruvians before you can stop the Boens. You said you would take my advice, and that's what I am certain needs to be done."

"Fine, I'll discuss it with the council."

Aven raised her dark eyebrows, paused, then picked out pieces of the meal. She nibbled at a strip of salted tuckfruit, staring off into nothing in particular.

"This reminds me of when I arrived at house Colby," Raena said. "Do you think about that time we ate in the garden?"

"Sometimes."

"That was nearly a year ago."

An unreadable expression passed across Aven's face. "It seems much longer than that."

"I suppose it does."

"All of it is gone now, the gardens, the Colby's, the gardeners. It's all Boens in their place. House Colby is Boenaerya now."

"I know."

Aven shuddered as though being ripped back into her present surroundings. She focused on Raena. "It was theirs to take back, there's no question. We never should have been on that land."

"How can you believe that, when you lost your people? You lost more than anyone."

"And how can you be descended from Boens and not see the way they were mistreated and robbed of their land? They took what was rightfully owed them. Do I wish they would have given us the option to leave? Of course. I dream about that every night. But why would they trust us, when we slaughtered their families three hundred years ago, and for what? Resources? Greed?"

"We wouldn't have surrendered."

"Exactly. If I would have known what was coming, I would have rallied supporters and allies from every corner. There's no way Candor would have released the houses of East Shore to fall to the Boens."

Raena grinned. "I missed this."

Aven's lips turned downward with a sour twist. She poked a finger into the butter yeast, fixating elsewhere.

For a moment, the air was thick. Raena knew she had said something wrong, but pushed beyond the urge to apologize or hide away her feelings.

With a deep breath, Raena forced her thoughts to the surface. "I missed you. The way that you speak to me, the way you are honest with me. You don't try to tell me only the things I want to hear. You don't cater to me as if I'm a source of power to glean from. And…perhaps I have, but I hope I've never done that to you."

Aven lifted one shoulder in a half-hearted shrug, biting her lip and staring at the demolished bit of butter yeast.

"We can fix this," Raena began.

"We have fixed it. This is fixed. We are sitting together at this table, speaking to one another, and we are speaking openly. That's good enough."

Raena bit back the sudden well of anguish in her chest. "Is it? This is all you want for us? For me to be the prince, and you to be the advisor, and we sit and have meals together?"

"Yes."

Raena shifted in her seat. She had been trying to find the right moment to say what she needed to. She'd been waiting to have a chance

238

to talk to Aven, and now that they were alone together, this felt like the opportunity. But the tightness in her chest also screamed at her that everything about it was wrong. Raena clenched her hands together and ignored her instincts.

"Do you know that Jonn-Del is trying to force me to marry?" Raena blurted out.

Aven's face twisted with a grimace, but then the expression disappeared equally fast. "No, but I suppose that is logical since it's how you must be named king."

"Exactly, but I can't trust anyone except for you and Bell. I can't trust any other woman in my bed every night, in my chamber with me."

"I see."

The coldness pouring off Aven made Raena's heart race with fear. Against all better judgment, Raena rushed on with all the forced confidence of a naked man running into battle.

"Jonn-Del wants me to marry Bell, actually," Raena said, "because of her status and the…security. He's sent for her to ask her to do it."

"That's a sound idea."

"I told him not to. I put a stop to it. I want to marry you, instead."

Now the words were out of her mouth and hanging in the air between them. Raena had said it and she couldn't take it back.

"Oh," was all Aven said.

"I know this can't really be a surprise, and I hoped that we could have this conversation sooner, but now you're back within the citadel—"

"I don't think this is a conversation. We don't need to discuss this at all."

Raena pursed her lips and nodded. She was unsurprised by Aven's reaction, but her gut twisted all the same.

Aven sighed, "I am beginning to trust you, again. But what we have is broken. What we had before was built on…very little foundation. I'm beginning to realize how we barely know each other. We probably rushed too quickly when our emotions were high. It was passion. But that passion is gone. What do we have between us if we haven't learned enough to even have…a friendship? Mutual respect? I can't form a partnership with someone without those things. And do you even want what you're proposing, or is it simply to stave off the pressure from Jonn-Del?"

Tears were coming.

Heavy, thick, and swollen, like a wake against a dam. They were building within Raena and she knew she had nary a second before they would rise to her eyes and fall out of her. She couldn't think about the words Aven had said, much less try to answer the questions.

In her desperation, Raena rose from the table, the chair scuffing across the stone.

"Majes—"

"I have to speak to someone about this," Raena snapped, "I know someone who…I'll be back." She spun, moving before Aven had the chance to even stand. Raena was so brisk toward the door, she practically ran.

Aven was left there in the receiving room, likely wondering if Raena was upset. Raena prayed somehow she hadn't noticed. A stupid prayer, Raena knew.

As Raena jogged through the corridor, she thought of her destination, but first desired to wander and shake away her pain. She passed the stairwells to the royal wings, and continued downward. A knight passed and gave her a courteous nod, viewing her in his peripheral. No doubt he noticed the reddening of her eyes and the threat of tears, but he said nothing. Raena prayed she would not encounter a man of the council—or worse, Sir Jonn-Del—because they would not have any qualms about speaking up regarding her distressed appearance.

Raena wound further below in the halls, toward the kitchens and food stores. When she reached the lowest feasting hall, she didn't give a second glance to the peasants gathered, awaiting their meals. They were a fixture of the corridor, always hoping for food scraps once all the nobles and castle serfs were fed. They all bowed deep and mumbled praises to the prince, which Raena waved away. She rounded the archways and entered the kitchen, filled with stragglers, cooks, and guards to keep the desperate peasants at bay. She would find the man who knew too much—her secrets. Raena wasn't sure why she felt compelled to look for him. What could he offer her in this moment? More riddles?

But he had known Raena's identity, or at least that was how she interpreted his odd allegory. If he knew more secrets, he might know more solutions.

"Prince Trevin," a guard bellowed, dropping to one knee. The rest of the occupants turned with shock, most bowing or falling prostrate in her honor.

"Thank—" Raena sputtered, a few tears catching in her throat. She cleared it and tried again to speak. "Thank you. Please rise. I wish to speak with someone. A man, I've seen him here in the kitchens more than once. He is a diacon, or a leader to those who practice Libre. He has stains on his skin, purple stains. Do any of you know him?"

The serfs had stood and glanced at one another in a moment of confusion.

One of the cooks nearest a cauldron, whose face Raena almost recognized, meekly raised her hand. "Your Majesty, if I may."

"You may. Tell me where I can find this man."

"Yes, Your Majesty." The cook swallowed and hung her head. "You see, if only I could. There is not one man who matches that description, at least not anymore. The diacons have taken to soaking their flesh in berries from redroot and leaves of the bellun. They are coloring their skin to match the man they call The Chosen."

Raena huffed. "Then where can I find The Chosen?"

"He is a legend, Majesty. I have heard of him but no one has ever seen him. They speak of him as an inspiration, but he may have been dead for hundreds of years, or be a symbol of their belief. I'm sure the man you're looking for is any one of the dozens of diacons, and they wander in and out of the castle kitchens. They bring us harvests from their followers in exchange for meals."

"Fine," Raena said, "then where do I find all of them? They must frequent someplace, or gather elsewhere."

The cook shuffled. "They are everywhere. They live among all the people, urging them to follow Libre and to leave behind their dependence and need for control."

Raena nodded, as if she had some concept of it all, when the religion was somewhat foreign and notional. She muttered thanks and was met with a series of bows once more. In a way, she felt foolish for seeking the man, as though he might have an answer. Resolved to ignore him and the future followers who sought her out, Raena returned to her chamber, hopeful not to see Aven—or anyone—for the rest of the day.

CHAPTER 22
RAENA

Blade on blade

As the summer heat began to diminish and autumn drew nearer with each long day, Raena became certain that her kingdom would fall to the Boens.

She had begged the council to reconsider their refusal to offer a treaty, but they were old men, and there is no one in the world more stubborn and irrational than a man who has gone all his life used to everyone listening to him. Now Raena was surrounded by them, and at the heart of the insolence was Jonn-Del.

They sat on the balcony together at dawn before the desert air became intolerably dry and sweltering. This had become their tradition in recent days.

Jonn-Del sipped at a tonic; he'd been complaining of stomach pain.

"Hasn't it resolved, yet?" Raena asked. She leaned back in her chair made of stripped hides; her feet raised on a round stone between them.

"I'm afraid not. The pain seems worst in the morning, and settles by afternoon."

"Maybe it's something you're dreaming about."

Jonn-Del flinched. "It could be my worry for the kingdom."

"Do you doubt that I worry for Candor?"

The old man rubbed his eyes. "Of course not. You will worry for your kingdom as you worry for yourself. If Candor falls, what will your fate be, as its prince? It might be the end to a short reign."

"Thank you for the reminder," Raena mumbled. "Might I remind you that you're the one who volunteered me for this reign? You didn't think it was poor planning?"

Jonn-Del reached for his tonic and took a long, purposeful drink. His brown eyes focused on the land beyond the balcony, where the walls of Candeo ended and the deserts began. Raena followed his gaze, wondering what had his attention, but saw only the same familiar tan rolling hills with patches of pale, wild brush.

"There's something I've been meaning to ask you," Raena began. "It's about one of the letters you wrote me. I've pondered it—"

"Majesty, Sir Jonn-Del," a quiet man's voice alerted them from the entrance to the balcony. Raena was surprised to find a member of the council, Fjall, in the archway. Fjall gave a hasty bow.

"You're interrupting us," Jonn-Del snapped, out of turn.

Raena ignored the error. "What is it, Lord Fjall?"

Fjall was a lithe man with skin as thick and brown as tree bark, descended from countless generations of desert-dwelling Candorians. His lips appeared chapped and dry as he spoke. "Majesty, there is a problem at the north gate. I believe you should come to the northern tower at once."

Raena stood instinctively, but Jonn-Del waved his hands.

"Tell me Fjall," Jonn-Del spat, "what is this problem? Why does it demand your Prince's immediate attention?"

"It's hard to describe, but I may explain as we walk."

Raena shot a warning in Jonn-Del's direction. "That'll be fine. Let's take the east corridor over the rampart to get there."

"Then I will follow," Jonn-Del said, gesturing for them to lead the way as he stood.

244

Fjall began to lead with a purpose. His long legs carried him faster than Raena, and he had to deliberately slow to allow her and Jonn-Del to keep the pace. When they entered the eastern corridor, he apologized for his haste and assured them it was necessary.

He offered his explanation as they kept up a clip through the halls. "It's been nearly an hour, since before the sunrise. Seven men have been standing in a row beyond the gate, unmoving. The guards approached them and questioned their purpose. They will not answer or offer an explanation. We believe they want an audience, or perhaps they plan to conduct a demonstration, but their unwavering position gave us reason to be wary."

Jonn-Del scoffed. "So, you've disrupted us because seven men are standing someplace? How's that a matter worthy of yer Prince?"

Fjall glanced back in surprise but kept up his pace. "There's an ominous tone to these men. They are not Ruvians, nor peasants, nor serfs. They are covered in pale robes and their skin is stained as purple as a plum."

"Diacons," Raena said.

"Are they?" Fjall asked. "The diacons of Libre have been confined to temples, I thought. I haven't seen them ever look so...uniform."

They were over the rampart and entered the north tower. The stairs wound like a serpent ahead of them, and Fjall bounded upward with the energy of a younger man.

Raena had to take two steps at a time to keep up, calling after him. "Their faces are painted now. I have seen them more than once. I'm not certain the reason, but they are growing in numbers and gaining followers faster than ever."

"The rise in followers I understand," Jonn-Del added, "the diacons offer protection from bandits to the serfs. But like anything, their loyalty comes at a price."

Raena wasn't sure what price he was implying, as the crown protected the serfs and the guards should have been sufficient to guarantee safety of all her subjects. Though, thinking back to Aven's brother and the stories of the pig farms, Raena supposed her guards might not have been enough. What was more, she couldn't fathom how a diacon would give protection from violent bandits, unless it were to hide victims within the meager temples scattered through Candeo.

"We ought to go to the third story window?" Fjall asked when they reached a landing.

Raena nodded, pointing the way.

The three of them abandoned the staircase and walked the length across the narrow tower. The windows in question were off a landing, alongside a section of library that Raena had never used. If they would have continued up the stairs they could have reconnected to the prince's great room and another council chamber. Raena thought the library might be something for her to investigate at a later time. Her idea dissipated as she stepped up to the window, which was a broad opening at the furthermost north section of the citadel. Below them was the gate and outer curtain. Raena peered down to see a line of guards, legionmen, and archers gathered on the ramparts. It was far more men than needed, as though most of the castle's defense had clustered in one corner to observe an event. Then she followed their attention beyond the gates, out to the sections of desert that opened and stretched as far as the eye could see.

The seven men were stiff as statues, and perfectly distributed in a row, as if they had been measured with a straight line drawn by the Almighty's hand.

"There are seven Almighties," Fjall whispered. He was at Raena's left shoulder, and Jonn-Del was to her right.

Raena didn't respond, observing the men for herself.

Their robes were indeed pale, matching the sand at their feet. The material whipped around them as the wind blew, but they remained rigid and composed. Each man had vibrant purple skin, flaring out against the beige backdrop. Their hair was covered by an attached hood, leaving only their faces and hands exposed.

It was eerie and unsettling, but no threat to her kingdom. Raena felt unnerved by her guards being so easily distracted from their posts.

246

"Where is the master-of-arms?" Raena asked.

Fjall and Jonn-Del were quiet for a moment.

At their lack of response, Raena spoke louder. "I want to speak with the master-of-arms, immediately."

"Yes, Your Majesty," Fjall said, bowing. "I will return here with haste."

The moment he backed from the window, something happened in the desert. The diacon at the center of them all raised one arm, pointing upward, directly at the open tower. Raena couldn't be certain, but she thought she heard a short yip much like a brush fox or even a child's cry. At the sound, all seven men turned in-place, as though they were a tiny army responding to a marching command. The center diacon kept his arm raised, and Raena felt certain it was aimed in her direction.

"Wait," Raena said over her shoulder to Fjall.

He returned to her side in a few steps and a mindful silence fell over them.

The wind whistled as it moved through the openings of the stone castle walls. There were a few clangs and knocks from the guards shuffling along the rampart below. Raena felt the festering heat of the desert air, not softened a bit by the occasional breeze.

The seven diacons held their new position, firm and expectant.

Raena mumbled to the men on either side of her. "Do you think they could hear me if I shouted from here?"

Jonn-del shrugged. "It's worth a try."

Raena squared her shoulders and pulled in a deep breath to prepare her loudest voice. "Men of Stratera, I am your ruler, Prince Trevin. Your assembly today outside our walls is alarming. Tell us, what is the meaning of this?"

The silence that followed was harsher, somehow; as though they defied their Prince by refusing to respond when addressed.

Raena felt her heart begin to quicken at the realization that so many of her men were now watching her, and she had no idea what to do.

Jonn-Del whispered, "Ought we order the archers to fire a few arrows of warning? They won't stay still if their lives are threatened."

"What good will that do?" Raena murmured back. "And our 'archers' are invalids and farmer boys. Look at them. They have been firing arrows for two seasons, at most. What if they strike a diacon by accident? You and I would be better candidates for firing the warning arrows, if anyone must do it."

"We could," Jonn-Del said, "I will go to the rampart—"

"I was joking. Do not shoot arrows at them. For Almighty's gifts, the last thing we need to do is start slaying our religious leaders when we've already let the people of Candor suffer against a failed war and a relentless onslaught of Ruvian bandits."

Fjall shook his head. "Then what do you propose, Prince Trevin?"

Raena stepped forward so she leaned over the ledge. Her top half was exposed and clear to see from the ground, she was sure. It was from this angle she was able to make out another crowd of a different kind had gathered; peasants were tucked between the tower and the north curtain, clamoring to catch sight of the diacons through slits in the wall.

"We can't have an attraction like this," Raena whispered, "this sort of attention is likely what the diacons are looking for. They are making a statement about something."

"And your people see you catering to it," Jonn-Del grumbled.

Raena ignored her urge to lean back into the shadows at his accusation. Instead, she leaned further out, and raised her voice again. "Diacons! I am your ruler, Prince Trevin. If you do not explain yourselves to me, I will have no choice but to assume you are assembling for a…conflict! We will deal with you accordingly. My archers are standing by."

The center diacon lowered his arm. Even though he was half a furlong away, his face appeared somber. Raena felt the weight of his stare.

The diacon called out, "We do not bring conflict. We bring the end."

Jonn-Del muttered something indistinct beside her, but Raena held up a hand to silence him.

"Explain what the end is," Raena said.

"Your end. It is our beginning."

Fjall moved closer, speaking quietly. "Majesty, that's a threat on your life. You must strike them down for it—"

"Enough," Raena replied, then called out the window again. "You are here to ask for something. Tell me what your demands are so that we may move forward with this. I have other matters to attend to."

The diacon shook his head. "The end is not a demand. The end is a debt, and it is already owed."

Raena clenched her fists. The temptation to shoot them with arrows was building within her, and she might want to draw first blood. She thought back to that diacon—perhaps the same one—who gave her the cryptic message in the low chambers a season before. She thought of how his message seemed to allude to his knowledge of one person. She turned, her heart beginning to race, and stared Fjall in the eyes.

"I want you to fetch two people for me," Raena whispered. "The master-of-arms, as I said. I also want you to bring my East Shore advisor. Her name is Duchess Avenna. She might be in the bailey, or near the inner pig barns. You need to find her."

Fjall nodded, his brow furrowed. "Of course, my liege."

As Fjall made a hasty exit, Jonn-Del scoffed behind Raena. "She's no one. She's nothin'. This has nothin' to do with her."

Raena spun, her eyes ablaze. "These diacons know something. One of them spoke to me about secrets of the bloodlines. They have information that you, of all people, will never want to leave their mouths. You've pulled me into this, don't deny it. If I have to carry this and cover your secrets, then I will do it my own way."

Jonn-Del's jaw clenched. He spoke through his teeth. "Your threat is out there, beyond the curtain. Why don't you focus on the matters at hand?"

"The diacons have not moved. For all I know, they plan to be statues in the sand. I won't strike down men for standing."

Jonn-Del muttered something under his breath, and Raena didn't bother to ask.

She cast one more studious gaze out the window, scanning the outlines of their robes for possible hidden weapons, and finding no evidence. Her archers and legion men were restlessly shifting along the parapet without orders.

Then, Raena heard a new sound.

It was light through the desert wind, barely enough to make out. It was as though a whisper came from a sword in the distance and told a story of its conflict through the breeze.

But Raena heard it again, and again, growing in number.

"Jonn-Del," she whispered, staring out. She searched for any clue; rising patterns of dust, bumps in the ground, shadows across the sandy horizon.

"What is it, Trevin?"

"Do you hear it?"

Jonn-Del shook his head.

Raena grabbed him, cupping her hand behind his ear and motioning him closer to the window. "Jonn-Del," she repeated, "that sound. Blade on blade. That's an army. Do you hear it now?"

His brown eyes grew wide and his mouth dropped open with surprise and fear. He jerked backward, instinctively grabbing for his side sword. "I hear it. We must assemble the guards."

Without waiting for instruction, Jonn-Del burst out of the room. Raena sprinted after him, only a few paces behind. They ran down the stairs, clamoring to get through the tower and out to the parapets.

"Everyone is assembled near the diacons!" Raena shouted at his back. "We have to spread them across the walls!"

"I know!" Jonn-Del yelled over his shoulder.

They continued to run and reached a landing that separated the wing into two corridors. One direction would lead to the parapet, the other would wind down to the stables and livestockery.

Jonn-Del was already sprinting through the corridor to the parapet. Raena thought to tell him of her destination, but waited until he had rounded the corner instead. Without a word, she turned and gave haste toward the stables.

As she ran down another flight of stairs, she met with a cluster of three knights, carrying pieces of armor, training weapons, and dressed for banquet.

"Majesty," they greeted, out of breath.

"Go to the west corner," Raena directed, not breaking her stride, "we have weak sides, you must defend them."

"Defend from…?" a knight asked.

Raena was past them and yelled over her shoulder. "Get to the west, and take any men with you that you come across!"

She reached the lower chambers and broke into the hallway outside one group of servant quarters. Raena stopped; her way blocked by dozens of peasants assembled to wait in hope for a meal. They wrapped and piled up like grains in a trough, spreading too thick to count and winding through every archway. They may have filled every chamber and corridor beyond, possibly out to the bailey. Raena calculated her next move, wondering where she could run, knowing it was likely she would only have one chance to flow through the packed crowd.

"Make way!" Raena bellowed in her best princely command voice.

The peasants nearest scattered, pushing one another aside. They muttered "it's the prince" in hushed whispers. It had been loud with the echoes of their conversation, but now it was deafening as their panicked voices rang off the uncovered walls.

Raena pushed into the crowd, continuing to demand they make way for her. She hated the way they cowered and apologized, as though she was someone to fear.

"Majesty!" a distinctly noble voice called from behind her.

Raena felt a hand on her elbow and glanced to see Sir Taygar, a knight of renown.

"Prince, you need an escort," Taygar said, grumbling a bit. "These peasants are hungry and volatile. They are liable to turn against you."

Raena bit her tongue, knowing she was behaving foolishly. "We must prepare the castle. There is something afoot—"

"Yes, I have just seen Fjall. He is a panicked mess. I sent him onward to the master-of-arms." Taygar held out his arm to hold back a few peasants, shouting for them to clear aside for the prince. He kept one hand back to guide Raena as he took the lead.

Then Raena heard the sharp blast of the battle horn. The master-of-arms must have been found, and was alerting the troops for battle.

Pandemonium broke out. The peasants around reacted to the horn with panic and screams. Raena felt them begin to push from all sides as they disregarded her presence in their fear.

"Majesty!" Taygar shouted, his hand the only part visible through the crowd, reaching backward. Raena grabbed his fingers and clung to them while a particularly strong peasant boy collided with her ribs. She managed to not let go of Taygar, and he pulled her forward.

Taygar shouted again for the crowd to clear. It was enough to break through the remaining few panicked serfs blocking the archway. Raena followed close behind and they burst out into the open bailey. There were still far more peasants out in the courtyard than ought to be, now running and scattering, trying to scramble for their belongings and get to safety.

"Sorry, Your Majesty," Taygar said, out of breath, "the people are desperate for food. I've never seen them so defiant."

"It's alright," Raena dismissed, searching the bailey for any sign of Aven.

"Where do you need to be, Prince Trevin? May I help you get to the legions? They will be awaiting your orders by now."

"No, first I need to find the Duchess Avenna. Do you know her? Can you help me search for her?"

Taygar nodded. "Aye, the pig farm girl. We all know her; she's oft around the training grounds. Is she…to help with the battle?"

Raena shot the knight a glance, trying to say her authority ought not be questioned. But she was met with an open expression of curiosity from young Taygar. "Perhaps," Raena answered, "she may need protection. I need to find her."

"Aye," Taygar muttered. He joined Raena in scanning the bailey, a difficult task with the many people running about. "I can't see much from here. I could climb the guard ladders and get a better look. Will you wait here a moment, Majesty?"

Raena glanced at his weapons. "Do you mind lending me your short sword, in case the walls are breached?"

"Of course," Taygar said, "it would be an honor." He smiled as he brandished the sword, presenting the blade with a bow.

"Thank you."

"My pleasure. I will return in a moment," Taygar said, then he scurried toward the edge of the bailey.

Raena waited, searching, grasping and weighing the new sword in her hands. Something about gripping the hilt of a sword gave her a bit of peace in the midst of her fear. She would need a better weapon if the walls were breached, something that would expand her reach, like a poleax. For now, this was a hint of sanity and control among the chaos.

"Prince Trevin!"

Raena glanced about.

"Prince! Up here!"

She looked higher to see Taygar, dangling from the ladder with one arm. His other arm extended, pointing to the far eastern edge of the bailey. "There! At the carts!"

Raena snapped to follow his gesture, unable to see. Without wasting a moment, she darted into the direction he indicated. She shouted "pardon me" as she dodged a horseman, then a mother gathering up her screaming child. Raena nearly clipped an old man lugging a grain sack, only to step to the side and barely miss a pack of guards running together, shouting for everyone to move aside.

Another horn blast.

This was a blast of three distinct calls, trilling over the citadel. It was followed by the booming beat of drums.

The war drums.

The castle was indeed under attack, and the walls had been breached.

Raena broke into a dead run, sprinting through the bailey. Shouting continued all around her, and there was no point in trying to yell over it all. She was halfway across the generous grounds when she spotted the familiar figure of Aven at a distance.

The duchess seemed trapped in time, still, with her hands to her chest. She indeed stood near the carts, filled with wares and supplies to be counted for the castles' stores. Uneasy guards were in a ring around the carts, watching the panicked citizens, prepared for the worst.

Aven was a beacon, and Raena was the ship in the storm, steady onward to her destination.

"Prince! You must get to safety!" Raena heard someone cry. It was a familiar voice, perhaps Jonn-Del?

She wasn't turning back now. She had to reach Aven.

CHAPTER 23
RAENA

The arena

"Aven!" Raena shouted.

Her hazel eyes seemed to snap out of the trance she was in. Aven was wearing a purple noble lady's dress and holding a small jar of seeds, out shopping from the traveling merchants in the bailey. Her eyes were alight as though the growing chaos around her had caused her to pause midstep in confusion.

But Aven jolted forward at the sound of Raena's voice. She dropped her jar into the dirt.

Another band of guards ran between them, stopping Raena in her tracks. The moment they cleared, Raena and Aven were united.

She couldn't help the overwhelming emotion, and Raena reached for her, pulling Aven into a tight embrace. At first, Aven was firm, startled, but after half a second perhaps, she melted and returned the affection. Her hands tentatively wrapped around Raena's back, holding them close.

Raena spoke into Aven's unruly dark hair. "There's a battle coming. I think the diacons have something to do with it, but it may be the Boens."

Aven squeezed, shrinking as her face pressed deeper into Raena's shoulder. "The Boens couldn't have come so soon. They are waiting for the treaty."

"Perhaps they changed their minds. You must get up to the towers. I will take you to the royal wing."

Aven pulled away, surprise in her eyes. "You have to defend the castle. You have to lead your army."

"The master-of-arms and the generals will lead them. Come on," Raena reached down to take Aven's hand.

"No, Ro—Trevin. Prince. Please," she lowered her voice, "you cannot protect me before your kingdom. I will see myself to the tower."

Raena leaned in and whispered once more. "It's madness in this bailey, and it's madness in the castle. You will never make it to the tower if I don't see you there. Please, come with me. I will fight this battle when you are out of view."

"My life is not this important, Trevin. It's not worth saving above the thousands of your—"

"It is this important."

They held each other with stubborn gazes, Raena reflecting the same insistence she saw written on Aven's face.

A second passed without either one of them relenting.

"Prince?" a man's voice interrupted.

Raena glanced to see a guard from the circle around the carts, breaking ranks to address her. "Yes?"

"My liege," he bowed, "ought we stay here with the grains, or join the others at the parapets? I'm sorry to ask you, Your Majesty, it's only that…there's no one else here to give orders."

Raena nodded. "Of course. Leave your post and go find the next legionmen to direct you. Make sure you have enough weapons to fight."

The guard pursed his lips and bowed again, muttering his gratitude.

Raena didn't wait for more of an argument from Aven. "Come with me, Duchess, I promise I will lead this fight once you are in the tower."

With a light pull of her hand, Aven consented. The two of them began to run.

Raena led them away from the kitchens and servant halls where the peasants were likely to still be clustered, perhaps worse than before. She took the long way around the banquet halls, nearly toward the training grounds that Prince Zander had built for the Knight's Trial. As they entered the streets of the citadel, Raena's memory flashed back in an instant to that day: the day of the Trial. She kept Aven close to her side as a cart and horse passed by, reminding her of how she and Finn had ridden borrowed horses and later walked through the citadel in their full suits of armor. There were obstacles to dodge—mostly market tents being packed up or abandoned by their merchants. Ahead were the smithy hovels, anchors, and hot open ovens lining the side of the streets. Raena tried to give plenty of room, putting herself between Aven and the flames, but the rest of the quick-paced crowd was doing the same. It was as much madness as she'd seen in the bailey.

"We're going away from the tower," Aven shouted, making herself heard over the chaos.

"I know," Raena yelled back, "we have to go through the proving ground."

Aven tensed, her fingers tightening between Raena's with a hard squeeze, but they pressed onward.

When they reached the corner of the proving ground, Raena was struck by how vivid her memory was. It was the exact same moment she had relived in her dreams for over a year. It was the same tent flap she had imagined herself going back to when she thought back to that moment.

Raena reached for the canvas flap and pushed it aside, pulling Aven into the darkness. Her eyes adjusted immediately, and Raena could see everything as bright as day. They were inside the assembly tent where the knights and squires had been gathered before the Trial. She remembered the nervous clang of metal as she and Finn anxiously anticipated the start. She remembered the roar of the crowd, not unlike the sounds she heard now, but coming from the opposite direction of inside instead of behind them. She remembered the pages calling for them all to enter the arena, without any idea of what to expect. Raena could still smell the blood in the air and the scent of horses and the metal of their weapons.

"Where are we?" Aven asked, her voice sounding timid.

Raena tensed. In her dreams and fantasies, she went back to this exact place, so many times. She imagined herself on that day, refusing to jump the walls, and calling to Finn not to break the rules. She imagined fighting through the labyrinth of Prince Zander's hideous game, endangering her life but emerging according to his sick plan. She imagined never receiving his attention, simply being lost among the other knights, with some other poor bastard named the victor of the Trials.

But then she imagined seeing Aven's face in the crowd, speaking of her beauty, and wooing her.

Raena felt a well burst inside her, flooding her. It was the memory of Aven: innocent, open, unafraid. It was a different Aven, a woman who had not seen the death of her family, the death of her brother, her duchy torn to ruin, and the betrayal of her true love.

Raena turned and pulled Aven closer to her in the dark so their bodies were nearly flush. "Duchess, I'm so sorry."

Aven's hesitance was clear. She stiffened at their proximity, her body tense. "What...why?"

Raena leaned down so her lips hovered at the edge of Aven's ear. "All of it. I'm so sorry, I've been such an ass. This is the place I was right before I saw you for the very first time. This is where we came before the Trial."

"Oh," Aven whispered.

"If I could go back to that moment, there is so much I would do differently. But most of all, I would go back and start it all over again with you."

Aven sighed and her shoulders relaxed. She tipped her shoulders, letting her arm brush against Raena's chest. Her voice dropped lower when she spoke, "What...what would you do?"

258

"I would choose to follow you back to East Shore. I would have rushed to show you that I was there to serve you. I would have followed you to the other Houses, the same as I did, except this time I would be more careful. I wouldn't have rushed to touch you. I would have been slower to get to know you, and to tell you my secret before we kissed."

Aven chuckled, her breath warm on Raena's face. "You act like that was all up to you. I'm the one who kissed you first, remember?"

"Of course, but…I would have told you who I was. All of it. And then I wouldn't have left your side. I should never have gone."

"You can't be upset with yourself for that forever. I was the one who asked you to leave."

There was a bang outside, as though something large fell to the ground, followed by a few urgent shouts.

"Rae…" Aven whispered, "we have to hurry."

"I know, but I need to say this," Raena said, pulling back to look into Aven's eyes. "Can you even see me now?"

"Yes, a little. There's not much light in here. You can see just fine, can't you?"

"Yes."

Aven nodded. "What is it?"

"I promised you after the Boens came that I wouldn't leave you again. I can't forgive myself for breaking that promise. I can't even live with myself after what I've done…how I've hurt you."

"Rae, stop. We've talked about this. You didn't mean to leave me behind the caravan, you didn't even know that Jonn asked me to leave. How could you know what he said to me?"

"I should have."

Aven grimaced and turned her face toward the ground. Her cheek was toward Raena's chest, nearly resting there, hiding. "Did you even…look for me?"

Raena balked, "I sent Allyn to look for you. All of the time. From the moment we arrived in Candeo and unpacked the caravans. I didn't see you there. I knew you were likely furious with me but I demanded he find you so that I could at least know you were safe."

Aven was quiet.

Raena resisted the growing urge to kiss the top of Aven's head. "I'm sorry. I never should have trusted him. Of course, he didn't tell me he'd found you until he had found a way to make it hurt me and benefit him somehow. I should have gone to find you myself. I should never have tried to…manipulate you into pretending with me. It was his fucking idea."

Aven lifted her chin, "Pretending? You mean that night in the caravan?"

Raena nodded, "he told me that no one believed I was really a man because I was too chaste. He said I had to convince you to 'spread your legs' for me and he would bring a crowd. So, they would finally stop gossiping and believe I was like any other man. But…"

It was quiet for a moment. Aven lightly pressed her fingertips to Raena's chest. "But, what?"

Raena sighed. "But I was hearing what I wanted to. No one was questioning my secret, and I knew it. I was trying to brag. I was trying to be like him. I was jealous of how he got all the attention of those girls, the way he didn't care about them, the way he was always so arrogant and calm. The way he acted as though everything belonged to him, simply because he had a big mustache and a cock. He was such a prick, especially after he knew my secret. When he found out about you and I, he was always angry. You were the one girl he couldn't have. And he never let me forget that he could…that he could give you something I couldn't."

Aven shook her head. "I never wanted that. I never wanted him."

"I know. Of course, I know that now. I just wanted him to see us together. I wanted to show him that I could…make you happy."

"Make me 'happy'?" Aven laughed. She leaned back and looked up at Raena, her hazel eyes wet with tears. She wiped one away as it began down her cheek. "You wanted him to see that you could fuck me, that's what you're sorry about."

"Yes. I'm ashamed…but yes."

"Why did it take you so long to understand that?"

Raena shook her head with a sigh. "I thought…I wanted to be one of them. I've always wanted to be one of them. One of the knights. One of the men."

"That's who you had to be to survive."

"No, it isn't. Not really. I had to pretend to be like them, but I never meant…I don't know how it happened. I wanted to be a man like Lord Sylas, or like Finn. Honorable, respectful, chivalrous. But one day I woke up and I was with Jonn and Allyn and I realized that I was one of them, instead."

Aven nodded, her eyes opening with recognition and reflection.

"I think…" Raena continued, "I think I just want to go back. Before all of this. I can't change everything else that has happened, but I want to go back to who I was."

Slowly, Aven slid her hand upward until her palm covered Raena's cheek. "You are better now than you were then. You are growing into a better leader, a better person. You are someone to be proud of. You are someone deserving of love."

Raena let out a shallow breath, fighting back the threat of her pain escaping in tears. Before she could, Aven pulled her forward, bringing their lips together in a searing kiss. Aven's lips tasted of sweet and salt, and felt warmer than Raena remembered. Raena struggled to catch her breath between the urgent presses of their mouths.

It was so overdue. It was coated with passion that Raena hadn't felt between them since the moments they had been in the forests—before Ediva, before the death of the Queen, before the cursed caravan.

The heat of their kiss held everything. It held love. It held forgiveness. It held sorrow. It held sex and desire. Raena felt her heart race into a pulse that shot through her spine, screaming at her body for attention from beneath every inch of her skin.

There was another chorus of shouts from outside the tent. Raena heard the clang of metal and she pulled away, holding Aven at arm's length.

"We must go," Raena breathed. "I am…I missed you. But we have to go."

"Wait," Aven said, pulling Raena in for another kiss. Her lips pulled with insistence, her tongue darting out to brush against Raena's with a quick flutter. When she moved away, the air between them was thick with her panting breaths. "Yes, now. Now we should go."

Raena nodded, unable to form words. She grabbed Aven's hand and led her through the darkness across the long tent. She could have closed her eyes and found her way, so familiar with every piece of her memory of this place.

She easily found the other side, grabbing the far opening and pulling the tent open. A wave of nausea hit her as they entered the arena. She remembered thinking of the walls akin to the layers of a croissant, folding endlessly over one another. Oddly, it felt smaller than Raena had remembered.

The training dummies were still there, along with the boulders and the upper "nests" for the archers and crossbowmen to sit. Ahead, along the wall, Raena spotted a hanging display of weapons. She ran to it, Aven staying close behind.

"How are you with a sword?" Raena asked.

"Not as good as I'd like to be. I'm better with a butcher's knife."

Raena raised an eyebrow, glancing with a wary expression.

Aven smirked. "What? You know that I am."

"Might be too soon to mock his death but…forget it, you're damn right." Raena reached up to grab a short scythe, the pole holding a curved blade. "What about this? Did you use one of these in the fields for your pigs?"

"Sure, to cut grain."

"Good. You can slice a man's knees with it." Raena handed it to Aven. "Take this too, you can wear it on your back." She took down a square shield with a leather strap, helping to fasten it over Aven's thin shoulders.

"This is heavy, I won't be able to run with it."

"You can throw it off if you need to, but hopefully it won't come to that."

Aven nodded, hoisting the shield higher. She looked a bit out of sorts, wearing her fine lavender dress, wielding a scythe and shield. But Raena reckoned that fashion would be damned if this battle evolved into war.

Raena grabbed for herself a short poleax and another side sword, attaching both the short weapons to her hips.

"Don't you need a shield?" Aven asked.

"I'm the Prince. If anyone gets close enough to me for that, I'm already fucked."

Aven swallowed audibly. Raena chose not to acknowledge it. "Come on, I'll carry your shield. We have to climb up to the stands, unless we want to jump these walls."

"Oh, you aren't going to teach me how to do it, Sir Wall-jumper?"

Raena giggled. "I could, but then you wouldn't be so enamored with me when you see how easy it is."

They jogged to the edge of the arena and Raena dropped to one knee, offering her hands. Aven stepped up, and Raena lifted her to the sidewall, standing to push Aven up higher until she could clear the structure. Aven rolled, falling into the stands on the other side. Raena tossed the shield, then the poleax up and over. With a quick leap, Raena grabbed the edge, then climbed with her feet up, making her body an arch until she managed to swing one leg over the top.

"How did you make that look so easy?" Aven marveled.

"Boen sorcery. I'm basically a fox with a girl-body."

"I miss that girl-body."

Raena blushed, stumbling as she picked up the shield and poleax. "W—we...we better go. This way. Erm..."

Aven was still laughing as they broke into a jog across the stands toward the royal viewing box. It was a long distance and climb, but they could make it. There was no one else in the arena.

As they climbed over the barriers dividing the seats for the peasants into the seats for nobles, Raena heard the telltale signs of conflict growing outside the arena. Battle had a smell, a taste, a feeling in the air. Raena had learned it well. She knew the shouts of men who were fighting for their lives.

She called for Aven to hurry; they were nearly to their destination. She held the weapons to allow for her duchess to make it without struggling. They both entered the upper viewing area where Prince Zander had been seated during Raena's Trial. She shuddered at the thought of him that day, smug and belligerent, so proud of the arena he demanded for. So spoiled and arrogant.

At the opposite end of the platform was an entrance to the noble tower. Normally it would have been guarded or patrolled, but there was no one in sight. Raena led through, prepared to answer questions from anyone who might approach them as they walked through the arch and entered the castle once more.

It was a short distance to the noble wing. They passed a few lords, knights, and guards running through the halls. Each of them seemed far too preoccupied to give care or notice to who Raena had in tow. The guards were the sole men who bowed and greeted Raena, the others were lost in their haste.

Raena came to her quarters, the only room still guarded. The two young men on either side of the door were glancing nervously about, as though they were sure to be cut down by invaders at any moment.

"Your Majesty," the first guard said, giving a bow. His voice squeaked as though at the start of puberty.

Raena nodded. "Gentlemen, I need you to maintain your post. This is Duchess Avenna of East Shore. Her life is to be defended at all costs. If you abandon this room or leave her behind, you'll be jailed for treason. Do not leave this post, no matter what happens."

The guards nodded, but then the first opened his mouth, starting a question.

"What is it?" Raena asked, "Go ahead."

"So sorry, my Prince," the guard muttered, "but if the horn blasts five times, all men are to respond to war. That's…do you mean that we ignore the battle call?"

"Yes, I do. That's a good question, lad. You are to not leave the duchess, no matter what happens. If you must leave, it will only be to aid in her escape and take her out of the castle."

The guards glanced at one another, then nodded in compliance.

Raena turned to Aven, handing her the shield and scythe. "Stay in the chamber, unless you think you must escape."

"Of course, my Prince."

"Whatever happens, I promise I'll be back for you."

Aven smirked. "I'll pretend I haven't heard that before."

"Ouch, my Lady," Raena covered her heart, "please don't wound me before I've even had a chance to join the battle."

"Oh, is this the time for us to jest? As we probably say goodbye?"

Raena shook her head. "No, it's absolutely not the time for that." She leaned in and stole a deep, passionate kiss, ignoring the uncomfortable sound of shuffling from the juvenile guards to her side. As they pulled away, Aven glanced toward the young boys, seeming dismayed that Raena had kissed her so boldly and openly.

Raena turned to the guards and winked. "Not a word about that, lads. You're both going to be heroes if you save the future Princess, or perhaps the future Queen."

"Now you're proposing marriage, Prince Trevin?"

Raena stepped back, fighting a pink tint to her cheeks. "Erm, I'm afraid I must lead my men into battle. No time for…talking."

Aven raised an eyebrow. Within a moment, Raena was bounding off, running to the stairs and through the tower.

Running into the sound of battle.

CHAPTER 24
RAENA

A battle

The legions were at the gates. They were so thick they surrounded the crack in the curtain like flies swarmed atop discarded meat. When Raena left the castle and entered the space between the walls and the curtain, she could make no sense of the fight. All she could see were the heads of men, buckling on top, moving as one jumbled mass. They shouted and seemed to pull from one side to the other.

Raena ran. Her feet pounding in to the dry straw grass and sand until she reached an open space where she could see in more than two directions.

The eastern curtain gate was splintered. It somehow had been rammed or perhaps closed on itself and ripped by its chains. On the parapets above, the archers were restless, staring down without clear targets to fire upon. Raena's own legion army blocked the shots, fighting in such disorder that she assumed some of them might have struck their own battle partner if they swung an arm.

Raena turned and cupped her hands around her mouth, yelling up toward the parapet. "Let me up! It's I, Prince Trevin. Let me up!"

She saw a few men disappear from the wall, then a long rope ladder rolled down. Without wasting a second, Raena ran to it and ascended as rapidly as she could muster.

When she reached the top, she searched the rampart for anyone wearing a general's collar or even a knight, finding only a bumbling crowd of archers.

"Where is your commanding officer?" Raena asked.

A few of them muttered unintelligible replies.

"Answer me," Raena snapped.

One of the archers pointed below, toward the gate. "General Ursh had command, but he joined the fight. We are waiting for Sir Han'black to return, he went to the other side of the castle."

"What's at the other side? The western side?"

"Another breach, Your Majesty."

Raena bit her lip. "Who is commanding the legions? General Ursh?"

"Yes, and General Phall. He is…we're not sure where he is."

Raena shook her head. "Not anymore. I'll speak to the master-of-arms, and the generals. You are under my command now." She cleared her throat, then spoke loud enough to call across the rampart. "I am your Prince, and you are now under my command. Your first order is to spread along this wall! Lift your arms out from your sides and move until you cannot touch the man beside you! Now!"

With haste, the archers spread, complying. Within seconds they were spread so far that they disappeared around the corner, likely stretching to the northern and southern sides of the castle. Raena looked up to the higher ramparts, seeing the other archers following suit.

Without the men gaggled together, she was able to freely run past them along the ramparts. At the halfway mark, she could see over the curtain to where their enemy was gathered, attempting to climb the curtain and simultaneously push through the curtain breach.

Diacons.

There were hundreds of them, dressed in the same white robes. From the looks of them, they may have been peasants, serfs, or the like. Perhaps some of them were even Ruvians, for all Raena could reckon. Every last one of them had painted their faces and hands shades of blue and purple, even the bearded men. Their morbid disguises were reminiscent of a person being choked to death.

They were holding crude weapons of all kinds: butcher tools, blacksmith tools, farming tools, sticks, branches, pieces of chain.

They were not unlike the bandits that were constantly attacking the farms. Except this was not the prince's farm, this was the castle.

Raena's fist clenched around her poleax as she felt the anger bubbling inside her. She was tempted to make the same mistake as General Ursh—no wonder the man had seen himself fit to rush into the battle. Surely, he got a glimpse of the 'enemy' and felt he could destroy all of them in a light afternoon. But Raena wouldn't be so brash. Arrogant mistakes could cost them far too many lives for such a wasteful conflict.

She clenched her teeth, angry that she hadn't fired down on those seven leaders from when she first had that chance. Angrier too that Jonn-Del had been right.

"You, you," Raena gestured to two of the archers, "follow me. I hope you are good shots."

The two archers were young boys, like all of Raena's men seemed to be. At least one of them had begun to grow patches of hair on his chin.

The boys followed as Raena sprinted around the parapet, due north. They kept up as she shouted for everyone to stay out of her way. She rounded the corner and was met with another long wall ahead, duly supplied with a single-file line of archers. At the far corner, Raena spotted another cluster of men. She charged toward them, knowing at once they were knights.

When she came closer, they turned in her direction.

"Sir Taygar," Raena greeted, catching her breath as she approached.

Taygar bowed, as did the other two; Jaye and Ja'quill.

268

"Your Majesty," Taygar replied, "we are watching this curtain. It appears the enemy is climbing beneath that section. They have made some sort of tunnel."

Raena peered down to see the tunnel in question, but the terra appeared undisturbed. "How can you tell?"

"It's not easy to see," Taygar said, "but we know there was a line of them, and now that line is much smaller. We think they have a place that they emerge from, just inside the castle."

Raena squinted, covering her eyes from the harsh sunlight above. It would be far easier for her to see in shadow or the dark. But she could make out a line of the men, robed like the others, disappearing into the curtain.

"We were about to climb down," Taygar explained, "there's no one covering this section."

"We'll all go," Raena replied. "How many of them do you estimate?"

Taygar shrugged. "Perhaps two dozen, if they've all come through."

Raena nodded and turned to the two archers behind her. "I want the two of you to follow behind us, and stay on the ground a few dozen paces behind. We are going to find you a way to get outside the curtain. When you've found it, we'll call for more archers. I want to get a least fifty archers outside the curtain, into the desert. You'll stand back-to-back and fire every arrow into these crowds of…robed people."

"Right, yes Your Majesty," the archers muttered, gazing at one another with uncertainty.

"It'll be alright," Raena assured. "I'll find a way out for you, and all the others will follow. Now, let's get down there."

Taygar nodded, grabbing a rope ladder and tossing it off the edge.

Raena was the first to descend.

She peered down between her legs as she moved down the ladder and spotted them. They were hanging tight to the inner wall, hugging the bricks where they wouldn't be seen by archers above. There were a dozen so far, and another crawled from a hole in the dirt as Raena watched.

She took care to move as quietly as she could, thankful that the ladder ended above the ground where they hadn't yet noticed. When Raena reached the end, she felt the jerking motion from the knights above joining her on the ladder, making their own descent.

Raena grabbed her poleax from the hook on her back and brandished it, then dangled from the ladder rung with one arm. She listened as the mock diacons whispered to one another, helping another from out of the ground tunnel. Raena glanced to either side, assessing where to go, then let herself drop with a thud.

As soon as her feet hit the ground, they came rushing toward her.

Raena swung, the blade of her poleax connecting instantly with a man's face, slicing through his cheek. He fell, and the next was right behind. Raena caught his shoulder on her backswing, driving the blunt end of her weapon against his torso, then it bounced and sheared his nose clean off. He screamed before the blood began to flow, already a monster, raising a farmer's scythe.

His arm was above his head as he lunged forward, leaving his chest open. Raena hit him in the sternum with the tip of her blade, driving it in and ripping upward. There was a catch as she felt the poleax sinking between his ribs and she jerked downward before he could fall forward and trap the weapon. He collapsed, giving way to two more of them, rushing her.

Raena darted back, then ran. The gap between the castle wall and the outer curtain was ten meters. If she could make enough space, her archers would have clean shots. That is, if her archers were worth their salt.

When she was ahead of them at the curtain, she turned to brace herself for them to follow. They had and were running toward her. Raena cast a glance upward at the archers along the parapet. A few of them had raised their bows, tracking the invaders, but none of them were firing.

"Scared bastards, come on," Raena muttered, shaking her head. She shuffled to the side, putting more space between her and the oncoming invaders. It was to no avail. A few arrows dropped, far off into the sand, nowhere near their targets.

270

It was a pathetic attempt.

"Guess I'll kill all of them, then?" Raena grumbled. She raised her poleax as the group made it to her.

The pack was grouped as three, and these robed men were definitely Ruvians. Their braided hair and beards were painted blue, but their white dresses were filthy and made from canvas sacks. Raena knew before they attacked that they could fight.

The center Ruvian swung a blacksmith hammer, and Raena flipped her poleax to hit him in the chin with the handle. She continued the circular motion to strike the man to his right with her blade, burying it into his shoulder with a pop. Her weapon was still sunk in when the third man reached wide and spun. There was nothing Raena could do to stop or block as he connected a butcher's chain into her ribs. She grunted as it wrapped around and whipped her back with a brutal blow.

Raena used the leverage of her poleax as a beam, holding it with stiff arms and swinging both her legs upward. She tucked, then kicked the Ruvian nearest her. Her feet landed square in his chest, and he flew back. The weight of her bearing down on the weapon caused the man with it lodged in his shoulder to crumble and collapse to the ground.

Raena ripped her poleax free and ducked half a second before the chain came whipping over her head, barely missing her right ear. The wind rushed around her with a whistling sound. From below, she had an easy shot to the chain-wielder's knees. She shot backwards, still crouched, and yelled as she swung the hammer end.

The Ruvian screamed, his leg contorting to an unnatural angle. He buckled and dropped his chain, crying on the ground.

Raena looked beyond the three Ruvians to see the next onslaught of robed men had been intercepted by Taygar and the other two knights. Beyond them, the two archers were shaking with fear at the castle wall, waiting near the ladder.

Before any of the three men could get back up, Raena swung her hammer down as if chopping a block of wood. In three rapid swoops, she crushed their skulls.

271

Then she ran.

She avoided the knights and their robed opponents, running around them to get back to the interior wall. When she reached it, she gestured to the archers.

"Come on, get right behind me. We're going through."

The two archers stared at her as though they didn't understand. There was no time for their defiance or questions, and Raena dropped to her knees, peering into the tunnel.

She could see into it until it curved. Of course, it was pitch dark inside. She looked over her shoulder and said; "No matter what happens in there, don't make a fucking sound, you understand?"

It was clear by their expressions the archers thought their Prince was a madman, but they came closer, falling to their knees.

Raena hooked her poleax to her back and climbed down into the tunnel, dropping underground.

The first thing she felt was comfort.

The dampness of the terra. The musty smell of the ground. The enveloping darkness, suited to her eyes.

Raena shook her head, hating how right it felt to be underground. Hating how much it felt right to be…a Boen.

She crawled through an opening, almost like a throat, and into a stomach-like cavern where the area opened up. It was barely enough for her to stand. Ahead she could see a straight chamber ahead, with the looks of what had once been a usable connecting series of tunnels. It was definitely part of the old Boen caves, or maybe dwellings older than that. No doubt someone in the kingdom had discovered this path under the curtain and was waiting to use it for the right moment. But why had they given it to the diacons?

The two archers were breathing behind her, bumping into one another.

Raena turned to them and whispered, "Just stay right behind me."

"Your Majesty, we can't see you," the archer whispered back.

"I know. Just keep moving forward, then."

She felt them grasp blindly to touch her back with their fingertips. When she moved forward, they kept on fumbling ahead, too.

Then she saw it. Movement at the far end of the cave.

Two robed men were feeling their way, their hands on the wet walls, taking a snail's pace ahead.

Raena pulled out her shortsword slow, easy, and silent. With her other hand, she placed a palm on the archer's chest, holding him still until he nodded his head, understanding. The two archers were still. Waiting.

Raena walked through the chamber alone. Her feet were light and silent, like a fox. She crept, crouching halfway, watching the two robed men.

They had no knowledge of her presence. They whispered to one another, stumbling in the darkness, their faces taut and squinting, hoping to see something ahead but failing.

Raena studied them. They were Candorian, she could easily tell. Peasants, perhaps. The taller of the two men had allowed his hood to fall off, and he wore a brother's braid in his hair. She hated to kill one of her own servants, especially one who had a brother, but she shook that thought from her mind. This was a battle. These men were committing treason against the crown. Whatever reason they decided to turn against her, they threatened Candor.

Raena was close enough to hear them talking. She stopped for a moment and waited, listening to their whispers.

"But what if we die?"

"Living this way has been worse than death. Don't forget what Zander did to our families. This new Prince is no better."

"But if we're dead—"

"This is the only way. We either starve to death, or we die heroes building a new Candor. Your choice."

Raena wanted to scoff at them. She wanted to tell them how stupid their plan was; how wrong they were not to trust her. She wanted to remind them that Zander had also been her enemy, and correct them for thinking she was anything like him. Most of all, she wanted to tell them they didn't know the first thing about how fucking hard it was to be a prince, and how many times she had to make decisions to help them. They would be grateful if they knew the truth.

But then she glanced at the makeshift weapons tied to their sides. They had made a choice. They said it themselves; they were willing to die for this grievance.

In a heartbeat, in the total darkness, Raena held her shortsword up and drew the blade fast across the taller man's neck. He cried out, gripping the wound and gurgling a warning. The second man tensed, startled. His hands raised but not in time. Raena slit his throat as she had done to the first, then grabbed him by the hair to help him down, out of her way.

She stepped on their bodies, which were still convulsing on the wet ground, then she ran through the rest of the cave. At the other end, another portal, and another tight opening. She squeezed through easily and found a crude wooden ladder to grant her way out.

Two pairs of eyes were peering down from the hole above, and they disappeared when she ascended.

As Raena emerged, she watched with caution to see how many men she was up against. But all she saw were the white backs of their robes as the invaders fled, running across the sand.

Then she heard it.

Five horn blasts.

A general had fallen. The legion had fallen. The invaders were taking the castle.

Raena would now be the only one to lead her armies to defend Candeo. And all of her 'armies' were untrained and unaccustomed to battle.

The horn blasts meant that every man who was able to fight was demanded to do so. Even her peasants. Even her farmers. Even the religious. But what if those men able to fight had already joined the battle—on the other side?

Raena scrambled back down, this time bolting through the tunnel. She was through in a few seconds, shouting for her archers to follow. She left them behind to find their own way as she exited the portal, back within the curtain. She reckoned it would take her less than five minutes to reach the stables and take a horse, if no one blocked her path.

Again, she passed the knights fighting the small group of invaders. The invaders were fewer now, she counted six still standing. But only two knights against them. As Raena ran, her legs pumping in a sprint, she scanned the bodies that had succumbed to the battle, and spotted Taygar among them. His eyes were open, staring up to the sky, gone from the world.

Raena ran onward. She rounded a corner of the castle and saw the far arch that led from the bailey to the stables. She remembered when she and Finn had gone there together, and he had pissed in the sand. She saw the dry, desolate fields. The grain had been harvested and the crops couldn't recover with the lack of water to share through the kingdom. It was everywhere she looked: this desperate and dying Candor.

She heard the sound of battle, deeper within the citadel. There were bodies scattered around as she reached the arch, but no one to stop her. She passed a small group of guards running toward the sound of the fight, and she cheered them on.

"I'll be right behind you, lads!" Raena said.

It was clear from the panicked look in their eyes that they weren't reassured. After all, they were boys in men's clothing, headed to die.

Raena burst into the stable and ran to the first paddock she could see. The horse was a rouncey, not much for war, but it was good enough. She pulled him out and hooked a rein through his teeth. Raena didn't bother to saddle him, jumping on his back and riding bare. She shouted for him to gallop, and they set on well. He wasn't an easy ride, probably too young to be fully broken yet. It didn't matter, she would make it work.

As soon as they crossed the threshold of the castle into the bailey, Raena saw how degraded the state of things had become.

Where the peasants had been gathered to wait for food, not an hour before, now there were hundreds of white robes, fighting the prince's guards. Above, in the parapets, robed invaders climbed and clamored to attack the archers. Raena was certain there hadn't been this many robed men in the desert beyond the walls, even at the corners.

They had come from inside. They were her people.

She kicked the horse and directed him forward to the other corner of the bailey. She unlatched her poleax, ready to strike anyone down who came close, but they scattered at the sight of her.

"It's the Prince!" someone shouted.

"Prince Trevin!" shouted another.

Raena couldn't discern if they were her guards or her enemies, but she rode on, ducking when she and her horse passed into a wide corridor toward the gardens, and toward her throne.

CHAPTER 25
SYLAS

Legions live in secret; if our enemy can be trusted

The Hornes packed Cames's wounds with dressing and left him in the caves. Isla tried to keep the site clean, but it was nearly impossible and cut away from the sparse amount of drinking water.

A few days after Lenon had cut the young man, Cames developed a fever. Sylas knew the signs of an infection and they had to remedy it immediately. So, when some of the Hornes came to the cave, pointed gruffly at Cames, then led him away, Sylas was relieved.

"Do you think they are going to give him medicine?" Isla asked, worry fraying her tone.

Sylas rubbed his eyes. "They need all of us, especially young warriors. They'll want him to live."

Isla was bending over the fire, stoking it with wet sticks and giving them a moment to steam before she tossed in another. "That's not the answer to my question."

"Isn't it?"

Isla flashed him a tight-lipped gaze that said volumes more than words would've.

"I'm sorry," Sylas blurted out, "I didn't mean to argue. I think they'll give him medicine, yes. If they wanted to let him die, they would've left him here to do it, in the cave."

Isla let out a sharp breath that caused the sparks below her to flare into the smoke momentarily.

Sensing that he was doomed to say everything wrong, Sylas stood, patting his thighs. "I'm going to check and see if there's anyone around, outside the cave."

Before his motives could be questioned, he was on the move.

To his surprise, magnificent sunlight met him at the entrance of the cave. The rays glinted off the wet shards of rock on either side, bringing out flecks of color he'd never noticed in the harsh formations. Dozens of yards below where the ocean spray hit the island, the water arched into a mist that the light touched and created a rainbow of color. He admired the prism for a few quiet moments, observing the pleasant and calm sensation it gave him low in his gut.

Perhaps it was the warmth of the sun on his face, or the sting of the sea salt so thick in the air, but Sylas felt water fill his throat and eyes. He couldn't pinpoint what inside him led him to cry, but it was short-lived. As soon as he wiped his face with a rough, dirty hand, the sensation was gone.

A grunt to his right caused Sylas to seek out the source. Stumbling along a steep trail, one hand holding his wounds, was Cames.

"Let me tend to ya!" Sylas shouted. He charged up the island trail as fast as he could manage while minding the precarious rocks. In a few bounds, he reached Cames, and wrapped an arm around the knight.

"I'm all right," Cames muttered through heaving breaths.

Sylas eyed the wound under Cames's hand; the bandage appeared to be the same blood-soaked wrap he'd been wearing for days. "Didn't they clean you up?"

Cames grunted, unable to answer.

Sylas noted the sweat on the younger man's forehead and slipped his shoulder under Cames's armpit in response.

"Come on, lad," Sylas groaned, bearing his weight.

Cames relented and leaned heavy against Sylas.

With short, labored steps, they made it back to the cave together. Only a pace inside the entrance, Cames collapsed, unable to make it any deeper.

"I'll fetch you water?" Sylas asked.

"In a moment," Cames panted, "don't leave me."

Sylas raised an eyebrow but didn't respond. Now that they were still, he could inspect Cames's wrap more thoroughly. He dropped to one knee and leaned close to see fresh blood seeping through. The smell was the worst indicator, though. Even ten hands away, Sylas caught a whiff of the sweet and sickening air around the wound.

"Why didn't they clean you up?" he groaned, shaking his head.

Cames shrugged, "Maybe they are running out of supplies. There are many wounded men in their capture."

"How many?"

"A thousand able-bodied, but—" Cames bit his lower lip, stopping himself.

The two men's eyes met and Sylas could see a flush creep into Cames's cheeks.

"What aren't you telling me, lad?"

"Nothing," Cames whispered, his light eyes glancing away.

Sylas stood, peering down with an authoritative stance. "Cames, you're not under my command here, but you still owe me respect. Tell me now, what're you up to? Where've you been? What did they want with you?"

Cames continued to stare at the dirt floor. Silent.

"You better tell me, before Isla sees you," Sylas said, "she'll figure out what you're hiding in a moment. You know you can't get a single thing past her."

Cames nodded, "I reckoned. I'll...I'll tell you. Please, give me a moment."

Sylas threw up his hands and slapped them down against his thighs; the sound echoed into the cave. He had a burst of energy that he hadn't felt in days, and he reckoned that might be anger cracking through the dull numbness. It slipped through his chest like a warm bath after a day of hunting in winter.

Cames cleared his throat. "Our people won't beat the Hornes in this war. Not if they join with the Boens."

Sylas leaned back against the cave wall and slid to the floor beside Cames so they were eye-to-eye. "What makes you think you know that?"

"It's hopeless. There's no way we can stop them."

"So then, what are you not telling me?"

Cames sighed, "Lenon asked me to be a general in his army. He wants me to...he wants me to lead a legion of Candorians into Boenaerya."

Sylas clenched his fists and felt a ball of rage rising from the pit of his stomach. He consciously slowed his breathing to try and maintain an air of composure. "I see. That sounds a bit like a death march, don't you think? You, leading a thousand men through the thick of Boenarya and over the mountains into Candor? How will you feed them? Most of them have been prisoners for—"

"It's not only those thousand," Cames interjected. He brought a shaking hand to his brow, wiping away the beading sweat threatening to drip into his eyes.

In another long pause, Sylas wanted to shake the young knight. He visualized his hand gripping Cames's shirt and thrusting him against the wall to demand answers. But on the outside, Sylas remained as steady and cold as the forsaken island they were trapped within.

"He won't tell me everything," Cames said, "but he said he will have a hundred-and-fifty thousand men when he descends on Candeo. He promised me that if I am loyal and I lead the thousand, I will not only be spared but given command of a great legion."

"He's lying. No kingdom has that many men. Not Ediva, not Candor, and definitely not the Hornes."

"He said they will be three armies, joined together."

Sylas furrowed his brow, contemplating what that could mean. Without more information, he turned the conversation back to Cames. "But you told him you won't do it?"

Cames shook his head and let loose an abrupt, quiet sob. "What choice do I have? My only hope of surviving is if he takes us to land to begin the war. Perhaps then I can slip away, even free a few of the others—"

"So, you will dishonor yourself?" Sylas whispered harshly. "You'll agree to build, train, and lead a legion for that monster's army?"

"I tried to do it with honor. I asked him to free some of the others in exchange. I asked him to free Lady Isla and the other women if I do it."

"And what did he say to that?"

"He…he didn't say much. I hope he's considering it."

"You hope," Sylas couldn't mask the sardonic tone that clung to his words.

Cames gazed down to his lap, fidgeting with the frayed edge of his bandages. "He won't be stopped. Those creatures he told us about, in the ocean?"

Sylas was too angry to speak, letting his silence encourage Cames to go on.

"Well, he said they can travel up the rivers. Right into the mountains. But he said they can cross the mountains and swim to Candeo, then fight on land."

Sylas scoffed, but inside his guts were twisting.

"I know it sounds impossible but…he even has maps of our land. The Houses and keeps marked out. The number of men in each army. The outposts. I think the other prisoners have been giving him the information."

Sylas pounded his fist against the stone floor. "That's why you have to stand your ground! That's exactly why, don't you see? Look how much betrayal costs. Other men would betray Candor? They would tell him these secrets?"

Cames didn't respond, staring somberly at his own hands.

"You can be better than this," Sylas whispered, leaning in closer. "You can die for Candor. With honor."

Unable to stomach another word between them, Sylas stood and walked to the back of the cave, rejoining the others. When he approached, Isla shot him a questioning glance, and he muttered that Cames was back and needed tending. No one asked for further explanation, and he was grateful, because he couldn't have predicted what would fall out of his mouth if provoked.

He sat at the fire, staring into the flames and letting his thoughts echo and roll inside his head. When he heard the women's voices in the mouth of the cave, he quickly went to his beddown space before he could see if they were bringing Cames back with them. He couldn't face the boy again for the day; perhaps tomorrow his anger would give way to compassion. He knew Isla would've scolded him, if she knew. She would tell him some tender words to melt through the burning in his chest and give way to empathy. He didn't want it. He wanted to stew in his moral absolute and believe that every man who had helped Lenon was a coward and a failure. He laid on his side with his back to the fire, watching the reflections and shadows cast by the flames, dancing over the cave walls.

"Sylas?" Isla whispered, from behind him. "Are you awake?"

Sylas shut his eyes.

He'd pretended to be asleep as long as he had to until eventually, true sleep had overtaken him. When he finally woke, Sylas rolled over to see the others, quietly tucked in their own beddowns. Time was usually meaningless in the constant darkness of the cave, but that didn't stop them from trying to maintain a semblance of a routine. Sylas mustered up and took a few swigs of water. He poured some out and rubbed it over his face and beard, struggling to feel fresh.

He wouldn't be able to go back to sleep, he knew that well enough.

With care, he stepped around the others softly and left the comfort of their confined dwelling. When he ventured out of the cave, it was indeed the middle of the night. The sky was clear with infinite stars, yet a light drizzle of rain fell on him from clouds he couldn't locate, mostly due to the strong gale wind. It pressed against him and pushed, as if trying to force him back into the cave, in a warning. But Sylas could see the familiar paths winding up the island and grit his teeth.

He started up, scanning for rocks jutting out that would remind him of their journey. All he truly knew was that he needed to continue north, and the rest relied on pure luck.

They had taken that journey in the dark, so surely the footholds should be familiar, Sylas reasoned. But with every step on the jagged island, he held more doubt.

Mere minutes had passed, and Sylas stopped to get his bearing. He turned round to assess where he'd come from and saw foreign formations that appeared insurmountable. At his side was a cliff face, and he swore the drop hadn't been so steep a moment before. If he didn't know better, he could've been convinced that the ledge was even shrinking beneath his feet.

Disoriented, Sylas leaned to one side, reaching out. His hand connected with a razor-sharp outcropping that dug into his palm. The sting to his flesh made him recoil to check for blood. In the dark, all he could see was a shimmer of wetness that could've been blood, or simply the product of constant mist and rain.

"How do you find such a place?"

Sylas shivered at the words from above. Chilling, deep, and now the voice that haunted his nightmares. He craned his neck up to see Lenon, crouched over a ledge with an amused expression.

Lenon shook his head, "You can fall. That is not a way to walk. Did you not see the end ahead?"

"I thought it…" the words died in Sylas's throat. He did not need to entertain the Horne leader's jest.

As if driving in the humiliation, Lenon chuckled and bound down the cliff face in a few expert swings. In seconds, he was behind Sylas. Lenon's bare, webbed toes gripped the ground beneath them and his languid arms reached out. He didn't make contact, but rather his hands hovered on either side of Sylas's torso, like a mother ready to catch her toddler standing for the first time.

"Come back, slow," Lenon said, his tone soothing.

Sylas clenched his fists so hard his forearms shook, but he did as instructed. He sensed Lenon moving in tandem as he took short steps away from the ledge. He tried not to show his fear, but his breathing was louder than he could control.

"There," Lenon said, dropping his arms. "This is a place."

Sylas turned now that it was safe to do so, and to his embarrassment, recognized they stood on a distinct junction of two connecting footpaths. He must have passed the exact point yet stumbled onto a dangerous precipice, nonetheless.

"Thank you," Sylas muttered, gritting his teeth.

Lenon laughed. "I can't let you fall to your death. What would be the point?"

Sylas didn't reply.

There was a quiet moment between them. Neither man spoke, though Lenon made a small clucking sound with his tongue. The Horne

284

leader rolled his shoulders as though bored, and began up the northern path.

Sylas had nearly forgotten his reasons for leaving the caves. At the sight of Lenon's retreating form, he realized his anger was burning again in his gut, almost as fresh as he'd felt it when speaking to Cames.

"Wait," Sylas groaned.

Lenon turned.

"I want to know what you're planning with Cames. He's like a son to me. If you're going to enlist his help, at least keep him alive. His wounds are beginning to turn."

"His wounds will heal when we give him the Change."

Sylas raised one eyebrow, searching for clarification. Without it, he continued. "May I see the others? I want to speak to the other Candorians. I can…help."

"No, there's no need for that. I have my generals; I have my army. They will be soon ready."

"You have a thousand men? That's the army you need?"

Lenon's laugh cut through the night. In a few quick bounds, he was back to the landing where Sylas stood. Their noses nearly touched when Lenon leaned in to speak. "I have thousands upon thousands of men waiting for me. When we reach land, I will have your kind. They will follow me into battle, once they see we will not be defeated."

Sylas swallowed hard. "My kind? Do you mean more Candorians?"

Lenon nodded. "Another fifty thousand."

"What…where are they?"

Lenon squinted as though contemplating if his next words were worth saying. He stared at Sylas for a moment, blinking away mist on his layered eyelids. "They are under your world. The Tunnel-Men you call Boens? They are soft. They never kill the way Hornes kill. They take all prisoners and keep them alive."

Sylas's heart began to race inside his chest. "You are telling me that the armies of Candor, Prince Zander's armies? They all survived?"

285

"Perhaps," Lenon said, "perhaps not all. But most. The Tunnel-Men have them."

"The Boens have them—and you believe they will join your war?"

Lenon turned and glanced down the island. "Can you find your way back? Don't fall off the cliffs. Your cave is that way."

"Wait," Sylas said. "I don't understand."

But his words echoed into the night, unanswered. Lenon was halfway up a rockface and clamoring over another cropping of shale without so much as a glance back in Sylas's direction.

CHAPTER 26
AVEN

Unity in Candeo, but none under the prince's rule

The fight was growing closer.

The guards had decided to enter the room and barricade the door, shoving all manner of furniture in front of it. They waited with Aven inside the Prince's chamber, trembling with fear.

Aven tried to occupy them with friendly conversation, but there was little point.

Since the five horn blasts had sounded, she knew the battle was already lost.

And she knew Raena wouldn't surrender.

The two guards were pacing, muttering to one another, checking every few seconds to ensure the barricade was secure. They sheathed and unsheathed their weapons multiple times as if to be certain they would fare well in the inevitable battle.

"We won't be able to exit," the shorter guard said to his companion. He was a dark, hairy lad, with eyes that reminded Aven of Barton Colby's.

The taller guard, who seemed younger, shook his head. "At least we'll protect the Princess."

"Duchess," Aven corrected.

The two guards glanced in her direction, startled.

"My apologies, Duchess," the taller one said with a bow, "I thought Prince Trevin said…"

"He was being coy," Aven replied. "He was teasing me, that's all. Besides, I'm not much of a duchess now, my duchy was sacked by the Boens."

They nodded, as though uncertain how else to respond.

The noise outside had died down for a moment, but then there was a crash and a scream. It sounded close enough to be immediately outside the door. Aven realized she was clutching her bodice, and she wiped her sweating palms on her dress.

"Prince Trevin!" a man's voice shouted from outside the door. He shouted again for the prince, pounding on the entrance. It sounded as though he were kicking or shoulder-slamming the door and the walls.

The guards held their swords, poised for a fight.

"Prince Trevin!" the man yelled again. "Are you in there? It's Jonn-Del!"

Aven felt her chest clench. It did indeed sound like Jonn-Del's voice.

The taller guard glanced back at her as if wondering what to do.

Aven stepped forward, closer to the barricade, and called out. "Sir Jonn-Del, he's not in here. He's gone to fight."

There was a weighted pause, and the knocking stopped.

Then Jonn-Del's voice squeaked as he responded. "Aven? Is that you?"

"Aye," she said, "the prince brought me here to wait. What's happening with the fight?"

Another pause, then he spoke in a stern tone. "We've lost a general. The peasants and Ruvians have all joined the zealots. We are losing. Prince Trevin must call a truce and meet their demands. If he doesn't, he'll be usurped."

"Usurped by whom?"

"They have a leader of some kind. They will give him the throne. Please, I need to know where he is."

Aven sighed. "I truly don't know. I'm sorry. He is likely to be near the frontlines of the fight."

"The last men who saw him said he disappeared into the ground. Do you know where that might lead?"

"No, I'm afraid not."

There was an audible groan from Jonn-Del's side of the door. "We're running out of time."

Aven pursed her lips, unsure of what more could be done. She searched her thoughts, considering the options, thinking of times she might have known Raena to disappear in the citadel. Altogether, she came up with nothing. The idea of Raena beneath the ground, roaming through tunnels like a true Boen gave her an unsettling sick feeling, yet it simultaneously felt...right.

"I'm going to the throne room," Jonn-Del said, "you should come with me. If they try to usurp the prince, they must seat a new ruler on the throne. We all have to stop them and kill whoever they send."

The two guards turned and were studying her now, waiting for her answer. Their tension was palpable, as though they hoped Aven would know the right move because they surely didn't.

Aven set her jaw. "Alright, give us a moment. We have to clear the door."

The guards didn't waste a second and pulled away the benches and wardrobe they had stacked, freeing the portal.

When Aven opened the door, she was surprised to see Jonn-Del had a gash across his forehead, leaving a trail of blood down his face. Blood trickled down and soaked the tunic under his chest plate. Even his sleeves were red and brown.

"You're...wounded," Aven said with a gasp.

"Aye," Jonn-Del mumbled, "come on. We have to run."

The guards took up the rear and Jonn-Del led the way. They ran through the royal corridor. It wasn't far from the prince's chamber to the throne room, but Aven heard echoes of the battle all around them. The sound of swords and men's grunting shouts filled the halls so it was impossible to discern their location. As they ran past a window, Aven peeked out to see down into the bailey, where a mob had formed. A few horsemen were trying to fight but appeared grossly outnumbered.

They turned the corner to the final hallway before the throne room, and Jonn-Del skidded to a stop.

There, ahead, were seven diacons of Libre.

Aven had seen them before. The last time she remembered encountering one, he'd been in the shadows at the farms. He'd stuck out in her mind, his familiarity. She felt instantly that she'd known him from a previous world, or perhaps a previous life. These seven were different. They were caricatures of the man she'd seen, like portraits painted of a king, capturing a persona but through an artist's interpretation.

They were in a line at the edge of the throne room, along the archways that separated it from the corridor. Aven peered beyond their white robes and spotted Raena.

She wore her Prince's crown and leather tunic bearing the fox sigil of House Schinen. Beneath it was a filthy muslin shirt, caked in mud—or blood. There were streaks of red and brown across Raena's pale face.

Aven couldn't breathe.

She didn't realize she was running forward until she heard a shout.

"Avenna, stop!" Jonn-Del cried.

But she was through the line of diacons, into the throne room, between them and Raena.

It was forty steps from the entrance to the throne, and Aven made it half the distance before she stopped and fell to her knees.

"Your Majesty," Aven breathed, her voice cracking. "I'm...I'm at your service."

"It's alright, Duchess," Raena said.

Aven glanced up, scanning the throne room. It was so much larger than she remembered ever seeing. She had been there a handful of times to address Queen Zarana or Prince Zander, but every time it had been filled with nobles lining both sides. Now it was akin to a tomb, long and hollow, filled with statues and columns that seemed to whisper of doom.

She rose from her bow, moving wordlessly to the side of the room. Raena nodded at her as though to affirm that Aven was standing in the right place. From the side of the room Aven could observe both Raena upon the throne and the line of diacons, locked in a sort of defiant stand-off.

"We have our demands," one of the diacons spoke. He stood at the center of the seven. His purple face gave Aven an unpleasant chill across her back.

Raena clasped her hands together, squeezing her palms. "I'm interested to hear them. You have stormed my castle, turned your followers against their own brothers, slaughtered your own. You've made my kingdom an unsuitable place for our own families. So, your demands must be something...truly spectacular."

The diacons did not react, their faces remaining stoic.

"We wish to place our own ruler upon the throne of Candor," the central diacon said.

Raena scoffed aloud, throwing her head back. "Of course, you do. That's what everyone wants. Do you not remember a season ago when the throne's heir was up for debate? Why didn't you produce your ruler, then? I'm afraid you are several sunsets too late for this."

Aven spotted Jonn-Del easing his way into the throne room. He held his armor and weapon close to keep them from clanging as he snuck along the far wall.

The diacons continued, "We will continue to beckon the people to fight. We will die for the Almighties and for Candor. We will fight until there is no one left."

"You're fools, then. Our kingdom will be divided. Then we'll be taken by Boens. We barely had a chance at survival, and now that you've invited treason—"

"It was already divided."

291

Raena raised her hand to point as she stood from the throne. "You have splintered this kingdom! We were already fighting with one hand behind our backs, and now you've bludgeoned the knees of the men beside you! Where is your loyalty? Certainly, you want to see Candor crumble and fall to the Boens!"

The central diacon bristled, showing emotion for the first time. He didn't move away, merely replied in a monotone. "We were dying at the hands of bandits. We were dying in the fields. Your kingdom is filled with unrest. Women raped and murdered while they slept. Children stolen from their beds. Your people are dying of starvation—slow, painful death. We didn't have to persuade them to fight, they were ready to demand a new rule. We will feed them. We will lead them to peace and prosperity."

Raena had dropped her hand, but her fists clenched at her side. "I'm not interested in your ideas. You will call off your fighters. We will settle this, but not with more death."

"We have called off our fighters, Prince Trevin. Have you?"

Raena shot a curious look toward Jonn-Del, who shook his head. She turned her back on the diacons and paced, bringing her fingers to her lips in thought. Aven could see now the worry on Raena's face, as well as the sluggish and tilted way she moved. Raena had been wounded, somewhere on her side or hip, Aven was sure of it.

"How about this," Raena said, spinning. "Your leaders will have a place on my council. Voting rights. I am not yet king, so your vote will carry the same weight as mine."

The diacons glanced at one another as though seeking committee. The central one shook his head. "That is only a plan until you are king. Then your vote holds more weight, and we will have no voice to give our people."

Raena nodded, "Of course. That's why you will have another seat on my council. I will give seats to five of your leaders."

The diacon opened his mouth, then closed it, considering the offer.

Aven watched out of the corner of her eye as Jonn-Del slipped back out of the room, from the same pocket he had first come. He wasn't subtle, but no one else appeared to be paying attention.

"We want seven," the diacon said, gesturing to the men on either side of him. "We are all seven diacons. We each represent the seven Almighties. We represent our seven factions. We speak for our seven groups of peoples, and each has a voice."

"Then what are you?" Raena snapped. "Why are you the only one who speaks at all?"

The central diacon nodded. "I am not who you think I am. I am a vessel for the Chosen, who defied death to give us all life. He will take my place. I am connected to him; I may speak his thoughts. We are all in his service, as he has died to see the Almighties for himself. He controls our thoughts, our minds, our mouths. He speaks through me."

Raena cringed. "Well then. If one dead bloke speaks for all of you, then you don't need to all have seats on the council, taking up space. You can have five seats, and you'll leave my throne room, now."

The diacons appeared to consider it. Aven realized for the first time that it was as if they were communicating, thinking as one, discussing the notions within their heads. It gave her an unsettling chill. Their eyes moved, but no other body parts, and she wondered if they were sending messages with their minds, something she had never heard of or considered possible.

"We accept," the central diacon said. "We accept five council seats."

"Good," Raena said, "you have a quarter-hour to stop and call off your attacks. If your people continue their uprising, I will kill all seven of you."

"A new seven will be called. He will speak through—"

"I don't care!" Raena shouted. "Then we'll kill him, too!"

The diacons didn't flinch. They paused for a moment, perhaps communicating, then they turned in unison and walked out of the throne room.

Aven waited until they were gone, then she ran forward to Raena, who was rubbing her tired eyes.

"You stopped them," Aven said.

Raena dropped her hands and shook her head. "For now. There will be another uprising. I cannot supply an army and feed the people. Those diacons are right, we are losing more to starvation than we will lose to the Boens."

With her shoulders drooping, Raena stumbled through the room and slumped into the throne, leaning far to one side.

"Are you wounded?" Aven asked.

"I doubt it," Raena muttered. "I don't know."

"Can I send for a healer?"

Raena shook her head. "No, I will wait for the guards to start coming back from battle. When it's over, they'll need the healers. Maybe I just need some ale."

The mention of guards made Aven remember the two men who had protected her, and she looked toward the arches to see them, waiting without purpose beyond the threshold. She called for them and asked them to fetch ale and clean water for the prince. When they were gone, she approached the throne.

"Will you need to address your people?" Aven asked.

Raena shrugged; her lips turned down into a pout. She rubbed the head of a bronze beast attached to the arm of the throne. It appeared well-worn, as if many kings and queens had rubbed it quite the same way.

"Allow me to rephrase that," Aven said, drawing a breath, "I think you need to address your people."

"Why? So, I can tell them that they've won? That they can fight against me whenever they want, and bully me into the corner?"

Aven sighed. She lifted her skirt and then lowered herself to sit cross-legged on the floor at Raena's feet. Raena raised a skeptical eyebrow, then returned her attention back to the little bronze creature.

"You think this is about winning and losing," Aven said, her tone soft, "but you didn't lose today. Giving your people a voice isn't losing.

If they have chosen to follow Libre and believe in it, surely you can empathize with them."

"I can't, actually. They are idolizing foolish hopes. We will have a true war, one that I cannot stop. And today they wanted to stick their hands into a snake pit and shake them around. If they wanted to put their fussock leaders on the council, they should have petitioned for it."

Aven raised an eyebrow. "Would you have granted their request?"

Raena huffed, biting the inside of her cheek. After a moment, she muttered something.

Aven didn't need to hear it to know it was likely denial. She pressed. "Do you remember when we were in House Deen together?"

"Of course."

"Do you remember when we were in the hallway? You, and I, and Fitzduncan? You kept begging me to think of how I ruled my people, and implore Duke Claue to enter the streets of his duchy to be among them. To see their burdens firsthand instead of hiding away."

"But I've been doing that. I've done that. I was in the streets and in the kitchens, eating sloppy pig-fat soup when we arrived in Candor."

"You haven't shown them that you are concerned for them," Aven said. She reached up to the throne and offered her hand, palm raised.

Raena eyed the gesture for a moment, then placed her hand on Aven's with hesitance. There was a warmth in Raena's gaze that felt friendly: comfortable. But there was something more, something that Aven didn't want to see.

Affection.

Aven pushed past it, all business. "You can connect with these people. You have to open up, show them who you really are. Show them the human side of you."

"Who I really am? You don't mean…"

"No. Not like that. Show them your story, your fears. Show them you care about them. Make them believe in you because you care about them."

Raena scoffed. "That might be easy for you. You're one of them, that's why they love you. Even though I was a lower nobleman, I still had a luxurious life in comparison."

Aven nodded. Gently, she pulled back her hand, placing it in her lap. She thought about what she wanted to say, the idea she wanted to propose. She knew it would help Raena, but she felt that it was too soon.

When Jonn-Del burst into the room, Aven was glad she'd not spoken what was on her mind.

"Majesty," Jonn-Del said giving a brisk bow as he walked, "the citadel is quieting. The followers of Libre have quelled. They stopped fighting. Shall I direct the guards and legions to arrest them?"

Raena glanced at Aven, then shook her head. "No, allow them to go back to their lives. Spread the word that I will address the kingdom tomorrow."

Jonn-Del's face was grim. "Alright then."

Aven caught a flicker of animosity between them, but there was no challenge stated. With a silent glare, Jonn-Del bowed.

"I will help you," Aven muttered, the two men still eyeing one another.

"Thank you," Raena mumbled, distracted.

"I mean it, I'm willing to do whatever it takes."

Raena's awkward reoccupation with Jonn-Del resolved, and she snapped her attention back to the Duchess. "I think I can handle it."

"Let me help you."

"Alright. We'll speak of it tomorrow."

CHAPTER 27
AVEN

An acceptance wrapped in obligation and duty

The diacons were self-righteous, arrogant, and insistent leaders. Raena was worn thin by their presence after a fortnight of allowing them on her council. Aven saw the dark circles around the prince's eyes and the weight of her expression. Raena's countenance now reminded Aven of the first time they saw one another after the Boen attack, restless yet weary.

Raena and Aven increased their meetings to daily consults as they tried to calm the turbulent kingdom under Raena's rule. The air between them had once again cooled, and they hadn't spoken once of the day the Librens attacked. It was as though those few passionate kisses were accepted as fear in the moment, and Raena and Aven returned to a position of political colleagues, nothing more.

Engaging the people of Candor had quelled some fires in the angered underbelly of the citadel, but discontent still prevailed. The bandits still attacked the farms. The peasants and serfs still begged for food. And the Librens were spreading lies.

"They say the Boens are a legend!" Raena shouted as she entered the chamber. Exasperated, she collapsed into a reclining chair.

Aven remained calm, sitting at the table where they took tea every morning and discussed the state of the kingdom. She poured, serving to both goblets, waiting for her Prince.

"How is something so absurd prevailing? How can they believe this?" Raena continued, one hand over her eyes. "Hundreds of thousands of people saw the Boens. Fifty thousand or more are dead. What do they think happened to the armies? That all of Candor's greatest warriors just fell into a pit one day?"

Aven folded her hands in her lap, listening.

"And fucking Jonn-Del and the fucking council are no help at all. Councilor Amanes suggested that I tell the kingdom there are no Boens so they will be validated in their theories. Why would I intentionally spread lies to appease people who are wrong?"

Aven cringed, biting her tongue.

"They say the Boens couldn't have done it all. We know the Hornes helped them. But the Librens think it's more than that. They think it was some sort of conspiracy, led by every kingdom and ruler. To do what? They aren't thinking it through."

There was a long pause. Raena sighed.

Aven gestured to the table. "Would you like your tea?"

"I might as well," Raena grumbled and took her place in her chair.

Aven thought for a moment while Raena sipped the hot tea. She thought about solutions, but her mind kept drifting back to the same solitary possibility.

"Thank you," Raena muttered, "I can tell when you brewed the tea. It's always stronger than the handmaidens make it."

"You're welcome, but you're incorrect. I taught them to brew it."

Raena grinned. "I've been telling them to brew it stronger for weeks. How did you manage?"

Aven shrugged, lifting her own tea to her lips. She was about to dismiss the question, but then a clever thought came to her, and all at once she knew exactly how to present her idea. She lowered the goblet back to the table and leaned forward with intensity. Her eyes caught Raena's and they shared a stare.

"I asked them," Aven said.

"What's that?"

"I asked them to brew the tea stronger, and they did it. They did it because I'm the one who asked them."

Raena scoffed, her pale brow furrowing. "All right..."

Aven leaned further still, her hand on the center of the table. "The common people care about what I have to say. They listen to me because I'm one of them. We've talked about this many times, how you have to get on their level."

"I know, Aven. But I can't—"

"What if you stop trying? What if you don't need to, anymore? I'm trying to make you the kind of leader that I was, and it's not working. If anything, it's worse than before."

Raena's expression soured. "Well, maybe."

"You know I don't mean any harm by it. You're trying your best, and I commend you for it. But the people of Candor are weary. The diacons of Libre appeal to them because they perceive the diacons as commoners, unlike you."

"Then you think it's hopeless? What are you saying?"

Aven shook her head. "It's hopeless, for you. You can't reach them."

Raena's jaw clenched, muscle rippling above her chin.

"But someone else can," Aven continued, "a commoner can appeal to them. A commoner can sway their opinion, and reunite this broken kingdom. In the same way that I was able to reach the handmaidens, I could also reach the common people."

"Yes, I know you can. Of course, you can. But how does that help me, any? Are you proposing that I give you the crown? A higher position in the kingdom? I'm barely able to convince Jonn-Del and the council that I have you as an 'advisor' as it is."

Aven squinted, choosing to ignore that last statement. "None of those. I am…accepting your proposal. I accept your offer to make me your queen. Or your princess, whichever it may be."

A sense of confusion seemed to pass over Raena, then she went even paler, her skin nearly white. She reached for the tea, abruptly, taking several rapid and long gulps.

Aven allowed it, saying nothing.

In the awkward silence, there was an uncomfortable tension. The only sound was the intermittent swallow from Raena.

When she'd practically guzzled her hot tea, Raena stood from the table, scraping her chair across the stone. She rubbed her hands together and took random steps, her mouth half-open as though she was about to speak, more than once, then thought better of it.

Aven would have laughed if she weren't feeling so suddenly discomforted.

"You accept…you want to marry me?" Raena said, spinning on her heel. Her periwinkle eyes were alight and her lips curled into a shallow smirk.

"For the sake of the kingdom only."

"Yes, but you want to marry me?" Raena smiled wider, stepping forward.

Aven held up both hands, stopping Raena in her tracks. "No. Rae…that's not what I'm saying. I'm sorry, but…I don't believe I have to explain why that's not what I'm saying."

"Well, I thought that you weren't ready to be with me, again—"

"And I'm not."

A dark shadow passed over Raena's countenance, and it was clear that she understood. Her eyes fell to the ground and she muttered to herself a few indistinguishable words.

Aven stood, her hands still in front of her. "I don't mean that we would be bound together in a complete sense. Only that I would…serve as your wife. As your Queen. I could reach the people of Candor in ways you've not been able to. I could give you what you need in order to become king, and make your pact with the Boens."

Raena's cheeks were reddening. "Yes. That is the most practical solution. That's what I meant to ask you, before. For the kingdom."

Aven lowered her hands and spoke softer. "You were right to ask it. I should have been clearer with you the first time you did, I'm sorry. I was being selfish to expect that we could have a different relationship, as if that is somehow a reason for a prince to take a princess."

"No," Raena muttered, "don't apologize. You shouldn't be forced to marry when you...you didn't want to."

"I was angry with you; I see it now. We should have done it the moment we were reunited in Candeo but I admit I was waiting because...I wanted something else. Now I see that this would be the best option."

"Something else? Do you mean you wanted to marry someone else?"

Aven scoffed, "No, never."

"Then what was it you wanted?"

"I suppose I...I hate to tell you this, I'm afraid it will hurt you."

Raena bristled, standing taller. "Nothing you say can hurt me. If we agree to what you're proposing, we must be totally honest with one another. I won't enter such an agreement without complete transparency at every step."

"Alright," Aven swallowed, bracing herself. With a deep breath, she let the truth flow from her lips. "I was hoping to fall in love with you, again. I hoped that my heart would change, once I was around you. I thought...I thought if I was here, in this castle, watching you as the prince? I might soften to you. I might feel the way for you that I once did."

"But you don't."

Aven felt the heat of tears beginning to roll from her eyes. "I'm sorry. I can't change what my heart is saying. And I can't make myself feel things for you that...aren't. I thought that I was only angry, but I'm not angry any longer. I look at you and I care about you, I respect you, I want you to be the king. But I don't..." she let the implication of her words linger.

301

She couldn't bring herself to say it. She couldn't bear to tell Raena that she didn't love her.

"I understand." Raena turned to the side, punching a fist against her palm. "It's alright. You tried. But this idea? Sure, it's a good one."

"Rae…I'm sorry."

"No, don't be. I will make some arrangements. I'm going to tell someone. Jonn-Del. I'm going to speak to him."

Aven suddenly felt the sensation that she'd experienced this exact moment before. She was taken back to the time Raena had awkwardly and abruptly tried a feeble proposal and Aven had rejected her with simple honesty. Raena had disappeared and not spoken to Aven again for several days. Aven reached out, her fingertips on Raena's forearm, begging her not to run off again.

The touch was enough, and Raena stayed planted in the chair, staring at the wall.

Aven blinked and a flurry of tears were let free by her lashes. They poured down her cheeks. She knew Raena wanted more. She wished she could let herself collapse against Raena's strong, comforting chest. She thought of the kiss they shared in the arena, and how she'd felt it was her gift to Raena, something Aven wasn't sure she wanted. She could give Raena something like that now to make the pain fade away. But that would be wrong. It would be wrong to take solace in Raena's arms only to ease her own guilt. It would hurt them both even more.

Raena didn't react to Aven's tears. She whispered, "I really should go. There will be a lot of arrangements to make. It will have to be a quick wedding."

With the absence of comfort, Aven wrapped her own arms tight around herself and nodded, murmuring approval. She held on as Raena stood, gave a brisk bow, and exited the chamber without another word. When she was alone, Aven let loose a gasping breath that she had been holding in, finally sobbing outright.

She knew that Raena was hurting. How could it not hurt? If Raena still held any feelings at all for Aven, the Prince's heart must be breaking.

But there was no way that Aven would be able to fake emotion or lie about what was buried in her heart. Letting out her truth stung as though Aven herself had been stabbed in the chest as she'd dragged her feelings out.

It was several minutes before she was able to gain her composure. Aven wiped her eyes and blotted her face with the sleeve of her gown. She was certain she would look a mess, but if she was fortunate, she wouldn't pass anyone in the halls. Once she felt confident, Aven left the chamber and completed the short walk to her boudoir where she was sure to be left in peace. No handmaidens would come for her until the midday meal.

She sat there for a while. She did some embroidery, her mind idle as she stitched. After an hour or two, she felt numb to the pain again, as if a great beast was returned to its cage.

A knock at the door startled her. Aven looked up to see Sir Jonn-Del and a man she didn't recognize, bearing the same desert mustelid sigil of House Lox.

"Sir," Aven said, standing abruptly to bow. She tossed her embroidery to the side.

"Save it," Jonn-Del grumbled, entering her room and slamming the door shut behind him. He took a seat on a stone stool. The second man remained standing.

Aven glanced at the stranger. He was tall, stocky, with thin skin. He was dark like any Candorian, but his face was much darker than his neck and hands, as though he'd been burnt by the sun too many times. His sigil made her uneasy. Not only his House, but the man reminded her greatly of Allyn.

Jonn-Del withdrew a dagger from his belt and held it to his fingernails. He began cleaning the beds, methodically, staring into his own reflection in the blade. "I've just spoken to Prince Trevin."

Aven knew he was trying to be intimidating. Of course, he was. But the man of House Lox, looming a few steps behind Jonn-Del, made her far more uneasy with his empty stare and statued pose.

"You think you know what's best for our common people, then?" Jonn-Del asked, raising one eyebrow.

"I think the prince does," Aven replied.

"Do you?" Jonn-Del muttered, "I suppose you told him this was his idea, then? You didn't offer him…some kind of promise of your flesh then, darling?"

Aven cringed. She glanced at Jonn-Del, but her hazel eyes kept drawing back to the man of Lox.

Jonn-Del sighed. "That's nothing to me. I think you understand why this is going to destroy his rule. This kingdom is fragile as it is, and now you want to come along and tear it apart."

The man of Lox nodded.

"I'm not…" Aven began, struggling for the words.

"Not what?" Jonn-Del said. "Not thinking of Candor? Of course not. That's what we're here for. Not only myself, and Baron Evandry, here. We understand what needs to be done, and we aren't going to allow you to get in the way. I have done my part to protect Candor all my life. You aren't the first meddling twat to think she gets to ruin traditions, sanctity, and the structure of civilization. I know I'll do what's needed, and when the time comes, Trevin will do it, too."

Aven's brow furrowed. There was something more to this that neither man was saying, and as she stared at the sigil on Baron Evandry's chest, it dawned on her.

They must know about Allyn.

Her palms began to sweat and she wiped them against her dress, trying to steady her fingers against the rough material of her skirt.

"I'd like to address a few things," Baron Evandry said. His voice was deep. Under better circumstances, it may have been soothing.

Jonn-Del sheathed his dagger, leaning forward on one knee. He stared at Aven.

The Baron stepped forward so he towered over the both of them. The window behind him was shining in the morning sunlight, making his body a silhouette and adding the darkness to his presence. "My brother is the Duke Lox, do you know who that is?"

Aven nodded, feeling her pulse rise so strongly it was as if her heart was in her throat.

"Good. I understand you were also friends with my nephew, Sir Allyn?"

Aven nodded, again.

"Sir Allyn was a good lad. He had only begun to secure his renown as a knight. He was bright, taking well to the task of keeping the libraries. He was eager for adventure, a true man of the hour. He had his pick of women and no shortage of friends. Everywhere he turned, he had a life of freedom, happiness, and a bright future."

Aven's head began to spin. She felt as if the air was being sucked from the room, swirling around her. Would they even give her a trial? Was a common-born woman deserving of a trial when she murdered a nobleman? Did they know that Raena had helped her to hide the body?

Would they kill her to protect Raena, or would they execute them both, together?

Surely, they were toying with her.

Baron Evandry placed his thick hand on Jonn-Del's shoulder, bracing himself as he hunched forward. He leaned so far that his face was a hand's length from Aven's, bearing down over her.

She shook with fear, despite herself. She could no longer ease her nerves as the certainty of her fate was looming. They might slit her throat. They might slice her artery, the same way she had sliced Allyn's, and leave her to die in the same fate.

Would she deserve it?

"Do you know what happened to him?" Baron Evandry whispered.

His mahogany eyes were hollow and deep, like little pools that lasted forever. He was fixed on Aven. She wanted to disappear, lost, drowning.

She prayed it would be quick. Aven glanced at Jonn-Del's hands, but they were empty. He had not redrawn his dagger, and Aven took that as a very bad sign that they must plan to kill her slowly.

The Baron muttered an insult, then repeated himself.

"No," Aven said. She didn't recognize her meek and trembling voice.

Baron Evandry's voice was quiet, but his breath was warm on Aven's face. "He was killed like a pig on your precious, filthy farm. He was slaughtered, like an animal, trying to help the likes of you and your worthless friends. You see, my nephew had no flaws, except for one. A very great one, it turns out. He had pity for you, little flecks of shite. He believed you were worthy of protection, and whatever else, instead of knowing that you are born in disease and waste and you live worthless lives until you die in disease and waste. So, he threw away everything, all his brightness and goodness and his heritage. He threw away a chance to be the next Duke of Lox, perhaps even more. The stakes were high, and what did he occupy himself with?"

Aven wanted to focus. She wanted to be calm. She wanted to appear collected. Surely, they would see her reaction as an admission of guilt. But against her will, she gripped her skirts until her knuckles were white. She felt a bead of sweat roll down the back of her neck, falling between her bodice and her shoulder blade.

"You," the Baron growled.

"I—I'm sorry," Aven stuttered.

The Baron acted as though he hadn't heard her. "You, and your lot, and every one of your fucking worthless farmer muck. You think you are so different, don't you? You think you're useful because you fucked a duke before he died of weakness? You think you have a place here? I've seen the way you act. We all have. Like you're some duchess. What are you the duchess of, exactly? A pathetic little place the Hornes squashed like a bug."

Aven couldn't hold back her breathing. She couldn't settle it. She took long, quaking breaths, as though she were about to vomit. Perhaps she was. Perhaps she would cry. Perhaps she would urinate herself. It was impossible to say that feeling of total panic inside her, and how her body was refusing to cooperate. Something was about to burst, and that was all she knew.

The Baron leaned back, resuming his place beside Jonn-Del. "You will not be a queen. You will not even be a princess. You are nothing, and you will be nothing, again."

She flinched; certain this was the end.

Jonn-Del's hands moved—for his blade?

Aven closed her eyes tight, she couldn't open them to see her end. She waited for death. In her mind, she began a prayer, the prayer of the Colby's. The prayer they gave to send their enemies to the world beyond.

Would Eathon be waiting for her? Would she remain his bride in the afterlife?

In the total darkness of her eyes clenched shut, she heard the shuffling of movement. She sensed Jonn-Del standing—felt the coolness of two shadows looming over her. She heard Jonn-Del's voice.

"You will go to Prince Trevin, and give him whatever he wants. Get into his bed, take care of his needs. I will tell his guards to say nothing, and do nothing to stop you from entering his chamber as much as he likes. I know he is bitter that he hasn't had a chance to…I've kept you and he separated. So, fine."

Aven found herself slowly opening her eyes, still wracked with fear, yet Jonn-Del's hands were empty and open. He was incredibly close, his belt nearly touching her ear. She couldn't turn her head or look up at him.

Jonn-Del continued. "You will give him your body, and be his mistress. He's a young man, I should have known he has needs. But you will not marry him, and this nonsense stops today."

Aven opened her mouth to form a question.

The Baron spoke before she had the chance. "Know your place, from now on. You can fuck a prince. You cannot marry a prince. You will tell him as much, or we will tell him for you."

It was quiet. They were waiting. They wanted something.

Aven's heart was still pounding. Her hands were still sweating. Her breath was still coming out in short gasps, though perhaps they couldn't hear it.

Then she felt the sudden, sharp tug of a hand in her hair. Baron Evandry grabbed her and held her hair in his fist. "Do you understand, peasant?"

Aven shook, but she forced out the words. "Yes. I understand."

"Good."

She felt him let go. She felt the breeze as they passed her. She felt the shift in the air, in the light, as the warmth of the sun through her window was no longer cooled by their shadows. She felt the lightness of space without their presence, and she knew that they were gone.

Aven slid down her chair, her legs giving out. She collapsed into the floor like a pool of water, seeping into the cracks. Her chest burned as she gasped for air. Bile rose in her throat, spreading an acrid taste through her mouth, but she did not vomit. Aven didn't know how long she stayed like that, or when she next opened her eyes, wasted from fear and distress.

CHAPTER 28
AVEN

Plans for a wedding

Baron Evandry and Jonn-Del's words still rung in Aven's ears the next evening. Raena had been locked in meetings with the council, including the five new diacon members, for the duration of the day. If Aven had to imagine, she would reckon they were discussing a way forward with the kingdom, and she hoped it would be fruitful. Her heart ached for the state of things, and a weight of doom lingered in her chest. Aven had a sense that danger was around the corner at every step.

Aven was in the hallway, passing the council chambers when Raena stepped out.

"I've been wondering when I would see you," Raena said, quickly closing the door behind her.

"Oh?"

"Yes, we have a lot to discuss."

Aven nodded and bit her lip.

Raena stepped closer. She was wearing her light leather House Schinen tunic and hooked her thumbs into the armholes. "I need to talk to you about…the wedding."

"Of course," Aven whispered. "I assumed you were busy with everything else."

"Well, I am. But I have a moment now if you do?"

"Alright," Aven replied, glancing up and down the hallway. "Can we go somewhere alone?"

"We can go to my chamber."

"Yes. Alright."

They walked through the hallways, quiet. Aven followed a few steps behind: the proper protocol for a woman of any stature and the prince. Raena led, winding through corridors, reaching the familiar location of her princely chambers. The same chambers where Aven had hidden from the battle. It was hard to believe that only days had passed when it felt like years.

Raena stood between her two guards, posted outside her chamber, and turned toward Aven.

Aven felt a pit of dread build in her stomach and then wane. She wondered if Baron Evandry and Jonn-Del had told Raena to take her as a "mistress". She wondered if Raena would choose to call off the marriage idea. Perhaps if Aven spent the night in the prince's chamber, it would quench the wicked games Jonn-Del was trying to play with Raena's rule.

"It's alright, Duchess, you've been here before." Raena gestured to the chamber door.

Aven cringed and realized she was stalling. She looked at the guards to see if they indicated some kind of judgment. One appeared to twitch, but she couldn't be certain if he was curious or if he simply had an inopportune itch.

"Yes, let's talk," Aven said.

Raena smirked, tucking her hands under her tunic. "We can talk. If you like. We can sleep. I'm sure my bed is more comfortable."

Aven felt her cheeks redden. "My…Your Majesty. Of course, if you wish."

Raena opened her mouth as though to speak again, then turned and opened the door, leading the way. As soon as Aven entered, Raena closed it tight and stepped into the ample and heavily-decorated boudoir.

"I'm sorry," Raena blurted out, "I realize that you probably felt obligated to say yes, because of the guards. If you don't want to be in my chamber tonight, it's alright. You don't have to. I only hoped...I would like to talk if you'd want to."

Aven furrowed her brow. "Are you expecting Jonn-Del to hear of it if I've been here?"

"No? Why would I?"

"The..." Aven froze, then started again. "Did Jonn-Del say something to you about calling off the marriage?"

Raena scoffed. "Of course. He hates the idea, but I told him to shut his mouth and accept that I'm the Prince now. He can't continue to boss me around, and he knows it."

Aven nodded, but her hazel eyes focused on the floor.

Raena's smile faded. "Did he say something to you? Did he try...what did he say?"

"It...I suppose it's nothing. He said that I ought to offer my body to you without the marriage. That I should...be your mistress."

Out of the corner of her eye, Aven peeked at Raena. The prince threw up her hands.

"What would be the point of that? If I wanted to marry you for...but this is a political union! I told him as much. I told him specifically that we were marrying to appeal to the common-born. Even he knows that's an excellent idea. In fact, it sounded even better when I was hearing myself say it to him than it sounded when you and I discussed it."

Aven wanted to accept the notion but the sting of Jonn-Del's words still lingered, repeating in her mind.

"Come on," Raena motioned toward a cushioned bench. "Let's get comfortable. Would you like anything to eat or drink?"

"No, thank you." Aven took the offered seat.

Raena poured a goblet of ale for herself, then a second, and set them both on a low table. She took a seat in a lounging chair, adjacent to Aven's bench.

"Do you mind if I remove some of this?" Raena asked, gesturing to her formal garments.

"Not at all."

Raena leaned down to pull strappings loose from her boots as she spoke. "We still want to do this, right? The marriage is a great idea."

"I suppose," Aven mumbled.

"Why are you hesitant? Is it because of me?"

"No…I'm sorry," Aven glanced at the two goblets of ale. "May I have one of these, after all?"

"Yes," Raena smirked, pulling her boots off. "I got that second for you. I knew you'd want it."

"Ah. You're already practicing to be my husband, then."

The tips of Raena's ears turned pink and she focused on unstitching the sides of her tunic.

Aven sipped the ale and swallowed before speaking. "Jonn-Del and Baron Evandry were very…intimidating."

Raena raised an eyebrow. "How so?"

"It was clear that if I don't listen to their warnings, they plan to go through with something ugly."

"Well, they couldn't. Especially if you are the princess. You'd be untouchable."

Aven took a deep breath. "What if they know something? Something that could hurt us both?"

Raena pulled free the last side stitch and removed her tunic. She shook loose the muslin undershirt. "Well, Jonn-Del can't tell anyone…that. He would incriminate himself. I've said as much to him and he knows it. He must take our secret to the gallows."

"Not that," Aven said. Though they were alone, she scooted to the edge of the bench and whispered. "What if they know something…about Allyn?"

Raena raised one eyebrow, her lips pursed. "No, they don't."

"They asked me about him. Baron Evandry asked if I knew him. He talked at length about how Allyn died because of me."

"Because...of you?"

"I don't know, I'm not sure if that's what he meant."

Raena leaned forward. Her face was twisted with concern. "Did he give any hints that he knew anything, specific? There's just no way that...I don't think he could."

Aven wanted to reply, but she found herself shaking. Her mouth closed tight. She wanted to shut her eyes again and escape from the moment, but it wasn't this moment she feared, it was the possible moment ahead. The moment where they would take her life and punish her for what she had done. Her arms wrapped around her and all of her body shivered.

Raena was wiping at her mouth, staring into the goblet, but when she caught sight of Aven she rose from her chair. In an instant, Raena was beside Aven on the bench, pulling her close. "Hey...it's alright," Raena whispered. Both of her strong arms wrapped around Aven, squeezing. Over and over Raena muttered calming, reassuring words.

"I don't know wh—what's wrong," Aven muttered.

"You're terrified, but it's alright," Raena said. "You're going to be safe. You're okay. You're safe."

Aven shook harder, as though the fear was fighting its way out of her skin.

Raena shifted, moving to where Aven's head was against her firm, muscular chest. The muslin undershirt was thin and Aven could smell the familiar scent of Raena's skin, flooding her with memories of moments when they were close. Most of them passionate, intimate, but some tainted with bittersweet saltiness.

"Nothing will happen to you," Raena mumbled, "I'm not going to let them do anything. I will kill them before they hurt you."

Though Aven believed the sentiment likely wasn't possible, Raena's confident tone brought her comfort. With a long breath, Aven felt her body release, and the shaking subsided. She lingered there a few seconds, letting Raena's warmth envelop her before Aven pulled back. They separated instantly, Raena sliding away on the bench.

"Are you alright?" Raena asked, her periwinkle eyes filled with serious concern.

"Yes, I…that's been happening a lot," Aven whispered.

Raena nodded. "It's a fear tremor. I understand."

Aven grimaced. "You do?"

"Aye, Finn used to have them. We shared a room when I was…after my body started to change. That was Lord Sylas's way of making sure the other boys didn't know."

"But he knew."

"Yes," Raena smiled, "he was the one I chose to share my secret with. We had a room together after that, forever. Really until I was sent to serve you, I was always with him. We slept on our furs. Sometimes we shared the same bed, because of his tremors. I would hold him like that, the same way. I would tell him it was alright."

Aven raised her eyebrows. "Did Sylas ever worry about the two of you in bed, like that?"

Raena chuckled. "No one did. No one would have. Not Lady Isla, either. They knew that Finn was…he's different. He's a different sort of man. He loves deeply and feels so much, but he doesn't have urges like other men do. I don't know how else to explain it without saying too much."

"Of course, of course. You don't have to tell me anything that's not yours to share."

"Right, thank you. If he were here, maybe he could tell you."

Aven reached for the goblet, holding it for a moment. "Do you think his tremors were because of anything? Some sort of pain. I know that mine are. I…I'm so afraid."

Raena shook her head. "We feared a lot, I think. Both he and I had to hide so many parts of ourselves. He never talked much about his brother, but I know they were close before he was taken to the gaol. He was afraid something similar would happen to him, and maybe to me."

"Was his brother..."

"He loved boys. He was found out. He was just barely a man himself."

Aven shook her head as if to forbid the thought. "I often forget how much harsher that is for the nobles in Candor. And I suppose I didn't think of it when I grew up here, because I didn't know it, about myself."

"But you aren't..." Raena began, then stopped herself. She reached for her goblet and took a purposeful drink of ale.

Aven waited a moment before asking. "I'm not what?"

"Sorry, I suppose I thought...I always thought you felt something for me because you didn't know."

Aven scoffed. "What do you mean? I don't understand what you're trying to say."

Raena began to blush but pushed on. "You know what I mean. You thought I was a man. You see me as one, so you have—had feelings for me. But it's just because I am a man, I'm sure. I don't think you would really think about all girls this way. And maybe you don't even think about me that way, anymore."

Aven let out a long breath through her teeth. "I can't argue with you on all counts, but you're mostly wrong. My feelings about you never changed whether I saw you as a man or a woman, and so you and I are clear, I do see you as a woman, I can simply hide it well. I imagine you're used to that. As far as I feel about anyone else, well, I've been attracted to all sorts of people. And I say people because some of them are men, some of them are women. I don't feel like I've ever preferred one or the other. Though, I never imagined myself being with a woman in any sort of...intimate way, before you."

Raena's neck had been red for a moment and it was spreading to her cheeks. She spoke in a hush. "Do you feel like I tricked you when I didn't tell you right away?"

"No, not at all. I understand perfectly. In fact, I've often felt surprised and privileged that you chose to tell me so quickly. I think when you did, I was relieved that you shared, but I was also frightened for you. If I knew your secret, others could, too."

"You were the first person I told since I was coming of age."

Aven reached out and placed her hand on Raena's forearm. "I'm honored. I protect your secret. I always will."

"Thank you," Raena mumbled, staring into her goblet. "I know you will."

There was a comfortable silence for a few breaths. Both of them hung suspended in the time together. Aven's mind centered on the peace that swelled through her. She let it drift inside her body, relaxing her. Though they were still in Candor and hazard was around every corner, she felt a sense of safety for the first time.

"So," Raena said, a smirk forming, "you're attracted to other women, then?"

Aven slapped the forearm she'd been holding. "I suppose I'm free to if I'd like."

"Nay, we're getting married. I'm going to keep you in this castle. No more handmaidens for you, either, I'll have to send the guards in to tend to you. I'll make sure they cover their faces."

Aven smiled, unable to bring herself to laugh after the tumbling wave of emotion she'd experienced for the night.

Raena gave her a playful nudge. "I'm teasing. I won't be a bad husband, I promise. And if you want to be with someone else, then this marriage is only—"

"Let's not jump ahead of ourselves," Aven blurted. "One pretend husband and diplomacy with an entire kingdom is enough for me to handle. I am not interested in additional pursuits such as lovers."

"Good, me neither. Not that you were wondering, but in case you were…I'm not interested in lovers, either."

"Well, that would be particularly dangerous for both of us."

Raena shrugged, taking the last drink of her ale and then standing to refill the goblet.

"How soon will we do this?" Aven asked.

"The wedding? There's no need to wait. We can begin planning as soon as I announce it. If we want to invite the heads of all the Houses, as we should? It will take them a few days to gather their traveling parties and arrive. I think we could hold the ceremony in a fortnight."

Aven nodded. Her stomach fluttered with nerves at the idea, but she ignored them.

"Your brothers will need to be brought in," Raena said.

"Brought in?"

Raena sat in the lounge chair once more. "Aye, I'm not sure where they all are, but I know I can send for them. C'olon is near Hawk's Keep, the last I checked. Faer was in the Scablands, but we can send horsemen north to reach him. I haven't been able to track down the others, but I'm the prince, I can order for their returns."

Aven felt the threat of tears, but none came. Perhaps if she had not cried so much lately, she would be able to. "Thank you."

"Of course. You don't need to thank me. You are about to be the princess, Aven. You will have the right and the authority to make these decisions."

"Yes, but…I didn't even know that you knew my brothers' names."

Raena shrugged. "Well, I decided to find out."

Aven smiled. She drained the rest of her ale. For a moment the only sound was a crackle from the fireplace. Without meaning to, she gazed across the boudoir to the door to Raena's chamber.

"Are you tired?" Raena asked.

"Yes, I suppose I am."

"Come on then, I'll show you to the bedroom."

Raena stood, but Aven hesitated. "Should I stay the night? Won't we want to wait…"

"For what? The wedding?"

Aven shrugged. "Isn't that the thing to do?"

317

"After what Jonn-Del said to you, I would prefer to keep you close at all times. If you are worried about how I'll behave—"

"No, no. I'm not worried about you. I just know that you have to worry about rumors and perception. You are the prince, and you have not yet announced our betrothal."

Raena smirked. "Duchess—and you are a duchess—my kingdom is under the communal hands of a bunch of lunatics, poisoning the minds of my subjects. My armies are children and infirm. My rule is tainted thanks to the miserable disaster that was the prince before me. Mentioning my name was treasonous a few seasons ago, and if I can't fix this, it will probably be treasonous again. As far as I can tell, sleeping with a common-born woman I'm about to wed will be the least of my scandals as a prince. If anyone has the energy to spread this rumor tomorrow, it'll soon be overshadowed by some other incident. So, I think we can safely say that you may sleep in my bed."

Aven slowly closed her mouth, her eyes fixating on Raena's.

"Come on, then." Raena walked into the chamber.

Aven took a deep breath and then followed. At the threshold, it was dark for a split second, but Raena was lighting candles that illuminated the ample bedroom as soon as Aven entered. And how it was one of the largest bedrooms she had ever seen.

The first thing Aven noticed was the stone bath built into the floor, with light steam rising from it, even though no handmaiden was there to draw freshly boiled water. There was another fireplace, crackling low, and Aven realized the room was a comfortable temperature because of it. There was a table filled with handfuls of food, varieties that Aven knew would be coveted by any member of the kingdom, desperate to eat something besides flat flour cake and pigskin soup.

The bed was a marvel of its own. Surrounded by hanging tapestries on the wall and draped with layers of delicate stitched blankets, Aven paused for a moment to admire the colors. The room was mainly desert orange and pale blue for House Schinen, but the bedding was a different shade. Dark ocean tones, like the sea at night, accented with silver drapes around the bedposts.

Raena stood before Aven, rubbing her hands together.

"Are those my…Colby colors?" Aven whispered, gesturing to the bed.

"Oh," Raena glanced, then her periwinkle eyes darted away. "Uh, I suppose. Yes. I was just wanting to be reminded of…I wanted to think of both Houses. I was part of Colby, as well."

Aven nodded.

"I can take some of the furs and I'll sleep on the floor. There's a spot on the other side of the bed. I'll just wake up in the morning, early, and get into bed with you before the handmaidens come in. If that's alright, I think it's best to keep up the appearances."

Aven shook her head. "Don't be silly. You shouldn't sleep on the floor. You're a prince, after all."

"Yes, but, well. No. You have made it clear that you want limits between us, and I respect your wishes."

"Rae," Aven stepped closer, holding out her hand. "You are respecting my wishes. You're being very courteous and understanding. That doesn't mean that you have to sleep on the floor. I'm sure we are perfectly capable of sharing a bed like two people who are thoughtful and…friendly with one another."

A shadow lingered in Raena's eyes for a second, then passed. "Of course. If you're comfortable, then that's all I care about. Thank you."

CHAPTER 29
AVEN

For breath upon your breath...for heart upon your heart

Aven hadn't known what being a princess felt like until now.

The morning of their wedding was a busy one. Raena had been whisked away before dawn to receive guests, and their bedroom was filled with a dozen handmaidens by the time the sun rose. All of them were bustling and moving about in a flutter. They worried over everything—chattering about gown stitching, hair, pins and hooks, and fretting with flower petals to make perfumes.

Aven was at the center in a perpetual state of dress and undress, like a child's doll being manipulated into various poses. She kept her mouth shut and her body pliable as the master-of-maidens, Duney, executed her vision.

This was her first day in her "Princess Room", a chamber equipped with a secondary nursery, already filled with furniture and accessories for a noble baby. The bed was also made for birthing, with a section that could be raised or lowered under the knees to allow a woman to take a comfortable position. She couldn't fathom the idea of pregnancy, knowing it wasn't possible with Raena. Somehow the thought of having any other "man's" baby felt wrong.

But that was putting the soldier ahead of the shield, so to speak.

As Duney weaved Aven's damp hair around a mould to shape it into curls, Aven remembered her wedding to Eathon. By comparison, that day had been simple. Quiet. A forest wedding with his closest family and a handful of nobles. This day would involve a whole kingdom, a notion which made Aven's heart race and palms sweat.

"You aren't holding still," Duney chided, repositioning Aven's head with a sharp tug.

"I'm sorry," Aven muttered.

Duney clicked her tongue. She was an elderly woman. Aven wondered if Duney had been the master-of-maidens for Zarana's wedding day, as well.

A few of the other handmaidens stepped away. Duney took the opportunity to lean in close and speak in a low voice. "I know where you hail from. I even remember seeing you when you were a young girl. A pig farmer's daughter."

Aven rejected the urge to cringe.

Duney smiled. "Today you become a princess. Don't forget that. In a few hours, you will be the most important woman in all of Calamyta. So, never apologize to a commoner like me again." Though her face was kind, her voice was cold.

"Thank you," Aven said.

"There."

Aven raised an eyebrow.

"You should turn all your apologies into gratitude."

"Ah," Aven muttered, as though she understood.

The other handmaidens returned and set to rustling the paper-thin muslin beneath Aven's skirts. Within minutes, the shape of her legs vanished and everything below her waist bloomed outward, like a feather duster. Aven could no longer see the floor around her feet, and hoped she wouldn't be expected to walk unassisted.

321

Someone asked what color to tint her face, and Duney muttered something about Aven's "delicate skin" that didn't come across as flattery. True to Candorian standards, the women pressed layers of damp scod grass to Aven's cheeks and forehead, leaving behind dusty residue until she matched the color of terra.

"Your husband will want you to wear this every day," Duney remarked, chuckling.

Aven smiled. "I'm sure I'll exceed his expectations, thanks to you."

"I do my best. And if his eyes start wandering after you give him his little princes, remember that I'm always here to help you remind him which woman to return to."

"Oh, I don't think that will be a problem with Prince Trevin."

Duney clucked her tongue. "That's what Zarana said about King Lyam. But I was there."

"Queen Zarana?" Aven asked. "What happened with—" she turned her head, earning a scowl from the maidens still painting her cheeks with rouge. But Duney was chastising one of the girls near the door, stepping quickly out of the room with a flurry.

"Please, Your Majesty," the maiden said, pulling Aven's chin back into place.

Aven accepted the continued rouge treatment, watching out of the corner of her eye for Duney to return. After what must have been an hour or more, the handmaidens were finished. Aven was a spectacle of grandiose beauty and nobility. She was covered in blue, silver, and dangling shapes cut from pure quorrilium that draped down her dress. Her hair was curled and then left in ringlets that cascaded over her shoulders. Her face was someone she barely recognized when they held up a mirror for her inspection. She looked more like Queen Zarana than any woman she had ever seen, and Aven supposed that must be due to the late Queen's affinity for similar extravagant make-up and clothing.

The maidens led her out of the chamber and toward the Viewing Room, another royal place that Aven hadn't known existed before this very day. She did not again see Duney, and wondered why the master had removed herself from preparations for the wedding.

The Viewing Room was a museum of sorts, lined with banners and tapestries that stretched through the chamber which was long and thin. There were affects belonging to the kings of historical Calamyta, spanning back three hundred years to the beginning of the known kingdoms, and then further to recognize the first seven families. The room was kept dark to preserve the artifacts, with candles encased in thin stone wraps.

Aven's eyes adjusted as she was sent into the room alone. She realized when the door behind her closed that it was the first silence she'd had since waking at dawn, and it was nearly the mid-day meal time. Gone was even the dull hum of the kingdom's people gathering outside.

She was meant to solemnly reflect on the nobles of Candor and find herself within the Viewing Room. She was meant to learn what rulers they had each been, cementing her own ruling style.

Aven couldn't help it as her mind drifted to Zander.

Had he ever set foot in the Viewing Room? Had he humbled himself to consider how to lead his people? Had he considered the things that Candor needed, instead of his own selfishness?

Aven walked slowly across the hard stone floor, each footstep echoing in the strange hollowness of the chamber.

When the door slid open and shut behind her, Aven turned and spotted the shadowed outlines of two men.

Instinctively, she bowed, unsure of their nobility.

"Isn't it us who is supposed to bow to you?" one asked in a jovial tone; a voice she had not heard in years but would recognize anywhere.

Aven practically sprinted to them, and the three embraced in an instant before another word could be said.

"Brothers," she gasped, through the onset of delighted tears. Gregor and Tennel laughed as they squeezed her between them.

"Let me see you," Aven said, pulling away.

"Aw, we're hideous," Gregor said.

Aven studied them both in the dim light. They were taller than her, as always, but they'd both grown broadly sideways with thick shoulders covered in the tunics of House Grent. Both men had beards, but Gregor's was thicker and hung from his chin. Their brown eyes carried more weight than Aven remembered ever seeing.

"What are…what are you doing here?" Aven said, aghast.

Tennel chuckled. "Your new husband sent a dozen men to rip us from our posts. We thought we were being imprisoned, the way they rushed in.

"Wait until you see who else is here," Gregor added. "Your new husband loves surprises. I guess he can do whatever he pleases, being the prince."

Aven didn't know how to reply, the words escaping her. She looked back and forth between her brothers with her mouth slightly open.

"Are you done in this room, then?" Tennel said, waving his hand. "We were sent ahead to fetch you and bring you down to the courtyard."

"Is it that time, already?" Aven muttered, finding her throat dry.

Tennel shrugged. When he smiled, hawk's feet formed around his eyes.

Aven gave a parting glance to the Viewing Room. She knew the end of the hall held the most recent rulers, and that's where she would find Queen Zarana's image and perhaps artifacts. But that would be for another day when she had more time.

"I'm ready," Aven said with a decisive nod.

She followed her brothers out to the corridors and they descended the tower. Both men chattered without ceasing, regaling stories of their unfortunate assignment to guard House Grent. Aven smiled and nodded every time they looked at her; the more they spoke the longer she could remain reflective in her own head.

At the bottom of the tower, the crowd of voices outside was so loud that Aven could no longer hear her brothers without them shouting.

Which Gregor did. "The whole bloody kingdom is out there!"

324

A tightness built in Aven's chest. She stared through the archway in front of her and wondered where they would possibly go to hold this wedding. In a surreal way, the crowd reminded her of the day the Librens had attacked the citadel.

"Come on," Tennel shouted, grabbing her hand. He barged into the edge of the courtyard and kept close to the wall, leading Aven. Gregor stayed behind, and in the moment they presented as true guards doing their job instead of her dear brothers.

They were only in the open courtyard for a moment. When they tucked back into an archway, a massive receiving party was waiting.

"Your Majesty," a noblewoman bearing the colors of House Lox said. She bowed and the others followed suit.

Aven vaguely recognized them all: House Payton, House Grent, House Lox, Hawk's Keep. No one from House Schinen, no one from Colby. No one to represent the married couples' true affiliations.

The nobles surrounded her in an entourage and they walked together with a man blowing a bugle at the front. The crowds parted for the bugle and within a minute the party was out of the castle and in the winding streets of the citadel.

Commoners on either side of them called out greetings and waved as they passed. Many were singing "The Joy of Candor", an old tune Aven remembered from childhood but had forgotten most of the lyrics to. The only line she could recall was "from the desert we bloom and flower before the tomb" which stuck in her mind because she never understood why Candorians sang about tombs. As Aven walked through the parted crowd, a diacon caught her eye. There were many men with white robes and purple faces, but this one stuck out. His face was not painted, but a natural sort of purple tone. Aven stared. He was so familiar; it was like looking into the past.

Zander.

She jolted and scanned again among the commoners. There were many diacons. Surely one of them had been the man she'd seen. Aven shook her head to banish the thought. She must've had Zander on her mind because she was being escorted into "his" arena.

Despite not knowing any words to "The Joy of Candor", she found herself humming when the small party turned and the nobles escorted Aven to the entrance.

There was so much to take in, Aven stumbled at the first step through the canvas flaps. The walls on the arena floor were gone—the labyrinth was dismantled. Mountain rock cobbles had been laid, spanning across the great space.

Aven realized she'd stopped, and the entourage was politely waiting ahead of her as she took it all in.

Nothing in the arena at all resembled the day of the Knight's Trials—except for the crowd. Even then, the seats were filled with peaceful and reverent citizens, not the bloodthirsty belligerence she'd seen over a year before.

Aven's eyes scanned across the arena floor. A pathway was highlighted by crushed spices and flowers, leading in a trail to the center, where a raised platform built of sand bricks was laid and surrounded by solemn noblemen.

"Take your time, Princess," a man quietly teased from behind.

Aven looked over her shoulder and was met with bright eyes and a crooked smile she would know anywhere in any kingdom. "Barton," she rasped, reaching for him instantly. She pulled him into an embrace which he returned with a suffocating squeeze. "What are you doing here?"

He chuckled against her hair. "Your Prince was rather insistent that your brothers attend." Barton stepped back, still smiling. "Even though I had to ride like the wind through Boenaerya to be here."

"I'm afraid I have no words. Thank you."

Gregor interjected. "Come on then, your reunions aren't finished. But your Prince and the whole kingdom are waiting."

Aven nodded, remembering again where she was, suddenly aware that the arena had gone quiet around them. Thousands upon thousands of sets of eyes were all on her, waiting, hanging on her every move. It was enough to make her heart race and her knees feel weak. Fortunately, Barton extended his elbow and Aven slipped her hand into it, steadying herself by his arm.

Each step felt as though she floated through the air. It was impossible for her senses to register it all. Though the arena was filled with thousands upon thousands, it was deathly quiet. She could even hear the crunch of flowers and spices between her feet and the cobblestone path. She stared ahead at the platform as they drew closer, searching for Raena. All she could see there was a line of noblemen stretching around the front, somber and expectant.

Barton leaned in and whispered. "I'm happy to see you marry again."

Aven glanced at him to see he was indeed smiling. "It has not yet been a double season. But here you are to bless me."

"I am," he grinned, "though it's not the double season, it is a different season. Indeed, when you should be wed. It's time for you to be a princess. It's time for you to save your kingdom."

"You believe that I can?"

Barton didn't answer, and they were near enough to the platform that Aven was suddenly not sure if there was any more to say. The nobles before her stepped aside and fell to their knees, bowing on either side. They lined her way and she paused, recognizing the final few steps ahead.

The platform was higher than it had seemed, raised on stilts to the same level of Aven's chest. There were flat stones leading the way, stacked into steps. When Aven followed the line of steps, the sight above her momentarily took her breath away.

Raena.

Glorious and dignified; she was the picture of a magnificent prince. Raena's hands were clasped and her shoulders raised, as though tense, but her periwinkle eyes beheld Aven with warmth. Raena was a menagerie of kingdoms and regions. Her golden hair was twisted behind her, the sides of her head freshly shaved and painted in the style she'd worn at House Colby. It was the first time she had cut the sides since they first rode to Ediva. Over her chest she wore solid copper armor, a breastplate emblazoned with the fox sigil of Schinen. Behind her were the flags of Schinen and Colby, flying side by side.

"Come on now, don't keep him waiting," Barton whispered.

Aven realized she had been staring stopped. With shaking legs, she stepped up the stones, Barton still at her side. When they reached the top of the platform, Aven knew what was expected of her, but felt unable to remember the steps. Fortunately, Barton took over and interceded. He pulled Aven gently to the place beside Raena and removed Aven's hand from his elbow, then held her wrist to steady her. Raena turned, her expression unreadable, and softly reached for Aven. Their hands connected and fingers intertwined, beginning the ceremony.

Raena acted first, lowering to her knees, their hands still connected. Aven waited, breathing a few long breaths, waiting for the invitation.

Raena stared upward and her face softened. "Duchess Avenna of House Colby, born to Gailia in service of King Lyam and Queen Zarana of House Payton, servant of Candor, leader of Boenaerya, widow of Duke Eathon Colby. I am humbled today before our kingdom, our families, and our regions. You have joined me upon this place where our eyes once met for the first time. Today I ask you to take me as yours. Will you belong to me?"

Aven felt her throat dry. Her heart raced as she recited the words. "And who are you, sir?"

"I am Trevin Schinen. I am Prince of Candor, Knight of Hawk's Keep, son of Stavin Schinen, born in service of King Lyam and Queen Zarana of Payton. I am a descendent of Coren Schinen, the third founder of Calamyta, sworn to the seven brothers. I am a humble prince, asking you to be my princess, and rule beside me."

She felt the words in her heart before she heard them, as though someone else were speaking. "I will belong to you. I will join you in life and death. I will wrap my soul into yours and find belonging." Then she lowered to her knees. Their hands still joined; Raena was close enough for Aven to feel her unsteady breaths. It was beautiful and surreal, and frightening all at once.

The men around them began to sing in deep, low tones. The diacon presiding over their ceremony was in black robes, holding a sceptre against his chest as his voice rang out. He was joined by Barton, Gregor, and Tennel, who stood behind Aven. Her three brothers placed their hands on her shoulders to give the blessing as their song rose.

That was when Aven followed the hands on Raena's shoulders, her eyes traveling up to find a man she did not expect; Sir Brande of House Galewind, the supposed pater of Sir Rowan, and therefore the man who had claimed a bastard to hide Raena's identity. Aven's eyes narrowed as she wondered if Sir Brande knew the reason he had been given claim to this bastard 'son', and why he had kept the secret. Would he reveal them now that Raena was prince?

"Join in our song," the diacon called out to the crowd.

Aven was ripped from her thoughts as the drone of singing rose all around them. The voices of thousands were deafening and beautiful, creating the chorus of the Candorian wedding chant.

Of the Seven Almighties
Of the seven families
Formed upon land that breathes
For breath upon your breath
For heart upon your heart
For souls to join as one together
As our seven brothers joined to sing
To end our troubles on this day
The Almighties make our souls one
The Almighties make our souls one

Against her will and all of her self-control, Aven felt warm tears forming in her eyes. She stared down at the ground, studying Raena's knees and the diacon's sandaled feet. She felt Raena squeeze her hands and gently begin to brush a thumb over the back of Aven's knuckles, but then stop as fast as she'd begun.

329

"The people have called for the Almighties to bless this marriage," the diacon spoke, his voice half-speaking, half-singing. "We ask for those closest to the Prince and Duchess to speak on their behalf. Sir Brande of House Galewind, you are here to bless Trevin. What say you?"

Brande puffed up his chest to speak loudly, as though performing in a theater. "I bless Trevin for this marriage."

The diacon nodded and turned to the men behind Aven. "And Lord Barton of House Colby, and gentlemen Tennel and Gregor, guards of House Grent, you are here to bless Avenna. What say you?"

"We bless Aven for this marriage," they replied in unison.

Aven felt them squeeze her shoulders, then let go, the warmth of their hands instantly missed. Now the touch of Raena's hands was even more apparent, and part of Aven wanted to let go and pull away. Yet the other part of her wanted to collapse and hide her face in Raena's shoulder, where she'd once found the most comfort in the world.

"Prince Trevin," the diacon continued, "there are many names you will call Avenna. You will call her princess. You will call her wife. And if her body is healthy and her heart receives you, then you will call her the Queen of Candor, mother to your heirs. For your love is not yours alone. Your bond belongs to your kingdom. Today, you accept this wife and promise to your people that you will honor the vows of Calamyta, as the seven brothers made. You will carry forth House Schinen through this union. Do you accept this task and promise to give your kingdom a queen, give your throne an heir, and give your wife your loyalty?"

Raena's palms were sweating as she spoke. "I accept this task. I will give my kingdom a queen, I will give my throne an heir, and I will give my…wife, Aven, my loyalty."

Aven felt her heart race as Raena's eyes fixated on hers. She could no longer look away and notice anything or anyone else. All had faded around them as Raena became the center of the universe. If she allowed herself to think of where they were, she may panic. Instead, she focused on the small things that had become so familiar: the few sparse freckles around Raena's nose. The unique blend of blue, grey, and lavender that flecked in her eyes. The long lashes that were perhaps the only facial feature that threatened to give Raena away.

"Duchess Avenna," the diacon said. "There are many names you will call Trevin..."

Aven resisted the urge to smirk at that, but caught a flicker of amusement cross Raena's face.

"...you will call him prince. You will call him ruler of the kingdom, your heart, and your body..."

Raena wrinkled her nose at that, and Aven couldn't stop her smirk. The sobriety was broken and they both fought to stifle laughter, Raena biting her lip.

"...but if you prepare your body and heart for him and you serve him before all others, you will bear him an heir and call him king. You will carry House Schinen forward into the next age of our kingdom, and you will be remembered for generations of Schinens to rule Calamyta..."

Raena scoffed, and Aven shook her head. They fought to regain their somber composure. But the mood between them had shifted and Aven felt the tension dissipate.

"...do you accept this task and promise to give your kingdom a king and a prince, give your throne an heir, and give your husband your loyalty?"

"I accept this task," Aven repeated, "I will give my kingdom a king and a prince, I will give my throne an heir, and I will give my husband, Trevin, my loyalty." Though she said Trevin, Aven repeated the words in her mind, and thought 'Raena' over and over once more.

The diacon lifted his sceptre over his head and waved it twice. Dust of crystals from beneath the barren wasteland shook loose as he did, scattering over them both. "Almighties seal your bond. Almighties fuse your souls. Almighties bless your bodies with health, fertility, and loyalty. May the Almighties make you complete with their gifts of Light, Air and Sky, Water, Earth, Time, Beasts, and Death. For this life and all future generations, you are sealed as one."

"We are sealed as one," Raena said.

Aven felt her breath catch. She had not said the words. It was as though time stood still, and she was certain her own look of anguish was reflecting on Raena's face. She felt the warm hands holding hers squeeze, pleading her to say the final phrase.

For an unknown reason, Aven felt a warm tear roll down her cheek without precursor or warning. She swallowed, then nodded her head to try again. "We are sealed as one," she whispered.

Satisfied, Raena nodded and looked up to the diacon.

"May it be known," the diacon called, his singing voice echoing through the arena, "on this day and forever, Prince Trevin has taken Avenna for his wife! Prince Trevin, kiss your wife, then stand together as one."

Aven's heart raced and all she could do was close her eyes and wait. How many times had she kissed Raena? A hundred? A thousand? Perhaps they had kissed even more times than she had kissed anyone else, even Eathon. Yet somehow on this day, their wedding day, the idea of feeling Raena's lips against her own terrified her to her very core. She knew she must not show any resistance or hesitation. There, before the bated breath and watchful eyes of their whole kingdom fixated upon them, her every move would be scrutinized. Aven could not show anything but submission and grace.

Raena was close. Aven felt Raena's breath on her cheek, then the lightest brush of lips there, on her skin. Aven's eyes fluttered open, afraid that Raena had decided to refuse the kiss. But then Raena was there, incredibly close, breathing the same breath as though they were indeed one. That's when Aven felt the press of those familiar, soft, full lips to hers. Her eyes were still open, but she tilted her head to accept the kiss with visible enthusiasm. Aven put her best effort into it, bringing her hand to Raena's neck and holding them in the kiss for an additional second. Only the two of them knew what was lacking; there was no subtle movement of their lips once they were locked together. It was stiff, as if they had met hours before and not once been lovers for two seasons.

When Raena pulled away, the crowd erupted into unintelligible noise. If the diacon spoke again, no one could hear it over the roaring around them. Raena held Aven's hand and pulled, bringing them both to their feet in unison.

As husband and wife, Prince and Princess, they walked down the platform. Aven knew that Gregor, Tennel, Barton, and Sir Brande would be following behind. She knew that the crowd was around them erupting in praise and likely throwing symbolic gifts of crystal dust, grain, rare threads, and even quorrilium slag to the arena floor. But she turned her head and beheld Raena as they walked out of the arena. Raena, her knight. Raena, her friend. Raena, her lover. Raena, her prince. And now Raena, her husband.

CHAPTER 30
AVEN

The child of Lyam and Larana Payton

The feast and party that followed the wedding had been so excessive and stimulating that Aven had hardly caught a glimpse of her Prince. She'd spent the night bowing to one noble visitor after the next, being given unwanted and inapplicable advice: everything from "don't spill blood of a servant woman unless she crosses you" to "don't close your legs after he puts his seed inside you, it will suffocate the children". Even if it were possible for Raena to impregnate Aven, she was well-aware that suffocation of seed was absolute horse shite. She bit her tongue and smiled at all of them, so much that her cheeks grew sore. She'd sipped wine, but only enough to ease the edge and stop her hands from shaking. At one point the wine had begun to warm her belly and she set it aside. After all, she'd been warned and briefed and coached to death on how to "act like a princess and not a fool".

Her solace had been the few moments she spotted one of her brothers across the room. Aven still couldn't believe they were there, returned to her, close in the castle. Barton alleged that he wouldn't stay long, but Tennel and Gregor had been given new assignments as castle guards. Even her mother Gailia appeared grateful, though she stuck to the shadows, out-of-place in the royal wedding feast.

They cheered and dismissed the newlywed couple at midnight. Raena and Aven held hands for the benefit of the guards as they walked the ramparts back to the royal chambers. When the moon was full over the citadel and not a cloud blocked the stars, Aven realized that her ears were ringing from the noise of the arena and the raucous music at the feast.

Raena was quiet, gazing at the stars while they walked. She remained somewhat aloof as the pair reentered the castle halls and wandered to the prince's chamber. Though Aven had been there before, now the expectation was higher. Raena seemed to feel the same as she fumbled with the hook and latch to open the door. A guard stepped forward first, scanning the room for danger and clearing it with a bow.

Raena bit her lip and waved at the empty chamber. "After you, Princess."

Aven blushed at the new title. It sounded sweet on Raena's tongue, as though she'd practiced saying it before this moment. Aven wondered if she would grow accustomed to it as she walked through the boudoir and into the deeper chamber.

Their room had been prepared elaborately for a clear purpose. The bed was covered in satin blankets, the finest threads, no doubt woven over a matter of years from the cocoons of thousands of nubile caterpillars from the Scablands. Aven had heard of such a thing, but never seen it for herself. Candles lit the room and the bath had been drawn; steam rising from the floor. Somehow, she knew the bed was warm without even laying in it.

She reached the side of the bed and admired the silk, brushing her hand over it. She felt a blush rise to her cheeks.

"If it's alright, I'll change my clothes first," Raena said.

Aven turned to find her wife at the doorway, about to step into the boudoir, holding a bundle of bedclothes. "Of course, but is there anything for me to wear?"

Raena glanced about with an air of panic. "I just realized that... I'm sorry, there isn't. Could I give you some of mine?"

Aven nodded. "If you wouldn't mind."

"I'd not mind at all," Raena mumbled, rushing to the wardrobe. She hastily pulled several muslin items and something smooth and dark, gathering them up, then tossed them out to display them across the bed. "They are men's, of course, but well...that doesn't bother me."

"It doesn't bother me, either. Thank you." Aven reached for the loose pants and tunic. "I've worn my brothers' old pajamas plenty of times."

"Right," Raena muttered. "Well then, I'll give you privacy. Just call me when you're done."

In an instant, Raena disappeared around the corner to the boudoir. Aven couldn't help but find it a bit strange for them to be changing separately, but she supposed it might have been equally strange for them to be nude in front of one another after all they'd been through.

Aven reached for the back of her dress and pulled at the ties, searching for the knots. She found a place the ribbons crossed over her back and tugged, trying to loosen them. Sighing, she held the elbow of one arm and tried again, stretching as far as she could, but it seemed to mock her by tightening. Her chest felt further constricted.

"Aven? Are you alright?" Raena called from beyond the archway.

"Yes, I'm fine."

"Are you sure? You're...grunting a lot."

Aven groaned, her eyes to the ceiling.

"Like that," Raena quipped.

"It's..." Aven sighed, "this dress is more elaborate than I'm used to. I think...I think I need your help."

"Should I close my eyes?"

"No, I'm still completely dressed, unfortunately."

Raena came in fast, holding her ceremonial clothes and tossing them onto a table before coming to Aven's aid. Aven turned to bare her back and pulled her hair aside. Raena seemed to stand there, studying for a moment.

"This is…complicated," Raena muttered.

"Women's clothing regularly is."

"Hmm, is it usually this knotty?"

"No," Aven said, "this is particularly elaborate for the ceremony. I probably should have fetched handmaidens to help me undress."

Aven could practically hear Raena puffing up her chest with pride at the mention of handmaidens. "No need. I'll get you out of this. I think I understand the problem."

Of course, Raena would see it as a challenge. Aven bowed her head and waited as she felt Raena's fingers setting to work. There was a series of tugs and pulls, then Raena's hand slid between the ribbons and Aven's back, causing her to shudder.

"I'm sorry, I should have asked," Raena whispered.

"It's okay," Aven whispered back.

"Almost done."

Aven nodded, biting her lip. She felt the warmth of Raena's hand and deep down she knew she longed for it to travel lower, brushing across her body, fondling and caressing her into the morning. But her heart was locked like a cold tomb, reminding her of how bitter and broken she would feel in the morning if she gave in to her body's craving.

"There," Raena said with an audible smile, "I think you could slide it down now?"

Aven looked over her shoulder to see the adorably gleeful look on her wife's face.

Raena pulled her hand free and clapped. "I'll leave you to it. Call me when you're done."

"Thank you, again," Aven replied. She waited for Raena's second exit then changed quickly. She got into the bed and pulled the silky blankets over her, taking a deep breath before she called for Raena to return to the chamber.

When Raena entered, her brow was furrowed, as though she'd thought of a new problem more challenging than the ribbons of the dress. She flurried about the room, blowing out candles, tidying the discarded clothes. She seemed unsure of what to do; Aven could sense the anxiety emulating out of her movements.

"Alright," Raena said, studying the ground. "Well, goodnight."

Aven frowned, perplexed.

With a forced smile, Raena blew out the final few candles. Shrouded in darkness, Aven laid in bed expectantly. She waited for a minute, then another, for the feeling of Raena getting in and under the blankets beside her. But that weight and shift of Raena never happened.

Aven heard a sigh in the room, somewhere away from the bed.

"Erm," Aven began, feeling odd about what to say.

"Are you alright, Princess?" Raena's voice asked, definitely far from the bed.

"Where are you?"

"Oh," Raena mumbled, "erm, I'm…I'm…Can you not see me? I forget what you can and can't see in the dark."

"No, I can't see you."

"Right."

There was a pause as though both of them were waiting to hear what the other would have to say. It lasted for a moment. Aven heard a rustling sound from far off, as though someone was shuffling in the hallway beyond the boudoir.

"Do you need anything? More blankets? A cold drink?" Raena asked.

Aven caught a glimpse of Raena's shadow, however slight, a few paces from the bed. "Raena…were you watching me?"

"When?"

"A moment ago, when you were quiet."

"I was."

Aven bit her lip and slowly pulled the blankets up to her chin. She couldn't help the blush that crept up her cheeks. She felt a throbbing in her chest that spread outward and filled her with warmth, and she was frustrated with her inability to name the emotion.

"Can you please light a candle?"

"Of course," Raena mumbled. In a second there was a flash, followed by a cool orange light. It illuminated Raena's face. Aven stared through the dark to meet Raena's gaze.

"If you're going to use your Boen sight, may I ask that you make it fair?"

"What do you mean?"

Aven struggled to think of the words, unsure what she wanted and how to ask for it. "I think...I think if you're looking at me in the dark, I want to know. And I want to be able to look at you, too."

Raena bit her lip and set down the candle on the floor beside her. "Of course. I will honor that from now on. Is there anything else I can do? Is there anything more you want?"

There were a dozen things that Aven wanted. She wanted to be told that Candor would be alright. She wanted to be told the Boens would never come. She wanted to believe that she and Raena could actually rule, and wouldn't be the bane of their kingdom. But need? She wasn't sure what she needed.

"I think I want you to get into bed," Aven said, quietly.

Raena smiled, "I can do that."

It was a comfortable arrangement; Aven on one end, Raena on the other, so their bodies were facing opposite directions. They had already grown used to it in a short time. Raena left the candle burning on the floor and took her place at the foot of the bed, burrowing into the furs and pulling them around her.

When Raena was settled, she spoke again. "It was a busy day. Perhaps neither of us are wound down enough to sleep yet."

"Are you happy with it?"

"With the day?"

"Yes. The wedding. Even though it wasn't really...it wasn't exactly what you may have imagined for yourself?"

Raena put her arm beneath her head and laid back, staring up at the ceiling. "It wasn't, no. But I'm not sure why. I always imagined that I would marry a woman, that's for sure. And I guess after I became Rowan, I imagined that I would be a knight when I married her. So, all of that was what I expected. But all of it was so extravagant and grand. It felt like the wedding was for the kingdom, but not really only…it didn't feel like it was mine, I suppose. Like I was watching it happen to someone else. Does that make sense?"

Aven nodded. "I understand."

Raena glanced in her direction. "Is that how it felt for you?"

"Erm…" Aven played with the blanket, twisting it between her fingers, while she thought. "Honestly, no. Not all of it felt right, but it did feel like it was for me. Moreso than it felt like it was for the kingdom when I think about it."

"Really?"

"Yes. When I married Eathon, none of my family was there. They wouldn't even entertain the idea of coming to East Shore. Queen Zarana was meant to come, but she wasn't able to travel because of something pressing in Candeo. But today…my brothers were there. Even at the end, I caught a glimpse of my mother. She was in the crowd, but I know I saw her. Perhaps that's why it wasn't perfect, but at least it reminded me of the weddings I'd imagined when I was a little girl."

"Perhaps."

They both fell into another contemplative silence, no strangeness passing between them. It was quiet for a few minutes. Aven continued to twist and feel the edge of the blanket, stealing glances at Raena in the candlelight. Her Prince's face was highlighted in angles and edges, appearing somehow softer and more ruggedly handsome all at once. Aven thought about all the moments she had stared at Raena, scanning for signs of what she knew she would never find: a beard, for one. But now Aven often found herself staring to reassure her mind that she couldn't see signs of Raena as a woman that others might see. As if she could 'catch' the details and protect Rae from exposing her truth. It must have been self-preservation.

"Maybe there's another reason," Raena whispered.

"Hmm?"

Raena rolled to her side and stared at Aven with strong intention. "Maybe there's another reason today felt special to you."

"I don't know what you mean."

"Aven...I have thought for a long time of something. I need to tell you. I'm sorry that I haven't before."

Aven felt her heart begin to beat faster, either at the intensity of Rae's stare, or the words she was saying. Either way, the room was growing warmer by the second.

Raena sat up. "Do you mind if I come to your side of the bed?"

"Of course not. It's your bed."

Even in the darkness, it looked as if Raena blushed. She turned and crawled to the middle of the bed, halfway to Aven, and rested on her elbows.

"You're a princess now," Raena began.

"Yes."

"Do you feel like perhaps you always were?"

Aven's brow pinched together. "What do you mean by that?"

"I think you always were. I think you're the princess."

"You mean that I am...I am a princess."

"No. I think you are the princess. I think you are the true princess. I think you're the true heir to the throne. I think you are the daughter of Lyam and Zarana Payton."

Aven broke into a laugh, but it sounded nervous. Scared. She laughed again, believing that Rae might join in, but the other woman was serious and steady. Their eyes met and locked. Raena's periwinkle stare was calm. There was no amusement or mischief anywhere to be found.

"What are you saying, Rae?" Aven whispered.

"I think if you let the idea into your mind, give it a moment there, you will realize it has to be true."

341

Aven blinked. She tried to hold the idea. But the words themselves were so foreign.

The daughter of Lyam and Zarana Payton.

"But Zander is their son."

Raena shook her head. "She hated him. She hated him to her core. You saw her in their final moments in Ediva, she did nothing to save him. She didn't even request that his life be spared. Part of me thinks she would have asked them to take his life and let her live. But the way she looked at all of us...anyway, I think I already knew, before then."

"This doesn't make sense. You're forgetting that I have a family. My parents and brothers raised me. I'm a pig butcher."

Raena grimaced. "You are? Then why do you have soft, pale skin like a noble? When your brothers are rough and dry like every other family of Candor who has worked fields for generations? Did you ever question why your mother had only sons, and then one day bore a daughter?"

"People have daughters."

"Not pig butchers. I asked your brother, Gregor, when he arrived. He told me that they didn't know what to do with you. They put you to work inside the castle, because there were no girls in the farms. He said something about the fields make girls rare. Girls weren't born to the other butchers, and you were the first. You were the only."

"It's rare, but it happens. What about my mother? She was born in the fields."

Raena spoke as if she were releasing fire she couldn't hold back. "I spoke to her, too. Her parents weren't pig butchers, but cooks for King Charl. It wasn't until she was older that they went to work the fields, when two warm seasons came and the river dried up. The kingdom needed more livestock, and her family became butchers then."

Aven shook her head. She wanted to say so much, but no words would form.

Raena didn't stop. "But that isn't even the reason I suspected it. I only asked Gregor because I already thought I knew, but I wanted to be sure. I wanted to be certain beyond a doubt when I finally told you. The

342

thing is, I've known this since I was in the gaol, since Zarana came to see me. I saw her close, in the gaol. I saw her face and I knew."

Aven couldn't say anything to respond, even if she wanted to.

"You look like her. More than Zander does, of course. And when she spoke of you, her eyes were always soft. Wistful. Like she was missing you, or she'd lost you. I think she almost told me the truth in the gaol, for some reason. It was like she started to explain to me how much you meant to her and why it was so important that I go back to Boenaerya for you. She was sending me to save…her daughter. Not just a duchess of East Shore. Certainly not just a butcher girl of Candor."

Raena pushed herself up on one arm, closer to Aven. She reached out her other hand and rested it, palm up, a kind gesture.

Tentatively, Aven responded, sliding her own hand across the bedsheets and placing it in Rae's. Their hands joined together with a comforting familiarity.

"I believe you're the true Payton," Rae whispered, "a true and proper princess. I believe our marriage is simply your destiny fulfilled. Perhaps it's a joke from the Almighties, to put you back in the place you belonged all along."

Aven squeezed the hand in hers, taking deeper breaths, trying to calm the crisis brewing within her. "Who else would know? If it were true…who else knows?"

"Perhaps Sir Jonn-Del."

Aven flinched hard. "He would have me killed."

"He won't. Not now. He wouldn't dare to kill the princess."

"What if he does it quietly? Poisons me? Makes me appear ill?"

"I won't let that happen. You will be safe. If anything happens to you, I'll have him executed. And I'll make sure that he knows it. He must protect your life with his own. Perhaps I will make him your personal guard, then he alone will be responsible for your safety."

Aven bit her lip. "This is all…this is too much."

"Right. Of course. I had months to think about it all, and I'm telling you everything as if it's easy to fathom. I'm sorry."

Aven glanced at their joined hands. "It's not your fault. I can handle it. I'm just…I don't think you're right. It's a good idea, but it doesn't make sense. Why would Zarana let her daughter be raised by pig butchers? Why my mother? Why would she send me as far as possible to East Shore?"

"And why would Zarana arrange the marriage of a pig butcher's daughter to a duke? Why would Zarana knowingly release Raena Schinen, daughter of her sworn enemy and a traitor, in order to save you from Boens? Why would Zarana have peace at her moments of trial and execution, knowing she and her heir son were to be the last of their bloodline? Unless, of course, she knew her bloodline did not truly end?"

"Yea," Aven whispered.

"I don't mean to overwhelm you. I'm doing it again."

"That's all right."

"We don't need to talk about it anymore. Perhaps I should have waited for another day to tell you."

"No…I think today was the right day."

"Oh. Good."

They were quiet again. Aven focused on the feeling of Rae's hand. Their fingers were entwined, but she didn't remember how they came to be that way. She felt connected, though she still felt a pull as if it wasn't enough. Raena's theory left her feeling pulled open—exposed.

"We'll stay very good friends through this," Aven whispered, staring at Rae through her eyelashes.

"Of course."

"We start ruling a kingdom tomorrow. Perhaps we should try to sleep?"

Raena nodded, a polite smile forming on her lips. She began to pull her hand away and slide down the edge of the bed toward the floor.

"Wait," Aven said, reaching.

"Hmm?"

The air between them was heavy and thick with words unsaid. Aven felt a similar pressure building in her chest. She stared at Raena, hoping perhaps her intentions would be understood without her needing to say them. But her luck wasn't that good; Raena simply stared back at her, blankly waiting.

"I think..." Aven began, then cleared her throat and tried again, "I'm feeling very scared, about all of this. It's a great deal to think about. I think I'll sleep better if you're here. Next to me."

Raena nodded, though her brow was furrowed. She opened her mouth then closed it and nodded again. "All right. Do you still want the candle?"

"No."

"Right."

It seemed to take a full minute, and Aven waited. She waited as Rae blew out the candle and then must have paused beside the bed. Then Aven felt the shift of the blankets and the mattress in the way she realized she'd been expecting now for some time. The feeling of Raena's body sliding in beside her was so familiar, it was like finding a favorite dressing gown at the bottom of the wardrobe and easing it on.

Raena rolled and adjusted the pillows a few times, working to get comfortable, then settled in.

Aven reached wordlessly in the dark.

Raena's hand found hers before she was at the midway point of the bed.

Without a word between them, Aven pulled, and then Raena was closer. Close enough they could hear and feel one another's breath. Close enough that Aven was surrounded by a feeling that washed over her: safety. The scent of sandalwood, leather, and terra filled her nostrils. She didn't have to ask for what she needed as Raena's arms carefully wrapped around her, and Aven melted into the sensation of being held. Her body relaxed. Part of her longed for more, but in so many ways, Aven was perfectly content. They both adjusted to the touch and Aven buried her face against Raena's chest.

"Are you comfortable? Is this all right?" Raena whispered against Aven's forehead.

Aven nodded, too relaxed to speak.

"You're going to fall asleep while I'm still talking, aren't you?"

Aven nodded again.

"Perfect. I won't be tired for a while. But that's okay, I don't sleep as much as you."

Aven smiled.

"One last thing I need to tell you, though. In light of this...secret, and the impending threat of the wrong people knowing who you are, I think it's best we prepare for it. Tomorrow, I want to start teaching you to fight. To defend yourself."

"I've defended myself," Aven mumbled.

"Yes, against an unarmed and unprepared intruder. How about I teach you to fight with a pike and sword? In case the castle is taken by Boens, or you're in a field and Ruvians come, or if we have to travel to Ediva...there seem to be endless reasons, now that I'm thinking of it."

"Aye," Aven whispered, "I'm closing my eyes now."

"Aye. Goodnight, Princess."

CHAPTER 31
BELL

Vicious and concupiscent

"I kept my promise to you, I've given you everything," Micha snarled, his fingers curling around the goblet. He held it in his left hand, which Bell knew mattered. His right hand was saved for swords and striking.

He had a right to be angry. So did Bell.

She moved through the King's council room with a purpose, her golden dress threatening to tangle underfoot. Bell drew closer to him where his eyes couldn't avoid her so easily as he had been. "I also kept my promise to you, or have you forgotten? We are both at each other's mercy. Yet you can't seem to leave me alone."

Micha shook his head and his crown jiggled as he did so. "You might live on the island now and be keeper of the Sandles, but that doesn't mean you don't still serve Ediva. Might I remind you that as my subject, you are called to arms whenever I need you?"

"You're a dictator, then!" Bell shouted, throwing up her arms.

Micha clenched his jaw. He had not yet shown a knack for knowing how to handle her emotional outbursts, and this made it apparent that today wouldn't be the day to break that pattern.

In the quiet moment, Bell folded her arms and look around the council room. She hadn't been there in months. She hadn't been in Ediva proper in months. She missed the smell of the ocean. She missed watching Finn swim in the frigid waves. She missed the way the wood was hard from salt in the air. Her new life on the Sandle Islands seemed serene. Cold, but serene. She and Finn had talked about starting a family when they were ready.

Bell should have known it was too good to keep. Micha had sent his boats for her; Bell and her hawks had been summoned and stripped right back out of paradise.

"I'm not trying to hurt you," Micha muttered, "but the truth is, I can't do this without your help."

"You don't understand what you're asking me to do," Bell retorted. "You want me to join your army and march upon my own kingdom. Do you understand what they'll do to me if I'm captured? What they'll do to my mother and father, if they are still within Candor's reach?"

"It will never come to that. This will never turn into an actual war. When they see the Boens coming, Candor will fight only one force. Your cousin, Rowan—"

"Trevin. He's called Trevin, now."

"Sure. Trevin. He's still the same man, prince or not. He will not take up arms against me, he swore it before he left. His armies will fight the Boens and leave above ground unharmed."

Bell paced, shaking her head. "Then what's the point? Why bring me and my hawks at all. I thought you said you needed Trevin to know that I'm there."

"I do," Micha said. "I need him to see you're with my army. It isn't because I doubt him but…the extra insurance won't hurt. Besides, if he doesn't fire upon us, we won't need to fire upon him. It protects both of our kingdoms this way. Only the Boens will lose men. And hopefully, it will be enough to send them back."

"Back to Boenaerya? It sounds like that isn't enough for them at all."

Micha set his goblet on the council table, splashing the ale over the sides. "I've already been through this. I wouldn't have sent for you if I didn't. My war strategists, my master-of-arms, my knights...all of them have done what they could to put a stop to this. There is no changing their minds anymore. The Boens have seen the Hornes readying to take Boenaerya. Once the Hornes come to the land, the Boens have nowhere to go. Except here...or Candor."

"Then put them under your ground. Give them a place of refuge."

"You know I don't have the resources, and half my kingdom is tundra. They won't be able to burrow through the ice. Why do you think they had to go around Ediva by boat, carted to the Horne islands?"

Bell pursed her lips in a defiant gesture. "I didn't think about it. I didn't think about how our enemies would try to destroy us. I choose to look for ways that you can stop them, instead. It seems you're afraid to explore that alternative, and would rather unleash them upon a weaker kingdom. Like a coward."

"May I remind you that I am still king? I could have you stricken down or hanged for the way you speak to me."

Bell stepped closer, enough that she could smell the pine scent in his furs. She smirked and gazed at him through her thick black eyelashes. "Ooh, please. Say more. You know I like that."

He groaned and spun away as if she were made of fire. "Not now. Not ever. Do not...don't do that. I am married. You know what that means."

"I do," Bell purred, "I also know you are asking me to march into war with you. Shouldn't we do something to rebuild our trust before we are united in battle?" She leaned her backside against the edge of the council table, knowing the way it would accentuate the curve of her ass.

When Micha turned to eye her warily, Bell reached for his discarded goblet. With her brows raised in a haughty expression, she took a long drink, allowing some of the ale to drip down her chin. A few drops rolled further, to her neck, to the tops of her breasts, into the deep crevice of her dress.

When she set the goblet back on the table, Micha's eyes were wide and intense, studying her.

"I'm so clumsy," Bell whispered, wiping at the ale on her chest. "I've been away from civilization too long, I fear. Have I forgotten how to behave myself like a civilized noblewoman?"

Micha balled his fists. "Aren't you…isn't Sir Finley your beloved now? You have him to return to on your island when this is over. I'm sure he expects you to be faithful, as my wife the Queen does."

Bell rolled her head back and laughed. "You don't understand. Finn isn't close-minded like most men. He expects me to have my needs met. And he knows that you and I…meet them."

"I will not betray my wife," Micha whispered.

"And I will not betray my kingdom," Bell snapped.

"So that's it, then? You would force me into bed if I ask you to perform your duties like any other of my nobles? I give you an island, I give you refuge from the war, and you still would defy my orders?"

Bell crossed her arms. "You forget that I am not a prisoner here. I don't have to belong to your kingdom, I chose to. I have stayed here in Ediva because there is nothing for me or Finn in Candor. But we can easily change our minds, especially when Candor fights and wins against the Boens. Perhaps I'll ride with you and take my hawks, but never return to your stupid ice kingdom."

Micha scoffed. "You're bluffing now, and it shows. You and Finn have everyone you care for back in Candor, especially Ro—Trevin. Why have you stayed here? Certainly, it's not for the ice, though you must love it since you happily took my island without protest."

Bell bit the inside of her cheek, debating what to say.

Micha smiled. "There it is, isn't it? You have nothing to say about that. I knew it was something."

"You don't know what you're talking about."

"Don't I? Then tell me why did you decide to stay here? Why don't you go on back? You were all the way at Hawk's Keep and yet you still returned. Could it be that your parents abandoned their post and left it for the Boens to take?"

"Does there have to be a reason?" Bell said, standing taller. "Not everything has a purpose. Everyone doesn't have a motive for every choice they make. I know you wouldn't understand that because you are careful, and reserved, and afraid to act because you're terrified you'll make a wrong move. You think that's the best way to be? Well, it isn't. I can enjoy my life how I want to."

Micha waved his arms as he spoke. "There's nothing wrong with being careful. Look at how it's saved my kingdom. Look at how I've protected myself from the Boens."

"Yeah? And how happy are you? How is it now to have the plain little wife, and be on the plain little path, and let your advisors weigh in on every step you take?"

"It's fine. I'm happy. My happiness doesn't matter as much as I need my lands to be safe from invasion and fertile and…I'm building a legacy for generations to come."

"You're building a boring one. You'll be remembered as a passionless king who never took risks."

"Riding on Candor is a risk."

"Yes, one that you've already planned for. One that you have completely strategized to death with The Jin and with Trevin, to ensure that it goes off as a true farce. In the end we both know that Trevin will give the underground tunnels to the Boens, and the Hornes will take Boenaerya, and you'll have a worse enemy at your southern borders than you've ever had."

"I've heard from the greatest war strategists in the kingdom, but amuse me." Micha stepped closer, leaning toward her. His chest grazed hers as he bent forward to take the goblet from behind her. When he stepped back, he raised the drink to his lips.

Bell smirked. "You are forgetting the greatest risk of all: that Trevin will honor his word to you. He is the crown Prince now, and recently took a bride. He may have changed his mind and decided to defend his

351

kingdom completely. He could even choose to fight you and ally with the Boens when they take underground."

"That's absurd. What would possess him to do so? His army can't take mine, especially after the Boens destroyed it."

Bell raised an eyebrow. "You don't know him like I do. He opposes everyone. Aren't you shocked that he married Aven? A butcher's daughter? Do you think that was for strategic reasons?"

"She is well-respected in Candor. The people love her because she's a commoner who became a duchess. She's—"

"And in Ediva, they both would have been killed for such a wedding. Don't you think he knew that? Do you think Trevin returned to Candor because you asked him, or because it meant he could take the throne for himself and have the woman he loved? It seems you were duped, dear King."

Micha paused. He opened his mouth, then stared away at the ground, fixated for a moment.

Bell stepped in as though she were circling her prey before a kill. "You might be a careful man, and so is my cousin. He wouldn't have done anything unless he had a greater plan. He holds his secrets tight to his chest. You misjudged him."

"I'm certain I did not. He is a man of honor. He will honor our alliance."

"He is loyal, indeed. But not loyal to you. His noble house, his kingdom, his bride? They all come first."

Micha shook his head. "You're not changing my mind on this, or any other thing. I've heard you out and you've given me nothing. I am readying my armies to ride at the first snowfall before the passes fill with ice. The Boens will follow along the northern edges of the river and traverse the mountain at night, alongside us."

"What a beautiful picture of winter. Enjoy your journey."

"You will come with me. You will ride behind me."

Bell laughed low and deep. "No thank you, King. I'm afraid I have other matters to tend to."

Without another word he slammed the goblet against the table. It splattered in all directions, ale sloshing out and the gold container echoing on the wood. The second his hand was unencumbered, Micha grabbed Bell by the throat and flung her, her back pressed into a chair.

His breath was hot and close, smelling of the drink. He panted, hard and even, his periwinkle eyes boring into her with unmatched aggression.

It took all of Bell's energy to hold back her grin of delight at his show of force. She put her hands behind her and thrust her hips forward slightly to confirm what she was already certain of; his arousal had grown and was threatening to escape from his trousers. As she leaned further into him, he suppressed a groan.

"You will listen to me," he growled. His lips practically touched hers.

Bell struggled to speak, though he wasn't squeezing nearly as hard as she would have liked. He never did.

"Do as I command," he whispered.

"Yes, Your Majesty." Bell replied.

"Good," Micha said. Then he pressed his lips into hers with the force of all his desire, crushing their mouths together. Heat rose between them like a flame brought back to embers that were never truly extinguished.

Bell sensed his hand relax as they kissed, his silent form of submission. She pressed her hips toward him to remind him that this was not a romantic, affectionate kiss. That sort of drivel might get Pearl Salish to spread her legs, but Bell needed him to take her with all of the power he used to.

Micha moaned, another loving sound, and his thumb gently stroked along her neck.

Bell pulled away, rolling her eyes as she opened them. "Come on, Micha," she whispered feverishly, "fuck me like a real king."

His eyes widened, and he nearly stammered. But then with a hard swallow and a dip of his chin, he grabbed her around the waist and turned her, pushing her down until her chest was flat on the table. As he pulled up her skirts, Bell turned her face so he wouldn't see the broadness of her delighted smile.

CHAPTER 32
BELL

Freezing in the snow and ice is worse than death

She couldn't say if it was worthwhile.

Fortunately, she'd had about thirty days to ask herself whether or not it was.

Thirty days of disgusting, tormented, aggravating snow. Ice. Mountains.

She was sick to death of eating roots, drinking cow's blood, and bacon salted so heavily it would last the next thousand years.

Micha hadn't spoken to her, nor even looked at her, since they left Castle Salish. He stayed far ahead on his horse. She had no way to escape or slip into the night; her hawks made sure of that. Everyone would notice her exit. Besides, where would she go? Under the Calam Mountains with the Boens? Into the river? Back into Ediva where his eyes and ears would call her a deserter and drag her before her lover King for trial?

Bell thought of Finn, often.

Micha had sworn before they left that he would send a messenger to the Sandles to tell Finn where Bell and the hawks had gone. What a sad day that must have been. What a pathetic fate, for Finn to be alone on that island with only a few keepers—the men who were the worst company and droll as a dead shrew.

"Regrets?" Bothell the Kingsguard said, riding up alongside.

"I didn't before now, but here you are. Thanks for that."

He laughed. "We did ride before. Same ride. Fun?"

"Do you mean is it more fun than before? No, absolutely not. When I did it with you and the Kingsguard, it took a fraction of the time."

"We bring whole army."

"Yes, I am aware of that," Bell groaned, "how could I forget the smell that offends my nostrils every moment of every horrid, long, stretching day?"

"I don't smell?"

She tossed a glance at Bothell, looking him over. She'd had him twice; once in Hawk's Keep, and once in the forests on their return journey. He had been the kind of male lover she enjoyed for a quick romp but was easily forgotten. He was naturally rougher than Micha and of course, nowhere near as intelligent. He couldn't match wits with her and she wouldn't have gone back for more if other options were available.

"You do smell," she said, "you smell as bad as every man ahead or behind us. And at this point, I likely smell as bad as all of you."

Bothell cracked a smile across his chapped lips. "You liked it?"

She wasn't sure if he meant the encounters before, or something now, or something different entirely. His broken Candorian left much to be desired. "Sure, I liked it. Whatever 'it' is. Maybe splash around in a river or rub some snow on your manhood to get the stink off, and I'll like it again. If that's what you're asking."

He scratched at his head. "Bathe? Wash?"

"Yes, Bothell. Please bathe, wash, and then come to find me. Do you know where my tent is?"

"Tent. Yes."

Bell could have sworn a few of the other Edivan guards cast sideways looks at the two of them, but she was confident they were making assumptions based on their tones. In her experience, no other guards could speak her native tongue as well as Bothell, which wasn't saying much.

Bothell puffed up his chest and gazed ahead as though searching for meaning. There was nothing but white sheets of biting snow, coating the air, coating the horizon, filling the world with one color and one temperature.

"Bathe, soon," Bothell said. He appeared to force one more smile, then he pulled his cowl over his chin to keep it warm, satisfied with her proposal.

As he rode off, part of Bell hoped maybe he wouldn't listen and come to her tent even before he bathed. The warmth of his body might soothe the never-ending freeze that had penetrated her to the core. She had been with worse bed partners for worse reasons than beating the cold.

As though he could sense that a topic of conversation happened that wasn't centered around his own name, King Micha appeared out of the blizzard wall. He was wearing majestic furs stacked over his shoulders. His little Boeny face was red and blistered, a stark contrast to how the Edivans fared in their natural environment. Bell wondered if she appeared as weathered as he.

"Lady Islabell," he greeted, pulling his horse alongside.

"King," she tutted, "you've picked a lovely day for a ride."

He rubbed at his nose. "This should be the worst of it. If you're catching a bite from the snow, I will send for a caravan for you to rest inside. We can also put you in a cave until it passes."

"A kind gesture, but you forget that if my hawks cannot see me, they will begin to mercilessly slaughter your men until I am produced again. They don't care much about whose army is whose, only my command."

"Right," Micha said, casting a wary glance to the sky, "I was afraid you would say that."

Bell gestured her arms outward. "There's something I've been meaning to ask you, so I'm glad you've finally graced me with your presence. Where the bloody fuck are the Boens? I haven't seen a single one emerge in a fortnight, if not longer. They were pecking out south of the river as if they were sparks from the fire. Now we're expected to believe they are somehow tunneling under the mountains? Is that what they convinced you of?"

Though his face wasn't moving, Bell could sense Micha was trying to grimace through his swollen cheeks.

"They are moving at night. They travel while we sleep."

"In the middle of your army? Have you seen them?"

"I haven't, but the word has spread. They are using my men as shields to get over the mountains. When we arrive in the Candorian desert, they will return underground and continue going forward to the citadel."

"I want you to remember that I said this was a stupid plan."

"And I want you to remember that I am the king, and I have a hundred military strategists advising me. You might know a thing or two, but so do all my advisors and counselors. Believe me, they would not take such a risk to ride us into a fruitless death."

Bell shook her head. "All you men are alike. That's why I enjoy fucking your brains out. You don't have much for them to begin with, so it makes my task easy."

"Bite your tongue, this is not the place."

"No one is listening," Bell said, "besides, I'm not coming on to you, I've already found myself a bed partner for the time-being."

She would have preferred Micha, but she didn't dare to tell him that; the jealous expression coating his face was far too satisfying.

"So," she continued, "did you come to tell me something, or did you just miss my company?"

"I wanted to see if you were all right. You and your hawks. This is difficult weather, I'm sure they are struggling too."

"Very kind of you. We're fine, thank you."

He nodded, his hands gripping the reins of his warhorse. "Listen, Bell, I don't expect any real fight to happen."

"So, you've assured me. Yet here we are, with a full army equipped for battle."

"Your cousin, Trevin. He and I can keep our kingdoms at peace."

"If my kingdom listens to him. He's been prince for the blink of an eye. They are still sore and broken after the last Boen war with a young boy for a king."

"We are all young-boy kings, it seems. The giants that were our parents have all been lost to war, old age, and disease."

Bell cocked her head. "Not your father, though. Why didn't they name him king, before you?"

Micha shrugged. "He wouldn't be chosen by the advisors. He is a noble, but my mother was not."

"Isn't there some law against that? Don't you all have to be noble blood, and so forth?"

Micha shifted on his horse. "It's difficult to explain. There are many ways the spiritual advisors see the bloodlines. They have a method to analyze them, and separate them based on the path that the Almighties have chosen. There are seven Almighties, there are seven paths. Each path can lead to the center, but all of them come from different origins."

"Like the center of your cities, and the courtyards. They all join in the center."

"Exactly. That's modeled after the seven paths and the one end. The one end isn't death, but it's balance."

Bell would have rolled her eyes if not for the way her lids felt frozen and numb.

Micha droned on, "One of the paths is to be a noble, with royal blood that is passed down to the next bloodline. This is the path that makes the most sense to you. It is the path assigned to outsiders, simply because the advisors don't take the time to recognize what path is chosen by the Almighties for every single person, unless they have a reason to. Another path is to be a martyr, to embrace death for a purpose. Another is to lead as an advisor, which is the path most of them take. Then there is a path of service, a path of solitude…"

"This sounds no different than assigning jobs within a castle. It's just a way to do it and claim mysterious divine intervention, so no one can argue when they're given a disgusting job to shovel horse shit."

Micha sighed. "It's not really important that you understand, but you were the one who asked. Anyway, to answer your question, my father wasn't chosen for the path of ruling. I was. It was between me and a few dozen others that the advisors tracked. I'm the one whose name was called and by a vote of the people, I was placed on the throne."

"But it's not a true vote. The advisors choose. It would be a true vote if anyone could be chosen. What if the advisors are wrong?"

Micha cast a glance over his shoulder. "I'd rather hear you say anything except blasphemy. I should have you executed for such a question."

"Thank you for sparing my life," she said, sarcastically.

"I can't show you endless mercy and endless favors. Even I have my limits."

For once, Bell nodded, not willing to continue teasing him down the same vein.

They rode in silence for a few more minutes, pressing ahead in the storm. She knew they would be above it by mid-day and she could enjoy the clear and crisp mountaintop. But for the next few hours it was a frozen form of hell.

"If you don't return, I'll understand," Micha said.

"What does that mean?"

"If you choose to stay in Candor when this is over, I'll understand."

Bell scoffed. "And leave Finn on your hideous island? No. I'm afraid you'll never be rid of me as long as that boyish knight lingers within your kingdom's borders."

Micha smiled in a tired way. "Well, thank you for joining me. I know that seeing your hawks above my legions will bring ease to Trevin, and therefore bring ease to the armies of Candor."

"How very comforting."

They shared one final look before Micha kicked his horse to hurry ahead and rejoin his men at the front lines.

CHAPTER 33
BELL

The hawks should get to do what they want

The descent down the Calam Mountains was far more peaceful. If snow made it to the western cliff faces at all, it was a powdery form that sprinkled like dust and melted away on one's skin. Bell had always loved the west side of the mountains, where the pines began and the forest floor opened up and every step was easy. The trees stretched down into the founts and peppered the land until they touched the edge of the Candor desert. She recalled many fond memories of hunting excursions into the foothills with her father, Finn, Raena, and their other squires. It was no surprise that she felt at home when she smelled the heady trees, the drying air, and felt the sun against her face. The founts were near again.

Bell yearned for home.

Images of Hawk's Keep, abandoned and left for the crows, flooded her mind though she tried to chase them out. She clutched the reins of her rouncey so tight that it left marks in her palms. For comfort, she imagined that her parents had returned, and the longer she let the thought marinate in her consciousness, the more she believed it was rational.

When they had traveled a day, she could spot the edges of the Western Founts in the valley. Hawk's Keep eluded her, but the outer lakes were defined in a familiar pattern. She had seen it from this particular view only a few times in her life, but she never forgot it. Bell always knew her way home. They had one final night to make camp in the high elevation, and Bell was restless at the fireside, uninterested in her tent or even attempting to sleep. The sun had set hours before, and she nursed a horn of kelpi alone while the Edivan warriors were passing out on the ground or long asleep on bedrolls around her.

"Shouldn't you be in your tent?" the King muttered as he approached.

Bell stayed comfortable on her log, though procedure demanded she should have stood and bowed. She glanced up at Micha, who stood tall and proud like a statue, staring into the fire.

"I'm not tired," Bell replied.

"It's been a long day of travel. You'll need your rest for tomorrow."

Bell scoffed, "Are you trying to sound like my father?"

"Do you need me to?"

Her hand tightened around the horn and she was tempted to throw it into the flames, but then she'd waste the precious kelpi that was numbing her rough edges.

"I'm sorry," Micha said, quietly, "we'll reach your keep tomorrow, and I know it will be difficult for you."

"Why would it be?"

"It's still abandoned. Your family has not returned."

Bell grabbed a heavy stick from beside her feet and flung it. When the wood connected to the fire, sparks shot out and singed the pine needles around them. "You don't know that for certain," she said, "they could be on their way. My father won't leave Hawk's Keep for long, and he's been away long enough."

Micha sighed.

In the distance overhead, Bell heard her hawks chattering in the treetop. They were increasingly restless as the traveling party drew closer to their home, reflecting the turmoil within her own heart.

"Are you staying awake for the birds?" Micha asked.

"What do you mean?"

"They are still in the trees. Don't they need to sleep in the tent with you?"

Bell sipped her kelpi, contemplating, then shook her head. "I kept them in my tent for warmth in the mountains. Here? They are as free as birds, as they say. They know where we are. They know we will soon be home."

"Have you given any thought to their names? I feel strange talking about them as if they don't mean anything to us. They are practically part of my entourage, after all."

"Yes, they are all named. The male is Samorr and the largest female is Queen. The gold-tipped wing one is Raena-bird and the small female is Alura."

Micha's grin spread across his pale face. "You named her for my mother?"

"Selfishly. She and I spent more time together after your wedding. I've grown fond of her. She's a lovely woman."

"I'd hoped you might call one Pearl; it would honor my wife—"

"Queen honors your wife. That's her title."

Micha squatted down beside her and bent to pick at the dirt. Now on the same level, he observed her out of the corner of his periwinkle eyes. "Will they be able to fight for my army, if called upon?"

"I thought you said there wouldn't be a fight."

"I thought that. But look around us," he lowered his voice, "no one has seen or heard the Boens. They are ghosts. How can I make a pact with your Prince cousin on behalf of an army that hasn't crossed the mountains?"

"Perhaps they couldn't find a way through."

Micha shrugged. "That's what my advisors believe. Once we reach Hawk's Keep, we will stall. We will hold up there, giving the Boens extra time—"

Bell twisted toward him, "You're seizing my father's keep?"

"Bell, there is no one—"

"You can't take it for yourself!" Before she could think better of it, Bell jumped to her feet, sloshing kelpi over her hand.

"Lower your voice," he whispered.

Bell bent at the waist and leaned over Micha. "I'll say what I need to. You think you won't have a war on your hands? You're inviting one by unlawfully taking one of the most critical keeps in all of Candor. My cousin Trevin will have your head for it. And my father will return and see that your army is laid to waste in the founts."

Micha threw up his hands. "Your father would, if he returned. But he abandoned the keep and so did all his warriors, his serfs, everyone. You know even the law of Candor dictates an empty fortress may be claimed by any king."

Bell scoffed and stood upright, taking a long drink of kelpi this time. She felt her chest clench at the thought. Of course, she knew they would pass through her home. Of course, she'd known that they might take refuge and camp within her father's keep. But waiting inside the walls? Taking sleeping quarters? The more she thought of it, the more her hands began to shake with rage. A voice within her mind began to scream and she feared she wouldn't be able to hold back from unleashing on the King if she stayed much longer.

"I'm sorry," Micha continued, "this is an opportunity I cannot pass—"

"You're wrong," she snapped, "the law isn't that simple. You can't claim a fortress without the permission of the King, even if it's abandoned. I am certain that's the law."

"Your kingdom doesn't have a king," he muttered, "it isn't up to a prince."

"I'm certain that Trevin can find a way to make the decision."

"Indeed, and his decision will be to grant me and my armies solace. He understands that we are coming with hopes for a treaty, yet prepared for war. He will maintain that agreement and act in kind, with peaceful intentions."

"How peaceful is it to steal the keep of a noble family?"

Micha stood to his full height, clenching his fists at his sides. "I've every intention of returning it if your father returns."

"When my father returns, you mean."

Micha let out a hard breath through his nostrils, flaring them. A puff of smoke cleared around his face, making him appear like a powerful beast in the firelight. "I hope you sleep well, Lady Islabell."

Bell huffed. "Ponce," she muttered.

Micha jerked forward and clapped his hands with fervor, as though he were preparing to shout in her face. But with a groan, he kicked a stick into the fire and stomped away, leaving Bell on her own.

She finished off the horn of kelpi with two long chugs, careful to close her lips enough that the chunks from the bottom didn't make their way into her mouth. With a grunt, she tossed the empty horn onto a pile of supplies and stumbled toward her tent. She chittered and clicked for her hawks to follow. When she reached the tent flap, she held it open to beckon in the hawks, but only Raena-bird and Samorr were there.

She had drunk enough kelpi to fall asleep. But after what could have only been a few hours she was startled awake by the birds, squawking and flapping their wings in warning. She opened her eyes to see Bothell, sheepishly hovering in the entrance.

"Steady," Bell murmured despite a throat dry as the Candorian desert. "Steady, you two."

"Visit?" Bothell asked.

Bell pushed back her fur covers and beckoned him to the bed. Her hawks continued to make alert sounds, but they didn't approach.

Bothell slipped in beside her, unwashed, as she'd expected. His stench was not as foul as she'd been imagining. Perhaps it was mostly soaked into his furs and leathers, because his hairy flesh wasn't unpleasant

365

once she had him naked. Every time she moaned with pleasure, the hawks began to squawk again and Bothell would stop to stare at them for a moment, intimidated by their presence. It made for a long night, and by the time they finished, the warm buzz of alcohol had left her system entirely. Bothell snored as he slept beside her and she stared at the dull top canvas above their heads, unable to drift off again.

She thought of where her mother and father could be. She tried to imagine them in West Twin, living in one of the stilted huts above the constant incoming tides. She thought of them taking boats out to sea with orders from Duke Gradeigh, or perhaps fishing for marler off the shores of East Twin. The idea that they would hide was plausible, especially if they were waiting for news from Candeo before they returned home. But surely, they would have heard such news by now? That was the piece that Bell couldn't reconcile and it spun around in her head like a caged animal.

When the sun rose, Bell felt she'd been waiting for it all her life. She dressed and packed for another day of travel faster than she had on their entire journey. By mid-morning, she was at the front of the riders, leading the way on horseback into the stretching pines on their mountain descent.

With Micha's well-equipped and well-fed legions behind her, Bell imagined she appeared like a goddess dragging an ocean of fire as her coattail. Above her, the hawks circled, joyfully

But when she gazed down again at the Western Founts, she didn't feel glorious and goddess-like. She heard the laughter of herself as a small girl, winding through the trees, chasing after Finn and Rowan. She smelled the salty brine of fish, caught from the mucky swamp edges of the outer lake, as she and her mother shared a bite. She tasted the sweet pop of golo berries in the spring. She heard her father's voice, laughing and calling after her, as she disappeared into the brush for another game of finders and seekers.

Bell felt the pull of her heart and everything within her, begging her honor, her allegiance to Candor, to Hawk's Keep, to her father, Lord Sylas.

His loyalty.

366

Where was his loyalty now? What could possibly exist in all the land of the Almighties that was worth abandoning his duties, his people, and his home?

One of the horsemen beside her gestured outward, laughing. He shouted something in Edivan over his shoulder and a chorus of laughter joined him.

Bell searched the valley for what they were pointing at. A flicker of movement near one of the lakes caught her eye. She squinted, staring, and pulled the reins of her rouncey to bring it to a halt.

Perhaps a furlong from the keep's curtain, near the bank of a fount lake, a gaggle of guards were bolting across the open meadows. Bell recognized their colors: Candor. She surmised they had been stationed in one of the outposts, perhaps there to watch for Boen or Edivan invaders.

Certainly, they were expected to stand their ground, perhaps even sound an alarm.

Yet no wonder the Edivan soldiers were laughing; the cowards were fleeing their post.

Bell felt a flush burn upward from her chest to her ears. Her breaths came short and fast.

"Shut up," she said, to no one in particular, knowing they wouldn't understand it.

A few of the soldiers brushed against her as they passed, sharing the narrow horse trail. She didn't urge her rouncey on. She was frozen to the spot.

"Move! Go!" a man called behind her. Bell didn't recognize his voice but didn't turn to see who spoke her language.

She snarled, her lip curling, and she tilted her head toward the sky. In the swirling blue and white overhead were four broad shadows, dark as black between her and the sun. As though her warhawks sensed her distress, Queen let out two shrieks to alert the others, and they all cried in response.

Bell raised her right hand, outstretched toward the valley. "Samorr!" She shouted the bird's name and before her heart could thump a single beat, he was diving from the sky. With his wings tucked to his sides and his beak aimed at the ground, he took on the shape of a sharp horn. He was near the treetops when she thrust both arms in front of her, indicating toward the retreating guards. "Attack!" she cried.

Bell had never used the word with her hawks to indicate anything larger than a field mouse.

They had trained for this as eyases, and trained again in a few short weeks, but Bell's chest clenched with anxiety as she gave the command. She realized too late that perhaps Samorr would misunderstand and attack an Edivan, which would surely draw fire from the rangers behind them. She heard a gasp behind her and she reeled to see the soldiers stopping.

Time slowed down.

In tandem, the Edivans around her had stopped. All eyes were trained, captivated, on the glorious warhawk.

Samorr swooped and dove, dodging high branches and trunks of pines, dipping lower toward the entourage. He would be among the ranks in seconds.

Bell kept her hands pointed toward the valley, praying the bird would understand her intended target.

With a screech, Samorr extended his wings, and his freefall came to an end. The air rushed around him in a deafening swoosh, and he shot out ahead of Bell and the army, soaring toward the valley.

Bell heaved a sigh of relief and let her hands fall to her rouncey's neck. "You old show off," she mumbled. With a shaking hand, she touched her chest to find her heart racing within her ribcage. Bell struggled to calm her nerves with deep breaths, focusing on Samorr.

Around her, the men were quiet, transfixed on the magnificent flight of the warhawk.

As Samorr drifted effortlessly over the sloping hills, descending further into the valley, he let out a series of long screeches. He was indeed a braggart of a creature. Bell imagined he was gleeful at the scent of fear from his target.

"What's this?" someone said from behind her. It was the same voice as before, so this time Bell turned to see a general, decorated in golden braids over his thick leather armor. He raised the layered face shield on his metallic helmet to reveal his round face, covered in thick reddish hair.

"General Vandy," Bell said through her teeth.

Vandy pointed with a sneer. "Who authorized an attack?"

Bell shrugged, resisting the urge to roll her eyes as she focused again on Samorr. General Vandy stayed quiet atop his horse to her left and they stared out into the valley together.

As Samorr ducked lower, the fleeing guards began to scream. They were sprinting through open fields, seemingly desperate to reach the next grove of pines ahead. There were few places to hide, even once between the trees. Bell supposed the only salvation the guards could hope for was to fall into a Boen tunnel.

Samorr squawked and dove, nose first. His wings spread, flayed out on either side, and then he ripped them downward. It was only when Bell heard a blood-curdling scream that she saw the guard flailing a meter above the ground, held tight by Samorr's talons.

Vandy squirmed. "Stop this, at once," he whispered, fascination and fear coating his voice.

"He'll stop soon enough," Bell replied.

"He...he'll put them down?"

Bell bit her lip. She couldn't answer because she certainly didn't have one. Though she feared for the safety of her bird, she couldn't call him off. Her curiosity had won over now. She had to know what the warhawks were capable of.

Overhead, the remaining three birds screamed out either in jealousy, encouragement, or criticism of Samorr.

The hawk was nearly ten meters into the air, and the guard had stopped struggling, likely afraid of being dropped. The man appeared too large to be carried, but the warhawk defied gravity.

Bell heard several gasps as Samorr eclipsed the treetops. A few of the Edivans shouted words she didn't understand.

"Stop this," General Vandy pleaded, "you must stop this."

Bell wet her lips, preparing to call the order for Samorr to stop. But then her attention drifted back to Hawk's Keep. The sight of her home stirred an emotion inside her that could not be sated or quenched. She wanted to deny that the men of Candor would ever abandon their posts. Hawk's Keep deserved guards who would fight to the death, tooth and nail, even with a full army descending upon them.

"They deserve to die," Bell said. She lifted her face and yelled to the sky, "Queen! Attack!"

The woosh of wings overhead was all the confirmation that Bell needed. She heard it before she saw the long shadow cast by Queen's massive form. With a screech, Queen was soaring through the open air, making a direct path toward where Samorr had the guard. In seconds, the two birds were circling one another in a showdown. Queen's attention was on Samorr and Samorr's beak was turned down to stare at the guard inquisitively.

As though worried the guard would be taken before he could be eaten, Samorr pecked violently at the guard, whose screams echoed through the valley.

The Edivans began to shout.

"No," Vandy murmured in disbelief, barely audible above the commotion.

Bell sneered and watched as Queen dropped from the sky to grab another guard. The female bird was not making a show of her stalking, as Samorr had done. Queen was efficient. When she swooped down, the guards screamed, but Queen didn't taunt them. She grabbed the smallest of the men by the shoulders, tossed him up two meters above the ground, and caught him again. She had one talon on his back and the other around his neck as she drifted higher. Queen was no more than ten yards into the air when the small man went limp. At the instant he stopped resisting, Queen hunched around him, convulsing, and her muscles rippled beneath her feathered body. Suspended in flight, she flayed her talons in opposite directions.

Queen's body blocked Bell's view, and for a moment she didn't know the status of the guard. But by the collective screams and cries from the Edivans, Bell was certain the guard had been killed by her bird.

Even Samorr appeared transfixed, hovering in mid-air. The male bird bent back to peck his prey again, and Queen turned.

That was when Bell saw it. In one talon, Queen held the man's body. In the other talon, she held his head, ripped cleanly away with most of his spine dangling behind it. With a disinterested squawk, Queen tossed the two pieces of the Candorian carelessly, as if casting aside the bone from a mutton leg after a meal.

Queen began a rapid dive toward another guard before the dead man's body and head even hit the ground.

Samorr seemed as transfixed as everyone else by the sheer power and strength of Queen's grasp. Unable to compete, Samorr twisted his body toward the sky and flapped with fervor. In seconds, he was a furlong above Ediva's army, among the clouds.

When Samorr dropped the guard from that height, the body flailed and flopped, like an old doll. The guard was plummeting, sure to die, and no one could save him.

Around her was a steady commotion. The men were scrambling— some were off their horses and running ahead, perhaps to get a better view. A few pushed past her and her rouncey groaned in protest of being shoved this way and that. Bell remained focused on the skies.

"Stop this, at once," a new voice said, stern and familiar.

Bell didn't need to turn around to know it was Micha, and he sounded furious.

"I can't call them off," Bell snapped, "it might confuse them. We don't want them to attack the wrong—"

"You can stop this, and you will."

Bell cringed. She wiped her hands on the royal purple dress she wore, frustrated with the dried mud and days' worth of sweat that had soaked into the beautiful fabric.

Out the corner of her eye, Bell saw Micha dismount and rush toward her. The soldiers cleared the way, squishing against each other on the narrow path.

"I gave you an order, as King!" Micha snarled. In two strides he was beside her, and he reached for her wrist.

Bell jerked her hand away and twisted. In the distance, Queen and Samorr had each disposed of their second guards and seemed to be in competition, racing to go after their third.

Micha withdrew his shortsword.

"What's that for?" Bell balked, "Are you intending to slit my throat, in front of all your army?"

There was a dull hum to the air as she stared defiantly at him, and he stared back. His cheeks inflated with every breath, as though his rage was boiling out from under the surface and he couldn't release it fast enough.

"We'll kill your birds," he whispered, "you know that, don't you?"

She knew he wasn't lying, and the realization washed over her, along with a pang of agony.

Bell searched for them without taking another second to consider it, and called out in her loudest yell, "Samorr, Queen, return!"

The screeches of her warhawks were punctuated by the scrape of metal beside her as Micha sheathed his sword once more.

"Please don't hurt them," Bell said, "this was my choice alone, they act on my command."

She turned to Micha, desperate, and reached for his hand but he stared at her and blinked, his periwinkle eyes gone from outraged to cold.

"We will speak of this when we reach the keep," Micha replied. He mounted his horse and returned to his position further within the ranks.

There'd been no one to defend Hawk's Keep. No one to resist them. The Edivans had simply walked in and made themselves at home.

372

Bell went to the royal wing without thinking much of it, walked into her own chamber, and shut the door.

Her heart ached at the sight of everything in its place, as though her parents had expected her to return from an afternoon of hunting. But where had she been instead? Snatched up by a childish, demanding prince. Dragged across a foreign land. Mockingly overthrown by a brutal army, somehow enlisting herself to join her enemy.

Briefly, she speculated that she could sneak into Micha's chamber, murder him, then methodically kill every general until someone put a stop to it. Of course, they would behead her, and then who would care for the hawks?

At the thought of the birds, she opened her chamber window wide and called for them. Queen shrieked a response from the treetops.

When the hawks arrived at the balcony, Bell beckoned them inside.

"I know, you hate being trapped, but I don't trust those soldiers. They are afraid of you, especially after today. Stay in here and I'll know you're safe."

Queen cooed in protest, flattening her wings against her sides and struggling to fit through the door. Bell wrapped her arms around the great beast's neck and pulled gently to slip Queen into the room. The other three were not nearly as large and they followed without a struggle.

Bell took the furs from her bed and flipped them onto the floor, generating a cloud of dust in her wake. In a moment she'd created a few nests in one corner, though it was only enough for the two smallest birds.

"I'll fetch more furs, you wait," Bell said.

The birds stared back as if personally disappointed in her failed effort.

Bell sighed, shaking her head, and hurried out of the chamber. She walked with light steps through the hall toward her mother and father's boudoir, already picturing their wardrobe stacked high with spare robes, furs, and coverings that would make for fine nests.

She rounded the corner and opened the door.

The first thing she noticed is that the candles were lit and the boudoir was not empty, nor cold, nor dark.

Then she saw the culprit. Micha was in a chair, holding a tome in his hands, lounging beside her father's bookshelves. He was freshly bathed, shaved, and dressed in soft night clothes.

Bell slammed the door behind her and charged toward him. "What are you doing in here? Put that back! Get out of here, at once!"

Micha set the tome on the floor and held up his hands. "Oi, please, calm down."

"Don't tell me to calm down. Get out of my father's room. You don't belong here. How dare you—"

"Bell, stop," Micha rose from the chair and reached for her forearms. Bell slapped him away and shoved him as hard as she could. He stepped backward, but didn't fall as she'd expected him to do. It only infuriated her more that she felt helpless to overpower him.

Bell pointed her finger at his nose. "I'm going to kill you. Do you understand? I'm going to murder you. I don't care what happens to me."

"Alright," Micha said.

The next string of phrases out of her mouth were indistinguishable, the words a jumble of curses, insults, and profanities. Her hands flurried, slapping and punching Micha's strong chest.

He backed away, his periwinkle eyes wide. His back hit the bookshelf and he stayed flat against it, arms limp at his sides.

Bell didn't quit.

She leaned in and swung her right arm as hard as she could, punching again and again into his chest. Micha flinched. She could feel him flex, muscles tightened, to take each strike. She didn't stop delivering them.

She wasn't sure what else came out of her mouth, but she knew she was shouting, or crying, or screaming. Her voice echoed in the chamber and back into her ears and she realized her words weren't meant for Micha at all.

They were meant for Sylas.

They were meant for her father.

"You left me. You left me. You fucking bastard," Bell heard herself say. And the weight of it, all at once, came crashing on top of her.

She couldn't breathe. She couldn't stand.

Her legs collapsed, shaking from the adrenaline, and she fell forward onto him.

Micha's arms finally moved, wrapping around her shoulders and embracing her. He held her up to prevent her from falling as she let all her muscles go limp. Her rage drained from her in one movement, though she were a bladder of water that burst.

Mouth open, unhinged, she sobbed against his shoulder. Her tears and saliva soaked into his shirt and formed a pool there.

Micha muttered soft words into her hair. His hands were firm on her back.

Bell let everything go.

CHAPTER 34
SYLAS

Honor is more important than life

Cames hadn't survived.

He'd died in Isla's arms, shivering, pleading to the Almighties for his life.

They couldn't give him a proper funeral, and that was the worst thing of all. Isla sobbed for days, inconsolable.

The Hornes took Cames's body when it began to smell.

It seemed to be the final straw that took Isla's hope. She stopped trying to convince Sylas that there was anything worth living for, and she remained huddled into a ball at the far edge of the cave.

He didn't know how many days had passed since then. He stopped going to the mouth of the cave to see when the sun rose and set. Everything was dark and grey, and time probably was passing quickly without Sylas tracking it.

The remaining few Candorians were in the same blasé state. All of them laid about, never talking, not planning an escape.

They were waiting for death. Sylas couldn't tell if the smell of Cames's body was lingering, or if all of them were inching closer to their demise and rotting from the inside out.

Besides dropping off food, the Hornes were rarely seen. Sylas knew enough about training for battle to recognize preparation when he saw it. They wanted an army. They wanted Boenaerya.

Part of him couldn't blame them; he wouldn't want to stay in rock tunnels either. But the Hornes had been in these islands for hundreds of years. There was no need for them to take any other land.

They didn't see it that way.

It could have been a fortnight. It could have been a year. Nothing much mattered beyond the cave. Except for one thing.

Sylas thought of Bell. He imagined her in a safe place, free, happy. She was his reason to go on. The image of her. If he closed his eyes tight, he could almost remember her smile. It gripped his cold heart and pumped life back through it when the rest of his body was frozen. His favorite memories of her; laughing at her coming-of-age feast, taking his hand when she nearly slipped into the lake, and riding on his shoulders home from a hunt. It was fading from his mind. Bell and Hawk's Keep seemed further away with each passing day.

It was night when Lenon came and led Sylas and Isla from the cave.

"You are going to lead my army now," Lenon said.

Sylas didn't argue. He merely followed.

There was a long line of Hornes ahead. They led down the winding path along the rocks like sea serpents glistening in the orange moonlight. Lenon was at the back of them, with Sylas and Isla trailing behind. Ice cold mist came in all directions, from both the sea and sky, as sharp barbs of water droplets stung his cheeks.

As they descended further down the island, a sense of dread filled his stomach.

"You like to swim?" Lenon heckled over his shoulder.

Sylas remained silent, wondering if his lack of response would provoke a change in Lenon's demeanor. As far as he could tell, Lenon remained cheery and jovial, chuckling after bantering in Hornish with the warriors around him.

Around another rock, and Sylas saw a flat plateau. There were four men assembled there—three of them Hornes, the fourth likely a Calamytan.

"Here is the place," Lenon explained, gesturing.

Sylas stood on the flat space, eyeing each of the men, wondering what the purpose was of this meeting. Isla was quiet. They waited for a moment, all eyes on Lenon.

The Horne leader drew a breath and then chuckled as he let it out. "Do you two men know each other?"

Sylas stared through the darkness at the Calamytan, who eyed him in return. The man's face was distinctly marked by red stains, like bruising, and it was indeed familiar but only from a distant memory.

"No?" Lenon asked. "Why don't you introduce yourselves then?"

"I'm Sylas, Lord of Hawk's Keep. Son of Archer."

The other man squinted. "I remember you. You're the one who brought the boy to the Knight's Trial that broke his arm. And Finn, he was one of your knights."

Sylas cringed, feeling pain he couldn't hide. His voice cracked as he spoke. "Cames was the broken-armed lad. He was here captive with us, but he's…perished. I haven't any idea where Finn is now. The last I heard, he was running from Boens and perhaps they killed him as well."

"Maybe," the man grumbled, "but it seems the Boens aren't much interested in taking prisoners. They brought us to the Hornes as fast as they could. I reckon they aren't keeping anyone underground."

"How many men do the Hornes have, then?" Sylas said, eyeing Lenon with a suspicious glare.

The man scratched his chin. "I reckon forty thousand. A bulk of the Candorian army."

"No," Sylas shook his head, "that can't be. Where would they keep you all? How would they feed that many? That's impossible."

The man shrugged, and it was silent for a moment. Sylas turned and studied the side of the rock-riddled islands, scanning the sides. His eyes followed the shapes of the grey rock faces, jagged and biting as though they nipped at the air and the frigid sleet nipped back. Unforgiving, but riddled with pockets. Sylas supposed there were indeed enough pockets to hold at least half of Zander's fallen army. Would they have slain the women, children, and infirmed captives of Boenaerya?

"Do you remember me?" the Candorian man asked. "I suppose that the toll of war may have changed me."

Sylas studied him again and shook his head.

"I'm Sir Han'gahan. I was a knight to King Lyam. Then to Prince Zander, along with your charge, Finn. I charged into the battle against the Boens. The bastards pulled me underground and kept me there, pissing on myself, until they turned me over to the Hornes. I've been on these forsaken death rocks, ever since."

Sylas nodded slowly. "Han'gahan. It sounds familiar. Like a distant memory, though."

"I remember you," Isla spoke.

Han'gahan shrugged. "Now, here we are. Pawns in a war against two of our enemies. Imagine that."

"Imagine it," Sylas echoed.

Lenon stepped forward and held up his hands. "Good, friends. You two are leaders. You two ruled the Calamytan. You will be my generals. You will lead my armies."

Sylas squinted, "We won't. We won't fight our own people for you."

"You will," Lenon said, "you will lose. I kill until you fight."

Isla and Sylas shared a knowing look.

Sylas spoke first, "The problem with that idea is assuming we have a limit to what we can lose. You don't have the leverage here. I'll watch you kill, and I won't stop you. There is no way for you to break me."

Lenon gestured to Isla. "How about her?"

Sylas felt his chest tighten, but he held his chin high. "My wife and I would both die for our kingdom. We are both prepared for death. You've tortured us long enough that mercy would be welcome."

"Very well, then," Lenon said. "Bring me 'wife'."

Sylas stepped in front of her as the two Hornes moved into action. "Leave her alone!" he shouted, but they were stronger and swifter. As he reached for Isla, one Horne shoved him in the chest, knocking him away. Sylas reached again and the Hornes twisted, wrapping their arms around Isla and pulling her. She struggled, her legs flailing, but they locked their hands under her armpits and dragged her across the flat stone. The third time Sylas moved toward her; he was stopped by two strong arms wrapping around him from behind.

"Steady there, Lord," Sir Han'gahan said, "we're not armed. Lenon will easily split us in two, I've seen it."

Sylas spat on the ground, staring at Lenon as Isla was brought to him.

"You don't need to fight," Lenon sneered. "I will show you something good."

Han'gahan held Sylas steady and whispered, "He's sparing us for a reason, just do as he asks."

Their eyes were on Lenon, filled with contempt, as he instructed his Horne followers to put Isla to her knees on the stone. She struggled, but they held her shoulders and bunched together the back of her dress to keep her in place.

Lenon paced in front of her, alternating between observing her and staring down the two Candorian men. "You use the metal for swords, shields, and crowns, yes? You find the metal under the surface, all over the land. Do you get the metal from under the surface, where the Boens are?"

"Do you mean quorrilium?" Isla asked.

"Yes, the metal. That is what you call it."

None of them responded, waiting to understand his question.

Lenon shrugged as he walked. "You use the metal for your swords, but do you know there is so much more to it? You do not even try. And when you kill a man, you can make him stronger. So strong he is able to fight the whole world and win. If all you would do is teach him to use the metal to make his body. He can eat it, drink it, he can bathe in it. His body would change and be better than any other man."

Han'gahan scoffed. "People have tried to make quorrilium into a medicine, to melt it into a drink. It kills faster than it heals. There is no truth to it."

Lenon grinned. "What people? Calamytes. Boens. All wrong. All doing wrong. There is a way to do everything, and the way you have chosen was wrong way. But we are here now, Lenon will teach you the right way. You see, I told you already about my garons in the sea. I told you that I had a powerful army. I think you did not believe me. What I have not done is show you. I thought that you could trust I was telling you the truth. But you don't. So, I will have to show you."

The two Hornes holding Isla moved so one was pinning her arms around her body. The second grabbed her hair and pulled her head back.

Sylas lunged forward, but Han'gahan held tight.

"You know why my army will defeat all?" Lenon asked, his hand slipping into a pocket of his thin armor, "because we can march on any lands. We have mastered the Change. We can make every Horne into a Boen when we are under the surface. We can become Candorian when we are in the desert. We can become anything we need to be. You will wait for generations, but we will become new men overnight."

As he spoke, he pulled out a tiny leather pouch and unfastened the top. He withdrew a pinch of black powder with two fingers and brought it to his nose to sniff softly. His eyes trained on Isla and she grew more defiant, fighting and shouting against the men who restrained her.

"Let me help her," Sylas snarled.

Han'gahan shook his head. "He didn't bring us here to kill us. Just stay calm."

Lenon glanced at the Horne behind Isla. "Open her mouth."

The Horne grabbed her jaw and tried to force it open while Isla twisted and wriggled her head in his grasp. The two Hornes were strong, and she couldn't resist for more than a second. Lenon appeared pleased as he peered down at her—her head back, mouth open, eyes watering. Expectant. There was nothing Isla could do but wait for his bidding.

"Now we watch together," Lenon said, extending his hand to her mouth. "You are small, and light. You will go through change quickly." He opened his fingers above her tongue and flicked them outward, expelling the black powder into her mouth.

Isla made a gagging sound, trying to spit it away no doubt, but the Horne holding her clamped her mouth shut and tackled her to the ground. The two men pinned her down flat on her back and kept her for a moment.

Sylas began to cry, though he couldn't feel his tears in the rain. "Let her go," he muttered, over and over again.

Lenon was smug, his arms folded. He stepped higher onto a rock. "Come on, watch the Change. It is truly special."

On the ground, Isla was breathing so hard that her nose expelled a glob of liquid onto the Horne's hand over her mouth. Her legs continued to kick wildly but somehow began to shift, as though they were rippling through fluid instead of air. She grabbed at the men pinning her down, scratching at their arms and chests, until her fingers moved as if they were linked together between each one was an invisible strand. She wailed. At last, the Horne pulled his hand away. When Isla screamed, her voice was garbled as though her throat were filled with wet barnacles. It drew Sylas's attention to her neck, and that's when he noticed her skin was stretching, rolling, on its own accord.

"What have you done to her?" Sylas screamed.

"It'll be over soon," Lenon replied, raising his voice to be heard over Isla's wails.

Isla bucked her knees and curled her body in a contorted fetal position. Her muscles tensed and her hands shook violently. Her cries turned to low groans of torment.

Sylas recognized the sound of pain and agony. He'd heard her moan in such a way when she'd labored with Bell, and never again after. He'd marveled at her strength when she delivered their perfect daughter, even though the healer said her womb was scarred and ruined from the labor. Would she be scarred and ruined from this Change?

"See there?" Lenon said, pointing down at her.

Sylas followed his gesture to spot the outline of new flesh. It was like watching growth happen in seconds, as Isla's muscle, bone, and skin reformed before their very eyes. Sylas blinked and then his wife was a different woman. Scales reflected the moonlight off her face. Gills burst open at her throat and sucked from the air. Sticky webs, clammy like the inside of one's cheek, clung between her fingers. Her feet had expanded inside her felt shoes and threatened to spring free. He could tell the outline of her bones; wide and flat like the flippers of a seal.

Sylas might've been amazed if it weren't for the grotesque evolution of his beautiful wife into a Horne monster.

"It won't last," Lenon remarked, "but I can soothe her pain."

As Isla's groan faded into whimpers, Sylas found himself desperate.

Lenon crossed his arms. "When we make landfall in Boenaerya, I will deliver this powder to all my armies. They will become men of the land. They will undergo the Change to adapt into the world around them. You see, now? Your wife is one for the Horne Islands. We will become one for Boenaerya. We will be stronger than Boens."

"We will die," Sylas spat. He felt bile rise in his throat, filling his mouth with the bitter acid. "You will fucking die. You detestable beast!"

Lenon showed no reaction.

"Easy," Han'gahan murmured, "let's not—"

"So that's it, then?" Sylas shouted. "You can turn your armies into people of the land? Fine then, good for you. Take your armies across the sea and leave us out of it!"

Han'gahan nudged Sylas, "Come on now, quiet."

"I will lead my men," Lenon said, "and you will lead yours. You will lead your Calamytes alongside us. We will all be men of the land, and we will take the world from the sea to the mountains!"

The wind and rain whipped across Sylas's face. He gazed down at Isla, writhing in pain, twitching and whimpering, grotesque gills protruding from her neck. He felt a shiver going through him to his bones as the reality of their predicament settled in.

They had always said they would be willing to die for Candor. But this death felt meaningless.

"If I refuse," Sylas began, "will you take my place?" He turned, eyes settled on Han'gahan with a heavy weight.

The knight did not reply, but his grave expression made clear that he did not intend to give in to Lenon easily. Besides, as far as Sylas could see, there was nothing for Lenon to leverage against Han'gahan, the way that he could use Isla.

"I'm growing tired," Lenon said. He reached to his waist and withdrew a scabbard, holding it up. The metal was crude and dull in the moonlight. "What's your choice, then?"

Sylas gazed mournfully at Isla, knowing this may be the last time he saw his wife alive. Her eyes were glazed over, unfocused, the pain likely too much for her to bear and be present for. He wouldn't be able to give her the proper goodbye that she deserved. He tried to focus on a memory of the past, a memory of a time with her that had been beautiful, loving, and peaceful. But all he could think of were days in that forsaken cave, huddled in the darkness, starving and angry. He tried to go further back to their moments with Bell, the abundant feasts in Hawk's Keep, the days with their squires and knights sharing in a hunt through the pines. Those were the brightest moments of his life. But they were gray in his memory, as if covered in fog that he could no longer see through.

Sylas stared at Lenon. His voice didn't waver as he spoke. "I will not join you. I will not serve nor lead your army. Kill us, then, if you must. But know this. You will be killing thousands. You must be ready to kill every man and woman behind me, because their loyalty to our kingdom is greater than mine."

Lenon shook his head, twirling the scabbard in his hand for a moment. "That's bad to hear. I'm sorry for you."

Sylas's fists were clenched. His eyes alight and his shoulders high with pride. "We'll die for Candor, then," he whispered. He didn't know if Isla could hear him, or anything at all.

Lenon said something to the Hornes beside him, and the three amphibious men moved, all at once. Sylas did not resist as the two Hornes grabbed him, their arms around his midsection, and lifted him off the stone. His feet dangled as they walked, carrying him like a petulant toddler. Sylas held still, resisting the temptation to fight back or close his eyes.

The two Hornes held him at the edge of the rock platform. With their hands under his armpits, they dangled him over the side. Sylas took care not to kick or thrash in fear he may slip from their grasp. Dozens of meters below was the icy, treacherous sea. Waves rolled and crashed over rocks. His mind could imagine the white spray of the ocean though it was almost too dark to see for himself.

Lenon's voice howled through the wind, rain, and ocean roar, "Lead my armies, Sylas!"

Sylas said nothing. He stared out, across the ocean. Somewhere in the distance was Boenaerya. Somewhere beyond, the Calam Mountains. And beyond that was home.

"Lead my armies, or you die!"

Sylas opened his mouth to whisper. "Almighties, hear me, do not let Isla be harmed, do not let Islabell be harmed, protect—"

The Hornes pulled him back before they launched him forward.

For a brief second, Sylas thought he was being returned to the land. But then he was flying.

He flew and fell through the air with violent speed. Rain whipped and hit his face, but from below, not from above, and Sylas realized he was moving faster than the raindrops.

It was seconds, only. Not even enough time to register where he was in space or how close he was to the water until it found his body and hit him.

Sylas thought at first that he'd hit the ground. The surface of the water felt like the blunt broadside of wet rocks against him. But when he realized he couldn't take a breath and water encapsulated him, that's when he knew he'd survived the fall.

Perhaps he could swim.

Perhaps he could make it back to the Horne Island, and stay on the rocks below.

But then what?

He was deep in the ice-cold, salt-ridden sea, so far that he couldn't determine which way could be up. He kicked, hoping his body would naturally float to the top. But it felt like he was suspended in the water, forever, and the ocean never stopped, it never would have a surface at all. Everything was water and he grew desperate for air, but he tried to remain calm.

That's when he saw the beast.

At first, it was a shadow. Moving through the ocean beside him like a bird glides through the air. The shadow was longer than a ship, and nearly as tall as a hovel. The shape twisted past and Sylas spun to try and follow it, but the beast disappeared further into the dark water.

He was so focused on finding the beast that he was surprised when his head popped out of the water. His body had floated to the top, and Sylas took a gasping breath of air. No sooner had he sucked it in before a wave careened over him and threw him back below. Sylas dove and kicked downward to keep from being tossed around like a plaything or cast into rocks.

There was a long moan from the sea, and he kept his eyes open, the saltwater burning them as he searched for the beast again.

When the shadow returned, this time it appeared smaller, perhaps half the size. But Sylas saw a slithering tail whip and two broad fins propelling from the sides, and he realized then that the beast was swimming toward him head-on.

There wasn't time for Sylas to swim away in any direction. Even if he tried, no doubt the sea creature was a hundred times faster.

Yet his instincts took over and he kicked, propelling his body backward, while his eyes stayed glued to the nearing beast.

In less than a second, the shadow was upon him. Sylas beheld it. The beast was greater than anything on land, air, or sea that he had ever imagined. Its head was topped with spiny spikes, its scaled skin reflecting all colors of the ocean with a blue glow. The beast was too tall for Sylas to see its eyes and nostrils at the same time. For a moment, Sylas felt humbled by the beauty and magnitude of such a creature, as though peace washed over him.

The beast opened its mouth to reveal rows of teeth.

Not a few. Not two or three or four. But teeth upon teeth upon jagged, razor-sharp teeth, even where a tongue should be.

The mouth stretched agape and Sylas heard a piercing screech reverberate through the water around them. The greyish tower of teeth grew closer and swelled around him like a mountain cavern.

He thought of Isla. He thought of Bell.

CHAPTER 35
RAENA

The war vote

"The Edivan army has reached the Western Founts."

The council chamber was quiet. All sixteen sets of eyes trained on Raena, waiting for their prince to speak.

Raena sat at the head of the table, leaning to one side of her royal chair, twirling a feather pen idly in her right hand while she contemplated the news. Around the table were her five diacons of Libre and her eleven councilors. She was the twelfth, with much less say in her kingdom now that Libre had bullied themselves to hold council chairs. She took a moment to gaze on each of the eleven Candorian faces staring back at her. She hated gazing at the Librens, with their creepy purple make-up and their constant white hoods; she'd asked them to remove their religious garb from political meetings but they insisted they must pay homage to their leader, The Chosen.

Amanes, the councilor of weapons, leaned forward to brace his elbows on the table. "If I may give the status of our armies?"

Raena shrugged. "Have they grown threefold since our meeting yesterday?"

"No."

"Then there isn't much point. We are outnumbered by Edivans five to one, and that doesn't include any Boens they may have with them. So, the status of our armies seems to be dismal."

Amanes bowed his head.

"We can hold the citadel," Salor Grent interjected, "we have enough people to keep the citadel and the duchies under siege. The war may settle two ongoing issues. We have the Ruvians and bandits to worry about. You know they won't return if an Edivan army is sitting outside our walls."

Raena scowled. "You're proposing we allow the Edivans to slaughter our peasants outside our gates and choke us from our resources so we can win a war that isn't ours? You want us to let our people starve, for what? So, we leave the tunnels unattended and the Boens can move into them? Nothing is to be gained there, it is the same result we would have if we proposed a treaty."

"No," Salor snapped, "if we fight Ediva, we have a chance to wear them out until Micha returns to his own land. Then we can fight the Boens, alone. We will drive them back out of Candor."

A few of the councilors nodded in agreement, but Raena caught Amanes grumbling to himself.

"What do you think, Councilor of Weapons?" Raena asked.

"It doesn't matter," Amanes grumbled, "everything must go for a vote."

"It must, and it will. But if you speak your piece as a representative for our armies, we might all vote with more informed consciences."

Amanes pursed his lips and let out a short breath through his nose, then he obliged the request. "There's no easy solution, and there's no guarantee. We cannot trust the Boens beneath our kingdoms. They could agree not to harm us, but they would always be an enemy below our feet. We also can't trust Ediva to retreat now that their armies are within our

389

borders. If we withdrew the rest of our forces from the desert and sieged the citadel, we have a fighting chance. When they run out of supplies, they will be forced to retreat to Ediva."

"If they haven't choked us out first," Salor said, echoing Raena's own words.

Raena held up her hand. "I hear only problems. Who is proposing a solution?"

The lead diacon, who called himself Air-child, spoke, "I speak for all of us."

Raena rolled her eyes. "We know how this works. You don't have to remind us every time you speak."

"Yes," Air-child mumbled, "we are sure the people of Candor must prevail. Our legacy is here. Our kingdom is the only true kingdom. Ediva is filled with lies, and evil, and blasphemy against the Almighties. Their armies ride under false worship and all of the world shall stack against them. They will lose every battle due to disease, drought, starvation, and injury. Let it be known that Ediva is cursed and Candor will erupt in victory, spreading the people of Calamyta throughout the world, spreading prosperity in all directions."

Amanes crossed his arms. "That's not a war strategy."

The men around the table all began to blurt out insults and groans at the incivility, except for the diacons who remained silent, likely communicating (or pretending to) inside their own heads. Air-child opened his mouth and made a long "oh" sound in response, staring at Amanes with a blank expression.

"Silence," Raena ordered, not needing to raise her voice. When the councilors fell quiet, she continued. "We have been at this for weeks. Every day we congregate to discuss what to do, and every day that army draws closer. I have spent more time arguing with the lot of you in here than I have spent tending to the ruling matters. I think I've seen Salor's face more than my new wife's; maybe I should try to create an heir with him instead?"

Salor grimaced and a few men snickered at the joke.

"We have to vote on this," Raena said, jamming her fingertip down on the table. "Whether we declare war or declare peace, we must have a decision. We either open our gates to the Boens and give them the underground, or we fight two armies and hope we get to keep a fraction of our men."

"I'm not prepared to vote," Salor said.

"You've said that for a fortnight. The decision has to be made. We need time to prepare, whatever the decision is."

Salor shook his head. "Then I would like it noted that I protested the vote."

"Fine," Raena snapped. "Who else protests the vote?"

No one raised their hand.

"Then I call for the vote."

Air-child nodded. "We second the call for a vote."

"One of you, or five of you?" Raena quipped, unable to restrain herself.

The diacons stared at her in unison, their dark eyes blinking in their unison stare, as if activated by a single pulse.

She sighed, regretting drawing their attention. "Let's have the vote, then."

Salor stood and fetched the royal decree log from the golden scroll table. He set it on the quorrilium pedestal and dipped his pen in an ink blotter. "We are now calling the official vote. All names and council seats will be identified in the log, and shall be here forward recorded. Prince Trevin is the originator of the vote, and I, Salor Grent, am the recorder. I have entered our names as the officiants of this vote. Let it be known that I have also recorded my protest to the vote and I have entered my vote as undecided."

"Unnecessary," Raena grumbled. "All right, the vote is for declaring peace with the Boens and surrendering our underground tunnels for their habitation. If you vote against this, you are content with us declaring war and fighting both the Boens and the Edivan army."

"There's not much choice," Amanes said, "since hoping a windstorm or drought kills them for us doesn't seem to be on the table for realistic consideration." He cast a pointed glare at Air-child, who seemed unaffected or unaware of the sarcasm.

Raena nodded at Salor, then raised her hand. "All those in favor of a peace treaty with the Boens, raise your hand."

Amanes's hand shot up the fastest. His was followed by Mujar, councilor of agriculture, then Poulo, councilor of coin, and Dwill, councilor of expansion. None of the diacons moved, it was as though they had gone into a sleep state with their eyes open, all staring straight ahead.

"That's fo—" Salor began.

"Wait," Raena said, gritting her teeth. She kept her hand raised, looking each of her councilors in the eye.

It worked, though it wasn't enough.

Two more raised their hands, their eyes apologetic, as if they knew that loyalty to her was pointless in the face of such strong opposition.

Salor spoke again, but quieter this time. "That's six votes in favor. One undecided. Nine opposed."

The irony was not lost on Raena. She slammed her hand down on the table. "I gave you bastards seats on my council. You fucking horses' asses with your fucking hideous face paint and your horseshit single-brain…shit! You fucking asses!"

Amanes was up from his chair and grabbed Raena around the shoulders, trying to pull her from her seat. He was muttering, attempting to appease her with calm words, but Raena couldn't hear him over her own rage. As he pulled her away, she launched from her chair and kicked it for good measure. A few of the men jerked in surprise, but the diacons stayed stiff as statues, not responding, not even turning their heads.

"Oh, come the fuck on!" Raena shouted, tugging against the restrictive arms around her shoulders, "What are you, dead inside? You all drink some sick poison every morning so your heads shut off and you listen to your fucking Chosen? Your Chosen boy is going to get us all killed and lose the kingdom. You know that? I hope the Boen's eat your fucking purple faces and laugh about it!"

They were at the door now, and Amanes was pleading her to calm down. As he pulled her through the threshold, Raena focused on shaking him off.

"Stop, stop, I'm fine," she said, insisting in a calmer voice.

"You don't seem fine," Amanes replied, still holding her.

"Let me go," Raena said, twisting. She put her thumbs underneath his biceps and poked upwards between the layers of muscle, breaking away in an instant.

Amanes may have once been a soldier in the Equinox, but he was an old councilor now. He cringed and grabbed at his arms where Raena had poked him, backing away from her in an instant. "All right, all right. Prince or not, you nearly struck a councilor back there. I'm doing you a favor. Let's go for a walk."

"They wish I would strike them," Raena muttered, pacing. "They probably want to be put out of their mind-controlled misery. Are they dead under there?"

"Who knows, I've stopped thinking about them and accepted it a while ago. You should try to do the same."

"I regret the day I ever caved to their demands."

"Well, they speak on behalf of many of your people. Like it or not, your kingdom listens to the diacons. The people believe everything they say is channeled from the Almighties. When the Librens find out that the diacons voted for war, then all of Candor will follow. They will embrace this. They will go into this battle with as much passion as they can manage."

"And they will die fools. We will lose everything."

Amanes stayed between Raena and the door, but he didn't argue. He watched her with steady eyes as she paced. She shook her arms to try and dispel the fury bursting through her veins like lightning charges, needing an outlet.

Amanes whispered, "Why don't you go rest. There's nothing more to be done today. Tomorrow, we will begin preparing for war. I will assign you generals and we will begin our tactical discussions and configuring the outposts. But for now? You've been at this for weeks. Go spend some time with your new wife."

Raena shot him a glare without meaning to.

"Come on," Amanes prodded, "you said yourself you haven't spent any time with her. Get her into bed, maybe the two of you can make yourselves a little prince."

"That's hardly going to save Candor."

"Maybe not, but you'll feel better trying."

Raena scoffed, but didn't protest. She was long-accustomed to feigning the idea that all men were sex maniacs, and she was as manic as the rest of them. If she wasn't, then she might not be a man, right? At least that was how Finn had explained it. He was as excellent of a faker as she was, if not better.

"All right," Raena mumbled, "you've got me there. I'll be with the Princess. Don't bother me until morning?"

"Of course, Your Majesty," Amanes said, smirking. "I'll tell the others you are to be left alone unless it's an emergency."

"The whole citadel better be on fire, or else it's not enough of an emergency, understood?"

His smirk broadened.

Raena turned her back to him and began walking before she rolled her eyes. She thought of what it would be like if she truly were a man named Trevin and she did go to Aven, making demands for her cock after just being forced into declaring war. It felt insulting to the memory of her father's name and House Schinen to be such a beast, but Raena played the part. Apparently, with men like Amanes, that was the kind of man he expected Prince Trevin to be.

CHAPTER 36
RAENA

Legacies and lies

War had been declared.

According to the messengers of Candor, the Edivan army had stopped to make camp in the Western Founts, taking shelter within the abandoned walls of Hawk's Keep. No Boens had yet been spotted or reported, but Raena was certain they were in the myriad of tunnels below her second home.

For three days, she had responded to the declaration by enabling the armies, supporting orders for them to take up arms and assemble. The legions of Candor would march to House Grent and try to stop Ediva from punching through. In theory, Ediva and the Boens would never reach Candeo. Raena knew it was a frivolous strategy; at fifty thousand men, Candor's army could hardly hold back one of their adversaries. They would be decimated fighting both.

The fall of Candor was inevitable and fast approaching.

After another heated exchange between her and General Wallen, commander of the archers, Raena retreated to her private library to collect herself and scribe for a few minutes. Once she had accepted the fate of Candor was to be destroyed and overthrown, she had taken to writing the stories of her friends and their glory. Sir Finley. Lady Islabell. Duchess Avenna. Lord Sylas. Sir Allyn. Sir Rowan. Heroes in battles against the Boens, and there to provide final judgment on Queen Zarana and disgraced King Zander.

Raena wondered if Prince Trevin would be written about as 'disgraced', as well.

A shadow darkened the doorway, then stepped into the library and closed the door.

"To what do I owe the pleasure?" Raena muttered, hardly looking up from her pages.

"It's time we put a stop to this," Jonn-Del said. He slid into a chair opposite her.

Raena glanced up, easily reading his face by the candlelight. He was sweating slightly along his brow, and pretending he wasn't out of breath. She assumed he ran to get there, but his brown eyes scanned the library as if he were nervously searching for something. Jonn-Del was wearing courtly knight's robes, suitable to take audience with a king, which was the second thing that struck Raena as odd.

"You must want me to guess what you mean," Raena said, "but I'm not in the mood."

Jonn-Del leaned close, his elbows propped on his knees. "We will lose this war."

"As I'm well aware."

"The Boens will likely spare your life, and some of your nobles, to leave as keepers of the above-ground farms. You'll be their slaves, at best."

Raena shrugged. "If I stay here at all, or if I don't fight to the death. I'm choosing to consider this one day at a time."

"You wouldn't abandon your new wife."

At the mention of Aven, Raena's eyes shot up and met Jonn-Del's. His expression was not of malice, but clarity. Raena realized he appeared worn down, the crow's feet around his brow more pronounced than usual. His chin, normally clean-shaven, was covered in greying hairs of beard growth a few days old.

Jonn-Del forced a smile and continued, "Whether or not I wanted you to marry her, that's done, now. The only thing to do is move forward and save Candor. I've spent the last few weeks thinking about what may need to happen in this exact scenario. You may not appreciate my outlook, but I am always prepared, and that's been necessary many times. I can do what must be done and most kings need men like that at their side."

Raena squinted, setting down her pen. "You know, I've often wondered how you were able to gain King Micha's trust. In the years before you served him, what did you do in Ediva?"

His smile faded, "I cared for the kingdom. I watched you from afar. I brought news to Lord Sylas to help him protect you. I still serve House Schinen first, forever, and to the death. Under any ruler, or any king, I will preserve the legacy that your father bestowed upon me."

"Of course. And your loyalty is unquestioned. Yet even though I am a member of House Schinen, you aren't loyal enough to ever be forthcoming with me. You want my trust in you, completely, but you won't give the same in return. How do you expect that to work?"

Jonn-Del scratched his hairy chin. "It may offend you, but you're still a child in many ways. When your father and I fought in the Equinox, we were young men. Not much older than you. So, I understand it might sound hypocritical. All I can say is that...our lives were harder, then. We were forced to grow up faster. We believed in King Zonn, and when Lyam was crowned, we believed in Lyam, as well. We fought alongside each other. We rode over the Calam Mountains in the spring and raided the Edivan camp at Hanford. I could tell you stories of battles with true glory, between equally matched enemies where the greatest man won."

Raena glanced at the pages she had been writing—the names of her friends. Their stories were heroic, but Jonn-Del made it sound as though fighting Edivans in war was the only way to be a legend.

"Enemies respect each other," Jonn-Del continued, "and we respected Ediva. They were noble in battle, and so were we. There is something to be said of fighting a clean war for your king."

"And that's not what this is."

"No, this is a shameful war. You and Micha will never be at odds. Both of you agree this isn't best for your kingdoms or for the lands. Despite what your council thinks, the people of Candor will not fight behind a hesitant ruler. They will sense your resistance to this war, and crumble."

Raena scoffed, "The armies will crumble because we barely scraped together fifty thousand farmers, boys, and peasants to stock our legions. We lost our warriors, our horses, and our weapons to Boenaerya. Everything we could have had to defend the citadel is underground in tunnels or likely in the hands of Boens on their way here to attack us. Fortunately for me the Librens will take up arms, and I gain a few religious zealots who now fight for me, in spite of their bloody incursion a month ago."

"Then make yourself king and declare peace."

Raena rubbed her hands together. "Are you here to joke? I have other things to do."

"I told you I'm prepared. I have the solutions for the problems you face, and I thought of them before the possibility even arose that your council may vote for war. I have planned your next move since we started that caravan from Ediva."

"Really?" Raena raised an eyebrow. "That's funny, because you never told me that you were making me take the name Trevin, nor that you would push me into being crowned prince—"

"I didn't tell you because you would have tried to evade it. And I haven't told you what I have planned now, because you will try to evade this, as well."

Raena stood from her chair and towered over him, her sternum inches from his cheek. He stared straight ahead. "What have you done, Jonn-Del?"

He shrugged, and began to open his mouth, but Raena snapped before he could answer.

"I am not your puppet or your pawn. You have given me the throne, and I will not act as your tool for your games. Tell me, now, what have you done?"

Jonn-Del stared at the floor as he spoke, "A caravan is coming from Ediva. Five Edivan handmaidens, along with guards. They are bringing a child. Half-Boen, half-Candorian. I'm assured by my messengers that the resemblance is uncanny."

Raena began to pace, her hand at her lips. She knew what he was about to say and her chest tightened with each word.

"The handmaidens are prepared to explain how the child came to be. You impregnated the Duchess of Colby when you were serving her House, as her knight. She had to hide her condition, both to protect you and herself. When the two of you visited the other Houses of East Shore, you were also staying away from Colby long enough that her subjects and Duke Eathon's family wouldn't notice her illness. After the Boens came, she birthed the child while hiding in a cave, and went on to hide it in Ediva."

Raena laughed, a dark, bitter sound.

"Then," Jonn-Del continued, "you left the child to be raised by Edivan handmaidens, receiving assurance from King Micha that your secret would be kept. You had no way of knowing you would go on to become the prince, and the child would be your heir. Now that you have the throne, you are ready to send for your son. Your son, the new prince, who makes you King of Candor."

Raena laughed again, this time more sardonic than the last. "You old fool, this is treason at best. You are wearing out your luck. How many lies do you think people will believe? How many of them know Aven has never birthed a child—"

Jonn-Del stood. "You underestimate me. The rumors have already begun. I've been circulating them for weeks, ever since you announced your engagement to Aven."

Raena stopped in her tracks, staring him down, her fists balled at her sides. "You circulated…what?"

"I circulated the rumors that you were marrying her because you sired a secret child. That you had slipped up while serving as her knight, and fathered a bastard."

Raena saw red. "How dare you fucking—"

"Stop and think about this. Think about how this will save everything. Swallow your pride for a moment—"

"This isn't about pride! Who is this child? Where did you take a child from? How have you convinced people in Ediva to carry out this lie for you?"

"You miss the point."

"I don't fucking miss the point. What do you think they will do to me? Are you forgetting that every one of these lies is stacked dangerously high on something rather fucking obvious?" Raena reached for his hand and grabbed his wrist. In a harsh tug, she placed his knuckles against the thick leather of her breastplate, shaking his limp fingers so they slapped against her chest. "What is your story going to be when they learn about this, then? Have you forgotten that I am just one public bath away from having us all beheaded?"

Jonn-Del whipped his arm back out of her grasp. "You've kept up your end. You've protected your secret. Now I'm protecting House Schinen and all of Candor."

"At what fucking cost?"

"Whatever it takes, which it seems you are not willing to do."

Raena leaned in so their noses nearly touched. She whispered like fire was expelling from her throat. "You don't give two shits about House Schinen. You want me to raise some child you found, from where, a peasant? How is that preserving my father's legacy? You want to put any random child on the throne?"

"That's a problem for the future. In the meantime, we solve our first problem, by making you king and stopping this war."

"A problem for the future?" Raena spat. "I've had enough of your 'plans'. From now on if you want me to agree to anything, you tell me all of it. The whole plan. I want to know exactly what your schemes are. Or else, I refuse." She stepped back and crossed her arms, staring him down.

Jonn-Del's lips were pursed, his face twisted into a scowl. He looked as if he wanted to strike her or shout, but he let out a hard breath through his nostrils and his expression softened. "All right, I'll tell you."

"Good. Sit."

He obliged, returning to his chair. He looked at Raena for a moment, but she didn't budge, continuing to stand there glaring down at him.

"All right," Jonn-Del repeated. "Once the child arrives, you and Aven will go to meet the caravan at the barns, on the edge of the castle. You will make it seem as though you are trying to keep everything quiet, but I have arranged for a troupe of guards to take up the barns as weapons storage, starting that same night. When they discover you, they will be alarmed to see the Edivans. You will call them off, and ask them not to tell anyone they have seen the Prince and Princess there."

Raena nodded, prodding him to continue.

"As I said, this rumor has been festering, especially among your guards. They have long suspected there must be an…alternate reason you took a common girl as your bride, when you could have had anyone you desired."

"How is that their concern?"

Jonn-Del shrugged. "Men who have very little love to fantasize about being in your shoes."

"And you can't help but take advantage of that, then?"

He glanced away, but not out of any shame or conviction. There was a bit of pride in his eyes.

"So then," Raena grumbled, "what's your plan for when this child grows older? You let him grow up believing I'm his father, and I lie to him for his whole life, and he thinks he belongs on the throne, serving Candor?"

"He will be given the choice."

"What do you mean, the choice? He'll get to choose to go along with it, or what?"

Jonn-Del sighed. His hand began to shake, and he pointed at the empty chair across from him. "Could you please sit? I will be honest with you, but there's something I should say."

Raena grabbed the chair by the back and with a steady gaze, she pushed it over. The wood clattered against the stone floor, echoing in the tiny space.

Jonn-Del didn't flinch. The two of them stared at one another in their filibuster, until the old knight cracked to the pressure.

"Fine, then," Jonn-Del said with a groan. "But you won't like what I say. Remember that I tried to make this news easier for you to swallow."

Raena raised one eyebrow, knowing exactly what she expected to hear.

"Your father and I were loyal to this kingdom, the crown. Henry and I were loyal to King Lyam. Did you know that he sometimes visited us while our fathers were talking. He was a bit older, but we would swordfight him. Your father and I trained in combat together, when we were young boys. I was a squire of course, and they were both lords. But your father treated me as if I were in the same category as the rest of them, as if I were destined to be a duke and not simply a knight. It helped that Lyam had four older brothers all in line to be king before him. We thought he would end up a knight or a lord, too. No one could have predicted how so many Paytons would fall when Ediva broke through the gates in the Battle of Grey River."

"Get to the point."

"No patience for an old man? That's a pity. There is so much you can learn. Aren't you a bit curious about the kind of person your father was?"

Raena grimaced. He had found her sweet spot. But she didn't need Jonn-Del's account of Henry Schinen; Raena could remember him. She had been eight years old; she had seen her father. He had been patient, kind, and strong. That was all Raena needed to know.

Jonn-Del seemed confident in his assessment and didn't hurry his account. "Everyone was shocked when the Paytons were slaughtered. We nearly lost the war; our king and all his princes were gone in the blink of an eye. The kingdom rose up with a vengeance, and we beat Ediva back all the way to Castle Salish. It helped that the people of East Shore stopped turning a blind eye. Even though they had tried to avoid the battles, that brought the war into their homeland. Your father and I were crossing the Scablands to infiltrate Ediva's vulnerable northern pass when they announced that Lyam Payton had survived the massacre. He was named crown prince that very night. The healers kept him alive, but he was always afflicted. He was weaker, like he barely survived to have not much of a life. Perhaps that's the reason why it was so hard for him to have a child with Zarana. Perhaps it was her age. But every time we thought it would last, she lost another one. All of those princes and princesses lost. But that's why we knew if she ever birthed a healthy child, it would be the only one. There was one chance to give Lyam the crown as king."

Raena's eyes narrowed. "I know this. I know all of this."

"Do you? Or do you think that you do?"

Raena stood taller. "What does this have to do with my father?"

"Henry," Jonn-del muttered, "you think that I am the one who plans for everything, but your father had years of plans for our kingdom. He knew how we would respond to every situation under the sun. He was ready to position himself to be the next king. And he would have been. That was the right decision. After Lyam, it would be Henry's turn. The three of us agreed."

"But Lyam had a son."

"Did he?" Jonn-Del asked, staring with a hollow expression.

Raena felt her legs buckling. She bent down to pick up the chair she'd pushed, setting it right and falling into it. "Go ahead, say what you mean."

"I think you already know. Zander was never Lyam's son."

Raena nodded. She'd known. Just like she had told Aven, she'd believed it, but it was something else entirely to hear it confirmed out loud by a man who definitely knew the truth.

Jonn-Del continued. "He was born the right day, at the right time. Henry had already found a handful of women, pregnant, peasants mostly. He was watching for the right one and when Zarana delivered, it was your father who went to the peasant woman and took her child. Henry delivered Zander to the Queen."

Raena pointed her finger in his face. "That's not true. Zarana took Zander from a pig butcher. She took Zander, and gave them Aven. Aven is the true princess, and the daughter of Lyam and Zarana."

"What? No. Whatever gave you that idea?" He reflected on it for a moment, then shook his head, chuckling. "No...sorry, lad. But the baby Zarana birthed was stillborn, like many of the rest. This one lasted longer than the others, but still, didn't live. We rushed it out of the room and Henry brought her a healthy little boy, minutes after. Your father made sure the kingdom would have the heir it needed, and Lyam was named King."

"My father wouldn't have taken some child from a woman in exchange for nothing. He would have given her another child to raise."

"He didn't. I know you were a child yourself but...your father was a great man. He did what needed to be done. He killed the woman and saved Zander from a life of filth and waste. He made that little peasant boy into a prince. If the woman had been given the choice, she probably would have wished that for her infant."

Raena balled her fist again, pounding it against her thigh. "I don't believe you."

"Believe it. And believe that we will do it again. We already are doing it again."

"Yeah? Because look how well it worked out. Zander was a disgrace. He was a petulant asshole who cared about nothing but himself. He drove Candor into ruin for his pride and arrogance. He couldn't take direction from anyone. Now you're telling me that it was your decision to create that monster?"

"We didn't know what kind of man he would turn out to be," Jonn-del sighed, "we never meant for him to rise to power. He was supposed to give Lyam the throne. No more."

"No more? So, what, your plan was to kill him?" Raena quipped, sarcastically. She began to huff at the notion but then realized that Jonn-Del was not responding in kind. He was silent, lips tight, studying the titles of library volumes against the wall.

"Jonn-Del," she pressed, quieter, "your plan was to kill him?"

He shrugged. "How much better off would Candor be now, if we had? Your father would be alive, and king. You would be Princess—"

"What the fuck is wrong with you?" she snapped. "He was just some child! He was just some regular, common child! You are the ones who stole him away. Maybe there was never anything wrong with him, maybe he was…hurt, from being thrown into a world where he didn't belong!"

"So now you have sympathy for him? This isn't about Zander. This is about Henry, and doing what's right. Putting the right man on the throne, who belongs there. And right now? That's you. You should be next in line, just like Henry should have been next in line, after Lyam. Then the throne would have gone to House Schinen. We all agreed, even Lyam. He would rule until the boy came of age, and then the boy…would have an accident. A tragedy. It wasn't going to be cruel. We wouldn't have let him suffer."

Raena felt blood rushing to her ears. If not for the chair beneath her, she might have fallen to the ground.

"We found someone who would do it. Turns out, we trusted the wrong man. That was mine and Henry's mistake. Instead of killing Zander, the ass betrayed us and ran to the Queen. He told her everything. And…that bitch. She couldn't just leave it alone. She sat with it for a year, waiting for Lyam to die. As soon as he was out of her way, she accused your father of treason and ordered the end of your noble house. Now you know the truth. Now you know what your father died for. He died for

405

this legacy, and you think that should all be in vain? You will throw it back in his face, refusing to take the crown? Because we might kill the wrong peasant boy?"

Raena bit her lip. Her mind was racing, searching for holes in his story. She tried to think of a way that timeline couldn't be correct, or her father couldn't have been involved. But her mind came up empty. Somehow everything Jonn-Del described was like a piece falling into place that had been absent from her story, all her life. She stammered as she talked, "Y—you plotted to murder the prince."

Jonn-Del rolled his eyes. "Maybe you're more like Zarana Payton than you are like Henry Schinen."

"Maybe I am," Raena muttered.

"I'll not sit here and let you make the same mistake. That's why I've told you. You think it's to inform you? No. You're right, I still don't trust you. Because I see you don't have the same drive as your father did. I don't know how to change that, but I keep hoping one day you'll wake up and see that ruling a kingdom isn't a bunch of promises and happy citizens and saving everyone. It's hard choices. People get killed. But in the end? Your civilization lives. That's worth more than every single, solitary life."

"So, murder is comfortable for you?"

Jonn-Del rolled his eyes. "What did you think it was going to be like? What did you think being a prince would be? That you could pour grain from the sky? That Ruvians would never attack your farmers? That your entire kingdom would be filled with singing and dancing?"

"There's a lot of gray area in between 'singing and dancing' and high treason."

"You seemed just fine with treason when it was killing the Queen for revenge."

Raena felt the muscles in her jaw tense from clenching.

"Your new son will arrive in a few days," Jonn-Del said, "that's enough time for you to prepare your wife and get ready for the throne."

There was an uncomfortable silence. Jonn-Del patted his thighs as he started to stand, but Raena leapt from her chair, blocking him.

"What will I do if the baby's family comes looking for him?" she blurted out.

Jonn-Del huffed, "They won't."

Raena relaxed her shoulders, preparing herself with a deep breath. "But his parents? What if they find him?"

"They won't," Jonn-Del repeated.

"And how are you sure of that?"

He sighed and stood from his chair, where his chin was squared with Raena's shoulder. At her right side, she would need to turn before she could strike him with a clean blow. Raena's heart raced.

Jonn-Del spied her from the corner of his eye. "I made sure. The boy's family is gone. You have nothing to worry about, Prince." He stepped toward the door, and was almost out of Raena's reach.

Almost.

She spun and clocked him in the temple with a left hook. Jonn-Del stumbled forward, grabbing the door frame to brace himself. Raena lunged after him and threw her right fist from above, striking the same temple a second time. That hit was far more powerful. He crumbled to the ground, appearing to be asleep.

Raena gripped her fist and paced for a moment. The thought crossed her mind to slit his throat, but surely a man who played with puppets had plans of insurance for such an assassination.

With Jonn-Del well and rightly unconscious, Raena burst out of the library.

CHAPTER 37
RAENA

The great plan

Aven would know what to do.

When Raena reached their chamber, she told the guards to double post, and not allow anyone in until morning.

"Not the council. Not a knight. Not a duke. No one." Raena instructed. She would have to bide time to deal with Jonn-Del. If he came to the door and demanded entry, the guards would turn him away—at least for one night.

Aven was sitting at the vanity, embroidering a flag, when Raena entered. The princess was dressed in a beige sleeping gown, with her hair loosely bound in a single braid. Raena typically saw Aven in this casual form, now that they were wed. Seeing her often didn't make her any less breathtaking, or make Raena any more accustomed to Aven's beauty.

"You're in for the evening early?" Aven asked.

Raena's hands were clenched. "Aye," she muttered. She walked through the chamber hastily, going to her wardrobe, then back to the boudoir, searching.

Aven continued her handiwork but watched Raena in sideways glances.

"Have you seen a canvas sack?" Raena asked.

"Is it for riding, or hanging weapons?"

"Erm, could be for both? But it has a rope around the top. It's good for traveling."

Aven nodded, setting her needles across her lap. "Are you traveling, Prince?"

Raena bit her lip. "I...I think I need to go take care of a few things."

They stared at one another for a long moment. Raena was suspended near the doorway, stopped at the midway point between the rooms of the chamber, as if she'd been frozen by magic. Aven was poised, calm, the picture of a woman who had decided to give her efforts and energy toward a battle flag in the face of a violent war. She folded said battle flag into a neat square and placed it on top of the vanity. With a short sigh, Aven stood, her hands folded in front of her skirt.

"Do you need to talk through it?"

Raena nodded. "Please."

Aven walked toward the bed and reached beneath it, rummaging for a moment, then producing a well-worn canvas bag. "Here. Let me help you pack."

"I'm not sure what I'll need, is the problem."

Aven shrugged. "Tell me what you plan to do, and I'll figure out what you need."

Raena cast her eyes to the floor, sheepish, but accepted.

The sun was still peeking through the windows, but by the time Raena was through talking and Aven had thoroughly packed the bag, the room was orange with the final moments of desert sunset. Tired from the conversation and the packing itself, Aven lounged on the bed, propping pillows behind her back, and set to taking out her braid. Raena had stripped down to her loose undershirt and trousers and sat propped at the opposite end—a mirrored image. It was a comfortable and familiar arrangement by now. They'd been sleeping that way since their wedding night, finding a compromise that allowed them both valuable rest while keeping up appearances of a 'marital bed'.

Aven twirled at her hair, half-tending to it and half-playing with it. "Do you think he's still on the floor where you punched him? What if he's dead?"

Raena spoke out of the side of her mouth as if revealing a secret. "Find me someone who would miss him."

"That's not the point. If he dies, we're all in danger."

"I hit him pretty hard but…I'm sure he's not dead. I've been knocked out cold, before. It's unpleasant, and sometimes you vomit, but it doesn't kill you."

Aven cringed, "What about what he said, about Zarana's baby being stillborn?"

"I don't believe him."

"Because you don't want to?"

Raena shrugged.

Aven stared at the blanket, deep in thought. She spoke as though she were dreaming, her voice carrying from away in a distant land. "When you told me that you thought I was her daughter, I didn't believe you. I didn't want to. I tried to ignore everything you said. But deep down, there was something inside me that said it had to be true. I know you wouldn't have reached such a conclusion without feeling sure, yourself. There was always something about the way she looked at me that seemed curious. As though she was trying to place where she had seen me before."

"You think she was wondering if you were hers?"

"Well, yes. But, no." Aven shook her head as though washing away a memory. "After something happened, I'm not sure when it was, she didn't look at me that way anymore. I think I was coming-of-age, maybe.

I just remember that one day she came down to the kitchens and asked to see 'the pig butcher's girl', and I heard her, but I hid behind the food stores. I was afraid my father would beat me if the cooks told him I wasn't working again. When the cook brought me out, she pushed me against the table. Zarana saw it, I know she did. I never saw that cook again. I think that was the same day Zarana took me to her library and told me to use the guards' stairwell."

Raena's brow was furrowed, intently listening. Aven glanced at her, looking for permission to go on.

"Zarana's expression changed around that time. I remember it because when I was in the libraries, I always read whatever I wanted. But this time, in her private library, I picked up The Tales of Gavin, and she pulled it from my hands. She gave me Zebulon Payton in Legend and told me to memorize it. She said that a girl of Candor needed to understand the mind of her king, and all kings before him, and why King Lyam sat on the throne. I was so nervous, I stared at the pages without really reading at all, until she left."

Raena rubbed at her jaw, amazed. "You've never thought of this, again?"

"Not significantly. Not until now."

"You're certain that her demeanor changed? Do you remember how close that was to the time of Lyam's death?"

Aven bit her lip and thought for a moment. "It's hard to say. But I remember when Lyam died, my father brought all of us out of the hovel and we stayed in a barn for a few weeks with another butcher's family, because he was afraid there would be an uprising. Of course, there wasn't...I remember it because I had my bleed, and I was in that barn with my brothers and the other butcher's sons. I had to hide it from them, and I didn't know how long to expect it. I think I had just come of age."

"Right. So, it was within the same time?"

"I think so. Close to the same time."

"That's when Jonn-Del said Zarana found out the truth about Zander and their plans to kill him. She must have also learned who her real child was, that you're the princess. Jonn-Del must be lying about you—"

"Or maybe he didn't know everything. He told you that Henry was the one who switched the babies. Perhaps your father told no one about me."

Raena grimaced, her lips curling. "My father was kind, and warm, and gentle. I remember him. He wasn't capable of any of this."

Aven tutted.

"What?"

"Nothing," Aven muttered.

"No, what is it? Come on, you might as well say what you want."

Aven groaned, rubbing her face. "I shouldn't…I'm sorry, but…your memories of your father were from childhood. As his daughter. He may have been a wonderful man, as you remember him, but he wasn't infallible. He was powerful, wealthy, and close friends with a brutal king. Lyam used to let his soldiers chase serfs to 'weed out the weak'. It was a plentiful time and the nobles believed they had people to spare. I have a hard time accepting that anyone in Lyam's inner circle wasn't…complicit."

Raena felt her face burning, and a stinging sensation filled the back of her throat. She wasn't sure if she wanted to cry or curse with rage. She swallowed hard, mulling it over, and caught Aven still and staring, patiently.

Raena adjusted the blankets and pulled one up to her chin. "I don't think he could have done this."

"Jonn-Del might be a lot of things. Conniving, certainly. But he's proud of who he is and who your father was. I think he told you what he saw as actions that you should be proud of."

Raena nodded. "That's exactly how he seemed. Like he thought this was a wonderful thing…Henry…I wish I really knew him."

"I don't think anyone can really know their parents. Clearly, if what you say is true and Lyam and Zarana are...well."

"Well? I guess we both had terrible parents, then."

Aven scoffed, "Then I'm sorry that mine killed yours."

"Almighty's breath, they did, didn't they?"

"Should we be sworn enemies, or something?"

Raena raised an eyebrow. "We're half enemies. Your parents only killed half my parents."

"Do you want to talk about that?"

"No, I want to talk about where I'll be tomorrow."

"I thought you decided," Aven said, "I packed your bag. You're riding at dawn—"

"And I'll stop the caravan. But what if I ride on, after that? What if I go on to Hawk's Keep?"

"Why?"

"Perhaps I can appeal to Micha. I can tell him how all of this has fallen apart. He doesn't want this war; he wants me to surrender the underground to the Boens. If I tell him that I couldn't, he'll have a chance to call off his army."

"Rae, listen to yourself. If you ride into the Edivan camp, they'll kill you. At best, they'll capture you. And the army won't ride with you."

"I won't take an army. I'll take a hundred of my best men and leave the rest. But regardless, Micha won't execute me or harm me; he's too dignified. He wouldn't win a war by assassination."

"Then what about the council? You return to Candor saying you made peace in spite of a council vote and they'll execute you for treason."

"Zander did it. He marched his armies on Boenaerya without council approval."

Aven raised her voice, "And Zander is dead. Lawfully and rightfully executed."

"He died for greed. If I die, I'd be dying to save Candor."

"And who would take the throne? Who would ensure that Candor is saved when you die? There would be no one to rule this kingdom with safety. There are so many things that you and I need to do, all of the things that we've talked about changing and making better for future generations. We want to make our Candor a safe place, a strong place, a kingdom better than it was before us. We've barely had the chance to begin."

"This war is stealing that from us."

"Maybe it doesn't have to. Maybe the war can help us get to our goals, somehow."

Raena tossed up her hands. "How?"

Aven went quiet, fixating her solemn gaze on the blanket between them. "This kingdom has been through wars before. Ideas can prevail. The throne can prevail and you can be the leader those people need. You are capable of bringing Candor to a singular goal and uniting them. The Librens, the Ruvians, the peasants, the nobles. Every group seems to have a different objective, but you know what they lack? A true purpose. A unified principle and goal, spoken from a leader, that's what would bring them all into the fold. One kingdom. A real kingdom. Your kingdom. King Lyam had that, because his goal was power and strength through weeding out weakness at every opportunity. People believed in that, because if they survived, they saw themselves as deserving."

Raena pressed her lips tight together, taking it all in.

Aven sat up, reaching to place her hand on the blanket over Raena's legs. "I know you can bring this kingdom together."

"But what better way for me to do it than by stopping the war? Surely then I'll have the respect of all Candorians."

Aven sighed, her eyes downcast. "I think part of me knows that's possible but…what if Micha says no? What will you do, then?"

"I'd rather…I'd rather not tell you."

Aven pulled her hand back and her lips curled into a frown. "Why?"

"I think you'll be angry."

"Then give me the chance to decide that, please."

Raena cringed. "Very well, that's a fair point. If they kill me, Barton will kill Jonn-Del. Or at least, that's what I expect to ask him to do. With Jonn-Del out of the way, I believe you can safely remain princess long enough to make some changes, to appease the council, to influence the future. You could even strategically marry the next king, and remain on the throne. You could raise the next heirs and teach them compassion. You could do this without me."

Aven was quiet. She bit her lower lip and stared into the space on the blanket between them. When she spoke, her voice wavered as though she had taken a large drink of water that was trapped in her throat. "It's not a bad plan. But I'd prefer you simply don't die."

"Well, I'd prefer that, as well."

"Good, then we're agreed. Can you please not die?" Aven's lips turned up at the corners to smile, then quivered; her voice had broken on the last word.

Raena watched, unable to find it in her heart to respond. After a second, a tear rolled down Aven's cheek, and it was as though a dam had finally broken. Raena's eyebrows knotted together and she felt an incredible pulling sensation in her chest. Aven lifted the blanket from her chest to her face and covered it there, her shoulders shaking.

Raena watched for a moment, frozen, as though she had never seen Aven cry. Perhaps she hadn't—at least not in this way, where Aven's very soul seemed to be leaking from her. Raena hesitated, then pushed back her coverings and crawled slowly across the bed. It was a sacred space they shared and kept divided, where Raena had become accustomed to staying on her own side. Separated. Moving across that forbidden boundary was an act of peace: an offering.

Raena was on her knees, crouching before her former lover. Her confidant.

Her wife.

Raena reached for Aven's shoulders, gently stroking them through the blankets. In the blink of an eye, Aven pushed the coverings away and grabbed the front of Raena's tunic, yanking her in. Raena fell forward, her head banging into the wall above Aven's.

"I'm sorry!" Aven gasped.

"It's all right, I'm all right," Raena mumbled, righting herself. She began to chuckle, and Aven smiled in response, breathing a sigh of relief. For a moment, Raena was on all fours, hovering, laughing quietly. But that faded fast when she saw the glistening tears over Aven's eyes and cheeks. She hesitated, then reached her hand out to wipe the wetness away with her thumb. To her surprise, Aven closed her eyes and pressed her face into the palm of Raena's hand.

"It will be alright," Raena whispered, her voice wavering.

Aven's eyes remained closed, new tears dripping from the edges. "I've believed that before. Somehow, I can't...I can't keep clinging to fringes of hope."

The words caught in Raena's throat and she swallowed them down. Somehow time began to slow, and for several breaths, they savored the same touch. Raena stroked her thumb as if brushing against a fragile and priceless vase she was afraid to break.

Without fully glancing up, Aven grabbed the front of Raena's tunic a second time, pulling with care. When Raena lowered down, Aven buried her face into the crook of the prince's shoulder. They locked together, both of their arms finding a way to wrap around one another. Raena relaxed into the bed on her side, Aven rolling to follow and staying tucked into the safety of Raena's shoulder as though it were a cave to hide in.

"I wish I could promise to stay," Raena whispered, her lips tickled by the top of Aven's hairline.

Aven nodded and turned her head to bury it deeper into Raena's neck. Raena felt the warm sensation of tears against her skin and soaking through the collar of her tunic. She could tell that Aven wasn't trying to

416

force herself not to cry. It was as though relief washed through them both and they relaxed into the emotion of sadness they shared.

"You always leave me," Aven said through a whimper.

"I know. I'm sorry. I can't seem to keep that promise."

Aven fisted the fabric of Raena's tunic. "I've thought so many times it might be the last time I would see you. Why is this time the hardest?"

Raena was quiet. She focused on everything about the sensation of Aven being close. It was not the closest they had ever been, by far, yet the way Raena's nerves danced within her like birds fluttering to the skies, felt fresh and new.

"Do you remember…" Aven began, then corrected herself, "of course, you remember. I was thinking about that time we were together in Boenaerya. When we were riding north to Ediva. The first night we were in the trees, and I fell asleep?"

Raena smiled. "Aye. Are you telling me that because you're about to fall asleep on me, again?"

"No, but cheeky of you. I happen to get tired, thank you very much."

"Of course. Some people sleep during the night, I've heard."

"Aye, we can't all be Boeny, Prince Rae."

Raena chuckled. "Prince Rae. I like the sound of that. Perhaps you can call me that in secret, forever."

"I like it. I'm tired of calling you all the different names. But," Aven shifted, peeking her face from behind Raena's tunic, "what was I saying? I was going to tell you something."

"The time we slept in the trees and you fell asleep—"

"Ah, yes. That time. That time I fell asleep and you were talking. That's not my fault, honestly. I don't know if I've ever told you this, but the sound of your voice is so soothing. When you talk, I feel so relaxed. Then I fall asleep."

"So, I'm boring?"

"Relaxing! There's a difference."

Raena let out a laugh. "Alright, I accept. I'm not boring."

"It's a compliment," Aven groaned, "it's so hard for me to relax. And, my point is, I haven't slept well. Or at least, I wasn't able to sleep well for so long. But I noticed that since we've shared this bed, even turned the opposite way…I'm comforted. I'm relaxed."

It was quiet again, and Raena allowed her hand to softly rub a pattern over Aven's back. She was careful not to drift too high where Aven's nightdress no longer covered her skin, and not to drift too low…

Aven shifted again, laying her hand flat on Raena's tunic and rolling back where she could gaze up and their eyes met.

Raena continued her pattern, growing lazier as the steady stare of Aven's gaze pulled her in. The pools of her eyes were enchanting, and Raena felt warmth flood through her. The way that Aven stared held something that Raena had not seen from her in many months. She'd forgotten how much she missed it. Raena cleared her throat, breaking the spell, but before she could speak, Aven lunged upwards and captured Raena's lips with her own in a searing kiss.

CHAPTER 38
RAENA

Lovers

The kiss was soft.

Aven's lips felt like returning home after a long battle and crawling into a familiar bed. Raena couldn't believe it was happening, yet the proof was the sensation of Aven breathing against her cheek. The sensation of Aven's hand on her chest roving lower to Raena's side. The sensation of their mouths joined in delicate passion.

Raena was afraid to respond too enthusiastically. As if it were a spell, she held practically still.

Aven tilted her head and deepened the kiss. Her lips pulled at Raena's, as though begging for more reciprocation.

Raena remained hesitant. She stayed there, her thoughts racing. Did Aven want only to kiss goodnight? Did she want to say goodbye? Was she trying to give Raena something to remember before the danger ahead?

She thought of the time they had kissed in the arena while the battle with the diacons grew in the citadel around them. Aven did have a habit of kissing Raena when mortality came knocking, she couldn't deny that.

Then Aven pressed her tongue to Raena's lips, begging entrance. When Raena opened her mouth to allow it and their tongues brushed together, Aven moaned.

The sound was low—pleading and hungry.

Raena's resolve crumbled like a sand wall in an earthquake. Raena broke the kiss and moved in an instant. Without precursor, her hand was on Aven's shoulder, gently pressing her lover back against the bed. Raena rolled to where she was partially on top and their bodies were flush together. When Raena started another kiss, their mouths were united in a feverish passion, far more desperate than the split second before.

Aven's sounds increased in volume to match their kisses, showing her pleasure.

Everything was happening at once. Raena felt Aven's hands moving everywhere. There was a question in her touch. The question was asking Raena for more.

When Aven pulled at the hem of Raena's tunic, the prince obliged. Raena pulled the offending article of clothing over her head and tossed it aside. The shift of her weight caused her leg to slip down between Aven's. Without much effort, Raena pressed her thigh against Aven's sex. Even through their respective clothing, Raena could feel Aven's heat.

Aven tilted her chin down and their lips separated. She spoke through panting breaths, "It's taken you long enough, Prince."

Raena felt her throat going dry with nerves. "Were you…have you been expecting me to…"

"To touch me? I don't know if I expected it, but I've been surprised that you haven't tried."

Raena's mind raced, trying to recall a time she may have had the opportunity. She couldn't think of a single example that Aven seemed to be interested in anything of the sort. If there had been a stolen glance, a longing stare, or even a hint of Aven's desire, Raena had missed it entirely.

"Do you mean after the wedding?" Raena whispered. "When we've been alone? I have wanted to respect your privacy and give you distance."

Aven's hand wound up Raena's shoulders and to the back of her neck. "You're not giving me distance now, Majesty."

"No," Raena swallowed hard. "Is there something you…will you tell me what's alright, with you?"

Aven nodded and lifted her hips. She rocked her core firmly against Raena's thigh. Her eyes fluttered shut and Aven let out a deep, long moan.

"Seven Almighties," Raena swore, lowering her lips to Aven's throat. She peppered the skin with kisses as their bodies rocked together. Raena could feel Aven's arousal building, and only a single piece of clothing had been removed between them.

Raena had to remedy that with immediacy.

She grabbed at Aven's sleeping gown, ripping it upwards, exposing the Princess's thighs.

Aven responded in kind, reaching down to pull the gown even higher until the material was bunched around her stomach.

Raena bit her lip, resisting the urge to scan and stare at Aven's body. She tried to calm herself with a few deep breaths through her teeth.

"Are you going to be modest now?" Aven asked, a smirk teasing at her lips.

"I don't know what you mean."

"Tell me Rae, do you want me?"

Raena shuddered. She paused and allowed herself to look fully into Aven's eyes. She opened her heart and resisted the urge to flinch and hide. They stared like that for a long moment, tenderly.

"Yes, I want you," Raena said, "I want you more than I ever have before."

"As your lover?"

"Yes. As my lover. And my…and my wife."

Aven gasped aloud at the word. She grabbed Raena's face and pulled her down into another kiss. As their lips tangled together with affection, Aven continued pulling at Raena's shoulders, as though desperate to feel even closer than they already were.

Continuing the kiss, Raena slid her hand down Aven's body, skipping over the bundle of fabric. She caressed the soft skin of Aven's side, her stomach, then her thighs. Raena paused at Aven's hips, eliciting a sigh of approval before she dipped her hand lower, nearly to her destination. When she felt the brush of soft curls against her fingertips, Aven grabbed her wrist to stop her.

Raena broke away, "I'm sorry—"

"No... it's not—I want that. I do. But, please."

"Slower?"

Aven shook her head, catching her breath. "Please, Rae. Let me...can I touch you?"

Raena felt her brow furrow. "Of course, you can."

"No, I mean, can I really touch you? Can I make love to you, the way you do to me? Can I put my...can I kiss you everywhere I want to?"

Heat spread upward from Raena's chest and into her cheeks. At the same instant, a very different type of heat exploded southward, giving way to a throbbing between Raena's thighs. Her stunned silence encouraged Aven to elaborate.

"You don't have to do anything you don't want to," Aven whispered. "I know you feel...you've always hidden your body. It's not something I'm pretending to understand. But I've wanted so long to truly have you. If you're comfortable."

Raena glanced down at her chest, bound and wrapped. Below that, her pants, where the fake pintle she wore strapped to her waist was dangling down, mocking a manhood. She thought back to the times they had made love. The first few times when she had been fully clothed and pleasured Aven. After that, she had only been naked with Aven once, and still too scared to let Aven do much more than fondle her and caress her. She wasn't sure if it was because of desire or simply habit.

While Raena thought, Aven affectionately reached up and rubbed her hands over Raena's back. It was reassuring and kind and was stirring Raena's desire to be touched even more.

"Have you thought about it?" Raena whispered.

Aven nodded enthusiastically. "You have no idea. I've thought about it so many times."

"Really? Even when you were angry with me?"

"Yes," Aven grinned, "don't judge me. Even when I wanted to scream in your face, I still can't help how I felt about your body."

"Oh really? And how is it you feel about my body?"

Aven stifled a giggle, and Raena found herself smiling in response.

"Come on," Raena teased, "are you trying to tell me you think about me naked?"

"Yes, that's exactly what I do."

Though the mood had lightened, there was genuine honesty in Aven's tone.

Raena raised an eyebrow. "And what…do you think about doing?"

"Touching you," Aven said. "Kissing you. Everywhere."

"When you say 'everywhere', do you mean…" Raena cast a meaningful glance downward, indicating between her own legs.

Aven nodded, her face becoming intensely serious. "Yes. I think about it so much. So often. I want to do what you like. I want to learn how you feel against my lips. I want to…" she stopped to swallow and then whispered almost inaudibly, "I want to taste you."

There was no ambiguity in Aven's meaning, and Raena felt another rush of heat barreling through her. The thought of anyone being intimate with her body in such a way had always terrified Raena, but she couldn't deny how badly she wanted it with Aven. She also couldn't deny how aroused she was.

More than once, after she had made love to Aven, she had felt so afire that she'd been unable to sleep. Raena had used her own hand the way she was desperate for Aven's touch, relieving the pressure.

Raena steadied herself with a deep breath. "No one has ever done that to me," she said, then thought how stupid that sounded. Of course, Aven knew that.

But the princess didn't mock her. "I know, lover. And I don't want you to say yes unless you truly want it."

Raena nodded, "Well, I mean to say, no one has ever done it, and what if I die tomorrow? What a tragedy that would be."

Aven's jaw dropped in horror. "Rae!" she gasped, aghast.

"What? It doesn't seem sad to you?" Raena smirked as impishly as she could, letting Aven in on the joke.

But teasing seemed only to pester Aven into resolve. With a brisk and stiff arm, Aven pushed Raena by the shoulder. Raena laughed as she rolled, falling back onto the bed. The coverings spun along with her, falling aside. In a second, Aven followed, flipping over and mounting Raena with confidence.

The laughter caught in Raena's throat as she gazed up at her wife.

Aven was the perfect image of beauty, all the more so due to her position on top of Raena. Her dark unruly hair framed her face, splaying outward in all directions and hanging down between them. Aven's dress had fallen slightly to cover her and draped over the tops of her thighs. Raena couldn't believe how badly she wanted to grab the nightdress and rip it in two to reveal Aven's perfect breasts. She was mildly obsessed with them, trying to remain respectful, but stealing glances at them far more times than she would ever admit. Raena would take that secret to her grave.

Aven bent down and kissed Raena's cheek, then whispered seductively. "Prince Rae...my wife?"

Raena groaned, "Yes?"

Aven rolled her hips, rocking them against Raena's. "I'll ask you again, lover. Will you please let me make love to you…with my mouth?"

Deep breaths. Raena's hands shook as she brought them to Aven's thighs and pressed herself upward, deepening the friction while they rocked together. "Yes…please. Yes."

Aven moaned in approval and captured Raena's lips with a kiss. It was passionate and warm and tender.

Raena wondered as their lips danced together. She wondered if Aven meant the word 'lover' with any implication. She wondered if Aven's heart had changed. She wondered if this act of 'making love' meant that they were wives in every sense and if Aven truly did love Raena again. They had confessed their love to one another before, but they had barely known one another, then. This time would be different. This time they wouldn't be desperate to experience physical pleasure out of attraction alone, surely now they had trust and respect for one another like never before. But Raena needed her to know. She needed to tell Aven how much she loved her.

But as Aven pulled at the soft tie and loosened Raena's pants, slipping her delicate fingers under the band, Raena forgot about everything else in her head. It was like her mind was blank and only her body existed.

Aven found the pintle and tugged at the string impatiently. "Does this come off or can I…move it aside?"

Raena mumbled something incoherent and reached down to unfasten the little disguise. It fell down her thigh and into the loose material of her pants. When Raena pushed her pants down and freed her legs, the pintle went along with them. She tossed both items to the side of the bed.

Aven's hands brushed over Raena's shoulders, then stomach and sides, and her hazel eyes were focused, admiring. "How about this, too?" Aven said, tracing her fingers over the binding on Raena's chest.

"Gladly," Raena muttered, popping the tight material free with a flick of her fingers against the clasp. In an instant, she was completely naked, all of her exposed. Though it wasn't the first time, it somehow felt new. Perhaps it was the candlelight that allowed Aven to see as well as feel her this time. Or perhaps it was the way that Aven knew so much more about who Raena was, instead of who she pretended to be. Was being naked any more intimate than having someone see your faults and know you for them? Raena didn't think so anymore.

But Aven didn't look like a woman thinking about faults. Her eyes widened with pleasure, taking in the sight of Raena. All of her. And Aven smiled as if seeing the sun after a storm.

In a flurry, Aven grabbed her nightdress and yanked it up. She freed her body from the garment and tossed it off the bed, somewhere near Raena's heap of clothing.

Raena was given inadequate time to stare at Aven's perfect breasts before her princess laid down. Their bodies naked, flush together, skin against skin in the best imaginable way. Raena felt pleasure and elation flow through her at the completeness and euphoria incited from the touch. Though she ached between her thighs for more, Raena had a burst of satisfaction.

Aven kissed the corner of her mouth, "Raena, I've missed you."

"I've missed you, too. So badly."

"When you return to me, don't let anything come between us."

Raena nodded and turned her head where they were looking once more into one another's eyes. "I won't."

"Do you promise?"

"Yes, I promise."

"I won't either. I won't ever again."

Raena gave her a soft kiss before whispering, their lips brushing together as she spoke, "Nothing can separate us now. You're my wife. I gave you all of myself that day. I gave you my heart, even if you didn't take it."

426

Aven sighed, "Then may I take it now, and give you mine?"

"Yes."

Raena saw the hint of a tear at the corner of Aven's eye, but knew it wasn't sadness overwhelming her.

Aven nuzzled against Raena's cheek. "Raena, I give you my heart. Again. Freely."

As if she could feel Aven's very soul opening up like the floodgates of a river and swallowing her, warmth spread through Raena's body, washing over her.

"I love you," Raena whispered, closing her eyes.

They breathed together as one in the dimlit chamber. Their hearts beating in their chests. Their bodies tangled and united. Raena knew then that it didn't matter what happened, it didn't matter if she lived or died. Anything could threaten the world outside that room and it couldn't change how Raena felt. Nothing anyone did would stop the pureness and strength of her love for Aven. Her bride. Her princess.

"I love you," Aven said. Then she pulled back and wiped a tear, smiling with a mischievous glint in her eye. She glanced downward and raised an eyebrow. "Now please, don't you think I've waited long enough to taste you?"

CHAPTER 39
AVEN

The monthly visitor most unwelcome

Aven was waking, immediately thinking of all there was to do. She had never felt more determined in all her life. It had been like this every day of the last week since Raena and Gregor had ridden away in the morning, and Aven had set her plans into motion.

She would make Prince Trevin a king, hopefully before 'he' returned.

She had three thoughts upon opening her eyes. She first remembered the plan she and Duney had laid out and the news Duney had given her the night before; they had found a Boeny man who could be a close cousin of Prince Trevin's. He was a sturdy build though late in years, likely descended from Candorians and Boens, not unlike the Schinens. He would be brought to the castle and offered a night with two women, discreetly; his seed would be collected and saved for the Princess. Duney had assured Aven for the past two weeks that she knew precisely how to produce an heir through this method. Though Aven found that confession alarming, she didn't ask more.

Aven's second waking thought was how dark her royal chambers were, and she recognized that the sun had not yet risen. She found it odd that her body had wakened her so early, so she stretched and wondered about the hour.

This led Aven to her third waking thought, and she felt a swelling pit of disappointment grow within her. She reached down to feel her nightdress, and her suspicion was confirmed by the wet sensation against her fingers. With a groan, Aven stood and walked to the lowered bath, pulling a string along the stone brick to call for her handmaiden.

When the maiden entered, Aven was already stripped of her nightgown and stepping into the lukewarm bath.

"Majesty," the maiden, Calla, began with a curtsy.

"Can you heat this water, please?"

"Aye," Calla eyed the discarded nightgown and the large red blotch, visible even in the low light. "Shall I call Duney, madam?"

Aven grimaced, fighting back a tear. Her bleed had not been due, had it? She honestly could not remember, which seemed foolish in retrospect. She was tempted not to involve Duney at all.

Calla didn't wait for a reply, going promptly to the fireplace and withdrawing a basket of coals then dumping them into the side feeders for the bath. The smoke and steam rose, heating the water at the sides.

"Madam," Calla muttered, squatting beside the bath, "I can send for a healer, or bring you a girl to give a massage?"

"I don't think so, thank you."

Calla pulled up a sleeve and reached into the water. Her eyes remained on Aven's with some unreadable intensity. "Please allow me, Princess. May I?"

Aven was unsure what she was granting permission for, but she nodded.

Calla's hand found its way to Aven's stomach, then slid lower, flattening against the top of Aven's hips. The handmaiden pressed, then kneaded, her hand moving beneath the water. Their faces were close enough for Aven to whisper, though she didn't.

Calla explained as she rubbed with increasing pressure. "I have three sisters, and a lover, I understand how to care for a woman through a bleed, Your Majesty."

Aven's cheeks flushed. She couldn't deny it felt soothing, and the cramps in her abdomen began to fade. "When you say you have a lover…"

Calla shrugged.

The room was quiet as Aven considered the implication. Neither of them said another word, Calla's hand continuing to rub in smaller circles, concentrating directly on the spot above Aven's pelvic bone. Aven glanced at Calla out of the corner of her eye, observing the young woman as much as she could. Something about the idea that Calla may have a female lover made her appear different. It made Aven notice little things: the lines around Calla's mouth from smiling, the furrow in her brow— were they from worrying about being discovered? Aven knew all too well the punishment and the law.

When the water was finally warmed from the coals, Calla stood and shook the water from her arm. "I'll fetch Duney now," she said, not asking permission again.

As the handmaiden left, Aven thought to herself that perhaps as a princess she should be more assertive and speak up, to keep her handmaiden from bossing her around. Yet she knew she didn't mind, and someone else's opinion shouldn't dictate how she behaved.

For a few moments, Aven soaked in the hot tub and watched the sunrise in her window. Shortly, Aven heard footsteps entering her chamber.

"You've gone and began to bleed then," Duney tutted. The older woman took a seat at the edge of the bath on the stones. Her gown had been tied shut instead of laced, giving her a haphazard appearance. Aven noted that Duney's grey hair was loose around her ears.

"I assure you, I didn't intend to."

"None of us ever do. If we could, we'd all put a stop to it."

Aven nodded, thinking instantly of Raena.

430

Duney sighed and tested the temperature of the water. "Nothing can be done now. Your body won't allow for seed in this state. We will need to wait, perhaps a week or two, then we can try."

Aven stared at ripples in the water, her eyes heavy. "Is there no way? Perhaps in a day or two?"

"Oh, child," Duney smiled, "have you ever been pregnant? Or did your mother tell you how it has to work?"

"I know how it works."

"You know how, but do you know when?"

Aven felt her brow furrow at the question. She couldn't fathom an answer.

Duney folded her hand on her lap as though about to impart a great lesson, and perhaps she was. "Conceiving a child is no great mystery, once you understand the timing of it. I know you understand it won't work when you bleed, and that's only part of the truth. Your bleed is a cycle, with each day holding a different meaning for your body and womb. Consider today the first day, like your birth. Consider the last day your death. Just as your body is only fertile in the middle ages of your life, so is your womb in this cycle. You will only become with child if we implant the seed rightly between each of your bleeds. I'm afraid that won't happen for at least ten more days, if not longer."

"What if the man you found…do you know where he lives? Are you sure he will stay in Candeo?"

"He's a smith for the crown, so likely will stay one," Duney said. "Don't worry about that, it's all up to me. I'll make sure that we find the man to plant his seed."

Aven nodded, unable to stop the sadness welling up behind her eyes. "But what about…that seems too long? By then, Prince Trevin will have been gone for almost a month's time. Won't people know it isn't his child?"

Duney chuckled. "The beauty of conception being a slight mystery is that very few people, especially men, question or seek to understand it. I could tell this kingdom you birthed a baby yesterday and most of them

431

would nod and applaud you for carrying it so delicately that they never noticed your stomach change or your demeanor worsen."

"I doubt that," Aven muttered, though she was already feeling relieved by Duney's reassurance.

"Please, let me worry about the details. I've already told Calla not to share that you're bleeding. She and I will be the only ones tending to you for a few days. Calla will keep this quiet. She has plenty of secrets of her own."

Aven thought of Calla's confession to a 'lover' and fought another blush.

Duney shook water off her hand and went to the fire to retrieve coals in the same fashion Calla had done a while earlier. "All of this will be alright. You need to stay relaxed." She gave Aven a stern look while pouring coals into the bath's side. "I can make it all work if you get pregnant in a few weeks, it'll be all right. But if you're afraid or anxious? It won't work. Your body won't take it. Your job now is to do everything you can to stay relaxed for the next few weeks."

"That's a bit much to ask of me. What with my husband running into our enemy's fortress and an ancient enemy coming up from underground to kill us all? Not to mention the Librens and the Ruvians—"

"Yes, yes. Plenty to worry about, isn't there? You know who sounded like you do now? Zarana. She couldn't relax during the Edivan War, then it was the famine, then there were two summers and the crops dried out. What else? Oh, she was worried her husband would father a bastard with all the women he was bedding. She probably worried her womb right out of producing an heir, until she calmed enough to conceive and keep one. That was a miracle. And look at all that happened to her? It was fine, in the end. She worried herself over nothing. She and Lyam had a good rule, at least until the Boens. There will always be another war, or another enemy, or another battle to fight. If you can't accept that, you'll drown in fear until your last dying breath."

Aven raised her eyebrows, surprised yet relieved. "Thank you, Duney. What do you propose I do today, then?"

"You're a princess, my dear. Start acting like one. Stay in this bath, then Calla and I will bring you meals, and we can fetch books from the library for you. There's no reason for you to do anything else at all."

"And what about my kingdom, shouldn't they want to see me hard at work supporting the council, or giving morale to the legions training for invasion?"

"The cocky fools on your husband's council and the amateur farmers taking up swords can stand to wait a few days. You are not the singular strand of hope tying this kingdom together."

Aven sighed, feeling torn. But the water around her began to heat and the cramps in her abdomen were returning, dull and aching. She succumbed to the comfort of the bath and believed Duney, closing her eyes and sinking into the water. She believed that comfort might come and perhaps even this enigmatic concept: relaxation.

CHAPTER 40
AVEN

When the horns sound nothing else matters

The night had been peaceful.

Calla and Duney were attentive, bringing Aven every food and drink she could desire. In a few days, she would return to her noble duties. Duney assured her that this would only perpetuate the narrative that Aven was carrying an heir.

Aven dreamed of babies. She dreamed of a giggling, straw-headed, periwinkle-eyed bundle. When she woke in the morning, she swore it must have been prophetic. Part of her yearned and ached, wishing she truly could bear the son of Raena Schinen. What a lovely child that would be, the innocent descendent of the most beautiful soul Aven had ever known.

By the second afternoon, Aven had spent most of her day in the same way as the first: indulging her body and answering every need.

"This is how it will be when I'm pregnant too, isn't it?" Aven asked.

Calla and Duney laughed, sharing an amused expression.

"How else could it be, madam?" Calla said.

Aven was about to answer when she heard a horn blast.

She waited, holding her breath, for the next sound.

Three long blasts.

The announcement was followed by shouts outside, beyond the window.

Aven sprung up from the bathwater. "Fetch me a dress," she said, pointing to the wardrobe.

Calla was already bringing towels to dry Aven when there was a knock on the chamber door. The pounding echoed through the boudoir and into the room.

"Majesty," a man's voice bellowed.

"Sir Jonn-Del," Duney whispered, throwing a red dress toward Calla. "Hurry, I'll be back."

Duney rushed to answer the door while Calla and Aven hastily worked to get the princess dried off and clothed.

Aven heard the muffled voices of Jonn-Del and Duney. Her ears perked at the word 'Boens' and she felt a tightness in her chest. She rushed Calla to hurry and lace her dress, though they both scrambled to finish as quickly as they could.

Though the dress was on, Aven's hair was wild, wet, and crimped.

"Madam, your hair," Calla said, grabbing for a brush from the vanity.

"There's no time," Aven replied. "Give me a veil…or wimple."

Calla grimaced. Wimples were long out of fashion, but this wasn't a showing or a ball. What was this, exactly? Perhaps a war.

"Majesty," Duney said, rushing back into the room alone. "Sir Jonn-Del and a dozen men are at the door. They said you must come at once. The castle is under attack."

"As I feared," Aven replied, breathlessly tugging a wimple over her hair. Calla did her part to tug and tuck.

"They've taken to the ramparts. I told him you would join him as soon as you are dressed."

"Aye," Aven said.

"Hurry with that," Duney berated Calla, reaching in to pull at the laces around Aven's midsection. They were stubbornly dangling, but there was little time to adjust them properly. Duney managed to tie them off at Aven's neck in a knot that wasn't protruding much.

"Did you give her a rag?" Duney asked.

Calla didn't reply, running to the wardrobe and searching the shelves.

"They're in the cupboards above the fire, warming."

Calla ran to fetch them and indeed found a rag where Duney had directed. She gave it a quick shake to unroll it and dropped to her knees in front of Aven.

"My Lady, may I?" Calla asked, looking up with deep brown eyes.

A pang of vulnerability struck Aven, but she shoved the sensation away. "Aye…of course."

Calla reached beneath Aven's skirts and fastened the rag between her legs without fuss or trouble. It was indeed as though Calla had done the same for many, many women before.

Aven heard the shouts continue and there was a thunder of footsteps echoing around them. No doubt knights passed her hallway and charged through the corridors.

"That's enough," Duney insisted, "you must go."

"Thank you," Aven said, gathering her skirts and pulling them up. She pushed her feet into a set of worn slippers she normally wouldn't dare to wear outside the chamber. She placed the thin wire crown meant for travel and dancing atop her head and fastened it against her hair. Aven gave a grateful half-smile to Duney, then set off down the hallways.

It was difficult to make way through the twisting corridors of the citadel castle. Men were bustling about in various states of preparation: armor covering their arms or chests, carrying weapons, holding armfuls of arrows. All of them seemed to have purpose and know their destination, which left Aven muttering prayers for each of them under her breath as she stepped aside to allow them through. Only a few bothered to mumble a quick "Your Majesty" as they ran and noticed her crown, the rest were justifiably preoccupied.

She reached the steps of the rampart after what felt like a great journey. Her legs even ached for no discernable reason. When she ascended the stairs, she looked ahead.

The sun was bright. The pale blue sky was the backdrop, and the shadows of Sir Jonn-Del and a few dozen other men were blurred in the foreground. They gestured to the ground below, observing and strategizing as they beheld the outer edges of the city. All of Candeo was visible though difficult to see, as the tower was high.

Aven joined them, standing along the thin walls, peering out. She placed her hand on her brow to shield the sun and scanned the rolling desert, but saw only various dark specks, scattered among the sand. They looked like sultanas in a bowl of porridge, shapeless blobs peppering against a lighter surface. Her first emotion was surprise, as this did not appear to be any opposing force. Indeed, she had expected an army in formation, poised tightly together for battle, ready to take on incoming arrows with shields and perhaps spears.

A few of the dark specks were weaving and moving. Some disappeared into the ground and then emerged, and she couldn't tell if they were coming from a new place, or if they came from a new hole.

"It's beginning," Jonn-Del said. He had side-stepped along the parapet behind the others to reach her.

"Are you sure of that?" Aven asked. "I don't see much of an army."

"This is certainly it. This is how they will come. They have begun to ascend from the ground, and then they fall back under. See, there? They are coming closer with every few minutes. I think in an hour or two, they will be underfoot and inside the castle walls. That is, if we don't stop them."

Aven shook her head. "They lack formations. There are maybe no more than...a thousand men?"

"That we can see," Jonn-Del said crossly. "Tens of thousands are surely underground. They think we will leave our castle to attack, and then they'll come under. They are trying to draw us out of the walls."

Aven's brow furrowed. "Wouldn't that be the best thing to do? To fight before they can fully assemble?"

Jonn-Del scoffed and didn't answer.

Aven avoided looking his way and her rage began to steep. She could assume he was rolling his eyes. How dare he defy the princess. The more she felt the arrogance rising off him the more her fury grew to a vile and bitter fire inside her.

She leaned forward and glanced down the line of men, recognizing General Phall, Sir Han'black, Baron Evandry, and Amanes, the councilor of weapons. Further in the line were more faces she knew, most of the leaders of the armies.

They were powerful men, but in the absence of their prince, they would only offer opinions. If Raena had been there, her vote would have decided the war strategy upon the advice of the generals.

"Your Majesty," Amanes said, as though he'd sensed her thoughts from her stare, "you may defer the battle decisions to the generals until your husband returns."

Aven pursed her lips. She realized she was still holding her skirts in tight fists, and she let them drop, holding her hands clasped instead. "The armies are readying for battle now?"

"Aye," Amanes replied. He gestured downward.

Aven followed his finger to lean against the side of the parapet, gazing down between the ramparts and the curtain. There in the fields where much of the city's farms and fields lay, men were assembling for war. She couldn't help but think of her brother Strand dying in that same spot, and somewhere was Allyn's decaying body, still within the city limits. Butchers, farmers, and milkmen were weaving among the legions, likely trying in vain to save their harvests before an army trampled through.

"Do you mean for me to abdicate command?" Aven asked.

Jonn-Del opened his mouth and was promptly interrupted by Amanes.

"You don't have command, madam. So, you cannot abdicate it," Amanes shrugged and shared a glance with Jonn-Del, clearly holding back amusement as it twinkled in his eyes.

Aven's jaw clenched and she let out a shaky breath. She waited for a second, hoping another man in the line would speak up, but when they appeared too fixated or too ignorant to offer a correction, she accepted that responsibility. "Gentlemen, I am sure that you are aware of the Rules of Engagement of Candor, which state in the third addendum that command of all legions changes hands when a war is declared. From the generals in times of peace, to the council in a time of war. With the king a sitting ruler of that council. However, the Tome of Law-and-Order states that a prince cannot rule a council and has a sitting vote at the same level of all other councilors."

"Of course," Amanes said, "this is hardly—"

"As you were," Aven snapped. "But the Tome also declares that the prince may hold the council as a ruling body to enforce all Rules of Engagement, does it not? Therefore, the prince would call a council meeting to determine the next step in war. In the absence of my husband, this meeting befalls on me. I will call the council at once—"

"Majesty," Jonn-Del interrupted. "That's fine if you're calling the council for a decision. But we have limited time. Not every strategy in a war can be decided by nobles and ruling classes. We give the authority to our generals to make battlefield decisions, as we always have. They are the experts and I would kindly request that you defer to them, as Amanes asked."

"I won't," Aven replied. "I will not abdicate. We follow the law or we have nothing worth fighting for. And if our laws are proven unrealistic and archaic, then I will pursue changing them when my husband returns and is crowned king."

Jonn-Del spun, leaning in so he was close enough to whisper. His tone was suddenly aggressive and harsh. "You think this is the time to prove a point? Is that what this is, getting the laws changed? You're nothing but a peasant, and you're about to throw our kingdom to the wolves over your stupid, selfish goals."

Aven fought the urge to tremble, but the only thing stronger than her fear was indignation. His insults cast fuel on the vindictive anger burning in her chest, swallowing all her other emotions with its flames. Without responding to Jonn-Del, she turned on her heel and walked across the parapet. "Gather the council. Send them to the chamber at once," she snapped.

She could have sworn she heard a few of the men laughing behind her.

Aven whipped her head around and caught them chuckling. Like children, they stiffened up at her hard, penetrating stare.

"Do you think it wise to mock your princess?" Aven boomed. "Follow that order and send the council. I'm not asking."

They nodded, sheepish and shameful like the cowards they were.

Aven lifted her chin and didn't stop walking until she reached the council chamber. She heard a commotion all around her, the continued assembly of forces gathering in all directions. Aven walked to the windows, twice her height and nearly as wide. She stood at the threshold, not bothering to step onto the balcony and peer down into the courtyard below. Instead, she gazed beyond. There were towers blocking her view, but Aven could see the desert past the citadel. She stared at the winding rivers which met in Candeo, bringing the only fertile soil to the western side of the Calam Mountains. She thought of Raena, hopefully safe at Hawk's Keep with Micha, planning how they would stop the Boens from moving forward. She clenched and unclenched her fist as she imagined her own battle that she was about to face—convincing a room full of men that war with their enemy would be futile.

When a few long moments had passed, Aven began to realize that she was still alone. Not even a guard or page had bothered to come and announce that the council was assembling.

Not even an update on the whereabouts of the councilors.

Aven crossed the room and broke into a jog through the halls. She rounded a corner and reached the outer assembly, jogging to the end of the long room to peer out an eastern-facing window. What she saw there made her heart sink like a rock in a pond.

The armies were lining up within the curtain, building a formation. By her estimation, there were fewer than a thousand fully uniformed and equipped, but more were bustling up behind to join the ranks. At the front was a general atop a horse, and a few knights flanking him on either side. They were shouting commands and bellowing in a cadence of words Aven couldn't decipher. Every few seconds, the budding legion would muck about, practicing their movements.

They resembled a hot bowl of popping beans more than an army.

Aven tried to see beyond the curtain to the Boens beyond, but her view was obscured by the towers and ramparts from this assembly room.

That was when she heard another horn blast. A single, long tweet, signaling an attack. Immediately there was a rattling sound that followed. Aven knew it distinctly; the chains of the gates were turning on their wheels and lowering for the legion.

She grabbed her skirt and pulled it up, breaking into a run.

Aven tore through the castle, searching for anyone who ranked higher than a guard. Most of the halls were empty now; no doubt the women and children had hunkered to the inner rooms, and the men had emptied the castle to join the fight. When Aven burst out of the keep and into the streets of Candeo, she saw much of the same. Peasants were scrambling to put away their belongings and scamper into safety, whether it was a barn or a shop. Children wandered lost without parents, or perhaps they were orphans, unaware of why the streets were rapidly abandoned.

Aven saw a gaggle of guards at the end of an alley, digging through a weapons store on a cart. She jogged between the mud sand walls to meet them.

"Gentlemen," she greeted their backs.

The guards turned with sour expressions, bothered, but then one's face twisted into recognition. He fell to one knee.

"Princess! Erm, Majesty, uh y-your—"

"That's fine, it's a war," she excused.

The others began to follow suit with their friend, but Aven waved her hands to stop them.

"It's a war, I mean it. Please."

They listened but shared dumbfounded expressions.

"Men," Aven continued, "what are your orders? Where are you going?"

"Erm, we're fighting the Boens, Princess."

"Right, so you are leaving the citadel? Going to the desert?"

The lead man shrugged. "Don't rightly know, but the horn has blasted, and we're all to take up arms. The marshal brought this cart and we all loaded up with all we can."

Aven resisted the urge to shake her head. "Where are you directed to go, once you're armed."

They stammered for an answer, looking to one another for help, but all six of them came up short for a reply.

"That's all right, thank you," Aven said. Before they could argue, she was running away, cursing herself for being lost in the action. She wound further out into the streets, past smith shops and stables, past a market, and into the peasant village. She was nearly at the edge of the city when she spotted a squad of soldiers. They were the first decent and orderly formation she'd seen that day: perhaps survivors of Zander's failed assault in Boenaerya.

Aven shouted for their attention, but as dedicated soldiers with true bearing, they did not give it. They marched forward toward the outer gates.

Aven ran toward them and shouted again when mere meters away. "Halt! I am your princess and I'm ordering you to halt!"

The soldier calling out the marching orders gave a command, and they stopped with a sharp jolt, perfectly synchronized. The lead soldier turned and stood as stiff as a board, staring as he rang off his name and title.

Aven didn't bother learning it. "Tell me your orders. Where are you marching to?"

"Past the gate to encounter the Boens."

"That's it? Nothing further?"

"No, madam."

Aven groaned. "And who then will stay to protect the castle?"

The soldier paused for a second before rattling off his reply. "Our orders are to fight the Boens, madam. Can't say what the general's plan is."

"Where will I find the general?"

"At the rear of the army, pressing them out to battle."

"Fine, then." Aven gave a lazy salute to dismiss the soldiers and ran back the way she'd came, searching for the stables again. When she reached them, she entered with hope. But that emotion faded just as fast upon finding the gates open and every stall empty.

Aven had one final effort.

She found the alley once again and bolted into it. The six guards were finishing up the buckles and ties on their weapon belts. They reminded her of her brothers in their father's clothes—mismatched and ill-fitted.

"Where will I get a horse?" Aven asked.

"Erm, a horse?"

"For fuck's sake," Aven gasped, "how is it that no man can handle a single question I propose today? Have you any idea what's happening? I need a horse. I need a fucking horse. Please."

One of the guards turned red as fire. The others seemed amused, cracking smiles at the Princess's use of a curse.

"Aye, y'right, Majesty. Come on wit' me." One of the guards stepped forward and led her around the corner.

Aven didn't ask questions when they entered a tavern, but she raised her eyebrows, observing while keeping up with the brisk pace of the guard. It was a seedy place she hadn't known or suspected to exist within Candeo. Patronage was light, but a few broad, hooded men were huddled at a table, whispering as she went by. Aven took them for Ruvians, and averted her eyes, though the question begged in her mind of how they made it inside the city.

Out the back door, the guard gestured into another alley. "Here, we din't know where ta put 'im. He were leadin' the cart."

Aven took in the sight of an ancient warhorse, probably twice her own age. He had scars around his barrel chest and his hooves were caked with mud and hay. His eyes barely cracked open at the attention from the two of them, as though he couldn't rouse from a nap.

"This horse pulled a cart?" she muttered, mostly to herself.

The guard shrugged. "Dunno any other horse for ya, Majesty."

"That's fine. Thank you."

As he turned to leave her there, Aven spun to call after him.

"Oi, guard. Take your time to join that fight. There's no sense in dying today. And that's an order from your princess."

He opened his mouth and then nodded. "And erm, you be careful, Princess. Be very careful, 'round this city. It's not at all safe fer ya. Another man might…any of 'em would mistreat a princess, if thinkin' it's a chance."

"I understand," Aven said. She quickly hoisted herself onto the warhorse, who did not respond or flinch at her added weight. She checked to ensure the old boy wasn't hitched or tied, then she gave him a kick.

The warhorse clambered forward, not so much as a trot.

Aven kicked him again and whipped the reins, giving a quick shout to command him. That did the trick, and the warhorse seemed to remember his past life. He clopped out of the alley and into the street.

Mere minutes had passed, but the streets had successfully been emptied of signs of life. Not even the stray urchin or beggar was to be found huddled in the doorways as Aven rode past. It was eerily quiet, save for the shouts she heard far in the distance. Aven could've followed the clang of metal and whistle of arrows out into the battlefield. She rounded a corner and spotted the gate ahead. With another kick to her warhorse's sides, Aven rode toward the fight.

CHAPTER 41
AVEN

Marching orders of defiance

The desert outside of Candeo had once been a flood plain, legends told. The rolling dusty hills were a testament to the waves that had danced atop the land, pushing from the Calam Mountains to the Scablands, to the easternmost reaches of ancient Calamyta. When the towering walls of water receded and left the rock beneath the terra, thick sand remained atop it to build new life. But little more than sagebrush, scrubs, and gris bushes could take root in the hostile ground. That made for unimpeded views, and Aven could sit atop her horse and stare out for miles.

The Boens were much farther away from the castle's curtain than they'd seemed when she was gazing down from the tower; she should have estimated that would be the case. Aven could barely make out the clash of armies in the distance: writhing black shapes jumbled together. The horsemen and knights were distinguishable in their movements, jutting from grouping to grouping, likely giving the commands.

Aven had seen battle against Boens before, but none of it was akin to the wars she'd read and studied as a young woman in the library.

Organized wars were a joining of forces, trained, equipped, unified. Fighting Boens was asymmetrical and disjointed.

She spotted a hill that raised into a plateau before dropping with a sharp cliffside made of stacked basalt. She charged toward it to wait on the edge and observe the battles below. As the warhorse's hooves pounded over sand and pale grass, Aven heard whistles and thuds nearby. Arrows were launched from the ramparts of Candeo, most of them reaching the far stretches of the desert, but a significant number were also falling short. Too short.

Aven was at risk of being struck, and so were Candor's forces. She shook her head, a tightness gripping her chest as she lowered herself perpendicular to the horse's back. Laying near his neck, she shouted for him to gallop faster. Her skirts whipped in the wind behind her and caught hold of her wimple. Before she could move her hands from the reins, the head covering was ripped away and flew behind them, joining the sagebrush and straw.

Aven heard a whistle and cowered, estimating that the arrow was mere meters from striking her.

"Come on, old bloke," she said, pleading. As they neared the hill, Aven realized that a vantage point would not protect her from the errant projectiles. In a clutch, she tugged the reins to the right, redirecting the horse. With a yank, he obliged, changing direction to aim for the space below the basalt cliff. Aven hoped that the structure would create a shield between her body and the rangers' arrows.

The cliffside was shorter than Aven predicted, jutting up a meter over her head while she was mounted. She drew back the reins and held the warhorse steady.

Panting for breath, Aven saw the battlefield with fresh eyes in closer proximity.

The Candorians had made an impressive advance, despite their untrained and unprepared legionmen. Knights wove over the hills on horseback, shouting in tones resembling a sick sort of glee. They waved swords and clanged against their shields to rally the troops below.

Even Aven could see there was no frontline; the soldiers were scattering out into the hot plateau. They were chasing ghosts.

Boens popped up from the ground, some of them crawling forth as if forced outward from their holes. Aven thought they resembled snakes slithering out of a pit.

She noticed an oddity on the terrain, growing and forming a broad blanket. At first, she thought it was a cloud of dust but then realized it was coated in a dark grey that could never resemble particles of sand.

Smoke.

Rising from the openings of the tunnels, perhaps.

It was spreading.

Aven scanned for the source of the fire, but there were no flames to be found.

When she searched, she spotted a familiar figure riding among the rear of the Candorian troops: General Phall.

Aven clenched her jaw and kicked the warhorse before she thought better of it. Together, they charged onto the battlefield.

The smell of iron and smoke hit her before she took in the source.

Her warhorse jerked to the right to avoid trampling an object, and Aven glanced left to see it as they passed.

A dead Boen, slain in the straw. He was sliced open at the chest and brown blood surrounded him on all sides, soaked into the terra. He reminded her of Strand, which struck her as strange. Something about his frame felt wrong, off.

His head was covered by a thick metal casing resembling a tubular helmet. Aven tried to study it, but her warhorse charged past before she could.

She fixed her eyes on the horizon, following General Phall as he flanked a squad of men. He herded them together, ordering them to tighten up their ranks.

Aven thought of herself gathering up pigs at night, leading them into a slaughter. In the back of her mind, she suspected she would be a casualty, as well, perhaps when the Boens began their real ambush. Almighties knew they weren't stupid enough to be picked off in the desert so easily.

"Watch the rear! Watch your columns!" General Phall screamed.

Aven rode up on the unsteady squad of at least a hundred men. They were marching out of step, their armor ringing and clashing without unison. The rear files were indeed trailing behind. A few of the soldiers had dropped weapons and were bending down to grab items, mucking up the order of columns.

"General!" Aven shouted, ignoring the desperation the man was absorbed in.

He didn't turn his head, continuing to wave a flag and bark out commands.

Aven navigated around the amorphous squad and rode up to the general's side, within a stone's throw but not close enough to startle him and risk accident.

"General Phall," she repeated, straining.

He cast a glance in her direction, the visor of his helmet raised to reveal his dark eyes and hooked nose. "Princess!" he proclaimed, startled.

With the element of surprise removed, Aven rode closer until their horses could have touched.

"What are your orders? Who gave the command to engage?" she asked without precursor.

Phall's grimace was apparent even with his face squished into the sides of his helmet. "This is no place for you, Princess. You best ride back to the castle. We are in the middle of a battle, here."

As if on cue, a hand punched through the sand, not two meters from her horse's hooves. When the fist emerged, dirt collapsed in around it, creating a new crater before their fixated eyes.

"Here's one!" the general bellowed.

As soon as the words left his lips, a dozen soldiers were racing toward the spot.

General Phall screamed at them to stay in their formation, but no one heeded his authority. Eagerly, the Candorians swarmed upon the gaping hole, slamming and poking their swords into the dusty pit. When the Boen's head and shoulders came free, Aven was shocked at his demeanor.

She stared between the feet of the soldiers as they danced around him.

The Boen wore a thick helmet, as the other had. It encased his head with a single narrow horizontal slit for the eyes, not enough to fit a blade through. He held no weapons, and his hands were gloved. He wore what appeared to be a brown sack, perhaps woven from crude wheat and twine. His shoulders were wide, not like the stringy Boens she remembered. Not like Raena.

As he crawled, he made a gurgling sound in his throat. Perhaps from being stabbed, but it sounded to Aven as if his mouth was bound or filled.

"Take his helmet off," Aven said, whipping her head toward Phall.

He grunted, "Princess, I'll not warn you again. This is a dangerous place. I would hate for the worst to happen to you."

Aven felt the hairs on the back of her neck bristle.

General Phall's face twisted into disgust—an ominous sneer. He kicked his horse and put space between the two of them. When he charged forward, he commanded his forces farther out into the battlefield.

Aven glanced back toward Candeo's walls, surprised to see it must have been two furlongs away now. She doubted the archers would reach this distance, though their barrage of arrows continued. For no discernable reason, they fired into an empty desert, devoid of enemies. In fact, Aven saw fewer Boens than she expected, making her heart race inside her chest.

"What are they planning?" she whispered to herself.

Aven watched as the legionmen marched away from the spot, following General Phall. They had completed their kill, and the torso of the Boen protruded and slumped forward from the hole, surely dead.

Around the edges of his body leaked slithering wafts of smoke, curling in the air above him. There was enough smoke gathering over the terra now to obscure the army from her view as they effectively disappeared beyond.

Aven dismounted.

She held the warhorse's reins to keep him near as she walked across the sand, feeling every bristle and rock through her thin slippers. Her wild hair, untamed and unpinned, whipped around her. Half of it was still wet from the bath and felt cool on her neck, a stark contrast to the scorching desert air and the beating midday sun.

Aven reached the dead Boen and felt the urge to retch. Her fists tightened and she breathed deep, staving off the fear. She glanced about, ensuring no one else was nearby.

Aven let go of the reins and dropped to one knee, crouching in front of the Boen. She counted for a few seconds, listening for any sign that he still lived. When his chest didn't move, she was satisfied.

She stared at the brown sack he wore up close and realized it was layered with another thick fabric underneath, like a pale leather. She had taken it for his pale skin before. At the left shoulder, he'd been stabbed significantly and there were several punctures from soldiers' blades. She steadied herself.

Gritting her teeth, Aven grabbed at his helmet and pulled, trying to tug the cumbersome metal free. His neck stretched in a way that surely would have hurt if he weren't dead.

She jerked again, yanking it forward, then back, and finding the effort totally useless.

Aven leaned back to catch her breath, gasping for air from the brief exertion.

That's when she saw it.

Flesh.

Dark, leathery, brown flesh.

She lurched forward and ripped at the gaps in his clothing. Beneath the brown sack was a layer of something glued to his skin. It didn't come away easily, as if he'd been wrapped in adhesive and coated in sheepskin. She peeled it with her nails, finding a place to separate it where blood had caked underneath. With another budge, the coating came loose, and Aven felt his skin at his collarbone.

Indeed, he was of dark skin. There was no way this could be a Boen.

She hooked her fingers under his chin, finding a hard edge there, like wood perhaps. It held the bottom of the helmet. She felt for a clasp to release it.

A sudden flash to her right caught Aven's eye. She whipped her head to see as a man leaped from horseback, tumbling into the dirt. He kicked up brush and sand into her face as he rolled.

Aven flinched, the dust in her eyes stinging instantly.

He was back up on his feet.

Her eyes barely opened to see his hand grabbing her by the collar, hair in between his fingers. He yanked her off the ground and Aven heard a ripping sound from her scalp.

"Run, idiot!" he screamed, throwing her forward.

Aven's hands raised to break her fall, catching the side of the idle warhorse. She continued to stumble, her face slamming against the beast's quarters.

"Run!" the soldier screamed again.

He had no sooner disappeared as a hundred more men his equal followed suit. Aven caught them emerging from the smoke in chaos.

Some flung their weapons carelessly as they bolted at full speed, charging from the battlefield. They were splaying in all directions—some toward Candeo's curtain, others out further into the desert cliffs.

Aven cowered against the warhorse's side. She gripped his leg as though wind was trying to drag her down and he could keep them upright.

"Get the fuck off this plain, Majesty!" a familiar man's voice shouted.

Aven gazed up to find none other than Sir Jonn-Del, mounted on a black horse nearly matching his own color. He paused his ride long enough to reach for her hand.

Thundering steps and a weak bugle echoed around them. As many as a thousand men were shoving, dodging, running by.

Aven had little choice.

She extended her hand and accepted the mercy of Jonn-Del, who pulled her into the saddle behind him with ease. He kicked his capable horse and they charged off the battleground. He shouted out for the soldiers to make way for him, not giving much effort into avoiding the mass. A few sneered as they passed. Some called out for direction, begging for orders in the confusion.

"What happened?" Aven asked. Her arms were gripped around his stomach, which she loathed, but feared falling off the steed even more.

"The Boens emerged suddenly," he said over his shoulder. "Several thousand came up, we can't fight them all. We must go back and leave room for the archers to knock them down."

Aven swallowed hard. "Are they fighting back?"

Jonn-Del scoffed. "The fuck do you mean?"

"Are they fighting? The ones I saw, they weren't fighting, they were just crawling out of the ground."

"That's because they send the first batch to make the holes wide, then they all come out. We need to retreat, gather the forces—"

"Who gave the marching orders? Who approved this war?"

Jonn-Del's shoulders tensed, obvious when a mere breath from Aven's face.

He waved a hand and shouted at a group of guards who'd fallen. They were piled atop each other, shifting and pushing. Jonn-Del navigated his horse away to avoid trampling them at the last second.

They were within a furlong of the curtain. Aven held tight and turned to look behind them. The smoke was rising and revealing a wall of Boens.

Standing in the desert, they were as she'd seen them before. Not advancing, not charging into battle. Perhaps not armored or equipped, either.

"They aren't even trying to fight!"

Jonn-Del shook his head at her observation.

When they had ridden another dozen meters, Aven could hear the shouts of archers atop the ramparts. They were readying to let loose a rain of arrows, no doubt.

She glanced back to see some of the Boens heading closer toward the castle, still no sign of weapons in their hands or attached to their backs. They moved stiffly, encumbered. Aven assessed and believed they were all bound by the strange pale leather as the one she'd encountered.

She took a sharp breath, readying herself. "Jonn-Del, listen to me," she said with confidence, "those men, they aren't Boens. They are someone else, but they are not Boens. You have to see the way they aren't even fighting."

"That's enough, really," Jonn-Del grunted.

"I am positive. You have to hear me. We are making a terrible mistake—"

He grabbed the reins of his warhorse and clenched, bringing them to a sudden halt. There in the center of the open field, armies marching or running on either side, Jonn-Del twisted in his saddle to glare at her sideways.

"You made the mistake," he spat, "you have been trying to stop this war and leave us to drown like flies in a honeypot. I ought've left ya out in the open where the Boens could've killed ya, and I'd've saved this kingdom!"

"Killed me? With what weapons? They aren't even fighting!"

"Then ya wanna go back out there, Princess? Be my guest!"

Aven's hands were at his waist and moved along his belt before she registered the action, grabbing the hilt of his dagger. She flicked it free of the sheath and held the blade against the tender indent of his thigh.

Jonn-Del's eyebrows raised with surprise.

Aven mirrored the expression, alarmed at her own fortitude. She cleared her throat. "Listen to me, knight. I am soon to be your queen. I will find out who gave the order for this war. I will put a stop to it. And when it comes to light that you betrayed the crown, you might wish that I'd finished the job here." To emphasize her last word, she pressed the blade for good measure. It split the cloth of his riding pants open, baring his dark skin beneath.

With a shove, Aven dismounted, keeping the dagger.

Jonn-Del huffed, cursing under his breath.

"Fuck off, Jonn-Del," Aven roared. She slapped the ass of his horse to send them along.

With her dagger in hand, she joined the fleeing teams of soldiers, praying she'd find a way back into the castle.

CHAPTER 42
AVEN

When the thunder comes

Aven kept to the swarm of soldiers and reached the curtain. The gate was still down, defended by the onslaught of arrows.

Not that Aven believed the gate needed defending, at all.

She made it into the citadel and had another obstacle; she had to get back inside the castle. Somehow Aven doubted the guards would be keeping anyone out, or even patrolling.

The legions were trying to assemble in the stockyards, training yards, and gardens. Aven struggled to push through their endless formations where they gathered awaiting orders.

When she made it into Candeo's streets, she felt relief to finally be out of the fray. The literal fog of war behind her, Aven walked along the tan cobblestones that led to the castle, holding her dress and Jonn-Del's dagger.

Aside from the occasional soldier dashing alone, the areas near the markets were still as deserted as they'd been before.

"Come on then, Princess?" a man's voice snarled from the shadows.

Aven cast a rapid glance, careful not to encourage interaction. She spotted the two Ruvians from the tavern, skulking in the shadows of a doorway.

Her pace quickened and she stared ahead, determined.

"Oi girl," the Ruvian called out, "wouldn't ya like a real cock once in a while?"

Aven's stomach lurched at the concept, but then she fought the urge to turn and engage him. Her mind raced with the notion that perhaps the Ruvian knew something about her wife that he shouldn't.

But she pressed onward, between a walk and a running pace, her legs aching with the added activity of the day. She rounded a corner hastily and ran straight into a soldier, her face colliding with his leather-covered chest.

"I'm so sorry!" Aven exclaimed.

The soldier lifted the visor of his helmet. "Aven?" His face revealed none other than her own brother.

"Tennel!" Without considering it, Aven fell forward against him again, this time wrapping her arms around his thick tunic and collapsing in his embrace.

He stiffened, then returned the hug with a few friendly pats to her back. When she pulled away, the reason for his hesitancy was clear; behind him were at least a dozen more men, likely Kingsguards ready to fight as soldiers.

"What are you doing?" Aven asked. "You can't leave the castle to fight in this battle."

Tennel shrugged, "Those are exactly our orders. They've given us scraps from the army to take up. I managed to get a decent poleax, though. What do you think?"

Aven grabbed his shoulders. "Who gave the order? Who ordered you to the battle?"

"Erm, our watch captain."

"But you're the Kingsguard. Who could give such an order to send you out of the castle for battle?"

457

Tennel bit his lip. "I haven't been long on the job, but I know it takes the prince's seal, or the king's seal, even. Maybe the council can do that? I'm not sure—"

"Yes, the council. That's what I thought."

Tennel fidgeted with the handle of his poleax hanging at his side, adjusting the weapon across his back.

"Come on, you're taking me back to the castle," Aven said with certainty.

"What? Aye, no, I have orders—"

"No. I'm the princess. You're coming back with me."

Tennel's mouth hung open and he turned toward the others, but they merely shrugged, none of them bold enough to challenge the princess.

"All right," he sighed, "please don't let me be hanged for abandoning my post."

"Who could hang you? Not my husband, of course."

"Seems like a conflict of interest, but yes. Let's go."

With a begrudging sigh, Tennel handed his poleax over to another eager guard, happy to obtain the superior weapon. He and Aven were no more than ten meters into their journey toward the castle when the horn blew. This time it blasted two short alarms.

"That's the sound for intruders inside the castle," Tennel said. "The Boens must have found a way in."

Aven shook her head. "Tennel, you need to know something I saw. These aren't Boens we're fighting. I think somehow, they are men of East Shore, perhaps. I can't be certain."

"Come on, we need to get into the castle faster. Whoever they are, they might be coming up from the ground. Do you know of any tunnels beneath the street? Any way they can get in? We'll avoid those."

He took her hand and they broke into a jog.

"There are places everywhere," Aven raised her voice over the hammering of their feet. "There are drainage tunnels, sewage tunnels, all of that beneath the city. But no one uses them, except rats and orphans."

458

"And Ruvians. And Librens, now." Tennel rounded a corner and pulled Aven into an alleyway. It was unfamiliar and perpendicular to where they needed to be, but she trusted that he knew his way.

When they reached the end of the alley it opened into a dead-end of smithies and a bakery from the looks of it. At the center of the circular street was a drainage hole for rain and waste. It caught Aven's eye as smoke wafted out of it.

"It's smoking," Aven gestured, "the holes in the battlefield were smoking, too. There's something to this."

"Aye, that's odd," Tennel said dismissively.

"No, we need to get down there."

"Fuck no, we're not going in the sewer. We need to get into the castle. Now there's a way through here, in the back of this smithy's shop."

Tennel pulled her arm but Aven resisted, trying to get closer to the hole. She won the tug-of-war and managed to step to the edge of it, peering down.

The hole was about the width of a bread loaf and reinforced with a metal-cast tube. The tube ran into the ground where presumably the opening led to wider sewage and waste areas underneath. Aven remembered as a child going to holes like this and pouring used bathwater into them, helping to rinse away the foul smell that would drift up from the sewers beneath on a hot day.

She twisted out of Tennel's grasp and waved her hand over the hole to brush away the smoke. When she leaned in, she was able to see down through the tube into the darkness.

But it wasn't only darkness looking back at her from the other side.

A man's face stared up at Aven. The wide whites of his eyes were bursting with fear. His mouth was filled and splayed open though he was unable to close it. He made a gurgling sound, and Aven recognized it as the sound she'd heard the helmeted man make in the desert.

Aven stumbled back. "There's a man in there!"

Tennel drew his dagger, "It's a Boen!"

459

"No!" She leaned in for a second look of confirmation. "No, he's Candorian. I'm sure of that."

"Is he Ruvian? A bandit?" Tennel's curiosity won over and he leaned over the hole to see for himself. He complained about the smoke, batting it away.

"The smoke is getting worse," Aven echoed. "We need to get him out of there."

"There's no way," Tennel said, "he has to keep going and find another way out. You hear me, friend? You have to keep going! Find another way out!"

Aven pushed away the smoke and this time squatted down to the ground to see even better if the man was listening to their advice. What she saw then was so terrifying it sent a chill through her spine.

The man was pinched between the walls of the narrow tunnel, and on either side of him in both directions were rows and rows of others.

Men in thick metal helmets, all pushing, moving. Like rats in water. Trying desperately to move forward. Why he didn't have a helmet was a mystery, but one that Aven was grateful for. The smoke grew too great for her to look anymore and her eyes burned when she rolled away, sitting on the ground.

"Tennel," she gasped, "there must be thousands of them down there. They're our men. They're Candorians."

"That's impossible," he shook his head. "What do you mean?"

The smoke was practically billowing out now.

"We have to find a way to get them out. We have to find another entrance to this tunnel. Quick, where does this lead? Where is the exit of the sewer?"

"The exit? It...I think it goes to empty in the river, at the edge of the city."

"Does it? Is there a way to get men through?"

"No, it raises up and goes out a tube, but it's a five-meter drop into the river, at least. The best ways out are going to be the waste chutes. The same ways that orphans and Ruvians get in, I'm sure."

Aven shook her head. "Those are small holes. No wonder the men are stuck in there. And perhaps our soldiers are killing them one-by-one as they try…" she covered her mouth with one hand.

"Our soldiers are killing our own people? Are you sure about this?"

She reached for Tennel's hand and allowed him to pull her upright. "You saw him yourself. You saw his face. That man was no Boen."

"Aye but…how did he get down there? What was in his mouth?"

"I don't know. But we have to stop this. We have to stop the armies from killing our own people."

Tennel nodded, "We can go to my watch captain. He would have received the order. He will know how to call the army back, I think."

"How long will that take?"

"A few hours, if we can find him. He'll have to issue the order and it will go through the generals—"

"That's too long. All those men will suffocate or be slaughtered by then."

Tennel bit his lip, eyeing the smokey hole warily.

"What is the signal to call off an attack?" Aven asked.

"What do you mean?"

"If your watch captain were going to call off the attack, how would he do it?"

Tennel folded his arms. "He would have to alert the generals and they would blast the horns to notify the troops. But they would request permission before the horns would blast, I think. In the meantime, they would communicate to the legion commanders—"

"That's it, then, come on."

"What?" Tennel called out.

But Aven was already on the move. She had her skirts bunched around her waist again, running toward the blacksmith shop entrance. Her near-black hair was fraying in all directions around her head and shoulders, flowing behind her as she ran into the shadows. She didn't look back to ensure Tennel kept up, she knew he would call out where to go as he jogged behind her.

With his commands for where to turn, they darted inward toward the center of the citadel, reaching the heart, the castle, in no time at all.

"Am I taking you to the watch captain?" Tennel asked, his voice lowered, when they were at the round side of the castle's southeast towers.

"No," Aven whispered over her shoulder, "take me to the top, where the horn is kept."

"The horn? Sister, you're mad."

"Then I'm mad. But you're following orders of the princess. Do this for me."

Tennel's nostrils flared with a short breath, letting out a sigh of frustration. "Fine. It's a death sentence. It's treason."

"It's not treason if you're the princess."

"I think you're the only one who will see it that way."

Aven narrowed her eyes and elbowed him in the back. "Let's go."

As they walked briskly around the bottom of the tower, Aven watched another sewer drain out of the corner of her eye, seeing the smoke rise. She thought of the men beneath, innocent of this crime against them. She wondered if they were knights or soldiers she had known. She wondered if one of her other brothers were among them. She didn't want to think such a gruesome, gut-wrenching possibility, but then she clenched her jaw and forced herself to imagine it. She would accept a charge of treason for saving her brothers from suffocating in smoke with a metal helmet glued to their jaw. She had to be willing to die to save the men of Candor. They were brothers and sons, too.

"Through here," Tennel whispered, jiggling away a metal latch and sliding open a stone door. It was a peasant entrance, undoubtedly.

They stepped into the shadow and nearly stumbled onto the many huddled bodies of frightened women and children, gathered on a straw floor. The room was little more than a hallway entrance, but it was lined with cowering bodies that tucked back as tight as they could toward the walls at the sight of Tennel. Aven closed the door behind her and muttered something about how she wasn't there to hurt anyone. Lining the walls were symbols of Libre that reminded Aven of her mother's hovel; the figurines of the seven Almighties were on tiny brick shelves. But Aven paused when she noticed an additional symbol, a painted portrait of a man with a purple face. His likeness was the same as the man she'd seen in the crowd on her wedding day. His features, his beady eyes, his defiant thin smirk. He may have been in a white robe but he was the spitting image of Zander, without a doubt.

Tennel nudged into her back and then charged ahead through the center, stepping over a leg or two, ignoring the peasants underfoot. Without much choice, Aven followed, resisting the urge to ask them about the portrait. Of course, there wasn't time.

After turning a few corners in the stone hall, they reached a room for laundering that was well-lit by upper windows. Stairs led to each portal, about two meters off the ground. There was no other door or exit.

"Damn, this doesn't connect," Tennel said, "it's just a wash chamber."

"What about those windows?"

Tennel shook his head, "They're a chute for the cleaned laundry. Would go into a rag pile or a cart to be gathered by the handmaids."

Before he finished his sentence, Aven was bounding up a set of stairs to see it for herself. She reached the top in seconds, peering through the window with both her head and shoulders through it.

"Don't do that!" Tennel warned, "You can't see where you'll land! Besides it's not strong enough to hold you!"

Aven observed the chute go down and through another window, into another tower of the castle. It was easily a three-meter drop on either side, out into the open street, with cobblestone that would catch her fall and break most of her bones in the process, most likely.

"Come on down!" Tennel begged. "We'll find another way in!"

Aven peered upward to see what was above the next tower and saw a corner of the parapets. Her destination.

"Come on brother," Aven retorted, "not much time to muck about." She grabbed her skirts and held them over her lap. When she crouched, she took care not to put her full weight upon the chute, but one leg at a

463

time to test if it would hold. Tennel was voicing his disagreeance louder as he ran up the stairs. But by the time he reached the landing, Aven was out of the window, flat on her back, her feet flying ahead of her rigid body like the tip of an arrow. She had nary a second suspended in the air on the slippery chute before she was through the second window and enveloped in darkness.

Then she was falling.

Her arms and legs flailed out in separate directions and she tried to right her body so her feet would hit the ground first. She was unsuccessful and the first contact she made was with her ass to the floor in a terrifying thud. The wind was knocked from her lungs and Aven tried to gasp, but had nothing to pull with, or so it felt. She recognized that she could suck in a breath at the same second, she realized she had landed in a moderately soft pile of laundered clothing. She could see the end of the chute hovering above her.

Then Aven heard a clang, and another clang, echoing from the window she'd passed through. Realizing what the sound could mean, Aven rolled to one side. Twice, thrice, she rolled, desperate to get out of the way.

Not a second later, Tennel was barreling down the chute, screaming at the top of his lungs, and falling from the higher window. A piece of the chute broke off and followed his descent. Aven rolled again to avoid it and in doing so she went right off the edge of the laundry and onto the stone. She heard metal and rock bashing together as the chute met the spot she had just been laying, along with the grunt of Tennel landing in a heap.

"See," Aven said, gasping for breath and standing shakily to her feet, "this was a fast way in."

"Princess," Tennel groaned as though it were a slur, "we could have both been killed. Then we'd accomplish nothing."

"Hurry up. We need to get to the parapets."

Tennel crawled across the soft and unstable pile. "I can't move any faster, thank you."

As soon as they were standing again, Aven bolted to the door. She knew the clean laundry would go up a back entrance toward the royal wing, where serfs and peasants would change bedding, bring fresh clothing, and otherwise prioritize herself and the rest of the nobles. Her instincts were correct. Halfway up the staircase was a landing to go onto the second floor, exiting the tower.

"Shouldn't we go that way?" Tennel prodded.

Aven shook her head and continued running up the stairs, too out-of-breath to form words.

At the top of the stairs was a heavy stone door. Aven heard the sound of the wind, whistling through the cracks. She pushed the door but it didn't give.

Without asking, Tennel stepped forward and joined, putting his shoulder into the port and heaving. After a second of groaning, the door budged free, swinging open with a rush of air flowing past them.

It was a guard post, abandoned, the opposite door left broad open. The hot wind from the desert flowed freely in, creating a harsh tornado-like tunnel that had made undue pressure on the door.

Aven ran ahead, giving no thought to what was beyond on the parapets.

Her feet pounded along the high stone walls. She had little regard for Tennel behind her, though she knew he must be there. The sun was drifting lower on the horizon, but still made all of the desert bright and the sky so pale it was almost white. Aven squinted as she continued. Far around a corner she could see archers, as they'd been most of the day, readied to fire between parapets. She wondered if they were still equipped with arrows, and prayed perhaps they'd run out. Aven couldn't see far to her left, with more towers of the castle blocking her view. But she knew instinctively there was a way to reach the horns as long as she stayed on the eastern side of the castle, facing the Calam Mountains.

"Up there!" Tennel yelled from behind her.

Aven rounded a corner and gazed up. At the top of the next inner rampart was a small guard post. She couldn't see to the top of it, but she knew Tennel must be calling it out to her. Aven scanned the walls for a way to reach it.

"We have to circle the entire castle to get there," Tennel explained, shouting over the wailing wind.

Aven turned back, her hair covering her face. She tried to push it aside futilely. "We don't have time. We have to get up there."

"There's no way to reach it!"

"Then the men underground will die! We have to find a way!"

Tennel leaned against a parapet on either side of the wall, searching. "There is a way down, but from the corner, and maybe it will lead around."

Aven followed where he pointed, seeing a gaggle of soldiers on the stairs in question. They were focused on a spot near the ground, which she was certain was another hole. The smoke gathering above their heads answered her question.

When she began to run this time, her legs burned. Aven knew her body was beginning to give out. She had been healthy and strong from working the pig fields, but it was nowhere near the hours of running, climbing, horseback riding, and desperation she had experienced in this one day. Her survival instinct was beginning to fade, and as Aven descended the stairs, part of her hoped the soldiers might take pity on her and end her life quickly. It was as if she had nothing left to fight with except a tiny flame.

But then one of the soldiers caught Aven's eye. He was tall. His skin was pale for a Candorian. At a distance, he almost had the complexion of Raena. At once, Aven felt the flame inside her rekindle, and she was bolstered with a renewed strength.

Her legs, though exhausted, pumped with fervor. And she was down the steps and into the short stone landing in an instant, shouting for the men to step aside.

One or two murmured a protest. A chubby hand grabbed at Aven's arm to restrain her, but she twisted her shoulders and broke free, the momentum of her run slipping her out of his grasp.

Tennel shoved through and commanded them to return to their duty. "Unhand the princess!" He shouted, as if he had authority over them all.

It worked, and the men slithered aside.

Aven bolted. She was at the opposite staircase and climbing it, panting for breath, but maintaining a steady pace.

When Tennel caught up to her, he was calling out between labored gasps. "You...you're bleeding. Aven." He yelled, his tone apologetic.

Aven glanced down at her skirts, continuing to ascend the stairs, and saw that indeed her rag had filled and overflowed. Blood covered the center of her skirt from her abdomen downward, forming an odd triangle. She assumed it had created a similar pattern on the back, where Tennel could see.

"Not much to be done," Aven shouted back.

"Can you...are you hurt?"

Aven couldn't help but roll her eyes. Of course, her brother, despite having a mother and sister for all his life, had never been expected to know or understand how a woman could bleed. Yet this was no time to explain it, and Aven resisted the urge to belittle him for the lack of knowledge. Aven felt ashamed and embarrassed, but steadily determined.

"I'm fine," she said. "I said, there's nothing to be done about it."

If he replied, Aven didn't hear it. She was at the top of the second rampart and the wind was howling in her ears. It felt as though the wind could blow her right off the wall at any second, and she crouched as she walked. The temptation to look down was strong, but Aven knew they must be near the top of the castle, and she'd always avoided putting too much thought into the view of the ground below. It would only turn her stomach.

The guard post was straight ahead, about ten meters. It was adjacent to the rampart, with a stone door for access. Aven could see where the top formed a cone, unlike the other parapet covers, to allow for the horn's sound to echo in all directions. There were windowed slats below the cone, opening for the guards to face out.

467

Aven clenched her jaw as she walked, thinking desperately about what she was about to say. She didn't know the first thing about ordering an army to step down. For that matter, neither did Tennel. She prayed at least the horn blowers would.

When she reached the stone door, she didn't need to open it. The door gave way before her and a horn blower welcomed her into the small space with a bow.

"Your Majesty," the guard muttered. "To what do we owe the pleasure?"

Aven entered to see what was less of a post and more like a bedroom. There were two of everything. Two cots, two chairs, two cases with a few books, and two tiny wardrobes. There was only one table, however, but it held two half-eaten meals.

"Do you mind?" Aven said, reaching for a plate of meat.

The horn blowers eyed one another and bowed again.

"Of course, Your Majesty, make yourself at home here," one said. He mumbled an appropriate greeting to Tennel.

Aven took a few bites of meat. She was famished: shaking. The exertion and the loss of blood had her on the verge of fainting, and the men seemed to notice. They eyed her skirts, pretending not to notice. One blushed to his ears while he stared at the wall, rather conspicuously.

"Thank you," Aven muttered, returning the plate to the table. "I don't think I've eaten today, to be honest."

"Aye, well, it's a war," the horn blower said.

"It isn't, though," she replied, "not anymore. I need you to call it off now. It's ended."

The horn blower who'd faced the wall turned, his jaw dropping as he bore into her with beady eyes. "Madam?"

"You heard me," Aven continued, "the fighting must stop. We are against our own men in those streets. What sort of horn blast would send that message?"

Tennel stepped in, holding up a hand. "Gentlemen, what the princess means is that we must call off all our troops and return them to

468

defensive positions, to allow the enemy to advance freely, uninhibited. We are pulling the enemy out, luring them, rather. It's the right strategy. How can you signal the troops to…retreat."

The horn blowers turned to one another and leaned in close. The beady-eyed one got on his toes to whisper in the taller man's ear. Aven watched them, trying to read their lips, but failing to do so. After a few seconds of whispering, she grew impatient.

"Gentlemen, we really don't have time. I am your princess, and anything you have to say will be said in front of me. You need to follow this order, at once."

The taller man shook his head. "I'm sorry, Your Majesty. We were given strict orders. This morning, in fact. We were reminded to only follow commands from General Phall, or the head of the prince's council, until the prince has safely returned."

"Well, I am proxy of the prince. I am his wife. I may speak on his behalf during a conflict such as this."

The shorter man made a sound of disbelief, "I don't believe that's the law, madam. I haven't seen a law such as that before."

Tennel put a hand on Aven's elbow to quiet her. "What're your names?"

"Cordov," the shorter one said.

"Sheer," replied the taller.

"Alright," Tennel replied, "Cordov? You seem to be a bit older. You've done this the longest, then?"

Pride flashed in Cordov's eyes. "Aye, and my father was a horn blower. I've been at this post for twenty years."

"Then you know what you're doing," Tennel said.

There was a flash of metal to Aven's right. Before she could utter a word, she heard Cordov scream. Tennel burst forward like a fox, his right hand lunging out from his side and plummeting the end of a dagger into Sheer's chest. With a twist and a popping sound, Tennel drove it deeper. Sheer reached forward to grab Tennel, but it wasn't enough to do anything. His hands slid, weak, down Tennel's frame. The two men collapsed against each other, breathing hard, as the last few seconds were drained out of Sheer's body.

Tennel ripped the knife free and stepped back, allowing Sheer to slump to the floor.

Cordov's hands covered his mouth. Wide-eyed, he yelled through his fingers. "That's…it's treason! You'll be executed! Horn blowers are in service to Prince Trevin!"

"And so is this princess!" Tennel shouted, a vein bulging on his forehead. "she told you to call off the fucking armies, now it's time for you to decide. Would you rather die?"

Aven swallowed hard. She felt her neck heating, likely red from the fear she felt creeping up inside her. Her brother's temper had been short when they were children. He had been a careful boy, terrified of risk…until he would snap from the pressure. It had put him in fistfights with the others that Tennel won, showing no mercy. Aven was reminded of that boy again, throwing punches against his larger brothers without thinking of the consequence.

Cordov shook his head. "I'm dead either way."

"Then die following the orders of Her Majesty, the princess, who is willing to die herself for this kingdom. You should take a cue from the woman risking it all to come to this tower, bloody and spent, because she knows she's on the right side." Tennel sneered. "As opposed to, let's say, whatever gutless coward told you to do his bidding, and is probably hunched up behind a few thousand men right now to protect his own ass."

Cordov nodded, "All right. All right. Don't kill me. You're swearing to me that…I must blast out the call for a retreat?"

"Yes," Aven said, "the armies of Candor must retreat."

"Yes, madam. As you wish."

With a heavy sigh, Cordov went to the edge of the chamber and pulled a horn from the wall. It was smaller than seemed capable of making a sound to alert all the kingdom. Aven raised her eyebrows as she watched him set the broad end against a hole in the wall she'd not thought much of before. He took a few long, deep breaths.

"You may want to cover your ears," Cordov warned.

Aven and Tennel quickly did as he instructed, without a moment to spare. As soon as Cordov's lips touched the brass, there was a dull hum around them. Aven could feel the vibration of the sound through the walls, and she realized that the chamber itself must amplify the noise and project it outward. It was as though it came to life, and Cordov's few preparatory breaths into the mouthpiece were the lungs around their bodies.

Then the thunder came.

His long two blasts, followed by one flurry, filled the world with sound. Aven felt her insides shake until it was over.

Cordov took his mouth away from the horn, his eyes cast toward the ground. "It's done," he said.

Aven nodded. "Thank you, you have done the right thing to honor your princess."

He shrugged. "I believe you. I'll be put to death, I'm sure."

"Not if I can do anything about it."

Cordov gave a weak half-smile, but his eyes remained sad.

"Tell me," Aven prodded, "who was it that told you not to follow any orders except their own? Was it the general?"

"No," Cordov said, "it wasn't. A new head of council was named in order to direct the forces, at the start of the war. They put it to a vote and elected him. He is giving all of the orders. It is him who gave the order to attack."

Aven nodded, encouraging him to go on. Before he spoke the name, Aven already knew what would come from his lips.

Cordov's beady eyes trained on hers. "He's a knight from the old Candor, he served when my father was a horn blower. They call him something else now, but I know him as Sir Jonn."

CHAPTER 43
SYLAS

CHAPTER 44
RAENA

The Baby

The guards leading the caravan had put up a valiant fight.

Their first mistake was being equipped to fight Boens, not knights. They brandished weapons for close contact: pikes and shortswords. What they lacked were arrows for long-range, which Raena and Gregor both possessed.

When Raena had spotted the caravan, they'd already been wandering around the desert for about four days. She had sent her hundred men onward to make camp, where they wouldn't see her and Gregor disappear over the dunes. It had been so obvious which traveling troupe was their target in question; all others stuck to the roads in formation. Raena kept her eyes trained on the sole lonely caravan among the sprawling sagebrush, a blight against the sand. They took a discrete path along the northernmost road, near House Lox.

Then Gregor and Raena sat atop their horses at a plateau for an hour while it drew closer, like allowing prey into a trap. That was the first time Raena and Gregor had been alone to talk to one another, and it was pleasant. They chatted about House Grent, Gregor's childhood, and his affinity for whittling. Raena resisted the urge to bring up Aven, again and again.

"Have you ever fired an arrow?" Raena asked when the caravan was in range.

Gregor murmured, "Not at a moving target."

"Ride behind me, then," Raena commanded, digging her heels into her horse.

She charged toward them with Gregor loyally following behind. She raised her bow and took a few deep breaths. She remembered the last time she'd hit moving targets with an arrow; it had been the Knight's Trial. That was longer ago than muscle memory would help her. Fortunately, they weren't yet alerted to her presence, although she was riding directly toward them as fast as her rouncey could gallop.

Raena let go of her arrow and it sailed through the air, landing true, striking the first guard in the chest. Before he fell, she had the second arrow loaded up. The second guard panicked and searched for the assailant, spotting Raena. He turned to run, but Raena was letting go. Her arrow flew through the air and struck him in the back. She couldn't load and fire fast enough for the third, though. He disappeared behind the caravan.

Raena dropped her bow and tugged the reins, slowing her rouncey. She raised her hand at Gregor in caution and he slowed up alongside her.

"Don't fire," Raena said, "we can't risk penetrating the canvas and killing the women."

Gregor nodded, holding his sword at his side dumbly atop his rouncey.

"We'll have to kill the other guards in combat," Raena said. "We'll wait for them to come out and fight."

They rode closer to the now unmoving wagon, then sat on their horses, waiting.

Out in the open desert, they stayed like that for another half hour. Gregor, a natural Candorian, didn't sweat in the sun. Raena wore a white hood, not unlike the Ruvians often bore, in order to protect her from the scorching heat of the afternoon.

"The Edivans must be wanting to die, in there," Gregor remarked. "Why do you reckon they didn't travel at night?"

Raena smirked. "Boens, I'm sure."

"Must be miserable, then. They can't handle heat like ours."

"Nah," Raena agreed. She eyed the caravan and sighed. "It's been long enough. I'm tired of waiting. How about I draw them out? I'll try to chase them from one end, you cut them down at the other?"

Gregor shifted nervously atop his rouncey. "How many do you expect?"

"Three, at the most."

"I dunno if I can take three guards."

Raena chuckled, gesturing to his poleax. "You don't need to take them. You're the one on horseback, just swing your poleax until I get back around."

Gregor pulled his weapon from behind him, clutching it with white knuckles, and nodded.

They both rode closer, paces away from the caravan.

"Stay there," Raena said, then kicked her rouncey. She rode around to the other end, where the canvas opened.

As she rounded the tent, she spied an Edivan guard with his head and shoulders protruding from the canvas. Their eyes met and he reeled back, disappearing into the folds of fabric. She heard a commotion inside and raised her bow. She aimed it at the tent, careful to take slow, long breaths.

Raena heard the voices in the caravan quiet, and she pulled her bow tighter, her fingers beginning to ache against the tension.

The caravan flap opened, and the guard burst forth. He appeared aggressive, brave, his sword raised. But his eyes widened. His momentum was already set and it was too late for him to react.

Raena let out a breath, no need to aim, and released the arrow. It whistled through the air and made the short journey in a fraction of a second, buried instantly in his throat. He stumbled forward, gasping for air in a hollow way, his free hand clutching the exposed shaft of the arrow. Raena guided her rouncey backward a few steps as the guard fell into the desert sand where hooves had been a moment before.

While the guard was sucking in his last breaths through the hole in his windpipe, Raena heard the clamber of the Edivans in the caravan. They were scrambling for the opposite end, as she predicted. She kicked her rouncey in the side and rode.

Gregor had his poleax out, swinging wildly as he'd been instructed. One guard was already in the sand and at Gregor's weak side, making jabs with the end of a pike.

"Stay there!" Raena shouted as she closed the gap.

Another guard emerged, screaming as he ran forth toward Gregor.

Raena knew that her brother-in-law couldn't take them both, he was barely managing to evade one.

"Hey!" Raena shouted at the guard, but they didn't budge.

The second guard raised his pike and Gregor swung again, leaving his side open and unprotected as his arm went forward. It was the exact sort of chance a real warrior was trained to spot, and the guard saw it as easily as Raena did.

Fortunately, she could ride faster than he could lift his pike.

Raena slashed downward in a wild swing of her poleax, striking the guard in the shoulder with the blunt end. The blow made the guard scream in pain as he dropped the pike, a hand's length shy from Gregor's ribs.

The second guard pulled back, glancing between Gregor and Raena as he adjusted his grip on his pike.

"Wait a moment," Raena shouted to Gregor.

Gregor did as commanded, holding tight to his poleax, staring down the Edivan guard.

Raena watched, the guard's eyes darting from side to side as he appeared to consider his options. Then in an instant, he dropped his pike and ran. He bolted toward a line of sand dunes in a straight line away from Raena.

Raena sighed and reached again for her bow, arming it in less than a second. As she raised it, Gregor gasped.

"Prince Trev—" Gregor protested.

But the arrow was released. Raena let it fly and it sunk dead center into the Edivan's shoulder blades.

The air was quiet. For a moment, it was as though the world had stopped.

Raena hung her bow on the saddle beside her boot.

"Sir," Gregor mumbled, "respectfully, may I…"

"Speak to me, brother."

"I don't believe you ought've shot him down. He was running."

"Ah. It pained me to do it. Unfortunately, I had to. He may have gone on to a house of Candor and told Sir Jonn-Del we were the ones to kill his counterparts."

Gregor nodded, swallowing hard before he spoke. "I see. Then will we also have to kill the handmaidens inside?"

Raena stared at the caravan, knowing all that remained there were women and the child. "No. You see, it's a funny thing. It's both tragic and…a benefit to us. But no one listens to handmaidens. Their word won't have much weight if they go on to Candeo. But also, there's this." Raena reached for her white hood and pulled it tight, wrapping it twice around her face at the top and the bottom. When she secured it, only a slit across her eyes opened to show any part of her face. She would be recognizable only to someone who knew her well.

Gregor sheathed his sword. "What will you have me do, Your Majesty? We don't look much like bandits or Ruvians. They're likely to know who ambushed them."

"They'll have an idea, but won't be certain. Go on, we'll bind them all up like we talked about. I'll hold the baby while you pack up any food and diapers they have for him. We'll take one of the handmaidens and set the others free when we're ready to ride out."

When Raena and Gregor rejoined the hundred men, the soldiers all seemed to skeptically eye the baby and the handmaiden, Macall. But the men had the sense not to ask their prince why the two new guests were joining them or where they'd come from. Raena knew enough to know that soldiers talked, and she offered no explanations.

It was another nine days' ride to Hawk's Keep with such a lumbering group. Raena kept Macall nearby. Though her men were honorable, they were still men, and Raena didn't trust them with a foreign handmaiden alone, especially under cover of night. Both Macall and the baby slept in Raena's tent behind a partition. Since they couldn't refer to him as 'baby', Raena suggested they call the infant Davyn, which delighted Gregor.

They kept to the northern edges of the desert as much as they could, staying on the crest of hills that overlooked the winding snake valleys and the trickling river coming off the Calam Mountains. That would be the path of least resistance for Micha and his army, should they begin their assault. The valleys also had the only route with underground tunnels, as far as Raena knew. She assumed they weren't able to support most incursions, but the Boens would likely find a way to dig out the tunnels and create connections.

At one point she spotted the remnants of her own noble house, House Schinen, far to the south. It pained her to see it, even after all the years. With the haze of the heat bouncing off the sand, it was almost as though she saw smoke still rising from the ashes of her lost keep. House Schinen now appeared so small, like it could be whisked away with one strong gust of wind.

Soon after dawn of the third day, they could see down to the pines and lakes of the Western Founts. The number of soldiers surrounding Hawk's Keep in all directions was breathtaking. Raena estimated the camps held close to eighty thousand, and she regretted underestimating how much of an army Micha had. There were still legions of soldiers making their way over the mountain passes, by Raena's estimation, up to another twenty thousand more were yet to come. An army of that size could hold up and recover from the journey in Hawk's Keep for a full season. They would need supplies, but of course, Micha would have accounted for that and planned something to tide them over. Then the question truly was: how many Boens were underground?

By that afternoon, they began a descent down the hills and reached the outer edge of the Founts. They stopped at a stream to prepare to cross and a horn blast pulled their attention toward the keep. Through the pines, Raena couldn't make out the walls but knew their location by heart.

"We need to get out into the open," she shouted to her soldiers. "We will show all signs that we are not here to attack!"

Raena led the charge. She raised one hand as a signal and spurred her horse ahead. As she scanned the trees ahead, her heart began to race. What if Micha didn't see their colors? What if Micha wasn't there at all, and it was only his army? Surely the generals would order an attack on a hundred lone Candorian soldiers, never realizing the prince was among them.

And baby Davyn.

She rode alongside the creek, knowing where it would lead. The Founts were a series of lakes in a pattern she'd memorized by her ninth birthday. This stream was like a vein that would wind into a second lake and if they followed its shore, they would be in an open meadow that was visible from the ramparts of Hawk's Keep. Raena remembered avoiding that meadow purposefully as a young squire when she needed to relieve herself and they were outside the castle, hiding from view of anyone who might see.

She gripped the reins and spurred her rouncey to ride as fast as he could muster. Leaning down, Raena's cheek was to his ear. As one, they whipped through the air like an arrow.

She peeked under her arm to see if her men had kept up, pleased to see a few riders at the head of the pack, racing with fervor to stay behind her.

Raena was rounding the shore of the lake when she heard a sickening sound she had never anticipated.

A screech from above.

The whoosh of wings like thunder.

Raena didn't need to gaze at the sky, she already knew.

Bell's warhawks.

They had been friendly and playful when Raena was young, though Bell had allowed them to live a solitary existence in the outer forests as the girls grew older. Raena hadn't paid the birds attention in many years.

When she saw the length of their shadows stretching across the ground in front of her, spanning a dozen meters in both directions, Raena nearly retched.

Ignoring her curiosity, Raena shouted to her horse to speed ahead, as if he could go any faster than he already was.

Behind her, a soldier screamed.

Raena heard another screech, this time much closer than the last. She sensed the bird dipping closer to her. Perhaps she could feel the wind on her back or the shade from its wings, but a chill surged up her spine. Something sharp and strong grabbed at her shoulders, scratching over them and losing grip.

Raena ducked, laying nearly flat on her horse.

"Keep going!" she cried, both to her rouncey and the men behind her.

The men's screams increased.

Raena muttered a prayer that Macall and Davyn were safe. She kicked herself for not telling Gregor to take them to the back of the herd and watch over them. But she couldn't change that now and she couldn't turn around to search for them, as she felt the bird descending onto her a second time.

The talons clawed at her back, trying to find purchase. They squeezed, curling over her muscles as if hoping to rip her off the horse. When the bird was unsuccessful, it settled onto Raena, perching on her shoulder with surprising weight.

"Get off!" Raena shouted, bucking and rolling.

The bird was unphased, settled. Its claw tips pierced through Raena's leather and stung the skin of her back each time she rocked along with her horse.

A hard and fierce pointed beak slammed into the back of her head.

"Get off, go back to Bell!" Raena cried. She reached for her shortsword, but in her prone position, it was pinned under her. When she tried to pull it free, she nearly fell off the horse.

Raena scrambled to recover and felt a second nip from the hawk's beak.

At this rate, she would never reach a view of the keep. The birds would kill her.

She felt the warm and wet sensation of blood in her hair, trickling down to her ears.

The rouncey jumped over a log that Raena hadn't even seen coming. The sudden leap threw her body high enough that her knees lost grip. She was momentarily suspended over the rouncey's back, connected only by her hand to the reins.

When Raena landed back on the horse with a groan, she noticed the hawk had let go.

For a few moments, she felt the relief of losing her unwanted passenger.

"Don't come back, you beast," she murmured.

But Raena wouldn't be so fortunate.

With another screech, the hawk returned with fervor. This time, it didn't bother to land on her. The bird hovered above Raena, flying alongside her, pecking viciously at her shoulders, her head, her left arm.

Raena tried to punch and kick, but to no avail. The hawk was pecking closer to her face with every lunge.

Her arm guarded her face, but in a flash, Raena's eyes met the hawk's.

A rush of familiarity passed between them, and the bird appeared to recoil. Though it still flew, and drifted, it tried to turn its head and stare at Raena.

"Whoa, whoa," Raena commanded, sitting upright on her rouncey and tugging the reins.

She stopped there at the lakeside, a few meters from the meadow. Safety, perhaps, was ahead, but safety was guaranteed if she could connect with this hawk.

The bird flapped a few times, then settled to the ground. Perched, the wings stayed stretched outward, as if to threaten her. It was successful. The wings spanned at least the length of three men.

"Islabell. Bell," Raena said, pointing toward the keep. She patted her hand to her heaving chest. "Rowan. Rowan."

No recognition flashed in the bird's amber eyes.

They stared at one another a moment longer. Raena felt blood dripping down her neck.

"Rowan," she repeated, "Finn? Sylas?"

The bird did not respond, though its wings seemed to sag and relax.

Raena took a deep breath, then remembered something. With the screams of the soldiers behind her, she thought of the time she, Finn, and Bell had played "assassins" in the pine forests. They must have been thirteen because Raena had begun her bleed. The hawks had smelled it on her and chased her. When she'd told Sylas about it afterward, he'd begun bringing her the strange tea from healers, the one that made it so she never bled like a woman again.

That day was vivid in Raena's mind, just like the day shortly after that she woke with a fever and a horrible stomachache, screaming in pain as the tea worked its magic inside her.

Bell had known how to stop the hawks from hurting Raena that day, hadn't she? Just like Isla had known how to soothe Raena's stomach pains.

Beads of sweat rolled down Raena's forehead into her eyes.

With a deep breath, Raena said, "Hawk, return." She pounded her fist twice to her chest and then cast it off in the direction of the keep. "Hawk, return."

At the command, the bird tilted its head to the side.

Raena twisted round on the back of her horse. "Hawks! Return!" She roared as loud as she could muster. Again, she struck her own chest and then cast her arm toward the keep.

Behind her, a few of the soldiers who were still upright and alert stared at her, before pulling their own horses to a halt.

"That's right!" Raena yelled, "say it with me! Hawks! Return!"

In unison, the few soldiers joined her.

It was about ten of them, but that was enough.

Raena saw now there were four warhawks in total, and the other three had been busy attacking her men. At a glance, at least six soldiers were dead or injured on the ground, but there was no sign of Gregor, Macall, and Davyn.

The largest of the hawks screeched. Raena could tell she was a female, and she was glorious—almost twice the size of the one that had been attacking her.

"Hawks! Return!" they chanted again.

With an indignant screech, the great hawks seemed to reluctantly obey.

"Hawks, return," another voice joined their commands. A quieter voice. A woman's voice.

The birds took flight and soared, low to the ground, headed toward the lake.

Raena spun atop her horse to watch them go, then her eyes scanned ahead for the voice.

There, at the edge of the pines, between Raena and the meadow, was Bell.

CHAPTER 45
RAENA

The king's deal

Bell was a vision. In purple robes, she stood tall and regal among the pines. Her brunette hair was dark yet somehow glowed around her face. Raena felt warmth and relief spread through her chest at the sight. She stumbled as she dismounted her rouncey, aware that she may be lightheaded from the loss of blood, but mustering her energy as she walked toward Bell.

Before Raena reached her sister's side, a large troupe of soldiers marched up from beyond the pines. At the front of their formation was King Micha in all his formal gold and maroon, flanked by two impressive Edivan generals.

Raena's steps slowed at the sight of the soldiers, bearing pikes and shields. When she stopped to behold them, they were three meters away, and she had no weapon, save for her shortsword.

Raena dropped to one knee. "Your Majesty."

"Prince Trevin," Micha greeted. "Please, stand and approach. But leave your men where they are if you don't mind."

From the ground, Raena called a command over her shoulder. "Don't come any closer, and tend to the men downed by the hawks."

She heard an affirmation from Sage, her lead horseman of the group.

"Did my birds kill your soldiers?" Bell asked, smugness in her tone.

Raena ignored the jest; it was ruder than she expected her sister to behave, especially after they'd been long separated. Rising as the king instructed, Raena walked toward the Edivans with tentative steps, her eyes dancing between Bell and Micha. She supposed she was searching their faces for signs that Micha was planning to order his soldiers to fling a pike through her heart, then and there.

When they were a few paces apart, Raena stopped. Her hands dangled at her sides, palms open, conveying her intended surrender.

The king spoke first, "Did you hope to overrun me with your legion of…fifty men, is it?"

"A hundred," Raena said, "about half of them scattered when the hawks attacked. And of course not, Your Majesty. I hoped to gain your audience."

"Well then, you've succeeded."

Raena nodded, swallowing hard as she considered her next words. The steady stream of blood down the back of her head was forming a distracting puddle along her collar.

Bell impatiently interjected. "You're lucky, Prince. My birds might've ripped your limbs off. They've been known to do it."

"I'm sure they have," Raena tutted, "they've grown at least twice in size since I last saw them. Lord Sylas would have been impressed."

Fire burned in Bell's eyes and the lady's jaw rippled with tension.

Raena resisted the urge to grin. She always could flip a switch of emotion in her sister. They could read each other's minds and hit exactly where it hurt if they were feeling spiteful enough.

Bell pointed a shaking finger at Raena. "Tell me, Rowan, was it all your idea to kidnap me like Zander did so you could impregnate and marry me, or do you plan to blame that plan on someone who 'coerced' you into it?"

487

Raena felt as though she'd been punched in the gut.

"Let's not," Micha said with a sigh. "Let's not bicker about…that."

"Oh, you're not, Your Highness," Bell said, "but my dear brother and I are."

"Well, save it for when you're alone, please? Prince Trevin and I have a more urgent discussion than your…strategic marriage plans. Besides, friend, we've heard you have already wed, haven't you?"

Raena nodded. "Indeed, Avenna is now my princess." Despite the tension of the situation, Raena felt her heart clench with the comfort of an embrace when she said those words aloud. "And I heard the same of you, Highness? Congratulations on your union."

"Hmm," Micha mumbled. "So, then what could have persuaded you to leave your new bride and ride to find me, risking death by pecking?" He gestured toward the hawks, who were now settled behind Bell, reminiscent of children hiding in their mother's skirts.

"I am here to ask for peace," Raena said, her head high, "I hope you will honor our relationship, our good intentions, and we can stop a war before it begins."

A few of the generals laughed, and Raena realized they must speak Candorian. Micha made no sound, but the skin around his eyes wrinkled with amusement.

"Peace?" Micha asked. "What does that look like to you? I may have asked that before. I have the full strength of the Boen army under our feet. They will not stop now. We have crossed the mountains. We know we outnumber your army ten-to-one. Even if you siege your castle, which I doubt you have the crops in stores to do, we will breach your walls in a day. Especially if the Boens find their way through the tunnels underground."

Raena's cheeks flushed with both humiliation and rage.

Micha continued. "I don't want to flatten Candor, and I don't want to lose you as an ally. But you've known this was coming, and yet you declared war. Now you are here—"

488

"I didn't declare war," Raena snapped. "I fought with my council to align with you, and they defied me. You forget that in Candorian law I am only a prince. I did everything you and I discussed. I tried, King Micha. I have never stopped trying. But I could not make myself king fast enough to turn the tide of my subjects and councilmen."

Micha shook his head. "I'm sorry, Trevin. I really am. I believe you. I received your messengers. I know you've done your best. But in the end, some old lessons are true. We have a saying in Ediva: not every ruler can lead. It seems that's the problem for you."

Raena stared at the ground, unable to hide her shame. It flooded her from the center and flowered out leaving a white-hot sensation in her bones. She wanted to hide, or vomit.

"So that's it then," Raena muttered, "you will give the order, and your men and the Boens will take Candeo? Can I spare their lives if I surrender?"

"That's noble of you," Micha said.

The air was thick with silence for a moment as Raena awaited the answer to her query.

Micha let out a long, belabored sigh. "I would love to ask your surrender, but my honor won't allow it. There's something I haven't been forthright about. Since you are being vulnerable with me, here at the risk of death, I will be honest with you."

Raena raised her eyes and locked them with his once again.

"The Boens have not shown their faces in several weeks," Micha explained. "We don't know if they are still intending to take Candor. We've been waiting here in hopes they would rejoin us, but the last time they surfaced was before the Calam Mountains."

Raena bit her lip, thinking. "Any chance they couldn't find a way under? The rocks may have been too much."

"We thought that, at first, as well. But the lava tubes are extensive and hundreds of meters wide. The Boens used them for perhaps a thousand years before they disappeared. The mountains should have been the easiest place for them to traverse through. Almost like walking through an open field."

"I see," Raena said, putting her hands on her hips. "So, you're waiting here in Hawk's Keep? That buys me time to build my strategies, assemble my armies…but we both know I don't have enough time, no matter how long you wait."

"Of course," Micha said, "that's why I have no qualms about telling you this."

"What if the Boens never come? What if they leave you here all winter? Will you turn back, then?"

"No. We will attack Candeo before winter falls."

Raena's face pinched with anger. "For what purpose? Our kingdoms were at war when we were children. Who did it serve? Haven't we learned better than to let Ediva and Candor be enemies?'

"You have proven you are not fit for rule. I'm sorry, but we both know it's true. Your kingdom is in shambles. Ediva is stronger than ever. We will give your people the order, discipline, and economy they've lacked for two generations. Our systems are superior, our division of resources is superior, and our leadership is superior. Not only because of me, but because we're blessed by the seven Almighties."

Raena resisted the urge to roll her eyes. She knew Micha was speaking for the benefit of his generals and she doubted he believed a damn word of it.

"What would it take to change your mind?" Raena asked.

"Hmm," Micha said. He turned to the general next to him as if to seek the answer. When met with silence, Micha stepped forward. His eyes seemed more tired and earnest than how Raena remembered him.

"Majesty," Raena began, "you have no reason to show Candor mercy. But now…I'm begging. You haven't given me a chance. I can be the leader they need. Candor and Ediva can be the greatest of allies, especially now."

She extended her hand, trembling. It felt like it was made of deadweight, and Raena realized some of her blood had run through her sleeve and spread into her riding glove.

Micha eyed the extended hand with a raised eyebrow. "I can shake your hand, friend. But it's meaningless. Your kingdom is the one who declared war. You've admitted you have no power to stop it. I align with you? Candor could attack me tomorrow. It's best we let that kingdom fall to dust. We can start over. We can rebuild something better."

"You and I?"

"No...we can," Micha gestured behind him. "We, the Edivans."

Raena swallowed hard and lowered her hand, unshaken by her ally.

"But there is one thing you can do," Micha said. "There is one thing that will turn the tides."

She raised an eyebrow expectantly and waited for him to go on."

Micha pulled at the toggles of his regal red robe, adjusting it around his shoulders. "I've feared that perhaps the Boens have changed to another strategy. Perhaps there is something we need to know from them. You and I...well, they won't harm us. I learned when they first invaded Boenaerya that they are keen to listen to me. You can go underground and find them. Find out their plan."

Bell gasped from behind him, but Micha paid her no mind.

"Drop under Hawk's Keep," Micha instructed, "and find out where they're hiding. Perhaps the Hornes have already slayed them, in which case? I can't spare my armies to fight yours, since I'll need my men against the Hornes. That's the only scenario I can think of where I would return to Ediva and request peace with Candor. But aside from that? We will march onward to Candeo as I've said."

"Alright. What choice do I have?" Raena asked, rhetorically. "Perhaps they'll kill me. Perhaps you will. I have the best options available." She faked a smile that Micha didn't return.

"You're seriously doing this?" Bell chimed in.

Raena shrugged, still grinning. She imagined she looked boyish and charming. "Well, on the bright side, I might bleed to death from where your birds pecked me. So, I might as well go out with some glory? Please tell Aven my death was really marvelous, like say I fought off a thousand Boens with my biceps alone."

"Sure, idiot," Bell retorted, "I'll say you squeezed each one to death until his head popped like a blueberry inside your arm."

"Perfect!" Raena rubbed her hands together. "Can we tend to these wounds before I hop into the tunnel or do you want me to go right now?"

Micha's mouth was slack with shock at the casual, dark banter between the two of them. His brow furrowed and he shook his head. "Erm. Yes, my healers will take you in. You can descend the tunnels tomorrow?"

"The sun is getting low. I'd prefer to go at night. That's when I feel the most awake, after all."

"Of course," Micha said. "Tonight, it is."

CHAPTER 46
RAENA

The Underground

Raena drank plenty of water and ale and had a few legs of mutton in hopes to replenish her lost blood. She was feeling weak, but rejuvenated when she dropped into the tunnel.

Bell had begged her not to do it, but to no avail.

"I've done plenty of dumb things and you couldn't stop me from those, either," Raena had told Bell before kissing her sister on the cheek goodbye.

It took mere seconds for Raena's eyes to adjust to the total darkness. She couldn't see perfectly, but she could make out enough of the path ahead.

It was damp, musky, and cold. The sensation of the tunnel wrapped around Raena like a familiar old blanket. She hated how much her Boeny body craved spaces like these to drop down and hide. She hated how right and perfect it felt to be underground.

Raena listened as she headed east through the clear passage, closer to the Calam Mountains. Micha had made it clear that he had no reason to believe the Boens had marched any further west than Hawk's Keep.

As Raena walked, she was silent on the outside, but her mind was racing with loud, busy thoughts. She thought of Davyn, Macall, and Gregor. She thought of her hundred men, waiting outside the curtain of Hawk's Keep, sitting among their Edivan enemies. She thought of Bell's stupid hawks, and wondered if they would shred everyone to pieces the second Bell was busy or went to bed.

Raena was tempted to whistle or sing a tune to pass the time. She knew she'd been walking more than half the night. Somehow, she had a sense of the night sky and moon above even better when she was under the cover of ground or a ceiling, something she'd never understood until Zarana had pointed out the depth of her Boen heritage.

Under her breath, as soft as could be, Raena sung a melancholy tune.

"Lover, I've needed you,
though you say no one could stay.
Lover, I've yearned for you,
every time you'd gone away.

From the Horne Islands to the secret Ruv'spokan,
you pushed me away and my poor heart was broken.
But I never stopped loving,
I never stop yearning,
oh lover I'll find you again.

Lover, I've followed you,
though you hid your heart deeper still.
Lover, I've known you,
better than anyone ever will.

From the top of the Calams to the swamps of the Twins,

494

you'll look into these eyes and you'll love me again.
When I hold your hands and look into your eyes,
you can't say you don't need me,
you can't say you don't love me.

When I reach the—"

The scent of smoke drew Raena out of the song, and she held out her hands, scanning the cave. There was a quiet rustle; the first sign of life within the tunnel she'd heard yet. Raena knew it wasn't her own echo, nor was it like the occasional drips of water she'd started to ignore.

With another rustle, Raena crept forward, hunching down to make her footsteps as light as possible. Her worn leather boots allowed for the pointed stalagmites to poke the balls of her feet, but she couldn't focus enough to avoid them.

"I remember you," a low, whispering man's voice seemed to slither around her in the dark.

Raena's eyes darted around the walls and came up empty. She held still, knowing she'd already been spotted. "Yeah? Do I remember you?"

"Perhaps," the voice whispered back.

"Any chance you'd like to come say hello, then?"

"Rowan."

Raena nodded. She put one trembling hand on the hilt of her shortsword and let the other hand dangle near her dagger without revealing where it was hidden against her thigh. "I go by Trevin now, but that doesn't matter. Call me Rowan, if that's how you remember me."

"Rowan."

"Yea, that's me. And you are?"

There was a quiet chuckle that reverberated low around the walls, sending an eerie chill up Raena's spine. She realized something artificial was projecting the voice. If that were the case, he may be watching her from any distance away. Regardless, she was in an open span of the cave with two meters to spare on either side, so if they wanted to ambush her, she would at least see them coming. Raena let out short, choppy breaths to try and settle her building nerves.

"I like you, Rowan."

"Great, that's a good start," Raena said, "we can be friends. You know what friends are? Friends means that we talk and we don't hurt each other. You're friends with Micha, right? He wants me to be your friend, too."

"Yes, friend Rowan. We can talk."

Raena felt the hairs on the back of her neck stand up at his tone and the familiarity of it. "You're...the King? Jin, we call you. That's who you are, isn't it?"

"Jin, yes. Jin and Rowan friends. Jin and Micha friends. Jin and Lenon friends."

Raena raised an eyebrow at that, but continued. "Good, Jin. We need to understand what to do. You and Micha had a plan and he hasn't seen you or your men for a while. He's...worried. He feels unsure. Can you help us? Can you tell us what you need?"

"Friends."

"Yes, we're friends. We want to know your plans. Can you tell your friends your plans?"

"Friends put down their weapons."

Raena glanced down at her shortsword, fully understanding his implication, though deciding to pretend she didn't. "You want the army to put down their weapons? Have you decided not to fight against Candor?"

"You put down your weapons, then we will be friends. Then we will show you. We will show you all of it."

Raena let out a long, shaking breath. Her chest clenched now that the moment of truth had arrived. Though she'd known entering the tunnel was likely a death march, the reality of the moment arriving caused more fear than she could bear. "Courage is doing the thing you're most afraid of," she whispered to herself. "Those brave enough to be vulnerable are rewarded." She unclasped her weapon belt and fussed with the buckle.

"All are afraid," the Boen voice said, now close and speaking at a normal volume.

Raena's eyes popped up to the cave walls, and she saw the shadow of Jin leaning against it. She dropped her belt, the metal clanging against the stone at her feet. "That's…right. You know the seven virtues of Coren Schinen?"

The Jin nodded.

Raena couldn't make out his facial features nor his body well enough to see if he brandished any weapons, but his posture was relaxed at least.

Raena spoke the next virtue aloud, "Trust in another man is the bravest thing any man can do."

"Or woman," The Jin said.

Raena froze, stiff and silent.

A moment passed with neither of them saying a word. Raena became painfully aware of the steady drips as water leaked down from the ceiling and splashed puddles that had likely formed before the beginning of her life.

"Rowan," The Jin said. "Put down all your weapons. We have no secrets."

"I suppose we don't," Raena said. She pulled up the tattered tail of her tunic and extracted the dagger, allowing that to also clatter to the ground.

"Now come," The Jin said, "I will show you."

He left Raena with no choice as he disappeared into the dark. Her fingers twitched at the notion of leaving her weapons. She let out a low growl of protest before shaking it off and following into the pitch black and well-hidden tunnels ahead. As Raena entered a smaller chamber, she lost sight of the Boen, but there was only one way he could have gone. She continued deeper, winding through a snaking tunnel with multiple walls. Every time she turned a corner, she was surprised to see she was still alone and there was another disappearing bend ahead.

497

The tunnel began to descend and Raena was going further underground. She had a sense that she may be getting close to the Calam Mountains because if the tunnel was a lava tube, it would have created a steep decline.

"What about having no secrets?" she called ahead into the empty space. "Can you tell me where you went? Are you still there?"

When no one answered, Raena sped up. She charged ahead at the safest speed she could muster, watching for sharp stalagmites and carefully scanning for drops or deep waters.

"Jin?" Raena called. "Is this even the right way? I'm getting lost. I'm pretty certain this is north, and—"

"Shh," someone whispered. It came from behind her.

Before Raena could turn, she felt the hands encircle her. They were cold as death, one arm around her shoulder, one around her neck. Raena dipped her chin to escape the chokehold, but it was too late. The thin, icy arm slipped easily around her throat and began to squeeze, locked in tight. Raena knew it was hopeless to fight, though she struggled anyway, and her last thought was how she wasn't surprised at all that she was losing consciousness.

———————

"Ey're not dead."

"Then when will ey be done sleeping?"

"Do you want to give another slap? Splash water? Let em rest."

Raena heard the whisper of men's voices above her and felt the pounding strain of the world's worst headache. Unable to stop herself, she groaned as she rolled to the side, nausea overwhelming her. She expected to vomit and was surprised when her stomach resisted, but she was tempted to believe it would happen soon enough.

"Where am I?" Raena rasped.

"King room," a man's voice said.

Raena rubbed her eyes.

"Oh, ey're awake!" another voice exclaimed. Raena recognized it as The Jin's, though she'd never heard him so happy or even pleased.

"King Jin…" Raena mumbled, "why did you do…what are you doing to me?"

"Friend, we give you the information," Jin replied. "This is where."

Raena's splitting headache made it hard to open her eyes, but she forced herself to take in her surroundings. The first thing she noticed was that it was so bright, that she thought they must have gone to the surface. Then she realized they were still in the cave, and she searched for a light source but saw none. It was indeed a room of sorts, with a few chairs, a table, and food service items that were mostly carved from stone. There were three men around her; The Jin and two Boens dressed in gowns. Their braids contained duck feathers, small rocks, and bits of quorrilium. Raena had no doubt they were princes, lords, or the equivalent. She was laying on a crude couch, covered in fabric, though it felt hard as a rock. Perhaps it was.

Raena tried to sit up and her stomach protested as though the muscles inside were ripping her in half.

"Did you poison me?" Raena groaned, clutching her sides.

"No, we are showing you," The Jin replied.

"Showing me what? Am I going to die? Just please, have mercy, don't torture me—" Raena couldn't finish her words. She turned to one side and her body lurched. There wasn't much in her stomach, but she expelled it all. Bits of undigested mutton, ale, and thankfully water splashed against the cave floor as they violently projected from her open mouth.

The Boens stepped back, likely repulsed, and waited for Raena to be done. When she'd stopped, one of them fetched a goblet and filled it with water for her. She sipped it hesitantly, confirming it had no flavor.

"I guess you're not poisoning me," Raena quipped, "or why give me water?"

"Not poison," The Jin said, "you may think it medicine."

"The water is medicine?"

"No, we give you medicine. We give some when you sleep. When body is ready, we give more."

Raena's stomach clenched but this time it was from fear, not nausea. She sat up fully and rested her feet on the stone ground. She could see The Jin's periwinkle eyes when she stared at him, it was like staring at Micha, or even staring into a mirror.

"What did you do to me?" Raena asked again, her voice low and steady.

The Jin held up a small pouch and smiled weakly. "The Hornes taught us about medicine. It makes a Change. You are already Boen, but weak. We don't hurt with the medicine. We make you stronger Boen. We give you the Change."

She didn't understand and yet she understood all at once.

Raena wondered what else it changed besides her eyes. She rubbed at her face, afraid to ask. Her hands were shaking either from the fear or the fatigue from vomiting.

"What's…what's going to happen?"

The Jin took a seat in his rudimentary chair, more like a chiseled hollow than a throne. "You are Boen. You will be Boen. Strong."

Raena flinched and squeezed her eyes shut. "And if I say no?"

"You can be asleep for next medicine, too."

"Right. I don't get a choice."

"It's best," The Jin said.

Raena let out a sigh and then gazed at him, trying to implore him by conveying as much earnest affection as she could. "Before you knock me cold again then, can you please tell me what your plan is with your armies? Have the Hornes already pushed you out of Boenaerya? King Micha is awaiting your men to rise to the surface. He needs to know what's next. That's why I'm here, to convey his wishes on his behalf."

The Jin smiled and rubbed his hands together. He said something in his own tongue to the other two men and they nodded. In a few seconds, the two Boens left the chamber and disappeared into a passage. The Jin and Raena were alone.

The Jin rubbed at his cheek in contemplation. "Do you not know about the prisoners?"

"Prisoners?"

"Yes, the angry men. The men from the desert and the forests. Surface men, like you, but not Boen. Our fight near trees."

"Candorians?"

"Yes!" The Jin exclaimed, clapping. He laughed with a rolling click sound in the back of his throat. "Cand...those. That is the word. We sent them home. Do you not know?"

Raena's brow furrowed. "You sent home the Candorians? Do you mean that you sent home Micha and the Edivans? Today?"

"No. Prisoners. Men of Zarana. You know Zarana? We give her to Micha. We keep her men. We keep the men of Zarana...and feed, bathe, make them well. But now? We cannot keep. Hornes will come, Hornes are coming. The Boens need food, Boens need water. We cannot share. We send men of Zarana home."

"Did you...the men of Zarana...did you make them go through the Change?"

"Some. Not all. We test."

Raena clasped her hands together and wrung them in her lap. The weight on her shoulders grew, and she realized she was forgetting exactly why she was there. The questions swirled in her mind and she knew less than she'd known ten minutes prior. "How many prisoners?"

"Five of ten thousand."

Raena's heart raced. "Five of ten...fifty?"

The Jin shrugged.

"You sent fifty thousand men of Candor home?"

"Perhaps more."

She put her hand to her mouth and gasped into her palm. A well of elation, joy, and shock burst inside her. She prayed that this was not a trick, and tried to rationalize all the ways she should trust The Jin, though her heart was begging her not to believe the excitement she felt.

"Fifty thousand men…that's…but that's enough to bolster Candor. That's enough for a siege. Y-you won't…why would you do that?"

The Jin reached for a goblet and took a few slow sips. He wiped his mouth and spoke. "You will have a message for Micha. Micha is friend. Rowan is friend. Lenon is friend. Boens will stay in Boenaerya and no one else will fight. We want quiet. We want no one else to come. Do not come to Boenaerya."

Raena nodded, "I understand, but the Hornes, are they still taking Boenaerya from you?"

"Perhaps. Boens will be ready. Boens prepare."

"You aren't…you aren't going to attack Candor?"

The Jin narrowed his eyes and shook his head. "No time. Hornes are fast. Hornes have the sea dragon, ey is their pet. Sea dragon will swim up the rivers and into Boenaerya," he modeled the movement with his hands, pantomiming a creature moving through water. "Sea dragon fights for Hornes and cannot be killed. It is a legend."

"Everything can be killed," Raena muttered.

"Boens return to Boenaerya and prepare for fight."

Raena thought for a moment, but her head felt clouded. She couldn't make sense of his intentions and was tempted to return to the same questions. But she didn't need to know everything, all she needed was to know what happened to Candor next. "Then we agree not to attack one another now. We are in a stalemate. Do you know what that means?"

"We are not enemies."

"It's…close to that. Yes."

"Boens going home."

"To Boenaerya. And I'm going home to Candor."

The Jin's lips tightened. "Rowan? Home can be Boenaerya. Rowan is Boen."

Raena smiled, "No, thank you. I want to be in Candor, that's home to me now. Maybe someday I can return to Boenaerya, but I'd like to live above the surface."

A flicker of mischief crossed The Jin's face and his periwinkle eyes twinkled, but then the expression faded once more. "We finish the Change."

"No, thank you," Raena said again.

The Jin stood and gave a slight bow. Raena struggled to stand and return it but found her legs were shaking and weaker than she expected. Feebly, she managed to dip slightly in respect.

"We are happy to have Rowan for friend," The Jin said, "one more missing piece. Three more, the wheel is complete."

Raena's brows stitched together at the strange expression. She meant to ask about it, but The Jin swiftly exited the chamber. Almost before he disappeared around the corner, the two Boens from before were rushing in, as if they were assuring Raena wouldn't try to leave.

The taller of the Boens held the little pouch of 'medicine' in his hand and immediately began to pull at the leather lacing.

"Come on boys," Raena said, rising to her full height. She wobbled, then steadied herself by bracing one hand on the table. She lifted the other in front of her, forming a fist. "We don't need to do this, alright? How about you tell your king you did, but then you...don't? His Candorian is shite, he won't figure it out."

The shorter Boen stepped forward and pulled a smooth wooden staff from his belt, no longer than six hands in length.

"Don't knock me out again? How about that for a deal?" Raena negotiated. She focused on them both, watching their moves as her other senses dulled. She had always been able to fixate on movement like a hawk during battle, but now that skill seemed even more enhanced. It was as if time itself slowed to a stop and Raena could take in every tiny twitch, every pulse of their veins, every leading gaze as their eyes darted and gave away their next moves. She wondered if the powder in the pouch was the reason, and thought for a brief second perhaps more of it would make her more powerful.

She watched the tall Boen reach in and extract a single pinch of the black powder, rolling it between his fingers.

503

It reminded her instantly of Sylas, fixing her tea, asking her again if she was sure it was what she wanted. "It'll change you, and you can never change back," he'd warned.

She'd known without a doubt. Now she wasn't given any choice at all.

The shorter Boen lunged forward and snapped his staff low, striking her in the knee. She groaned in pain and her already weakened leg gave out. Raena fell forward, swinging as she stumbled. Her first punch landed on the Boen's jaw and his head twisted away with a sickening crunch. Her second punch was aimed for his gut, but was too high, and caught him in the ribs. Her knuckles smarted immediately.

Her opponent recoiled, bringing his staff to his chest. Raena charged forward, knowing that he couldn't maneuver the weapon if she was too close. She swung her head under his chin and butted him in the mouth. As she felt pain and dizziness through her skull, she regretted the poor choice. Her vision spun and the wooziness from when she'd first woken up came rushing back with a vengeance.

Unable to right herself, Raena's legs folded underneath her and she was sliding to the ground, most her body limp against the Boen.

They shouted something to one another. Raena rolled to her back and covered her head with her arms, trying to scoot to where she could kick them from the ground. She was pleased to see blood around the shorter Boen's mouth, which he wiped and spat away.

The tall one kicked her in the ribs before she could dodge it.

Raena pushed off with her feet, but the roughness of her tunic and the stone floor kept her from moving more than a few centimeters.

Both the Boens yelled something, then kicked her in unison. Raena felt and heard the snap of a rib and she rolled, screaming in pain. They continued to kick her back for a few strikes, then she felt the weight of one of them. He pushed her down and lodged his knee under her neck, pinning her to the floor. Raena kicked both legs, flopping like a fish out of water. Though she twisted and scrambled, there was nothing she could do.

She saw the tall Boen come around and crouch in front of her. With her cheek smashed to the cold stone floor, she stared ahead, spitting and cursing at them both.

It was unfortunate they didn't understand Candorian, because Raena's curses were particularly disgusting. Lady Isla would have slapped her mouth and sent her to bed without dinner if she'd heard the half of them.

The Boen on her back pressed his full weight to her shoulders then reached around and pulled open her lips with his icy, thin fingers.

Raena snarled and clenched her teeth tight, breathing like a beast.

She could only see segments of the tall Boen crouched in front of her, his knee on the floor, his bare foot beyond it, his hand holding the little pouch against his thigh. She saw his pinched fingers as they came closer, closer, closer to her face.

Raena tried to scream and whip her head, but they'd overpowered her.

She felt the cold fingertips press to the inside of her cheek, then one dipped into her mouth, curled like a hook, and rubbed the substance along her gums.

Raena tried spitting and they clamped a hand over her mouth, holding her jaw shut with one and her lips together with the other.

The metallic taste flooded her mouth and Raena knew it was too late to stop it. Whether it was poison, medicine, or the source of power, it was inside her.

As soon as she tasted it, she felt a sensation under her skin, as if something rolled and crawled through her, from her chest down to her thighs, then up and under her skull.

Raena screamed inside her closed mouth.

Twisting, turning. All of it coiled and sprung in her belly. She realized she was curled up like an infant, her knees to her chest, and the Boens had stepped away. Though they no longer touched her, she couldn't move of her own free will.

The 'medicine' had control of her now.

The Change owned Raena.

She tilted her head back and screamed. The sound that left her body was foreign. It was low. Gutteral. With clicks. It was the clicks the Boens made.

Boen.

Boen.

Boen.

"Boen."

Raena was yelling the word again and again. It echoed in her head. It was all around her. The lights brightened, her muscles ached and flexed and rippled under her. She felt her shoulders broaden and push her head further from the ground.

She rolled forward, hard, and her nose collided with the stone. There should have been pain, but there was so much pain, she couldn't feel any more.

"Stop! Stop this! I'm dying!" Raena screamed.

Her pleas for life fell on deaf ears. She could hardly breathe. The air itself was too thick. She couldn't get enough of it into her lungs, and they burned.

Raena punched herself in the jaw, hoping it would knock her unconscious. When the Boens didn't react, she did it again.

"Please! Kill me! Do something!" she screamed at them.

Raena could see their faces, dumbfounded.

They chittered to one another in their clicking sounds. Then the short one stepped forward, and the last thing Raena saw was the swing of his wooden staff.

CHAPTER 47
BELL

Good at keeping secrets unless telling them is more fun

They'd found Raena outside the curtain.

She was lying next to the mouth of a tunnel, under the shade of a pine, screaming about the sun and begging for death.

Bell hadn't been the one to find her, but the news traveled fast among the Candorian soldiers staying within Hawk's Keep. Gregor, Aven's brother, had told Bell that Raena had gone blind. Micha's men took Raena to the dungeon at first, unsure of what to do. Bell pleaded with Micha, and he relented, giving Raena a dark room at the center of the keep once she calmed down enough to ask for it.

For three days, Bell sat by her bed while Raena slept and moaned, in a stupor.

When the sun had set on the third night, Raena twitched and opened her eyes. Even in the candlelight, Bell was surprised to see that they were more purple than she had ever seen them.

"Can you blow out the candles?" Raena groaned.

"They are too bright for you, aren't they?"

Raena nodded. "And I need some water."

Bell had Fox in her arms and he'd been long asleep. She set the bundled baby on the bed, an arm's reach from Raena. "Can you see the baby, here? Careful."

"I see him. I see everything."

Bell smiled, then went to fetch the water. She didn't blow out the candles because she still needed them, and she hoped Raena wouldn't ask again.

"You've been sleeping for days," Bell said, handing the goblet to Raena. "Fox and I have been here, sometimes he cries, but it didn't even wake you."

Raena sipped the water, raising one eyebrow in response.

"Well, Fox hasn't been here the whole time. It's too boring for him. He's been getting plenty of walks around the grounds, in the gardens, the great hall. He's very well-traveled."

"Fox?"

Bell gestured to the baby. "That's what I named him."

"His name is Davyn," Raena leaned back against the headboard with a moan and closed her eyes. "I still hurt everywhere. But someone bathed me, I see. I hope you know who it was?"

"I do. It was me."

"Thank the Almighties then. I'm not ready for any of those men to see how big my cock is and get jealous."

Bell rolled her eyes. "No one can hear us, idiot. This room is away from everything. It had to be! You've been screaming and moaning so much, no one wanted to listen to that shite."

"Well…" Raena wet her lips, "thank you."

"Your body seems different. I remembered you had a scar, but I could hardly see it."

"What do you mean?" Raena asked. She pulled back the blanket with care not to disturb Fox and peeled up the bottom of her shirt. When Raena saw the faint scar on her ribs, her fingers traced it a few times. "What happened to it?"

"You don't know?"

"No…" Raena whispered, her voice filled with awe. "And my muscles are so wiry…I suppose it's part of the Change."

"What change?"

"It's a lot to tell. Can we talk about it later? I'm so tired."

Bell stood from her chair and took a seat on the bed. She reached out to pat Raena's hand, then pulled the blankets back over her. Fox was between them, so peaceful. Bell knew the baby looked like Raena, but now that they were side by side, it was uncanny.

"I've been waiting for you to wake up for days so I could find out what happened to you. I know you're tired, but maybe I can wake you up in the morning?"

"No, it's alright. I can manage. What do you need to know? What the Boens are doing?"

"Oh no, I could care less about that. Save that war strategy gobshite for Micha. He'll force you to talk about it for days, I've no doubt…no, I'm wondering what you plan to do next? Will you go home?"

Raena sighed, "Well, yes. If I'm allowed to go after this."

"Why wouldn't you be allowed?"

Raena opened her eyes, though she squinted as though staring into the sun. "Two reasons. Perhaps Micha will want to kill me when I tell him what I learned of the Boens. I know you said you don't care, but it's relevant. They have foiled his ability to march on Candor. They have returned fifty thousand soldiers to the Candorian army."

Bell scoffed. "Fifty thousand soldiers…how? How did they even get…"

"Zander's men. They captured them and kept them underground. They never killed their prisoners. And if Jin is telling the truth, all of them are back in Candeo now."

"But how would they even get them there?"

Raena flashed a crooked grin. "I thought all the war strategy didn't interest you?"

"I didn't know it was going to be unbelievable!" Bell slapped Raena's shoulder. "Alright, alright. So, you think Micha will execute you for that? What would be the point?"

"If he can't take Candor by force—"

"No," Bell snapped, "he's not that kind of leader. You know that."

"You're right. So, there's the second reason I can't go back then. I've betrayed my council. I've made alliances with Micha against their declaration of war. I'm a traitor, this time for more than what I'm pretending is between my legs, or the man I'm impersonating. I'll be beheaded, I'm sure. Jonn-Del will see to that."

"Jonn-Del is a ponce who won't kill anyone unless he gains from it."

"I can hope as much."

Bell rolled her eyes.

"What?" Raena asked.

"Oh nothing, you are just always the same, brother. You pretend everything is hopeless, then you come up with some perfect plan and you find the way out. It's boring, really."

Raena's mouth dropped open, but her attention was quickly diverted by Davyn fussing. He wiggled on the bed, kicking his tiny feet. Without pause, Raena lifted him to her chest and rocked, but that merely caused him to cry louder.

"This is painful to watch," Bell chided. In an instant, she swooped in and reached for the infant, pulling him from Raena's arms firmly and cradling him to her breasts.

With a few shaky deep breaths, Davyn calmed, nestling into the skin amply available due to Bell's dress's plunging neckline.

Bell cast a haughty look of arrogant pride in Raena's direction.

"Well," Raena grumbled, "if I had tits for him to rub his face on, I'm sure I'd've calmed him just fine."

"Oh, do you not have tits?" Bell smirked.

Raena folded her arms and raised an eyebrow. "Did I say I was glad to see you? Perhaps I'd prefer a random handmaiden to tend to me. Maybe one of your hawks can bathe me."

"I can arrange that. Samorr seemed to understand your body well enough to peck at it."

"How are those birds of yours, anyway? Micha doesn't mind them running around his soldiers liable to attack at any moment?"

"Who knows?" Bell said. "He won't dare tell me what to do in my father's keep. He knows those hawks mean more to me than anyone, besides you and Finn."

Raena reached out and placed her hand on Bell's thigh. "And Sylas. And Isla."

Bell lowered her head, suddenly focused on Fox's face.

"They'll come home," Raena whispered.

Bell bit back the hint of tears and then shook her head. "Well anyway, Micha is distracted. He's got a war to run. No time to worry about me and my hawks."

Raena was quiet for a moment, but her hand stayed on Bell's leg, surprisingly cold even through the layers of fabric. "Davyn really likes you. It's not only your tits."

Bell cooed, "He's a good baby. Where did he come from?"

"Another long story…but he's an orphan, now."

"If I didn't know better, I'd believe he was yours. You can't ever have a child, can you?"

Raena bit her lip and shook her head.

"Why don't you take Fox home with you? You and Aven can raise him. Everyone will believe he's yours. You can say you fathered a bastard but his mother died—"

"No. There have been enough lies in my lifetime to give me a world of pain. I want nothing more to do with the webs of deceit that Jonn-Del, Zarana, and my father spun."

Bell wondered what she meant by that, but before she could ask, Raena groaned, clutching her sides.

"Can I make you a drink for the pain?"

"No," Raena muttered, "I want my body to heal. Nothing for me except water."

"Can I ask…you said Fox is an orphan, and you're sure you don't want to take him to Candeo?"

"It's Davyn. I named him first."

"You named him? Well, you chose poorly. I named him after you, of course. Is Fox not your sigil? I thought it a compliment to you."

"It is, but he isn't mine."

Bell grinned eagerly. "Then you don't mind that I'll take him."

"Take him?"

"Yes," Bell said, "him and my hawks, of course. We can't stay here while Micha sorts licking his wounds and trying to save face. I'm tired of comforting him and hoping he'll keep me around. He is going back to Pearl eventually. I've done all I wanted to do for him, to build him up, to make him into the kind of man that is strong enough to serve a kingdom."

"You take credit for that? All right…"

Bell ignored the jest. "I'm missing Finn. He's alone on that island and I'm ready to go back. I know he would love Fox…Davyn as much as I do, if not more. If it weren't for Aven, I bet you would come with us. No responsibility, no stupid crown, no asshole Jonn-Del. Just the three of us, swimming in the cold sea, practicing our archery, making kelpi ferment in a stone pit, and raising this little Fox to be a cunning mastermind."

"Maybe that's enough for you and Finn, but it would never be enough for me."

"You're like Sylas in that way. And where is he, now? Probably dead, with his keep occupied by his greatest enemies."

Raena pursed her lips, letting out a short breath, but didn't argue.

"Anyway, I'm leaving here as soon as you're well," Bell promised, "it'll be hard to get over the mountains, but I'm sure Micha will give me a few men to escort me."

"And without you here, Micha will let me and my soldiers leave freely?"

"Of course, he will. Especially once you tell him that your army just grew by fifty thousand. You don't need me in his ear anymore, you have a strong kingdom again."

Raena shrugged. "Maybe. We'll see what state those former prisoners are in. It may be a long time before they are ready to fight."

"Well, you are free to come with me," Bell said. "Come to the islands with me, Finn, and Fox."

"I'll think about it," Raena said.

"No, you won't. We both know where you'll end up."

Raena scoffed, her lips twisting into a slight smirk.

"I love you, stupid brother."

"I love you, as well."

Bell kissed Davyn again. "Thank you for this gift, he's the best thing you ever could've given me."

"You're welcome. He'll be happy with you and Finn."

"Do you need to rest?"

Raena nodded, suppressing a yawn.

"I'll let you," Bell began, standing from the bed and rocking Fox as she did.

Bell took a few steps across the familiar plank floors toward the outer chamber. When she reached the candle and was about to blow it out, she paused and twisted back to look at Raena one final time. "I have a gift for you too, you know."

"Oh? Aside from letting me get some sleep?"

"Yes, aside from that. Something else I convinced your brother to do for you."

Raena shifted in the bed, her jaw hanging slightly open. "My brother...Finn?" she stared at Bell with an odd expression, both curious and confused.

Bell waited and the silence between them seemed to expand into infinity. Bell felt an adrenaline rush in the pit of her stomach, nearly gleeful as she realized what she was intent on revealing. She'd known for so long, and was giddy at the fact that Raena still hadn't figured it out.

Bell thought of when they were children, chasing through the fields, playing knights and ladies, having mock fights with sticks. Bell was always making the rules to the games and Raena was always finding a clever exception that she could exploit to win. Raena always wanted to be more clever, to outsmart Finn and Bell, and then insist that it was 'fun'.

Now Bell was the clever one.

It was fun, indeed.

Bell sensed the distress in Raena's face with every passing second. Raena appeared lost as if she were searching a tomb in her mind.

Bell chuckled and their eyes met, "No, silly boy. Your real brother."

Raena slid one hang under her tunic, touching her chest, maybe feeling her heartbeat for comfort. Her jaw slightly open, her bright eyes steadily fixed on Bell's. Raena had all the features of a predator on a hunt. Hunting for the truth.

"Of course," Bell sang without an ounce of concern in her voice. "Micha Schinen. Son of Henry Schinen and Alura Sterling. Who, honestly? Is the loveliest woman. You really ought to get to know her better. Now, if you'll excuse me, I really must be feeding little Fox, here." And because that satisfaction wasn't enough for her, Bell could not stifle her laughter. It echoed through the chamber as she picked up the sole remaining candle. With Fox and the light, Bell sped from the room fast enough that she wouldn't even hear if Raena called after her.

AUTHOR'S FOREWORD & ACKNOWLEDGMENTS

What a whirlwind of pandemic life I had between Traitors and Defenders!

First of all, everything in my life changed (for the better) between these two books. I want to thank my readers who stayed faithfully engaged with me after Traitors was released. The positive messages, reviews, and tags genuinely motivated me to keep going and not give up.

2021-22 was a dark time for me and writing took a backseat. I navigated through: 1. Leaving my abuser; 2. A messy, high-conflict divorce; and 3. A nasty custody battle.

But once my draft of Defenders was complete, I sat back and read it, realizing how much of my real-life agony had bled into this book and created beauty.

In these pages, you'll find my guilt and shame embodied in Raena. You'll find my resilience and survivor spirit embodied in Aven. You'll find my fear and resignation embodied in Sylas. And you'll find my determination to remain carefree and playful in Bell. All of these characters carried me through the hardest year of my life, and I hope they will benefit and support you in some way as well.

I've thanked my readers, but I must thank you again. Thank you for continuing to follow this series and trust me with your reading time and attention. Thank you for picking up another book from me and giving it a shot.

Now, in order of influence and their mark on Defenders, here's everyone else that I owe my gratitude to:

Ellie, my faithful publisher, who gives me endless second chances and holds me accountable.

Kassara Meek, the greatest editor ever, who probably knows the details of my writing even better than I do. I'm so sorry that I still don't understand how ellipses work…anyway you're a genius.

Shawna, my critique partner and alpha reader. Thank you for encouraging me through every page of this book.

Micah, an amazing idea man, author, and beta reader. Thank you for continuing to make this series great with your fantasy knowledge.

Amanda, my best friend, favorite near-sister, and surprise beta reader!

My sister EDR, who gets all of the Points for finishing Traitors first in our family. Yes, this fact shocks me.

My mom, who still gets Points for loving me and encouraging my writing, all of the time.

Patrick, who created the helmets for the Boens and, therefore, a major plot point.

Lisa, the world's biggest Raena stan. I'm glad you're here and I need you here for the next book, too.

The Black Crown Book Club, whose members' names are easter eggs scattered throughout Defenders. Now you all have to read the book, guys.

And finally, I want to thank my abuser who told me that my "childish, amateur" writing was a waste of time and that I was selfish for it. Here I am, another book written and living a beautiful life, all in spite of them.

About the Author

Cate Pearce was homeschooled on a Christmas tree farm in rural Western Washington. Through fundamentalist influences, young Cate was taught rigid rules around gender, courtship, purity, and religion. Spoiler: she abandoned most of those constructs and reshaped them into her own ideas.

Cate's journey as a writer began at age eight when she was fed-up with a plotline on Star Trek TNG. So naturally she began writing her own episodes on a Commodore 64. Her love of writing continued through high school, where she dabbled in underground newspapers, creative writing courses, and also discovered her Star Trek rewrite hobby had a name: fan fiction. In 2005 Cate attended The Evergreen State College, studying mostly business, but also honing her skills as a writer through the robust liberal arts program. It was while an undergrad student that Cate began a medieval fantasy short story retelling of Shakespeare's Twelfth Night, inspired that Olivia and Viola "should have stayed in-love." This concept morphed and grew over 15 years, eventually developing into Cate's first novel, Traitors of the Black Crown.

After college, Cate worked in hazard response and emergency management. She continued to write as a hobby but also in a professional capacity, authoring hundreds of technical plans, white papers, and newsletters. In 2017 she completed a Master's Degree in Emergency Management from Arizona State. Cate's expertise enabled her the opportunity to travel the world as an instructor/trainer in her field, visiting Asia, Europe, the Middle East, and nearly every state in America. Her love of history, geography, and travel continued to feed and inspire the settings and themes of her fictional fantasy work.

Somewhere in the midst of all that, Cate delivered two children at-home with the assistance of saintly midwives. Both children are small, brilliant, and avid readers. Cate co-parents with a strong, feminist, queer woman, raising their children in the PNW. Aside from writing, Cate maintains her "day-job", protecting communities from disaster incidents and emergencies.

Lightning Source UK Ltd.
Milton Keynes UK
UKHW010950060223
416537UK00007B/1569